ALL THE AIR drains from me, leaving me to pant from the unexpected use of magic as the tension on the man's face alleviates. Does he realize I used magic on him?

"A wall collapsed, my queen," he coughs. "Weren't expecting it, not there, but—"

Theron falls to the ground beside me, his attention boring into the miner in a frantic pull of pure, aching need.

"We . . . found it," the miner says like he can't believe his own news. He blinks at me, and I try with everything I have left to breathe, just breathe, *keep breathing.*

"We found it, my queen. The magic chasm."

ICE

LIKE

FIRE

SARA RAASCH

BALZER + BRAY
An Imprint of HarperCollins*Publishers*

To Kelson, who embodies the best parts of Mather and Theron even
when I'm the worst parts of Meira

Balzer + Bray is an imprint of HarperCollins Publishers.

Ice Like Fire
Copyright © 2015 by Sara Raasch
Map art © 2014 by Jordan Saia
All rights reserved. Printed in the United States of America.
No part of this book may be used or reproduced in any manner whatsoever without
written permission except in the case of brief quotations embodied in critical articles
and reviews. For information address HarperCollins Children's Books, a division of
HarperCollins Publishers, 195 Broadway, New York, NY 10007.
www.epicreads.com

Library of Congress Control Number: 2015943607
ISBN 978-0-06-228696-3

Typography by Erin Fitzsimmons
16 17 18 19 20   PC / RRDH   10 9 8 7 6 5 4 3 2 1
❖
First paperback edition, 2016

Meira

FIVE ENEMIES.

Five dented helmets sit lopsided over five equally dented breastplates; five black suns shine, scratched yet distinct, on the silver metal. More soldiers than I could ever take on my own, but as I stand in the center of their ring, boots planted in the snow, I cock an eyebrow at the closest one, the calm that precedes a fight descending over me.

My chakram already rests in my hand, but part of me doesn't want to throw it just yet, reveling in the feel of its smooth handle against my palm. Dendera thought herself so clever, hiding it where she did—but really, giving it to the Cordellan soldiers was almost too easy. Where else would I go for a weapon if not the weapons tent?

"Do it!" comes a high-pitched squeal.

"Shh, she'll hear you!"

A deluge of shushing follows when I snap my head toward

the row of boulders outside my ring of mock enemies. A cluster of small heads ducks behind the largest rock.

"She saw us!"

"You're standing on my foot!"

"Be quiet!"

A smile flutters on my lips. When I face the closest of the soldiers again, the pile of snow within the dented helmet and breastplate sags a little, knocked askew by the same gust of icy wind that beats at my skirt. The illusion wavers.

I'm not in battle gear—I'm in a sleeveless gown of pleated ivory fabric, my hair done up in elaborate braids. My "enemies" are stacks of snow that I hastily kicked together and dressed in the discarded Spring armor that litters my kingdom. My audience isn't an army, but a group of curious Winterian children who followed me out of the city. The chakram is real, though, and the way my body reacts to it makes this almost believable.

I'm a soldier. Angra's men surround me. And I will kill every one of them.

My knees bend, hips pivoting, shoulders twisting and muscles knotting up. Inhale, exhale, spin, release—the moves rise from my memory, as ingrained into my body as the act of walking, despite the fact that it's been three months since I last threw my chakram.

The blade breaks out of my palm with a hiss that punctures the cold air. It whirls into the closest enemy, rebounds off a rock, knocks into the next soldier, and sings back to my hand.

Every taut nerve relaxes and I exhale, long, deep, pure. Snow above, that feels *good.*

I let the chakram fly again, and again, finishing off the remaining soldiers. Cheers erupt from behind me, tiny voices laughing as snowflakes settle over the fallen bodies of my victims. I stay in the position of my last catch, hips bent and chakram firm in my hand, but the illusion is thoroughly broken now—in the best way.

A grin curves my lips. I can't remember the last time someone laughed in Winter. The past three months should have been filled with such joy, but the only sounds I've heard have been the thuds of construction, murmured plans for crops and mines, soft applause at public events.

"Can I throw it?" one of the girls calls, and her plea encourages the rest of them to demand the same thing.

"Better start with something less sharp." I smile and bend to scoop snow into a loose ball that I let slide from my fingers. "And less deadly."

The girl who first asked to throw my chakram understands before the rest of them. She drops to her knees, mashes snow into a ball, and hurls it at a boy behind her.

"Got you!" she squeals, and takes off, tearing over the field in search of a hiding place.

The rest of them lash into a frenzy, packing snow into projectiles and launching them at one another as they sprint over the fields beyond.

"You're dead! I hit you!" one little boy cries.

My smile slips.

We don't have to fight anymore. They'll never have to throw more than snowballs, I tell myself.

"Isn't this a little . . . morbid?"

I whirl, fingers spasming around the chakram. But I don't even get the blade up before I see who's entering the little clearing created by the foothills of the Klaryns on one side and rippling fields of snow on the other.

Theron tips his head, some of his hair falling out from behind his ears to swing in a brown-blond curtain. A question hangs in his gaze, the lines around his eyes holding concern.

"Morbid?" I manage half a smile. "Or cathartic?"

"Most cathartic things *are* morbid," he amends. "Healing through melancholy."

I roll my eyes. "Leave it to you to find something poetic about slicing off the heads of snowmen."

He laughs and the air grows a little cooler, a delightful chill that fizzles against my heart. His coloring looks harsh against the perpetual ivory backdrop of Winter—the lean muscles of his body are hugged by Cordell's hunter-green-and-gold uniform, the material thicker to account for Winter's chill and the fact that his Cordellan blood doesn't protect him from my kingdom's climate.

Theron nods back the way he came, toward the city of

Gaos. If the Klaryns were a sea, Gaos would be Winter's largest port—the biggest city with access to the most mines.

It's a place I've spent far too much time these past three months.

"We're ready to open the Tadil Mine," he says, shifting in what could be a shiver of cold, but could also be a shiver of anticipation.

"We just opened a mine yesterday. And two last week," I counter. I hate how my voice twists. Theron shouldn't be the recipient of my anger.

His jaw tightens. "I know."

"Your father's coming to Jannuari for the ceremony at the end of the week, isn't he?"

He reads my meaning. "The Autumnian royals will be here as well. You shouldn't confront my father with them present."

"Cordell is as involved with Autumn as they are with Winter. Their king probably wants to force Noam out as much as I do."

Theron winces, and I realize too late how callous my words were. Noam is still Theron's father and his king, and no matter how tight my chest gets whenever Noam issues a new order . . . we need Cordell. Without Noam's aid, we would have no army—the Winterians' physiques have just started to go from emaciated to healthy, and as such they've only recently become able to train at all. Without

Cordell, we would have no supplies, since Winter has no trade reestablished, and what crops we *can* grow in our frozen kingdom—thanks to my magic—are still freshly seeded and won't yield for months yet, even with the extra boost from Winter's conduit.

So I have no choice but to obey Noam's demands, because we are so indebted to him that sometimes I can't believe I'm not wearing Cordellan colors yet too.

"Fine," I concede. "I'll open this mine. I'll bring Noam and Autumn payment due for their part in Winter's salvation, but the moment the ceremony ends—"

What do I plan to do after the ceremony? Because that's all it is, a ceremony—a pretty performance to thank Autumn and Cordell for their aid in freeing Winter from Spring. We'll pay them with what goods we've mined, but it won't even be a fraction of what we owe. We'll be in the same situation after the ceremony as we are now: at Cordell's mercy.

That's why I've spent so much of the past three months trying to convince Dendera that queens can carry weapons. That's why I found my chakram and staged this moment of normalcy—because even though we have Winter back, I feel exactly the same as I did when Spring owned our kingdom. Enslaved at another kingdom's mercy. Albeit with less immediate threat, which is the only reason I've tolerated Noam for as long as I have. My people don't see Cordell's presence as oppressive—they see aid.

Theron reaches for me, but I'm still holding my chakram,

so he settles for only one of my hands, yanking me out of my worrying. He isn't just a delegate from Cordell; he isn't just his father's son. He's also a boy who looks at me with wanting, the same look he gave me in the dark halls of Angra's palace before he kissed me—a look he's given me a dozen times in the last three months.

My breath catches. He doesn't kiss me now, though, and I can't decide whether I want him to—and if I do, whether it would be because I want comfort, distraction, or him.

"I'm sorry," he says softly. "But we have to keep trying—and the work is good for Winter. If anything, your kingdom will benefit from these resources too. I hate that he's right, but we need—"

"Noam doesn't *need* Winter," I cut him off. "He *wants* Winter—he wants access to the chasm of magic. Why would you say he's right?" I hesitate. "Do you agree with him?"

Theron rocks closer, a cloud of lavender from the scented soap he uses drifting off his body. He moves his hands to my arms, the sleeves of his jacket tugging up, revealing his wrists and their jagged pink scars. Guilt leaves a vile tang in my mouth.

He got those scars while trying to rescue me.

Theron follows my gaze to his bare wrists. He jerks away, pulling down his sleeves.

I swallow. I should say something about it: his scars, his reaction. But he always changes the subject before I—

"I don't think he's entirely right," Theron stammers, steering the conversation back on course, though I don't miss how he keeps one hand on his sleeve, pressing the fabric to his wrist. "Not in how he's going about it, at least. Winter needs support, which Cordell can give. And if we find the magic chasm, we'll *all* be in a better place."

His eyes hold mine, wordlessly pleading with me to carry on like normal.

I relent. For now. "And how should Noam go about getting recompense for his aid?"

But as soon as I ask the question, I know the answer, and my body flares with a wave of desire that makes me rock toward him.

Theron leans forward. "I want my father to reinstate our engagement." His words are no louder than the snowflakes that drop around us. "If our kingdoms were joined, it wouldn't be one dominating the other, one indebted to the other—we'd be united, powerful." He pauses, exhaling a cloud of condensation. "Protected."

Icy tingles shoot down my body, conflicting with the parts of me that know Theron and I aren't destined for what we once were. Noam dissolved our engagement because he saw Winter's debt to Cordell as a sufficient link between our two kingdoms—and maybe a little bit because he felt cheated by Sir for setting up a marriage between his son, the heir of a Rhythm, and a girl who should have been a Winterian pawn, not a queen in her own right.

Noam wants our mines; he wants access to the lost chasm of magic. He knows he'll have them, thanks to our dependency on him. This way, he can treat Winter like the lowly broken thing we are—not a political equal. And honestly, I'm a little relieved to not have to worry about being married now.

But Theron has made it quite clear, many times, that he isn't pleased with Noam's decision.

As if to confirm my thoughts, his features shift and he angles toward me. "I'll always fight for you. I'll always keep you safe," he adds.

The way he says it is a promise and a declaration and a plea all in one. The words feed tremors that shake down to his wrists, highlighting the fears he doesn't dare breathe aloud.

Protected. Keep you safe.

He's afraid of our pasts too. He's afraid that what happened will happen again, nightmares that keep playing out.

"You don't have to keep me safe," I whisper.

"But I can. I *will*." Theron's declaration is so stern that I feel it cut across my face.

But I don't want to need him—or his father, or Cordell. I don't want my kingdom to need anyone. Most days, I don't even want them to need *me*.

I touch my locket, the empty piece of jewelry that stands as a symbol of Winter's magic to everyone else. They believe that once the halves were reunited, the locket resumed its status as one of the eight sources of magic in this world—the Royal Conduits. They think any magic I used before then—healing Sir and the boy in the Abril camp, infusing the enslaved Winterians with strength—was a fluke, a miracle, because every other Royal Conduit is an object like a dagger, a ring, a shield. It never occurred to them—or me, before this—that magic could find its host in a *person*.

They have no idea where the real magic is. And honestly, Cordell is the least of my worries—because something else sits inside me that could be far more dangerous.

I press my free hand to Theron's chest. Alone out here, with the snow falling and the cold wind twirling and the feel of his own pulse hammering under my fingers, I let us have this moment. Regardless of what we are now, moments like these, when we can forget politics and titles and our past, keep us both from falling apart beneath the stresses of our lives.

I press into him and lift up, catching his lips on mine. He moans and sweeps his arms around me, curving along the bend of my body, returning my kiss with a passion that undoes me.

Theron runs a hand along my temple, over my ear, and down my cheek, his fingers brushing aside the hairs that curl out of their pins. I tip my head to the side, leaning into his palm, my own fingers encircling his wrist.

His scars are lumpy and misshapen under my touch. My

heart—already beating erratically from the way Theron's lips are rough yet his touch gentle, and from the pang of need in my gut when he moans like that—spirals out of control.

I ease back, our exhales turning to frost. "Theron, what happened to you in Abril?"

The words barely come, but there they finally are, dancing through the snowflakes.

He hesitates, not hearing me for a beat. Then he flinches, his face awash with horror that he smoothes into confusion. "You were there—"

"No, I mean . . . before." Deep breaths. "You were in Abril before I knew you were there. And . . . you can tell me. If you ever need to. I mean, I know it's hard, but I—" I groan at myself, head dipping between us. "I'm not good at this."

Despite everything, Theron chuckles. "Good at what?"

I look up at him and start to smile back before I realize how he swept over everything I said. "Good at . . . us."

His lips explode in a smile that only reminds me of everything it covers. "You're better at us than you think," he whispers, freeing his hand from my grip to run his fingers the rest of the way down my face, my neck, until he cups my shoulder.

I offer a weak smile and shake my head. "The miners. I should get to them."

Theron nods. "Yes," he agrees. A burst of hope brightens his face. "Maybe this mine will be the one."

Unlikely, I almost say. We've started excavating more than half of Winter's mines, and none of them have yielded anything beyond the usual resources. The fact that Noam believes we'll find the place from which the Royal Conduits originated is infuriating. The magic chasm has been lost beneath the Season Kingdoms for centuries, and just because a Rhythm is now the one searching, he expects to unearth it?

These are Winter's mines, and he's forcing *my* people to use what little strength they have to dig them up. They spent sixteen years in Angra's work camps; they should be healing, not chasing power for a man who already has too much.

My anger flares again and I turn, leaving the carcasses of my mock enemies behind.

Theron walks beside me in silence, and as we weave around a few boulders, Gaos springs up before us as if the Klaryns had been keeping it hidden until my return. It looks much like Jannuari did when we first arrived, but at least parts of that city have been patched together since then. So few people have chosen to repopulate Gaos that we've been able to repair only the area closest to the mines, leaving most of the city in ruins. Cottages dilapidated from disuse line the streets; rubble fills alleys in hastily made piles. Snow coats everything, hiding some of the destruction under pure ivory.

I hesitate, just a twitch of a pause, when Gaos comes into view. But it's enough to cause Theron to thread his arm around my waist, tugging my body to his.

"It will be better in time," he assures me.

I peer up at him, still desperately clutching my chakram. His hand cups my hip, warm against Winter's perpetual coolness.

"Thank you."

Theron smiles, but before he can reply, another voice cuts him off.

"My queen!"

The sound of snow crunching under her feet follows Nessa's cry, which is just as quickly followed by her brothers' startled shouts. By the time I turn to face her, she's halfway across the remaining stretch of snow between Gaos and me, her gown flapping around her legs.

She stumbles to a halt, panting between smiles. Months of freedom are finally starting to show—there's a healthy plumpness to her arms and face and a soft glow in her cheeks.

"We've been searching everywhere for you! Are you ready?"

My face morphs into something between a wince and a grin. "How angry is Dendera?"

Nessa shrugs. "She'll be appeased once the mine is open." She shoots an awkward bow at Theron and grabs my hand. "May I steal her away, Prince Theron?"

He brushes his thumb over my hip bone in a movement that sends a shiver up my skin. "Of course—"

But Nessa is already hauling me across the snow.

Conall and Garrigan meet us just inside the first street of the city, Conall with a glower, Garrigan with an amused smirk.

"You should have taken us with you," Conall reprimands me. He realizes who he's reprimanding and clears his throat. "My queen."

"She's perfectly capable of taking care of herself," Garrigan defends me. But at Conall's glare he tries to hide his smirk behind a rather aggressive cough.

"That's not the point." Conall whips to me. "Henn hasn't been training us for nothing."

I almost echo Garrigan's words, almost lift my chakram for emphasis. But the lines of strain around Conall's eyes make me tuck my chakram behind my back.

"I'm sorry I worried you," I say. "I didn't mean—"

"Where have you been?"

A trembling squeak catches in my throat as Dendera comes storming up the road.

"I leave you alone for *one minute* and you take off like—" She slams to a stop. I try to hide my chakram even farther behind my back, but it's too late.

The look she gives me isn't the furious glare I expected.

It's tired, drained, and as she closes the space between us, her forty-some years hang even heavier from her face.

"Meira," she chastises.

I haven't heard her, or Nessa, or anyone but Theron call me that in . . . months. It's always "my queen" or "my lady." Hearing it now is a burst of cold air in a stuffy room, and I gulp it in.

"I told you," Dendera says, easing the chakram from my hand and passing it to Garrigan. "You don't need this anymore. You are queen. You protect us in other ways."

"I know." I keep my jaw tight, my voice level. "But why can't I be both?"

Dendera sighs the same sad, pitiful sigh she's given me way too often these past three months. "The war is over," she tells me, not for the first time, and probably not for the last. "Our people lived under war for too long—they need a serene ruler, not a warrior queen."

It makes sense in my head. But it doesn't make sense in my heart.

"You're right, Duchess," I lie. If I press too much, I'll see the same expression I saw on her face a hundred times growing up—fear of failing. Just like with Theron and his scars, and Nessa too—if I catch her when she thinks no one is watching, her eyes become hollow and glassy. And when sleep brings her nightmares, she weeps so hard my heart aches.

As long as no one mentions the past or anything bad, we're fine.

"Come." Dendera claps her hands, all business again. "We're late enough as it is."

Meira

DENDERA TAKES US to a square that opens mere paces from the Tadil Mine. The buildings here stand whole and clean, paths swept clear of debris, cottages repaired. The families of the miners already deep in the Tadil pack the square along with Cordellan soldiers, most bouncing from foot to foot in an effort to keep warm. An open-air tent caps the entrance to the square, our first stop as we file in alongside tables littered with maps and calculations.

Sir and Alysson bow their heads in quiet discussion within the tent. Their focus shifts to me, a genuine smile crossing Alysson's face, a sweep of analysis passing over Sir's. They're just as sharply dressed as Nessa and Dendera in their gowns—while traditional Winterian clothing for women consists of pleated, ivory, floor-length dresses, most of the men wear blue tunics and pants under lengths of white fabric that wrap in an X around their torsos. It's still strange to me to see Sir dressed in anything other than his battle gear, but he doesn't even have a dagger at his hip. The threat is gone, our enemy dead.

"My queen." Sir bows his head. My skin bristles at my title on his lips, one more thing I have yet to grow accustomed to. Sir, calling me "my queen." Sir, my general. Sir, Mather's father.

The thought of him seizes me.

I haven't really talked to Mather since we sat on our horses side by side outside Jannuari, before I fully took up the responsibilities of being queen, and he fully surrendered everything he thought he once was.

I'd hoped he just needed time to adjust, but it's been three months since he's said more than "Yes, my queen," to me. I have no idea how to go about bridging the distance between us—I just keep telling myself, maybe foolishly, that when he's ready, he'll talk to me again.

Or maybe it has less to do with him no longer being king and more to do with Theron, who, even though our engagement has been dissolved, is still a permanent fixture in my life. For now, it's easier not to think about Mather. To fake the mask, force the smile, and cover up the awfulness underneath.

I wish I didn't have to force it away—I wish none of us had to, and we were all strong enough to deal with the things that have happened to us.

A tingle of chill blossoms in my chest. Sparking and

wild, icy and alive, and I stifle a sigh at what it signifies.

When Angra conquered my kingdom sixteen years ago, he did so by breaking our Royal Conduit. And when a conduit is broken in defense of a kingdom, the ruler of that kingdom then becomes the conduit. Their body, their life force—it all merges with the magic. No one knows this save for me, Angra, and the woman whose death turned me into Winter's conduit: my mother.

You can help them deal with what happened, Hannah prods. Since the magic *is* me, unlimited within my body, she's able to speak to me, even after her death.

I'm not forcing healing on them, I say, withering at the thought. I know the magic could heal their physical wounds—but emotional? I can't—

I didn't mean that, Hannah says. *You can show them that they have a future. That Winter is capable of surviving.*

My tension relaxes. *Okay,* I manage.

The crowd stills as Sir leads me out of the tent. Twenty workers are already deep in the mine, as every opening has gone the same way—they go in; I stay up top and use my magic to fill them with inhuman agility and endurance. Magic works only over short distances—I couldn't use it on the miners if I was in Jannuari. But here, they're in the tunnels just ahead.

"Whenever you're ready, my queen," Sir says. If he senses how much I hate these mine openings, he doesn't say anything, just steps away with his arms behind his back.

I grind my jaw and try to ignore everything else—Hannah, Sir, all the eyes on me, the heavy quiet that falls.

My magic used to be glorious. When we were trapped in Spring and it reared up and saved us; when we first returned to Winter and I wasn't sure how to help everyone, and it came flooding out of me to bring snow and fill my people with vitality. When I had no idea what I wanted or how to do anything, I was grateful for the way the magic always just *knew*.

But now I realize that if I wanted to stop it from pouring out of me, surging through the earth, and filling the miners with strength and endurance, I couldn't. That's what scares me most about these times—the magic sparks and swirls up, and I know, deep in the throbbing pit of my heart, that my body would give out long before the magic would even consider stopping.

Pulled by some unspoken signal, streams of iciness whirl through my chest and turn every vein into crystallized snow. My instinct reacts with a choking burst of need to stop it, to rein it in, but reason clogs my certainty, since I know that my people need the very magic I'm trying to stifle, and before I'm able to breathe, the magic pours into the miners. I stand in its wake, trembling, eyes snapping open to look on the expectant faces of the crowd. They can't see it or sense it, unless I channel it into them. No one knows how empty I feel, like a quiver for arrows, existing only to hold a greater weapon.

I tried to tell Sir about this—and immediately choked it back when Noam came in the room. If Noam finds out that all he needs to do is have an enemy break his Royal Conduit and he would *become* his own conduit, he wouldn't have to find the chasm. He'd be all-powerful, filled with magic.

And he wouldn't need to pretend to care about Winter anymore.

I turn, hungry for a diversion. The crowd takes that as my dismissal and softly applauds.

"Speak to them," Sir urges when I move for the tent.

I curve my arms around myself. "I've given the same speech every time we've opened a mine. They've heard it all before—rebirth, progression, hope."

"They expect it." Sir doesn't yield, and when I take another step toward the tent, he grabs my arm. "My queen. You're forgetting your position."

If only, I think, then immediately regret it. I don't want to forget who I am now.

I just wish I could be both this *and* myself.

Alysson and Dendera stand quietly behind Sir; Conall and Garrigan wait a few paces off to the side; Theron made it here and converses with a few of his men. This normalcy makes it easier to notice how out of place Nessa suddenly looks next to her brothers. Her shoulders angle forward, but her attention is pinned on an alley to my right.

I shake out of Sir's grip and nod in Nessa's direction as I stride forward.

"They're back," she whispers when I reach her. Her eyes cut to the alley, and I can see from this angle that Finn and Greer stand at the edge of the light, motionless until my attention locks onto them.

Finn bobs his head and they move toward the main tent as if they've been in Gaos all along. They left Jannuari with us but split off soon after, creeping away before any Cordellans could realize that the queen's Winterian council went from five members to three.

Sir guides me to the tent as if afraid I'll refuse to do that too. But I push ahead of him, crowding around the table in the center with Alysson and Dendera. We all try to maintain a relaxed air, nothing out of the ordinary, nothing to draw attention. But my anxiety splits into frayed strands that loop more tightly around my lungs with every passing second.

"What did you find?" Sir is the first to speak, his tone low.

Finn and Greer push against the table, sweat streaking through smudges of dirt on their faces. I cross my arms. Such a routine thing—the queen's advisers returning from a mission. But I can't get the gnawing in my head to agree.

I should have gone on this trip to retrieve information for the monarch—I shouldn't be the monarch herself.

Finn opens his sack and pulls out a bundle while Greer

removes one from his waist. "Stopped in Spring first," Finn says, his attention on the table. Only Conall, Garrigan, and Nessa look out of the tent, watching the Cordellans for any sign of movement toward us. "The early reports that the Cordellans received were correct—no sign of Angra. Spring has transformed into a military state, run by a handful of his remaining generals. No magic, though, and no warmongering."

Relief fights to sputter through me, but I hold it back. Just because Spring is silent doesn't mean everything is fine—if Angra survived the battle in Abril and wanted to keep his survival a secret, he'd be a fool to stay in Spring.

And since we haven't heard a word from him since the battle, if he is alive . . . he definitely doesn't want anyone to know.

"We passed through Autumn on our way to Summer—both are unchanged," Finn continues. "Autumn was gracious, and Summer didn't even realize we were there, which made poking around for rumors of Angra easier. Yakim and Ventralli, on the other hand . . ."

I jolt closer to the table. "They found you?"

Greer nods. "Word spread of two Winterians in the kingdom. Luckily when we said we were there on behalf of our queen, they seemed to soften toward us—but they didn't let us out of their sight until we left their borders. Both Yakim and Ventralli sent gifts for you."

He nudges the bundles toward me. I pick up the first

one and pull back the matted cloth to reveal a book, a thick volume bound in leather with black lettering embossed on the cover.

"*The Effective Implementation of Tax Laws Under Queen Giselle*"? I read. The Yakimian queen sent me a book about tax laws she enacted?

Finn shrugs. "She wanted to give us more, but we told her we hadn't the resources to carry it all. She invites you to her kingdom. They both did, actually."

That makes me pick up the other package. This one unrolls, spreading over the table to reveal a tapestry, multi-colored threads weaving together to form a scene of Winter's snowy fields overtaking Spring's green-and-floral forest.

"The Ventrallan queen had that created," Finn notes, "to congratulate you on your victory."

I trace a finger down the twirl of silver thread that separates Winter from Spring. "We were in Ventralli and Yakim before Angra fell, gathering supplies and other such things, and people saw us, and never once did the royal families care. Why now?"

Greer's age deepens in the way his wrinkles crease, his body slouches. "Cordell has its hands in two Seasons now—Autumn and Winter. With such a strong foothold here, it would be able to take Spring easily too, if Noam chose to do so. Summer has trade agreements with Yakim, but no formal alliance. The other Rhythms know Noam is seeking the magic chasm, and they fear his ambitions.

They're testing Winter's allegiance to Cordell, to see if they can unseat Noam."

"They were both most adamant that you visit them," Finn adds. "Queen Giselle told us you are always welcome. Queen Raelyn said the same of Ventralli—she seems to be the one speaking for the king, though he was just as eager to meet you."

I shake my head. "Did any of those kingdoms show signs of . . . him?"

I can't say his name. Can't force myself to feel it grating on my tongue.

"No, my queen," Greer replies. "There was no sign of Angra. We didn't go to Paisly—the trip through their mountains is treacherous, and after the attitudes we observed in Ventralli and Yakim, we didn't think it necessary."

"Why?"

"Because Paisly is a Rhythm too—they wouldn't host an ousted Season king. Yakim and Ventralli were barely willing to host *us*. I don't think . . ." Greer pauses. "My queen, I don't think Angra is in Primoria."

The way he says that makes me shut my eyes. When I first suggested that someone search the world for Angra, everyone thought I was being overly cautious. He vanished after the battle in Abril, but most believe that the magic disintegrated him—not that he escaped.

"He's dead," Sir says. "He is no longer a threat we should concern ourselves with."

I stare at him, drained. He—and the rest of my Winter-ian council—still believes Angra was defeated, even after I told them that his Royal Conduit had been overtaken by a dark magic created thousands of years ago, before the Royal Conduits were made. Then everyone had small conduits, but when they slowly began to use the magic for evil, that negative use birthed the Decay, a powerful magic that infected everyone with the strength and need to enact their most awful desires. With the creation of the Royal Conduits and the purge of all smaller conduits, the Decay weakened, but it didn't die—it fed on Angra's power until Mather broke Spring's staff.

If Angra is alive, he could be like me, a conduit himself, unburdened by the limitations of his object-conduit. And the Decay could be . . . endless.

But if Angra is alive, why would he be hidden away? Why wouldn't he have swept through the world, enslaving us all? Maybe that's what makes Sir so certain he's dead.

Everyone watches me, even Conall, Garrigan, and Nessa. My eyes shift past them and open wide. One second, no one watched the Cordellans for one second—

"Trouble?"

A Cordellan soldier ducks into the tent, flanked by three others. The moment their armored frames fill the space, my council yanks to attention, casting off any pretense of ease.

I growl deep in my throat as Theron enters the tent too.

"I'm sure they're discussing how best to proceed with the Tadil's spoils," Theron guesses, moving to stand beside me. He tips his head at his men. "No trouble here."

The soldiers hesitate, clearly unconvinced, but Theron is their prince. They back out of the tent as Theron tucks his hand around my waist. The chill of magic palpitates through me, only marred now—I shouldn't need someone from another land to sweep to my rescue. Especially to fend off the very men who are supposed to be protecting us.

"Thank you for interceding, Prince Theron," Sir offers.

Theron bobs his head. "No need to thank me. You should be allowed to gather in your own kingdom without Cordellan interference."

I cock an eyebrow at him. "Don't let your father hear you say that."

That makes Theron tighten his grip on me, drawing me closer. "My father hears whatever he wants to hear," he says. "What were you discussing, though?"

Sir steps closer. My eyes flick to the side, noting Finn and Greer striding down the road, most likely heading to freshen up so as not to appear travel worn.

"We were discussing only—"

But whatever lie Sir might have been about to tell proves unnecessary. Theron unwinds himself from me and snatches the tapestry from the table.

"Ventralli?" he asks. "Why do you have this?"

Of course he would know where the tapestry is from. His mother was the aunt of the current Ventrallan king— Theron's room in Bithai is stuffed with paintings, masks, and other treasures from his Ventrallan side.

I glance at Sir, who holds my gaze. The same emotion coats everyone else—Dendera watches me, Alysson grips the edge of the table. All waiting for my response.

All wanting me to lie.

Finn and Greer's journey was supposed to be secret, one frail act of Winter in the face of Cordell's occupation. Proof that we could do something, *be* something, on our own.

But lying to Theron . . .

Sir's jaw tightens when I hang silent for a beat too long. "The rubble of Gaos," he says. "We found it in the buildings."

I don't realize until the words leave his lips that Theron might find out the truth anyway—if Giselle and Raelyn welcomed Finn and Greer, news will spread. Noam will eventually hear that his Rhythm brethren had Winterian visitors.

I choke, but the lie has been told. Backtracking now would only look worse—wouldn't it? I can't very well ask Sir's opinion on this—besides, he's the one who lied. Maybe . . . it's okay.

No. It isn't okay. But I don't know how a queen would make this okay.

"It's beautiful." Theron runs his fingers down the threads. "A Winter–Spring battle?"

He looks at me, expectant.

I actually manage a chuckle. "You're asking me? You're the one with Ventrallan blood."

Theron cocks a grin. "Ah, but I'd hoped some of me had rubbed off on you by now."

My cheeks heat, inflamed by the group of my advisers still watching us, by the way Theron straightens, tilting his head to me. I can't tell if he knows Sir lied—all I can see is the look he gets whenever something artistic is around, a softening at his edges. Seeing him like this is such a nice change from his recent tension, balancing on the edge of fear and memories, that I almost miss where else I've seen it before.

I jolt with realization. It's exactly how he looked at me on the fields outside Gaos, and every time he wants to kiss me—like I'm a work of art he's trying to interpret.

My heart thumps so loudly I'm sure he can hear. If we were standing in his room, he the prince of Cordell, myself a soldier of Winter, I would have swooned without another thought.

But I look around the tent, at Sir, Dendera, Alysson. Even Conall, Garrigan, and Nessa. They all look at me with similar gazes—like they've only ever known me as the queen of Winter, a figure owed reverence and worship.

But I'm none of those things. I'm someone who just helped lie to one of her closest friends.

This is what Winter needs. This is who Winter needs me to be.

I hate who I am now.

A deep rumble bubbles up through the earth. The vibration catches me off guard, numbness washing over me while the world quivers in a violent cacophony of tremors and belching thuds. A few abrupt seconds and it all falls as still and quiet as if nothing happened.

But something happened. Something that makes the families of the miners, still in the square, scream in terror:

A cave-in.

Clarity hardens every nerve and I launch away from the table. My skirt tangles around my legs until I bundle it and push faster, but just as I angle across the square, someone grabs me.

"My queen!" Sir's voice is his familiar tone of command. "You can't—"

"There are miners down there," I shout back. The people around me rush toward the mine entrance, crowding against Cordellan soldiers who fight to keep them in the square until decisions can be made. "*My* people. I'm the only one who can heal them, and I won't let them stay down there!"

I knew we shouldn't have opened this mine. And now, if some of my people have died because of Noam's insistence on searching for something we will never find—I'll kill him.

Sir's grip tightens. "You're the queen—you do not rush into collapsed mines!"

I almost scream at him, but nothing comes. Because over the ridge hurries one of the Cordellan soldiers charged with guarding the entrance to the mine.

"A miner!" he announces over the square to cries for details. "Coming up the shaft!"

Relief springs in my gut. The magic—it gave them endurance and strength. Maybe it let one of them escape to run desperately fast up the mine shaft.

Sir pushes through the crowd, letting me follow a beat behind.

When we make it to the ridge, the hill on the other side curves down before splitting around a path lined with boulders. The path leads to a cave that seems like any other—dark and fathomless. Sir and I sprint for it, and a trail of people—Conall and Garrigan, Theron, a few Cordellan soldiers—gathers behind us. As I focus on the entrance, I beg the darkness to relinquish the miner, for news that the cave-in wasn't a cave-in, but something else—

Just as we reach the entrance, the miner stumbles out and falls to his knees. He's so covered with grime that his ivory skin and hair are gray, and he hacks a funnel of dust into the sunlight. I drop before him, my hands on his shoulders. No thought, no chance to reconsider—the magic swells in my chest, a surge of frost that rushes down my arms and slams into the miner's body, clearing his lungs, healing the bruises along his limbs.

All the air drains from me, leaving me to pant from the

unexpected use of magic as the tension on the man's face alleviates. Does he realize I used magic on him?

"A wall collapsed, my queen," he coughs. "Weren't expecting it, not there, but—"

Theron falls to the ground beside me, his attention boring into the miner in a frantic pull of pure, aching need.

"We . . . found it," the miner says like he can't believe his own news. He blinks at me, and I try with everything I have left to breathe, just breathe, *keep breathing*.

"We found it, my queen. The magic chasm."

Meira

HANNAH? I TRY, and my magic sparks the slightest flash of cold. *Tell me he's wrong.*

But the emotion that radiates from her is the opposite of what I expected: amazement. Awe. The same winded shock that descends over everyone else.

We were so close, she gasps. *The Tadil, all this time—we were so close. . . .*

Her words fade, but I know what she means.

Before Angra overtook Winter.

The miner shoves to his feet, wordlessly leading me on. Sir lets me stumble after him without protest, trudging along behind me as if he's being dragged into the mine against his will. We're trailed by Theron, Garrigan, Conall, and a handful of Cordellan soldiers.

The morning sun lights the first few paces inside the mine shaft, but farther in, when the ground starts to slant around serrated rock walls, everything is coated in darkness. The miner picks up a single lit lantern, most likely the one he carried as he ran up the mine, and the rest of us take a few from a pile, strike flames to life, and follow him.

The cave flashes into view, tools littering a corridor two arm lengths wide and little more than a full man's height tall. Silence ensnares us the moment we enter the tunnel, the only noise the muted shuffling of our feet as we take cautious steps into the shadows.

Fingers brush my wrist, a delicate touch that grows bolder when I pull up a weak smile for Theron. He doesn't say anything, though I can tell by the way his mouth pops open that he wants to. What is there to say, though, beyond murmurings of disbelief?

I squeeze his fingers and tug him forward, leading him into the darkness.

More shafts open along the way, but the miner at the front of our group leads us past them all, plunging into the deepest tunnel in the Klaryns. The air smells of ancient, musty grime, coating my skin in thin layers that feel, somehow, just as Winterian as snow. That does little to abate the tension coiling in my gut when the tunnel before us ends at an opening.

The other miners' lanterns light up the puckered wall, clearly an unexpected expansion by the way rocks sit in haphazard clusters of debris along the ground. The remaining Winterian miners seem uninjured, which eases some of my worry. They all stand in the tunnel, gaping at the crack in the wall, too afraid to move inside, too awed to pull away.

When they see us, they step back, all eyes snapping to me. But I'm just as afraid, just as awed, the lantern trembling in my grip, light pulsing in dizzying flashes.

Someone *made* this space. Beyond the opening, perfect diamond cuttings turn the gray-black ground into a marble-like floor. The walls around the room are the same jagged rocks as the rest of the mine—but even that seems intentional, as it draws all focus to the back of the room, where the stone has been flattened into a smooth wall.

In that wall stands something that makes me gasp with astonishment.

I slide forward, past the crumbled heaps of rock, depositing my light at the threshold since the lanterns behind me brighten this new space. The moment I step into the room, the air crackles against my skin, a jolt like the electric charge of a thunderstorm preparing to unleash cascades of lightning. I shiver, bumps rising along my arms.

The air hangs heavy and humid with magic.

And I think . . . I think I'm looking at the door to the chasm.

Theron touches my elbow and I start. I didn't know he'd followed me into the room, but he seems the only one brave enough—or stupid enough—to venture after me. Everyone else remains pinned in the entrance, gaping in shocked horror at the same thing that draws my attention like a gnat to a flame.

A door towers over us, massive and thick, made of the same gray stone as the rest of the room. Four images are carved in the center of the door—one, a tangle of flaming vines; another, books stacked in a pile; another, a simple mask; and the last, the largest one centered above the smaller three, a mountaintop bathed in a beam of light with words arching over it, THE ORDER OF THE LUSTRATE.

I step closer, my boots tapping against the stone floor.

A beam of light hitting a mountaintop. *Where have I seen that before?*

And who is the Order of the Lustrate?

Theron hisses. "Golden leaves." He slides forward a step. "Are those . . . keyholes?"

I grab his arm, keeping us both from going too far into the room. This place feels dangerous, like it's waiting for something, and I don't want to find out what.

But he's right—in the center of each of the three small carvings sits a narrow keyhole.

"Do you think this is it?" I whisper, barely loud enough to stir the air.

Theron's hand encases mine where I hold his arm and he nods, dazed.

"Yes," he says, smiling like a piece of him is rising up over the walls of fear within him. "We found it. We're going to be okay now." He looks to me, back to the door.

"We're going to be okay. . . ."

I glance over my shoulder at everyone still clogged by the entrance. Sir's eyes meet mine, and I wheeze on the choking knowledge of what exactly this means.

The last time our world had more than just the eight Royal Conduits, the Decay was created. People began using their individual conduits for things that harmed one another, murder and theft and evil, and that birthed a dark magic that infiltrated people's minds, encouraged them to use their magic for evil, and started a cycle of despair.

And when we open that door, if it does guard the magic chasm . . .

We could be wrong. It could just be a . . . room. In a mountain?

What else could it be?

My throat clamps shut. This really is it, isn't it? I should have stopped Noam long ago. I shouldn't have let him do this to my kingdom—how did we even find this?

Theron's face is wide with astonishment. He's pleased with this find, he'll want to open that door, and seeing that expression on him makes me reel even more. I didn't think. I charged in here without remembering who Theron is, who he *really* is—not just a source of comfort, not just my friend. He *wants* this. Cordell wants this.

I back up, farther from him.

Theron reaches out for me. "Meira?"

Biting and sharp, a cold sensation cuts through my body

in a heave of magic. *My* magic, not the spark in the air. I slam to a halt.

Meira! comes Hannah's voice. She's upset. Afraid. Of what?

Theron follows my retreat. His foot hooks on the floor and he teeters forward, arms flailing as he collides with me and sends us toppling down, closer to the carved door.

Meira, get away from here!

So cold, *so cold—*

MEIRA! Hannah cries. *Mei—*

Silence. Utter, aching silence, like a door slamming shut, cutting off all noises beyond.

Fiery, determined heat eats at my body in mad snatches of relentless pain. Just as frigid as my magic is cold, this is hot, spreading in singeing fingers up my limbs and across my chest and neck. It cauterizes my throat into a lumpy, impenetrable knot, intensifying and raging against every nerve so that when I scream, it goes unheard.

Theron's body presses against mine, and all I know beyond the licking warbles of pain that eat up my insides and remain trapped behind the knot in my throat is that we're causing this. Or *me*—I'm causing this, because Theron isn't in pain. His brow furrows only in confusion.

"Meira, what—"

An invisible force launches us through the air, hurling us back at the entrance to the room. Our bodies pop with a chorus of blows against the stone wall before we collapse in a heap on the floor. Everyone by the door shouts in alarm and dives toward us, but somewhere along the way the knot in my throat released, and the pain comes rushing out of my mouth in a scream that doesn't even sound human. My body throbs and I curl into a ball, head to my knees, arms over my ears, rocking back and forth, trying to find some position that doesn't feel like I'm being burned alive.

HANNAH! I shout at her, at the magic, at anything that could make it stop—

Silence, still. Just silence, that's all I get from her. Dread plummets through me before thick darkness slides into my eyes and down my throat and fills me top to bottom in a prison I know far too well.

"Meira!" Theron's fingers bury in my hair, his arms fold around me. "Meira, hold on—"

A blink, and I'm left alone in darkness, fire, and ice.

Blackness subsides, unfurling in the yellow glow of torches. I'm almost grateful for the light—I'm awake; I survived; I'm okay—until my eyes adjust to the room.

A cell reveals itself in the flickering light, grimy black stones glinting with putrid stains. In the corner sits Theron, staring at the door with a concentration spurred by intense fear.

Because in that doorway stands Angra.

"The heir of Cordell," Angra announces as he walks forward and crouches before Theron, leaning on his staff. "You give new meaning to the word valiant. *What was your plan? Sneak into my city and free*

my latest Winterian slave?" He reaches out, grabbing Theron's chin and wrenching his attention up. "Or are you expecting your father to sweep in and save you both?"

Theron's stoicism breaks in a gasp that matches my own.

This is what happened to Theron while he was imprisoned in Abril.

Angra cocks his head as if he's listening to an echo. His expression flashes with a look I never thought his face capable of. Eyes relaxed, lips parted: shocked awe.

Angra recovers, stroking his thumb along Theron's jaw. "Do you really think he'll come?"

Theron's brows peak, a spasm of doubt that he might not even be aware of.

Angra latches onto it. "You and I are not so different. Shall I show you how similar we truly are?" He places his hand on Theron's head.

Theron cries out. Whether or not this already happened, I can't let him scream like that—I dive as Angra rips his hand back, letting Theron rock forward.

Theron's shoulders heave as he retches. "No" is all he says, his first muffled word. Then, with more terror, "No! He didn't kill her like yours did. . . ."

Kill her? Who? What did Angra show him?

Angra clucks his tongue. "He did, little prince." He pulls back and watches Theron squirm. "We're the same."

"Meira!"

I bolt upright in a haze of flickering yellow, clenching

fistfuls of fabric that tug against my grip. I'm in my cottage in Gaos, the brown walls misshapen and cracked enough that cold air darts inside. The small room holds nothing more than a cot and a few tables, but on every table, candles burn. Dozens of them, and I blink at the light, my eyes darting from flame to twitching flame faster than my brain can process a reason.

The fabric in my fists tugs again and I start.

Sir is here, his hands braced on either side of my legs, and I clutch his collar as if I might draw him into a fight. Theron is here too, hovering at the end of the cot, an unlit candle in one hand and a match in the other.

Angra. The memory. I cave forward, head to my knees, releasing my grip on Sir. Why did I see that? *How* did I—

"The magic chasm," I pant, and burst upright. "The door—there was a barrier—"

It all rushes back to me: the stone door, the keyholes in the carvings, the sensation of being burned from the inside out. A barrier prevented us from approaching the door. A magic fail-safe that launched both Theron and me away, but only affected me.

Maybe the chasm reacted like that because I *am* magic. Maybe it collided with the nearest person and dredged up memories, ricocheting my magic out in a frenzy. But Theron isn't Winterian—how did I affect him? Or was it not me so much as the barrier's magic reacting to my own?

Whatever it was, whatever the reason, it's only a spark in the fire of this horror.

"Whatever magic is down there, we can't touch it," I declare.

Theron gapes like it was the last thing he expected me to say.

"Here, my queen. Drink this." Sir tries to hand me a goblet of water, but I shove it away.

"We found the magic chasm," I state, forcing myself to hear it, to feel it. "Something's blocking it—a barrier of some sort. We cannot take down that barrier. If we access the magic, if it spreads out to everyone—"

Theron lurches closer to my cot. "That's exactly what needs to happen."

I hesitate. The sight of Theron before me clashes with my memory of him writhing on the floor of Angra's dungeon. Was what I saw real, though?

Hannah. I stretch out to my magic with tentative, uncertain thoughts. *Was it—*

Cold sparks up my chest. A normal reaction to seeking the magic, but where it usually flares and fades, this time—it doesn't quiet.

It spurs higher, plummeting down my limbs, gathering speed and strength as it races to launch out of my body. I rear back, slamming into the wall beside my cot.

No, I beg it, screaming in my head. *STOP!*

It doesn't listen. Not in time anyway—it leaves my body a beat before I fling my will out to it, spiraling out of me and into—who? Where?

Sir.

He flies to his feet, mouth popping open in a choking huff like someone slammed a sword hilt into his lungs. "What—" He gags. "What did you—"

He stumbles back, boots slipping on the wooden floor, and bumps into the closed door to the rest of the cottage. His hand drops to the knob and he shoves, but instead of twisting under his fingers, the entire thing breaks apart and clatters to the ground.

I leap off the cot, hands out.

Sir ripped the door clean off its hinges.

No—*I* did it to him.

I drop back onto the bed. I've seen the magic give people strength before—but enough to endure a day of labor, not rip apart planks of wood. And it always reacted the way it should—uncontrollable, but it did what my people needed it to do.

What *happened*?

Sir flexes his hand and shoots a questioning gaze at me. "My queen. Why did you do that?"

I shake my head. "I didn't mean to. The magic down there—that barrier—it did something. I don't feel . . . right."

My chest is so cold. My heart is ice, my limbs snow, my every breath should be a cloud of condensation. The magic felt awakened before, but now it feels—unleashed.

Sir eases forward. "We'll figure it out, my queen. We'll send someone else down there, someone who isn't connected to a Royal Conduit."

I launch to my feet again. "No, it's too dangerous. *No one* can go down there."

"We found it, Meira." Theron intercedes, his voice hoarse. "The magic chasm, after all this time, and you don't want to at least investigate it? The world hasn't seen such power in centuries. Imagine the good we could do with this!"

"And imagine the evil!" I shout, unable to keep my worry at bay. "Did you see what I just did? My magic could've hurt Sir! And you want *more*? Even if we could get to it, the world won't receive magic the way you want it to. You believe your father would use more magic for good? Maybe in Cordell's eyes, but how will it affect my kingdom?"

Theron drops the unlit candle and match he had still been holding and steps closer to me. "The world needs this," he states. "My father isn't the only one with plans—we could see to it that the magic would benefit everyone. Your people would all have their own magic. They'd have the strength needed to keep anything like Angra's takeover from happening again."

"You can't tell your father we found it," I beg. "I know why you fear Angra, but we are stronger than him. *You are nothing like him.*"

Theron's eyes narrow in confusion, darting over my face. I pause, waiting for understanding to clear his memories, but he only cocks his head, perplexed.

Doesn't he remember what Angra did to him? Wasn't that real?

A door opens deeper in the cottage and voices slam into us.

"Is she awake?" Nessa asks.

Dendera chirps when they stumble into the room. "What happened to the door?"

While Sir, Nessa, and Dendera drop into quiet discussion, I draw closer to Theron, lowering my voice. "Please don't tell Noam."

"My men saw it too. Your people know we found it. He'll find out eventually."

"Only a few of your men were down there, and my people will keep it quiet. Please, Theron. Just give me time to figure out what to do."

My heart knots up in the pause that follows.

"When you were asleep—" Theron finally says. "You sounded like you were scared."

He didn't agree to anything. He changed the subject.

"I dreamed of Angra. And you." I hesitate, not wanting

to hurt him, my words hammers and him a porcelain vase. "In Abril."

Theron jolts back from me.

I try to wave it away. "It was just a dream—"

He snatches my hand midwave and holds it, every muscle in his body stiff.

"I don't remember much about it," he whispers, each word weighted by three months of keeping it inside. "Whole days just . . . gone. But I do remember Angra telling me what he planned to do with you. What he planned to let Herod—" Theron's voice cracks. "Angra used magic on me in Abril, that much I do know. He shouldn't have been able to—Royal Conduits can't affect people not of their kingdom. And if a more powerful magic exists, we need protection."

My arms twitch to lean forward and wrap around him. But despite his pain, despite the memories throbbing in my mind of Angra's torture, I can't agree to what Theron wants.

"Then it's even more important that the door stay closed. If it's used wrong, it could aid the very magic you fear."

Theron grimaces. He's unconvinced, but Nessa rushes over to me.

"My queen, how are you feeling?"

She doesn't ask what happened, or anything about the

mine shaft, and I assume Sir filled her in enough. Conall and Garrigan take up their places guarding my room when Sir says something about going to check on Finn and Greer. He doesn't stay to make sure I'm okay; he simply tells Dendera to "ensure that the queen rests."

No help from him—and no help from Theron either, who also leaves. I try to go after him, but Dendera shoves me onto the cot, scolding me to lie down. Theron doesn't notice, vanishing without another word. What did I expect him to say, though? What could he do?

He could help me in this. He could stay, help me deal with . . . everything.

No—Theron is broken because of me. Because he came to save *me*. I saw what he went through—or at least, what he might have gone through. Even if he doesn't remember what happened, there's no way to know whether or not what I saw *didn't* happen. He doesn't need to help me; I need to help *him*. I have other people who can—

Sudden awareness drowns every other thought.

Hannah never responded. The moment I reached out to her, my magic erupted.

I almost call out to her again, but my chest seizes, and I can't tear my eyes away from the splinters of the door that Nessa brushes into the corner. Our connection was always mysterious—maybe the barrier severed it. The coldness inside me throbs as if sensing my dilemma, knowing I'm moments away from trying to rekindle my magic.

I'm afraid of it. But I can't be afraid of my magic. Now that the chasm has been found . . .

I can't be afraid of anything.

Mather

"BLOCK!"

Mather's sword cut through the air a beat behind his command, but even as the word left his lips, he knew how this fight would end. His opponent would stumble on the barn's uneven floor as uncertainty flashed through his eyes; then he would realize his mistake, overcorrect, and end up on his back with Mather's wooden blade pressing into his collarbone.

Seconds later, the man blinked up at Mather from the floor. "I'm sorry, my lord," he mumbled, and rolled to his feet, passing his practice sword to the next in line.

Mather exhaled, watching his breath collect in puffs of white in the afternoon air. At least his next opponent, a boy named Philip, was his age. A nice change from the older men, who stared at him with a mix of fear and desperate eagerness.

Of all the Winterians rescued from the Spring work camps, only six hundred had lived in Jannuari. Two hundred had come from western Winter, seven hundred from the center forests, and a mere one hundred fifty from the southern Klaryn foothills. Of those who had formerly lived in Winter's capital, little more than three-fourths of them had chosen to repopulate Jannuari. The rest couldn't bear the sight of their war-shattered homes and had dispersed three months ago into the now-untamed wilds of a new and unknown Winter.

Sweet ice above, Mather couldn't believe so much time had passed. How had it been three months since they'd returned to Jannuari? Three months since the battle in Abril where he had broken Angra's conduit and the Spring king had died. Three months of freedom.

And less than a month since William and Meira and a contingent of others had departed for the southern mines. In hours—moments, heartbeats—they would return, along with Noam coming back from one of his too-short breaks to Bithai. The Cordellan king would amble back into Winter's capital like the stuffed-up, overconfident ass he was, and swipe what riches the Winterians had been able to extract.

The rattle of armor jerked Mather's attention to the door of the barn. A pair of Cordellan soldiers sauntered past on their patrol through Jannuari's inhabited quarter, mocking grins spreading over their faces as they eyed the scene within.

Mather's grip on his practice sword tightened. But he found he couldn't hate the borrowed soldiers for laughing—what the Winterians were doing *was* laughable, training people so soon after years of imprisonment, expecting everything to instantly heal and fall into place. Most Winterians had only recently begun looking like people again instead of starved slaves. Making them fight when their eyes spoke of terror and memories still raw . . .

Mather turned to Henn. "This is too soon."

Henn leaned forward from where he was propped against the wall, observing the training in William's stead. "We've only been at it for a few weeks." He nodded Mather along. "Spar."

An order. Mather growled, the sound bubbling in his throat. Orders were all he had now. Orders from William, orders from Henn. Orders from his queen.

A jostling near the door tugged at Mather's awareness again, but it wasn't Cordellan armor. Boots, the rustle of fabric, and a voice Mather knew by heart.

"We've returned."

William.

No one seemed to notice the way Mather darkened at William's arrival, an event that should have made him fake a smile, at the very least.

Henn launched away from the wall, closing the space between him and William like a man intoxicated. "You're all back?"

Mather saw the unspoken questions ripple across Henn's face—*Is Dendera safe? Is she well?*—because similar questions filled him.

If you've returned, William, it means Meira is back too—is she safe? Is she well?

Does she miss me at all?

Blotches of red covered William's cheeks, telling of the cold winds that had chased their party all the way from the mines. He smiled at Henn, dusting snow from his sleeves. It scratched at Mather wrong whenever William looked like that. After sixteen years of William being stoic and hard and unrelenting, happiness looked awkward on him.

"Yes," William started, one eyebrow rising. After a pause, he waved at the door behind him. "Dismissed. Go to Dendera. She's just as eager to see you."

Henn slapped William on the shoulder and darted outside. Which left Mather as the sole person to report on the trainees' progress, and when William turned to him, Mather found his mouth had dried more violently than the Rania Plains at noon.

"Report," William coaxed, taking in the Winterians standing behind them.

What did he have to report? The most notable thing the

Winterian trainees had done since they had begun was to eat a full breakfast and keep it all down.

"They're not physically ready for this," Mather stated, his voice level.

William's smile didn't flutter. "They will be. Training will help."

"They need to heal first." Mather angled his shoulders forward, all too aware of how the subjects of their argument stood behind them, watching, listening. "They need to work through what happened. They need to *understand* what happened—"

Mather cut his words short. William's veil fluttered, a crack that showed whenever Mather pushed too far. Like when William had tried to explain his reasoning for keeping Mather's parentage a secret as a "necessary sacrifice for Winter," and instead of accepting that explanation, Mather had demanded why. Because it made sense, yet it didn't make sense, and while Mather had wept on the floor of the ruined cottage the Loren family had claimed, William had simply stood, told him it was in the past, and left.

But all William said now was "No, they need this. They need to get into a routine."

Which felt exactly like: *It's in the past, Mather. Look only to the future.*

Mather panted. He couldn't breathe, damn it. . . .

He shouted a warning cry and dove at Philip. The boy launched backward with a shocked yelp and caught a few of Mather's rapid blows before he tripped on a lump of straw and smacked onto the floor in an explosion of dust.

Mather wrapped both hands around the hilt of his sword. In one solid push of movement he leaped into the air, dropped down, straddled the boy, and rammed the sword against the floor a finger's width from Philip's head.

Everyone in the barn held silent. Not a gasp, not a cry of concern. Just dozens of eyes watching Mather and Philip and the wooden sword wobbling vertically in the barn's floor.

Philip's eyes wandered down Mather's sword, to the crack in the floor, and back.

"So." His lips relaxed in a smile. "This means I lost, right?"

Mather spit out a laugh. The sound released the tension, and a few of the men waiting in line chuckled as Mather helped Philip to his feet.

But Philip's eyes flicked over Mather's shoulder and the laughter died, an absence of sound that ignited all of Mather's senses.

He only had time to grab his sword out of the floor before William swung down on him. Mather slid to his knees, caught the blow, and danced around until he righted himself. William spun his blade and dove again.

Around them, Winterian voices rose in encouragement, Winterian cheers filled the air, so wondrously different from the life Mather had been living months ago that it saturated his every muscle, easing realizations into his mind.

If they're all happy, maybe ignoring the past is worth it.

Mather threw every bit of his frustration into the fight, letting the cheers dissolve beneath his sudden need to beat William. He sucked the cold air into his lungs. Winter's air. The kingdom he had been supposed to lead, protect, defend.

And it was all on Meira's shoulders now.

He didn't want to need her. But loving her was easy, something that had developed over time, like sword fighting or archery—a skill he had picked up methodically until one day he did it without thought. Needing a family, though? He would never in a thousand winters need it.

He would never be able to forgive William for letting him think he was an orphan.

Mather jerked to a halt. William's blade continued through the air and slammed into his shoulder, knocking him flat on his stomach. Mather glowered and sprang up, sword thudding somewhere behind him as he propelled himself at William. His shoulder connected with William's gut, sending both of them down in a tangled pile of grunts and limbs and punches. It didn't last long—in a few firm twists, William had Mather's arms knotted behind his back, Mather's cheek memorizing the feel of the rough wooden floor.

William bent down, his mouth to Mather's ear. "It doesn't matter if they fail a hundred times," he said, barely panting. "All that matters is that we're here. This is our future."

Mather grunted, sucking down dusty air. "Yes, *Sir*."

He knew William hated when Meira called him that, not that William would ever tell her to stop. Mather just wanted to see unease in someone else, so he knew that he wasn't the only one feeling it.

William's grip on him tensed. He held him on the ground for a beat before stepping back, and when Mather burst to his feet, hands clenched, he couldn't bring himself to face the group of now-speechless Winterians.

"That's enough for today," William told everyone as though nothing had happened.

Mather whirled for the door first. William caught his arm in a tight grip, yanking him to a halt as everyone behind them moved to put away the practice swords. "We brought a new shipment of goods. Sort them, and be at the ceremony tonight."

Orders. More jewels for him to sort through, counting out piles of payment to a kingdom that would demand even more. He didn't know why Noam insisted on storing the goods here and playing through a ceremony instead of shipping everything to Bithai. Maybe he wanted to taunt the Winterians even more, force Meira to hand each jewel to him, one by one.

Mather shot William a curt nod and hung back once he realized William too intended to head out. Returning to Meira and Noam, no doubt.

Mather lingered until the barn emptied, and only then did he let himself fly out the door. He was so distracted that he didn't notice the figure standing just outside until he slammed into it, shoulder stinging from where it connected with armor.

"Watch your—" he started, a mouthful of curses ready. Careless Cordellan scum—

But it wasn't just any Cordellan. It was Captain Brennan Crewe, the man Noam had put in charge of the soldiers stationed in Jannuari. Number two on the list of Cordellans Mather hated, behind both Theron and Noam, who tied for first.

Mather spun away, stomping off before he could register any reaction on Brennan's face. He'd gotten only a few paces when he heard snow crunch, footsteps that trotted after him.

"Hold a moment!" Brennan called. "How goes the training? By your scowl, I can tell it's going as well as I'd expected. My king still wonders why you bother training an army, when you have all the protection you would ever need from Cordell."

Mather stopped, boots shredding holes in the snow. The training barn stood to the east of the palace, connected by an expanse of snow and a disheveled path that covered with flakes faster than anyone could clean it. But they were alone, no soldiers pacing by in their patrol. And after his interaction with William, Mather didn't have the strength to keep his mouth shut.

"It's going well enough that you should tell your king not to get too comfortable here," he spit as he pivoted around.

Brennan's eyebrows rose. "You forget your place, *Lord* Mather."

Mather bristled but ground his jaw to steady himself. Being dropped from king to lord didn't bother him, not really—what bothered him was who had all his responsibilities on her shoulders now.

"My apologies, Captain. I did forget my place in relation to your own. I have such a hard time remembering that you aren't an actual soldier—you're a gift meant to protect an investment. It would make things so much easier if every Cordellan soldier walked around wearing bows on their helmets."

Brennan lurched closer. Mather rose up as he neared, but before he felt the sweet vacancy of instinct take over his movements, Brennan smiled.

"Gifts we may be," he said, "but at least we are wanted. Your queen is back, didn't you hear? But has she summoned you? No, I'd take it. You're probably on your way to continue the task of counting out *Cordell's* wealth. You act so sure of your importance to Winter, though we both know your role in this kingdom is little more than that of a peasant."

By the time Brennan finished talking, Mather couldn't see anything but the stars swimming across his vision, his body so hot with rage that he expected the falling snowflakes to sizzle on his skin. He moved, but he didn't remember doing so—all he knew was a sudden fistful of Brennan's collar, the fabric pulling taut out of his breastplate as he yanked the man forward.

"You have no idea what you're talking about," Mather growled.

Brennan's attention flicked over Mather's shoulder. His eyes widened. "Queen Meira."

She was here, now?

Mather released Brennan and spun, his boots twisting on the ice-slickened stones. He plummeted into the snow, his panic fading as quickly as it had come.

The path behind him stood empty.

Brennan laughed. "But you're right, Lord Mather. I have no idea what I'm talking about."

Mather leaped to his feet, tearing down the path as

though he could outrun his humiliation.

Did everyone know of his failures, how he was not only no longer the king, but no longer someone Winter's true ruler turned to at all? Did everyone recognize how far he had fallen?

Did no one else see how much stress and hardship were on Meira now?

And tonight Mather would have to see Meira float around the ballroom on Theron's arm, and pretend that watching her was enough for him. Though every part of him screamed to fight for her . . . he couldn't. She hadn't sought him out in the three months since their return. He'd seen her in passing, in meetings—but that was it.

He didn't want to have to fight for her. He wanted her to *want* him, and she didn't.

She wanted Theron.

As much as it pained Mather to admit, Theron deserved her. It was Theron who had saved her from Spring; Theron who had risked his life to draw Cordell's army to fight Angra.

And it was Mather who had done *nothing* while Meira had fallen unconscious at Herod's feet during the battle. Mather who had paced the halls of Noam's palace until the floors were nearly worn through while she spent months in Angra's prison camp. Mather who did nothing now, again, because he didn't know what he could do for her, and he couldn't stand being around her when she had . . . Theron.

He wasn't king anymore. He wasn't an orphan anymore. He wasn't in Meira's life anymore.

None of this was the freedom he thought he'd wanted.

Meira

THE TWO-DAY RIDE back from Gaos was too short. Even these final moments, hiding behind my horse in the frigid afternoon air as everyone else heads toward the palace, are too short, and I inhale the saddle's worn leather scent. My mount snorts away the snowflakes that land on his nose but otherwise remains unfazed by the cacophony around him.

"My king, welcome back to Jannuari!" a Cordellan calls, one of those who had accompanied us to Gaos.

Another whoops. "Tonight will be quite the party!"

I wince, the voices creeping up my limbs like fast-moving vines. Theron never promised he'd keep his men silent—and for all my certainty that I can handle this situation on my own, I can't think of *how*. I have no idea who the Order of the Lustrate is, or how best to keep the chasm door closed.

"You can claim exhaustion."

I start and whirl to Nessa, hovering beside me. Conall lingers a few paces away, watching the Cordellans with a barely acceptable glare of contempt, while Garrigan watches us.

"He already saw me ride up," I say.

Nessa shrugs. "It was a long trip. Claim exhaustion and come with us to the palace."

"Exhaustion wouldn't be a lie," Garrigan adds, his attention on my face. No doubt taking note of the circles under my eyes, the sallow color in my cheeks.

A noise pulls me away from Nessa and Garrigan, the steady *swoosh* of a sleigh bobbing over the uneven, icy road. I watch it glide past us, the silver-and-ivory details marred by cracks and chips in the paint. It was a discovery in the rubble of Jannuari, one of our few possessions that is entirely Winterian, not influenced by Cordellan assistance. This one is enclosed like a boxed wagon, meant for transporting goods, not people.

And goods it carries. Jewels, stones, all mined from Gaos, to be added to the other riches we've acquired for payment to Cordell and Autumn.

I toss a feeble smile at Nessa and Garrigan and walk out from behind my horse as the sleigh passes.

Noam stands in a group of his men, talking in a low voice to Theron, who seems even more exhausted than I feel. He sees me emerge and turns with a noticeable sigh of relief, drawing his father's attention.

Noam looks like Theron, only twenty years older, undeniably related and undeniably Cordellan—shoulder-length golden-brown hair going gray at the roots, brown eyes rimmed with lines yet glistening under the cloudy skies. His hip, as usual, bears the holster that cradles Cordell's conduit, the jewel on the dagger's hilt emitting a lavender haze of magic.

"Lady Queen," he calls, closing the few paces between us.

The Cordellan soldiers shift in their conversations, watching with interest. There are Winterians here too, busily fixing the buildings surrounding the square, hauling lumber and supplies. Behind it all, the Jannuari Palace rises up. The remaining wings sit in a U shape, cupping a wide courtyard with drooping willow trees, the exterior walls embellished by ivory trim and white marble, char marks and gaping cannon holes.

I pull my shoulders back. "King Noam," I start. I've made pleasantries enough by now that I should have one ready to spit out—*So glad to see you've made it back to Jannuari* or *I hope your trip wasn't too taxing*—but I'm too tired to pretend not to hate him right now.

"Any news on your progress?" he asks. "I keep hoping for the day when Winter will prove itself to be a better investment than expected."

My mask of political neutrality crumbles away. "We are

not an investment," I snap.

Theron steps closer to me. "Autumn will be here in a few hours. We should start preparing for tonight's ceremony—"

But Noam ignores him, his amusement warping into a sneer. "Do not mistake the reason for my presence." His conduit spikes purple light. "You are as aware as I am that the only worthwhile thing in your kingdom lies in those mountains. You have neither the resources nor the support to harness their use. You need me, Lady Queen."

"Someday we won't," I growl. "I'd fear that day if I were you."

Noam's face twists. "A threat? And here I thought you were finally above such things."

I catch myself. He's right. *I hate that he's right*—

A blanket of ice sucks my breath away.

I wheeze on the anxiety that cocoons around my anger, a deadly blend that makes my magic more agitated. It flares up my chest, fed by each word Noam says, each flicker of terror that I'm losing control. Again.

But I should be fine now—I encountered the magic barrier days ago. *My magic should be back to normal, shouldn't it?*

I almost call for Hannah. But even considering that option makes the magic rise higher, coating my tongue with frost and numbing my fingers into solid tubes of ice. I have to calm down—there are Winterians around me. *Lots* of Winterians, and I'm so cold that I feel like one strong exhale will send magic spiraling out of me.

Thankfully, Theron takes his father's arm. The movement distracts me, one beat of relief.

Until I hear what he says.

"We found it," Theron exhales, massaging the back of his neck like he has to coax each word out of his throat. "The magic chasm. We need your help to—"

"Theron!" His name splits my heart.

The magic must have muddled my brain, because surely he didn't say *that*.

But he never actually promised he wouldn't tell his father about the magic chasm. He knows how I feel about it, and I know how *he* feels about it—but I never thought he'd do this.

I didn't realize how desperate he truly was for the chasm, how that spark of hope in his eyes is so anchored to this discovery. Because now, as he stands there, hanging on Noam's reaction, Theron looks more like himself than he has in months.

He needs this.

Noam turns to me. Squints. And smiles. A smile to put all others to shame, cracking across his face like he's been saving it for this day.

"Did you, now?" he asks me—just me, like Theron isn't the one who told him.

No, I want to say. *No, Theron's lying, we haven't found anything—*

Noam steps to the side and waves me toward the palace, his eyes never leaving my face. "I believe we have a few things to discuss, Lady Queen." His smile hardens. "In private."

Sir comes up beside me. Too late to do anything, but he reads the aghast look on my face and spins on Noam. "Is there a problem?"

Noam grins. "My son just told me of your discovery. You're welcome to join the conversation, General Loren."

Noam nods at his men, and I feel more than see them surround us. They're not overtly threatening, and the hum in the square continues just the same—hammers pounding, voices buzzing in conversation. Even Conall, Garrigan, and Nessa remain by the horses, wholly unaware of the way Noam beckons us to follow him into the palace like it's his.

Sir throws Theron a glare when Noam gets a few paces ahead. "You told him?"

The bite in Sir's voice is the same growl he threw at me so often growing up. But this time, it's distorted with the smallest flicker of remorse. Not for himself, I realize when my eyes snap to his. For me.

He knows what happened. Understands it more than even I can at this point.

Theron betrayed me.

My lungs hitch.

The Cordellan soldiers urge us forward, and we start walking toward the palace.

"I had to," Theron says, beseeching, but when I don't look at him, he clears his throat and roughens his voice. "We have to open that door. We need Cordell's resources to figure out a way to do so—and I have a plan that will make my father need my help to open the door too." He leans toward me. "Trust me, Meira."

"But I asked you not to tell him." I finally look at him. "I needed time, Theron. I needed to figure—"

"How much time do you think we have?" Theron's brow pinches, and I know he's trying not to show his frustration. "How long do you think Angra will give us before—"

"Angra is *dead*," Sir cuts in. "You did this to fortify us against an evil that isn't even here?"

Theron's face sets. "I did it so that no matter what evils arise, we will never be outmatched again."

The doors to the palace open and Noam leads us through the entryway, down a hall, and into a study. When the door closes behind us, Noam stops in the middle of the room and locks his arms behind his back, not bothering to face us yet. Theron steps forward while Sir presses his fists into the back of one of the couches, caving in on himself as he tries to assess the situation. And I move to the window, the glass smudged and dirty but still showing a view of the palace's courtyard and Jannuari beyond.

"We found a door," Theron begins when the silence lingers. "In the Tadil Mine. It was carved with scenes—vines on fire, a stack of books, a mask, and light hitting a mountain with the words 'The Order of the Lustrate' around it. The first three had keyholes in the center, but we couldn't move closer to study them. There's a barrier that blocks anyone from approaching."

I know that tone. The slight air of distraction, like his mind rolls through things faster than his mouth can say them. I turn, and sure enough, Theron gazes absently into the air as he talks. He got the same look in Gaos when he stared at the tapestry—and me.

I fall against the wall.

That's where I've seen the Order of the Lustrate's seal before. In Bithai, Theron got this same look on his face when he helped me decipher that maddening book, *Magic of Primoria*.

The beam of light hitting a mountaintop—it was on the cover.

I find myself dangling on the precipice of asking Hannah about this, but that instinct shatters against my abrupt realization that she still isn't here. My mind is only mine.

I brace for a flood of missing her, but all that comes is a small, selfish knot of relief. I'm happy to be the only one in my head again.

Shouldn't I miss her, though?

Noam turns. "Is that all?"

"Yes. I returned once, after we found it." Theron rubs his shoulder, wincing like it pains him. "The barrier is . . . persistent. Each time someone tries to pass, it throws them against the wall. And there's nothing else down there."

I don't have it in me to be hurt that he went to study the door without telling me.

The Order of the Lustrate wrote the book I read in Bithai months ago. Most of it was cryptic scrawling or riddles, but maybe there's something in it that could be useful now.

I instantly groan. There's no way I could get it, not without alerting Noam to its importance. I could send someone to steal it from Bithai, but even when I had it, I needed Theron's help to figure out any of its passages. Maybe Sir or Dendera would be better equipped at deciphering centuries-old riddles?

"The carvings," Theron tells Noam, easing around the couches to stand in front of him. "We can't open the door now, but I think—I think the carvings could lead us to a way."

I straighten, eyes hard on Theron.

"How so?" Noam asks.

Theron exhales. "The whole place feels like a secret, but I think whoever made it wanted it to be opened. But not easily. Something like that *should* be difficult to open, and if I had set it up, I would have made it so only the worthy could access that much power."

Noam stays quiet, his arms folded.

"I think the carvings hold clues." Theron slides a paper out of his pocket and unfolds it, showing Noam as he talks. "I drew them as best I could. Vines on fire, books in a pile, a mask. On the surface, they seem unrelated—but they do have one thing in common."

Noam finally loses his patience. "So help me, if you—"

"Each symbolizes a kingdom in Primoria. Vines on fire—Summer, their vineyards and their climate. Books in a pile—Yakim, their knowledge. A mask—Ventralli, their masks and art. What else could it be? I think these symbols are meant to lead us to a way to open the chasm. I propose we put together a caravan to visit these three kingdoms and see if my suspicions are correct," Theron finishes.

Summer, Yakim, and Ventralli? I keep my face as blank as I can, but inside, unease takes root in my stomach. A Season and two Rhythms? Why would the Order hide the keys in those three kingdoms? Could it be that easy?

Theron certainly thinks so. And he *has* proven rather adept at deciphering cryptic things.

"But *where*?" Noam waves his hand west, in the general direction of Summer, Yakim, and Ventralli. "Where do you propose we begin? What are we even searching for?"

"The keys for each lock, I think. It seems right, at

least—three keyholes, three symbols. Once we get them, I'm hoping the barrier falls—it's a barrier of magic, so the keys might be magic too—"

"So you propose we search all three damn kingdoms?" Noam's annoyance flickers into anger.

"Yes—well, in part." Theron looks down at his sketches of the chasm door's symbols. "We could start by exploring the areas in each kingdom that are most likely to have what we seek. Areas of value, perhaps, that would have survived the tests of time. It's at least a start. We could ask—"

Noam jerks forward, one hand jabbing threateningly. "You are not to breathe a word of this venture to anyone. There is no *asking* anything. No questions of keys or mystical barriers or the Order of the Lustrate. If anyone knows anything at all about these things and hears you speak of them, it won't be difficult for them to figure out what we found." Noam grinds his jaw. "Leaving at all is risky. If word gets beyond these borders . . . no. There has to be another way to open that door."

Theron's brows lift. He seems close to arguing with Noam, his eyes sweeping over his father's face.

I step forward before Theron needs to say anything.

"Do you have a better idea?" I snap at Noam.

The Order of the Lustrate is out there. They exist; they wrote that book, they made the chasm entrance. They have to be out there still, or at the very least, there has to be someone in Primoria who knows them or remembers their teachings, and talking to someone would be infinitely more helpful than that mysterious book.

Maybe they can seal the door or tell me what their barrier did to my magic so I can get it under control—or even just reconnect my link to Hannah, so she can help me. However strange it was to have my dead mother in my head, she was useful sometimes.

"You want the door opened so badly?" I continue. "This is the only clue we have. Unless you'd like to go to Gaos and try running into the barrier yourself. I know *I'd* prefer that option."

Noam scowls. "Careful, Lady Queen."

"No." I curl my hand into a fist. "This is what you've wanted all along, and we found it. So we're going to these kingdoms, and we're going to find the keys or the Order itself or whatever we need to find." I glance at Theron, hating myself for the half-truths I'm telling.

But he's the reason we're here at all.

"We have to at least try," I say. And it isn't entirely a lie—I do want to try. But to get answers, not open the door.

They don't need to know that, though. Theron will go to these kingdoms—his passion won't let him sit idly by, even if his father disagrees. And if Theron goes, I will too. I'll be right there the whole journey, searching just as hard as him, and I *will* find answers. I'll track down the Order, or I'll find the keys before Theron does and in doing so, gain much-needed leverage over Cordell.

Theron seems appeased by my agreement. He looks at me with something like awe, and I shudder. He thinks I've changed my mind about wanting to keep the chasm locked.

Noam's eyes fly over my face. His lips rise in a slow smile again, tinged with condescending amusement, like he remembered something that puts him back in control.

"You propose to visit Summer, Yakim, and Ventralli," he says. "Didn't a few Winterians recently return from such a visit?"

I bite back panic. "What of it?"

"I've been told Yakim and Ventralli extended invitations to you. You already have a relationship with Cordell and Autumn—it will be expected for you to seek introduction to the world, and it will give us cover to search for the keys. And if nothing presents itself in Summer, Ventralli, and Yakim, you'll continue to Paisly. We won't leave a single kingdom in this world unsearched."

Noam's is the kingdom of opportunity. While Winter uses magic for strength and endurance to make its citizens the best miners in the world, Cordell uses its magic to make its citizens the best at analyzing a situation and coming out on top. That's exactly what Noam has done—woven this into something advantageous to him.

My heart heaves disgust, the same draining sensation as when my magic is used. Like I'm not human, not important, just some toy to be played with at the behest of stronger things.

I may not be Cordellan, but I can manipulate a situation too.

"It would seem that Cordell needs Winter as much as Winter needs Cordell," I tell Noam.

I'll play along, you arrogant pig. I'll pretend to be an obedient little queen until I can crush you.

But with what? I thought I'd have more time to arrange a way to break Cordell's hold over us. I thought we'd at least have a Winterian army, a small gathering of fighters. But even if everything works perfectly—I get the keys before them and find information from the Order about controlling my magic—I have no way of forcing Cordell out of Winter.

Or do I?

Because Noam smiles as soon as I finish talking.

"You're quite right, Lady Queen. Cordell does still have need of Winter, and will until all payment has been issued. Speaking of—do we not have a ceremony to prepare?"

I level a gaze at Sir, whose face rests in the emotionlessness he wears so well. He could be terrified or curious or any number of things, and I'd never know.

What I do know is that he didn't help me at all. Either because he thought I could handle it on my own, or because he's too shocked to intercede, I can't tell.

"I will get ready for the ceremony while you and the Cordellans make the necessary travel arrangements," I tell him, eyes on him in a way I hope he understands.

Keep them here. Distract them.

Sir straightens. "Of course. King Noam, if you please," he says, waving Noam to sit.

I exhale in relief and spin for the door before Noam can say anything else, before Theron can catch me and try to mend the tears in our relationship. I have travel arrangements of my own to make, ones involving our only other hope: our mines.

Yakim and Ventralli don't know that we've found the magic chasm—and if Noam has his way, which he most likely will, they won't find out until he can open it. Which means they still want Winter's mines to search on their own—and maybe Summer will be willing to offer support in exchange for payment, even if they have their own access to the Klaryns. While we search their kingdoms for the keys, I could forge an alliance based on a clearly defined trade, not this open-ended, deadly game that Noam plays.

I have no control over whether or not I find the keys before Cordell, or whether the keys are found *at all*, or whether I'll get answers on how to fix my magic—but even if the search turns up fruitless, at least Winter will come through this with *something*.

I will not return from this trip without a way to keep my kingdom safe.

Meira

THE CORDELLAN SOLDIERS who escorted us to the palace barely flinch when I dart out of the room. Only two people care, and their presence adds cool reassurance to my racing mind.

Conall says nothing, simply falls in behind me when I turn right, deeper into the palace. Garrigan closes in after him, just as silent, his face strained and questioning where Conall's is stiff and determined. They both probably wonder what happened, but for once, their station stops them from asking.

I gather my skirt into my fists and keep walking, my back straight. I'm the queen, and I'm behaving exactly as a queen would—orchestrating political maneuvers.

Luckily the Jannuari Palace enhances my illusion of being queen more strongly than anything else. The whole place feels regal—if I focus on what it could be, not on the ruin that it is.

Before I even knew I was queen, Hannah showed me her memories of the palace through our shared connection to the magic. I saw the ballroom, the great square unfolding from the marble staircase in a billowing cloud of such pure white that the entire room gleamed. She showed me the halls, each one taller than the last, lit by sconces that threw light onto the ivory perfection. Everything was white— carvings dug into the walls, sculptures in alcoves, moldings that danced in circles and squares along the ceiling. Everything was beautiful, and whole, and perfect.

All those images conflict with what I see now, creating a collage of old and new, whole and broken. The memories of white statues in every alcove and candles flickering on tables and the white-paneled walls mesh with the half-destroyed palace that exists now, holes gaping in the walls and rubble swept into piles.

A small flicker of longing sparks. Hannah showing me what Winter used to look like was one of the few good memories I have of her. Remembering it now . . .

I'll find a way to get her back. At least, I think I want to get her back.

I yank open a door that leads to the basement. Garrigan and Conall follow me into the even more frigid air, the gray walls a startling contrast to the ivory halls above. We continue until we reach a corridor, more stones forming a floor and walls that host heavy iron doors.

Like the mines that run under the Klaryn Mountains, a labyrinth of rooms winds deep beneath the Jannuari Palace, the stone floors worn smooth from years of tread, sconces caked in dust yet still able to hold twitching orbs of fire. These halls once housed offices or storage or even dungeons, but most of the rooms now remain closed and unused.

Except for a few toward the end.

I hurry on, footsteps tapping lightly on the stones. Right, left, right again, until I reach a short hall with three doors, all locked tight.

Or . . . they *should* be locked.

One stands open on my right, catching me in a brief spurt of worry before I compose myself. We just got back from Gaos—the soldiers haven't yet finished depositing our newest resources yet. It's only them.

But when I step up to the door, everything drains out of me.

"Mather?"

He doesn't rise from where he sits on the floor before a crate, a paper in one hand, quill in the other. The stones, still jagged clumps of rock coated in dirt, haven't yet been polished into the multifaceted, brilliant pieces they're meant to be. The light from the sconces behind me reflects orange and yellow onto the spoils: eerie and dancing, touching each piece and darting away.

Seeing him sends ripples vibrating through me, because aside from Conall and Garrigan, who linger down the hall a few paces, we're alone.

Mather looks up at me, his expression pinched as if he expects me to be someone awaiting orders. But when he recognizes me, his face spasms. "You're not a Cordellan."

I frown. "Should I be?"

He collects himself, his eyes sweeping from my head to my feet so fast I could have blinked and missed it. "I—why are you down here, my queen?"

This is the closest we've been to each other in months—and *that's* what he says?

"Why are *you* down here?" I throw back.

"Helping. You shouldn't be here—it's dangerous."

"Dangerous?"

"You could be crushed." He gestures to the stacks of crates around him.

None are higher than my hip.

His focus drops back to the paper and he scribbles notes, his hand shaking ever so slightly as he writes.

"Dangerous," I repeat. My jaw tightens. He stays quiet, feigning distraction, and the stillness lets the past hour—the past week, the past months—creep over me.

"You're worried about me?" I snap. "You'll have to forgive

me, since the only interactions we've had in the past three months have been in meetings with a dozen other people. So you can see why I might be confused that you think of protecting Winter's queen, when for the past couple of months, you've acted as though you didn't give a damn about her. But don't worry, I have plenty of other people in my life who have perfected the ability to pretend to care. You don't owe me any favors."

That wrenches his attention back to me. "I didn't—and— *What?*" He gapes, glancing around the room like he's trying to find an explanation in the crates. "I was just sitting here, taking inventory for your kingdom, when you come swooping in. What should I have said? Ice above, do you just need someone to yell at?"

"Yes!"

He flinches and my mouth falls open and all my anger drops away beneath an onslaught of far stronger emotions.

I miss him. So much my chest aches, and I can't believe the ache hasn't killed me yet. All I want is to say the right thing, to hear him laugh and joke about sparring with Sir. I need to talk to him, for us to be the way we were—two children standing together against a war. That's how I feel now, but this time . . . I'm not a child. And I'm not standing with him—I'm alone.

I stagger. "I shouldn't have—"

But Mather's eyes close in a scowl before he sets down his

quill and rises to his feet. Something about his demeanor breaks a little, and he widens his legs as if preparing for a fight.

"Okay," he says, arms crossed, the paper crinkling in his fist. "Yell at me."

I squint. "Yell at you?"

Mather nods. "Yes. Do it. I've—" He stops, jaw snapping shut with an audible *click*. He shifts away from me, back again, lips pursing in nervous frustration. "The least I can do is let you yell at me. We both know I deserve it. So"—he waves me on—"yell at me."

I square my shoulders, open my mouth, but nothing comes out. Yes, he does deserve it. But yelling at him won't undo all the times I searched for him in meetings only to see him slouched in a corner, participating as much as would be expected from a newly titled lord of Winter, but not as much as would be expected from my friend. I don't even think it would make me feel any better, because he'd end up just as beaten and forlorn as Theron.

Mather lifts a white eyebrow. "You don't have to actually yell, if you don't want to. Slightly elevated whispering would be fine."

I sigh. "You're not the one I should be yelling at."

"Someone deserves it more than me?"

He's trying for humor, but it tugs at my worries.

"How did you do this?" I whisper, my chapped lips

cracking in the room's frigidness.

Mather hardens. He doesn't seem at all confused by what I asked. "I focused on my duty. I put Winter first, above everything." The sudden heaviness in his eyes negates any advice he just gave. "But I think I messed up. Being king. I'd do it differently now if I could."

"What? How?"

He shrugs, his words coming faster. "I wouldn't focus on Winter as much. I'd let myself focus on . . . other things too. Winter isn't everything."

"Yes, it is," I counter. "You were right to focus on your duty. That's what I'm trying to do, but I feel like I'm barely holding everything together."

"Did something happen?"

Mather's expression is familiar—but it isn't what I expect.

There's no fear. No brokenness. Just strength.

I've been waiting for him to heal on his own. Hoping and needing and *wanting* him to somehow resolve the issues of our lives so I could have my friend back.

Has he figured things out? Has he accepted our new lives?

Or is he just hiding his pain like everyone else?

"We found the magic chasm," I tell him, easing each word out in a test of his strength. "And Noam is sending us in search of a way to open it. We're going to Summer,

Yakim, and Ventralli, and I thought I'd—"

"What?" Mather gags. "You found it? When? Where?"

"The Tadil Mine. A few days ago."

He pulls back, his eyes distant as he thinks. "Noam wasn't in Winter when you found it."

I shake my head.

"So why in the name of all that is cold did you tell him?"

"I didn't want to tell him," I snap. "Theron—"

Oh, no.

"No," Mather wheezes. "Theron told Noam?"

I say nothing, and my silence confirms it. After a pause, Mather groans, and I ready for a rant. This will be the moment that tells me where we stand now—how he reacts to Theron.

But Mather just pushes his groan into a sigh. "That was wrong of him."

My breath catches and my throat wells at the unexpected comfort he offers.

I cough, pulling out of the daze. "That's not why I came down here, though. I need goods. Separate from the ones we're to give Autumn and Cordell."

He squints. "You want goods? Why?"

"Ventralli and Yakim invited me to their kingdoms before this trip was planned, and I want to take advantage of their interest in us while I'm there. Give some of the jewels as a goodwill offering to symbolize trading ownership of a few of our mines for . . . support."

Mather's face lightens, his brows lifting as he grins. That whole-face, knee-quaking smile that constantly bombarded me as a child.

"You want to take some from the stores we owe to Cordell," he clarifies.

I nod. "More than you know."

He barks laughter. "I think I know pretty well." He steps closer and lifts the paper he'd been scribbling on, only now it's wrinkled from where he held it. "I'm one of the Winterians helping to sort the resources from the mines. And what we get is supposed to go straight to Cordell and Autumn tonight, but—" He pauses, mischief sparking in his eyes. "Giving them *everything* didn't seem like the best investment for Winter's future."

I cock my head. "What do you mean?"

"I've been pulling aside resources from every shipment to help rebuild our treasury."

Shock flows over me. "How . . . how much?"

Mather glances at the paper. "Five crates. Which isn't a lot, I know, but I didn't want the Cordellans to realize that some of their precious payment is gone."

He's been helping me, helping Winter, in ways I didn't even know I needed.

I surge forward and lock my fingers around his arm. "Thank—"

His eyes drop to my grip, every part of his body freezing at my touch. I don't pull back and his gaze lifts higher, rising up my arm. My other arm sits tucked inside a tight, ivory sleeve, but this one is bare to my collarbone. I hadn't realized how much more revealing it is than what I usually wear—or what I used to wear—around him. A shirt and pants and boots.

And when Mather's eyes meet mine, his cheeks flush such a deep scarlet that not even the dimness of this room can hide it. A coldness rushes down me, the biting sensation of falling into a pile of snow, every part of my body tingling and alert. I'm swarmed with the feeling of being exposed yet too covered up all at once, and the longer he stares at me, the colder my body grows.

I jerk away from him and coil my fingers into my palm.

He swallows, throat convulsing. "I'm glad I could help. But . . ." He stops. "You're already a better ruler than I ever was."

I shake my head to fight the way Mather looks at me, as if he's studying me, noting how close we are, how much closer we could be. I wanted him back in my life to have support, someone to help me save our kingdom—not another complication.

But my heart says otherwise, knocking against my ribs in deliberate, persistent pulses.

He helped Winter. He isn't dissolving at the mention of problems or trying to avoid issues.

"Five crates," I echo. "I wonder if that will be enough."

Mather shakes back into our conversation. "How much are you thinking?"

I smile. The lingering pinkness in Mather's cheeks deepens.

"More," I tell him. "A lot more. Enough to send one final message to Noam."

Mather nods. "I'm a proponent of any plan that irks him."

I laugh. The sound jolts through me, sharp and bumping, and I clap my palms over my mouth.

"You're allowed to laugh." Mather chuckles at my surprise.

The part of me that spent so long missing him sighs, content.

The sound of footsteps echoes down the hall, ricocheting off the stone like pebbles falling down a mountainside. I turn when Sir comes to stand beside me.

"My queen." Sir glances past me to Mather, who shoots up straight, shoulders rolling back in a sudden stance of alertness. But Sir doesn't afford him more than a glance, his attention dipping back to me. "We need to speak about the trip."

"I know—but not just yet." I turn to Mather again. The idea he planted sprouts roots and unfurls wide leaves, fostering recklessness similar to that of the wild girl I used to be.

But while that girl made mistakes, she is the reason I have a kingdom to rule. I owe it to myself to at least try to be her again, in some small way.

"Where did you put those five crates?" I ask Mather.

His stance relaxes and he waves his arm out for me to follow him.

Down another hall, up two rooms, Mather stops, leading the party of Sir, Conall, Garrigan, and me. He digs a key out of his pocket and unlocks a door, swinging it wide to reveal a grime-covered space even smaller than the rooms we were just near.

But in the back stand five crates, each stuffed with lumpy pieces of Winter's future.

I pivot to Sir. "At the ceremony tonight, bring only these five crates."

Sir blinks. "My queen, Cordell is expecting far more than this."

"They will get what they deserve in time. But for now . . . we have a greater need."

Sir's veil of formality lifts, showing a flash of his worry. "Cordell is our only ally, my queen. It is not wise to anger them."

I know, and I almost tell him that, almost break through my fragile certainty. What I'm doing is purely the old me, something rash and careless, the part of me that snuck away to find my chakram. The part of me that wails in fury whenever I have to use my magic or Noam tightens his grip on Winter. The part of me that wants to *matter*.

"Which is why I'm going to get us more allies," I tell Sir.

It's dangerous, but we need these resources to gain allies so we can get some leverage.

Noam will be *furious*.

And right now, that sounds wonderful.

Meira

DENDERA GIVES MY hair a final pat. "You're ready."

Nessa squeals and claps her hands over her mouth. My eyes flick to Dendera's reflection, heartbeat hurtling back and forth in my throat. Her enthusiasm is almost as palpable as Nessa's, if not as vocal.

I close my eyes, back straight, face impassive. When I look, I will see someone capable and composed, a warrior and a leader all in one. I can be both Winter's queen and the orphaned soldier-girl, as my act of defiance tonight against Noam will show.

I open my eyes.

My hair, half pulled behind my head in an array of braids, half curling around my shoulders, shines the most radiant white. My gown has silver clasps at the shoulders that leave my arms bare and a belt that curves tight around my waist. At my throat, nestled against the ivory of my collarbone, sits Winter's Royal Conduit, the silver, heart-shaped locket with the single white snowflake etched on the center.

I smile, trying out an expression the same way Dendera made me try on different gowns. The pretense cracks and my stomach tightens with the ever-lingering knot of worry that this is a mistake. That I'm wrong for what I have planned, that I need to not be reckless or impulsive or do things I *know* are dangerous.

But I hold that smile on my face until it aches.

I smooth the pleated skirt and follow Dendera and Nessa out of my room.

Conall and Garrigan drop in behind us, along with Henn, who takes Dendera's hand. I sneak a grin at her, but she's too absorbed in Henn to see.

My entourage and I weave our way through the palace, looping around to enter the ballroom through the door closest to the rear. I know what awaits us beyond it—a dais, along with Cordellan soldiers, Noam, Theron, the Autumnians, and my people, all excited for the ceremony.

I should be excited too. But a sudden surge of music makes everyone around me stiffen, as if no one is sure they're hearing what they think they're hearing. I tell myself to move through the door linking this hall to the ballroom, but I can't.

This music. It's airy and delicate, bouncing off the walls around me in a swell of unassuming perfection. If I could put notes to the sound of flakes falling, of water crystallizing into ice, of snow gusting on the wind, this would be it.

This is what Winter sounds like.

Dendera squeezes my arm, a dreamlike smile on her face. "The instruments are lyres, a discovery salvaged from the palace. It appears Angra did not destroy all of our treasures."

Yet, comes my instinctual reaction, shattering the trance of the music. But no—he's dead. Finn and Greer brought back no news of him. And even if he comes back somehow, I'll have allies united to stand against him. He can't hurt us anymore.

A door opens on our left, letting a flurry of musty air waft up from the stone halls below. Sir emerges, trailed by Greer and Finn, each with at least one crate in their arms. The goods I designated for Cordell and Autumn.

Sir narrows a look at me. "My queen, are you certain you wish to go through with this?"

I teeter on the brink of changing my mind. "Yes."

He shifts the crates he holds, his uncertainty reeling on his face. "I trust you, my queen. We all trust you to make the best decisions for our future, but I—"

I put my hand on his arm. "Please, William. Let me do this. Let me just try."

That silences him, and he holds my gaze in the stillness like he's searching for something in my eyes. But he says nothing more, and Nessa takes my hand to lead me toward the end of this ivory hall. I'm dragged back to all those times in Abril when she held on to me for strength or out of some dire need to make sure I was there.

My fingers tighten around hers, and Dendera opens the door.

The celebration unfolds around us, cupped inside a half-destroyed ballroom. The south side of the ceiling is completely gone, only a fraction of the wall remaining, which lets in snowflakes and the gray evening sky. A marble staircase against the far wall leads to the wing that houses my room and a few dozen more. The other walls tower three stories in the air, lined with the same ivory moldings and silver accents as the rest of the palace. Cracks run like jagged snakes through the walls; bits of mortar crumble from the broken ceiling in bursts of shattered rain.

But as I step inside, I couldn't have guessed that the ballroom had ever been anything but whole.

Everyone is here. Every resident of Jannuari, the Autumnian visitors, a few Cordellan soldiers, all mingling under the lyre music and snow-cloud sky. And every Winterian has managed to find at least some small piece of white clothing to wear in honor of our kingdom—a shirt or a scarf or a gown with white patterned over gray. Hundreds of white-haired heads in white outfits, twisting and moving like so many flakes of snow. Winter's blizzard.

The dais sits to the right of the hall I just exited, adorned by tufts of white silk and bundles of Winterian plants, evergreen sprigs and milky snowdrops. The fresh scent of pine and the honey-sweet floral aroma mix with the crispness of the air drifting through the ceiling, creating an atmosphere that saturates my every nerve with thoughts of Winter.

The atmosphere cracks a little when I see who waits on that dais: Noam, Theron, and two Autumnian royals.

I've managed to avoid Theron since our meeting earlier, keeping to my room or the basement. Now I meet his eyes, and I see there a question laced with concern wrapped in need.

My attention leaps from him to his father, both of them straight-backed in their green-and-gold Cordellan uniforms. Entirely normal, as if we didn't find the magic chasm's entrance at all.

Focus. Breathe.

Unlike Noam, the Autumnians have had the decency to remain in their own kingdom since Winter's rebirth to give us time to collect ourselves—which means I haven't met them yet. King Caspar Abu Shazi Akbari, whose line holds the connection to Autumn's female-blooded conduit, stands beside his queen, Nikoletta Umm Shazi Akbari, Noam's sister, whose marriage produced the female heir Autumn needed after two generations without a daughter.

Caspar watches me so intently that I'm worried about tipping over backward. He has the shoulder-length black hair, warm umber skin, and deep, black eyes of Autumn. His tunic of glistening gold over ruby-red pants seems too simple for a king, but the thin strand of interlocking gold leaves in his hair proclaims his station.

Nikoletta, by contrast, beams at me. Gentle waves of dark blond hair ripple over her shoulders, far lighter than the black-as-night hair of her Autumnian subjects. On her head sits a crown of rubies that hosts an array of dangling beads. Red fabric pours out of the back of the crown, blending into her bloodred gown, which is overlaid with golden flowers and more rubies.

"It is my deepest honor to present . . ."

I jump. Dendera has moved to the dais, her voice urging a hush over the music and chatting voices. Everyone turns to face us.

". . . the savior of Winter . . ."

Nessa tugs on my hand, bouncing in her excitement, but I can't join her. At the edge of the crowd, on the other side of the dais, Alysson grins up at Dendera, one arm tucked into Mather's. But he stares straight at me, eyes unblinking. His mouth opens like he wants to say something, but he catches himself in the heavy silence of the ballroom and hesitates. Trapped between those three months we went without talking and our interaction earlier.

Before anything can happen, Dendera's voice bursts out into the ballroom with such force that I expect the rest of the ceiling to crumble.

". . . Queen Meira Dynam!"

The crowd switches from watchful to cheering, a frenzied explosion that overwhelms the lyres as they start up again. Nessa eases her hand from mine and I move toward the dais with cautious steps, the cheers of the crowd ringing in my ears. My people, *applauding*.

No matter what happens, this ceremony was worth it, if only to hear my people so happy.

I draw their voices into my heart, lock them away deep inside me, and climb the dais, putting Noam, Theron, Nikoletta, and Caspar on my right. They're close enough that I know they can see me trembling, can probably hear me gagging on air.

The crowd's excitement ebbs until silence hangs heavier than any cheer. All eyes on me.

"We are here today . . ." Mouth dry, I push out loud words. "We are here today to pay our thanks for the brave acts of Cordell and Autumn."

I wave Sir, Greer, and Finn forward, each still carrying the crates. "These past months have allowed us to reopen our mines, signifying that Winter is a viable, living kingdom again."

The last part I say to Noam, staring at him though my voice carries around the room. His eyes flicker as my men flank me on the dais.

I motion Finn and his two crates forward. "To Autumn, the first of much that is owed."

The crowd breaks into a reverent applause as Finn lays the goods at Caspar's feet. Caspar bows his head in wordless thanks and Nikoletta applauds softly. Neither of them seems put off by the small offering—in fact, they simply seem grateful to be here at all.

I wave Sir and Greer forward. "And to Cordell. The first of many payments."

Noam eyes the three crates that they lay at his feet before glancing at me, at Sir, and even farther back, at the hall door. No one else moves to bring forward the rest of the payment.

His face twists. The glow around the dagger at his hip wrenches from delicate lavender to heavy indigo. "You must be mistaken." His words are soft, just for those on the dais.

Sir and Greer back away, joining Finn at the edge of the stage. I smile as serenely as I can, ignoring the way Theron watches me, silent, evaluating.

"Winter owes Autumn and Cordell much," I say, keeping my voice elevated. "And we will continue to pay both until our debts are cleared. We thank these kingdoms for their service and sacrifice." I start a heavy clap that catches and spreads, signaling the end of the ceremony.

The din of cheers and applause rises again, as does the lyre music, kicking up in a post-ceremony celebration. The guests turn into it, swaying in chatting groups, everyone pleasantly distracted as Noam grabs my arm before I can duck off the dais.

"This is far from over," he growls, his fingers bruising my bare skin.

I look up at him, but I don't see him. The stronger pull

of conduit magic living in my body connects to Noam's magic through skin-to-skin contact, and memories pour from his head into my own, the same I've seen before: Noam, at his dying wife's bedside, but something about his remorse is . . . off.

A flood of violent emotions hits me, overpowering everything else.

I will destroy her, Noam thinks. *I will not be denied what is mine by a child.*

Sir pushes Noam back. "None of that here," he growls through clenched teeth.

A movement on the edge of the dais says the Cordellan soldiers have readied themselves, waiting for Noam to give the order. Beyond them, the laughter and music of the party doesn't dwindle, no one besides us noticing the tension.

I lean close to Noam. "We will repay what we owe you, but Winter never agreed to the things you demand."

Noam eases forward, his hot breath bursting across my face. "You cannot win against me, child-queen. I will raze this kingdom as brutally as the Shadow of the Seasons if I have to."

Theron grabs his father's arm. "You don't mean that?"

Noam doesn't turn away from me. "I do." He tips his head, his anger lighting in a new expression: scorn. "What do you intend to do with the resources you kept? Go ahead. Use this trip to negotiate aid for your pathetic land. But know this—" He jabs a finger at me and I lurch back, shock making me pliable. He knows what I intend to do? "No number of allies will save you from my wrath. You think I fear the other Rhythms? No, Lady Queen—this is the final act of impudence I will tolerate. I will stay in Winter while you search the world, and if you return without a way to open that door, I will forcibly take your kingdom. No more games, no more stalling; Winter will be *mine*. Prove to me that you are useful. Make me glad I let you live."

Theron shoves his father back, teetering him toward the edge of the stage. "Stop."

But Noam is too far gone for intervention. His top lip flickers in a snarl and he catches Theron's arm in an unrelenting grip. "Don't think I don't know where your heart is, boy. This trip isn't just a test for Winter—prove to me that you are worthy to be my heir. I will tolerate no more games from *any* of you."

My mouth closes, muscles cramping so all I see, feel, think is a pulsing, reverberating panic that starts in my gut and spreads through my body. The magic rises up into a swirling, threatening gale, pushing higher and higher for the surface.

I swallow, choking. *No, not now—*

Before I can add more proof of my weakness to Noam's crusade, I rush off the dais, hand against my chest, trying and failing and begging the magic to compress back inside me.

I did this. Of course Noam would figure out my plan—it was stupid to think he wouldn't. And we have a deadline now.

Should I have let him bleed my kingdom dry? Should I have not fought back? No, of course not. But not like this. Not like . . . me.

The magic sputters, knocking the air from my lungs. I stagger through the door and dump myself back into the hall, the noise of the celebration muffling in the high, narrow walls. Someone says something to me, distant and fogged, and my knees crack as I drop to the ground. But I will not use my magic—I am not weak, I am not afraid, *I am the queen*.

"My queen!" Sir kneels in front of me.

I brace myself against the floor, gritting my teeth. "I . . . I did that. . . ."

Sir's face softens. *Softens.* "You tried, my queen. You understand now, though."

I blink at him. His words sink into my mind like stones plummeting into a pool.

He let me do this. And he isn't angry—he's expectant. Like he allowed me this one flash of who I used to be as a test of my growth. Hannah would have done the same—let me plunge ahead, knowing I'd realize my folly and come limping back to what was right.

I do understand. I always understood, but I thought—I hoped—that I could handle this as *me*.

But only a queen can handle running a kingdom, not an orphaned soldier-girl. No one else can deal with their past; why did I think mine would help us?

Around me, Nessa, Conall, and Garrigan hover, faces twisted with concern.

Sir remains kneeling beside me, expressionless. "Are you all right, my queen?"

"No," I growl. I hate him for not believing in me; I hate myself *for* believing in me. "But I swear, I will be."

Mather

WHEN MEIRA HAD appeared next to the dais, cheeks tinged the most enticing shade of pink, the fabric of her gown pulling against her legs—Mather understood more violently than he ever had the meaning of the word *perfection*.

And he would have hated himself for thinking that, if not for their lingering conversation from hours before. The one when they had felt like themselves again—he, capable of helping her, and she, an untamed girl with deadly ideas in her eyes.

Now he couldn't look away as she stood over the crowd, spewing niceties about gratitude and owing much to Cordell and Autumn. She was in there, somewhere. The girl he'd grown up with. She was in there, and he was still here too, and maybe, just maybe—

Reality crashed back over him.

They weren't themselves. He was a lord and she was a queen and Theron was . . . hers. Theron, who smiled at her now. Mather wished he could find even a flicker of dishonesty in that smile—but it was pure and true, and Mather hated him for it.

This was why he'd avoided Meira for so long. So he wouldn't have to see Theron too, and be reminded of how she had found someone better than himself.

Mather swung to his left, diving away from Alysson and into the crowd that remained transfixed by Meira's speech. He had just formed a plan to sneak out of the ballroom when a boy from the army training burst into his path.

"Lord Mather?"

Mather drew back, thoughts scattering. Applause and lyre music rose up—Meira must have finished her speech.

"Just Mather," he corrected. "Philip, right?"

"Just Phil," Phil returned with a grin, and motioned toward the city. "Some friends traded with the Cordellans for ale. You look like you could use a glass."

A laugh scratched its way out of Mather's throat. "Is it that obvious?"

Phil bobbed his head noncommittally. "Well, I figure there are two kinds of people here tonight." He glanced behind Mather, surveying the now dancing and chatting crowd. "Most are celebrating. The rest are trying to forget that Jannuari hasn't had such a celebration in sixteen years."

His eyes drifted back to Mather. "And you're definitely in the latter camp."

Mather shrugged. "I don't want to forget," he admitted, and glanced over his shoulder, all the way across the room, to Meira, still standing on the dais and talking with Noam, William, and Theron. Even from this distance, he could tell that her confidence had sputtered into anxiety—her hands clenched against her stomach, her bottom lip occasionally caught between her teeth in a wince that made him want to slide an arm around her waist, press his lips to her ear, and promise that everything would be okay.

"Ah," Phil murmured.

Mather turned back to him. "Ah, what?"

"Ah, you're no different from all the other Winterian boys." Phil motioned to Meira. "You're sweet on the girl who saved us. It's natural, I guess, to flip upside down over the person who made our lives less horrible. Don't worry, ale cures that too."

Mather blinked. Of course he wasn't alone in his love for Meira. But realizing that made him feel even more pathetic.

"Lead the way to this ale that cures so much," he said, and Phil chuckled.

Leaving the ballroom wasn't as difficult as Mather had thought—no one spared them a glance as they shot out of the doors and into the night. The palace walls muted the cheering and music, making the transition from the packed ballroom to the open night one of instant peace. Mather breathed in the dancing snowflakes, but Phil was already halfway down the courtyard, striding quickly into the dark city.

Though all work had been packed away for the night, the air reeked of sawed wood and sweat, and snowflakes stuck to everything in sight. Mather dug his hands into his pockets and tried not to analyze the cottages they passed. William would want that one to have a new roof—that one still needed a sturdier door—the windows on that one were salvageable.

Phil nudged Mather's shoulder. "You'll feel less pitiful when you're surrounded by people who feel the same way."

"Really?"

"No. But everyone else will be excited to meet the swordsman who pulverizes them on a daily basis."

Mather chuckled.

A few streets later, Phil jogged up to a cottage and rapped on the door. Laughter could be heard inside, sounding out of place in the damaged house. Repairs hadn't yet touched this area—warped gray wood wove into an ancient front door, the windows on either side hid behind jagged burlap. Every building on this street was vacant, with only the laughter coming from within this lone cottage acting as a barrier to the sadness.

The door opened to a boy, slightly younger than them, who burst into a grin and punched Phil in the shoulder.

"You're late! We started without you."

Phil grabbed his shoulder like the punch had actually hurt him. "As long as you Suns didn't drain the barrels yet. Eli, Mather. Mather, Eli."

Eli narrowed his eyes. "Once-King Mather?"

Mather's brows rose. He'd never been called that, but it had probably been thought in his direction. He couldn't believe it didn't hurt him now. "Just Mather."

Eli didn't seem convinced, but he disappeared back inside, shouting as he went that they had two more for the table. Phil moved to follow when Mather tipped his head. "Suns?"

Phil glanced back. The happiness on his face flickered, his smile breaking for the first time. "I guess you'd never have heard that, huh?"

Just as Mather waved his hand to brush it off, Phil spoke.

"You know how Spring soldiers have black suns on their breastplates? That got to be what we called 'em, in the Bikendi camp, at least. 'Suns are coming, better be quiet!' It's a joke now, among those of us from Bikendi." Phil winced every time he said the camp's name. He shrugged toward the people within. "They're all 'Suns.' Like worthless, you know? Unwanted. Sounds ridiculous explaining it, but there it is."

An invisible hand wrapped cold fingers around Mather's throat. Phil dove inside like he hadn't just pointed out the one biggest difference between Mather and everyone here.

Mather had been free while everyone else had been separated into four Winterian work camps in Spring—Abril, Bikendi, Zoreon, and Edurne. Would they hate him for it? Would his presence serve to remind everyone of how they had spent their childhoods cowering from Angra's men while Mather had spent his childhood with his family?

Mather stomped into the cottage and slammed the door behind him. The room sat in near blackness, lit only by a few candles, and holes in the ceiling let in barrages of snowflakes that poured over the single table in the center of the one-room cottage. Five of the younger boys from the training sessions, including Phil, crowded around the table, goblets in their fists, puddles of ale dyeing the wood dark brown. Another person sat away from the table, huddled in a back corner on a stool. A girl, her knees pulled up to her forehead, her hands working furiously at something as bits of wood flew about her. Whittling?

The door's slam reverberated through the room. The boys paused in their alcohol-encouraged laughter to survey the newcomer.

"Mather." Phil waved his hand in introduction from his spot at the table, pointing out people as he said their names. "Trace, Kiefer, Hollis—and you already know Eli. Kiefer and Eli are brothers. The ghost in the back of the room is Feige, Hollis's little sister."

Feige shot Phil a glare that would have unnerved the hardest soldier. "I am *not* a ghost."

Phil rolled his eyes. "Keep telling yourself that, little one."

"Leave her alone," Hollis said in a voice that, while soft, shot into everyone like an order from a general. He was a huge boy, broad shouldered, the oldest of the lot, probably twenty or twenty-one. He had his chair positioned so he could see everyone in the room, and kept glancing at his sister as if to make sure she hadn't vanished.

Phil shrugged at Mather. "They're all in denial. But I guess that's what this is about, eh? Liquid denial." He took a swig.

Trace chuckled into his own goblet. He was older than Mather, but not by much, with the lean muscles of someone who could be molded into a fantastic close-combat soldier. Knives perhaps, something easy to carry, a weapon that victims saw only when he wanted them to.

"Don't sound so righteous." Trace peered up at Mather as he spoke, though his words were still directed at Phil. "You're denying it just as much as the rest of us."

Mather plopped into a chair between Phil and Eli and grabbed the nearest cup. "Denial has nothing to do with it. There's no way to handle it at all."

That wasn't true. William handled it, and Alysson, and everyone else who clung to the joy of "At least we're in Winter again." Somehow, they'd been able to accept being back in Winter as enough to heal their pasts. He wished it could be that easy for him, but it wasn't. Which was why he didn't care what repercussions William might dump on him for drinking his problems away—and worse, for condoning other Winterians' drinking their problems away too.

Kiefer glowered across the table. "What would you know about any of this?" he hissed. His question shattered the cloak of ignorance that the others had been holding on to, and everyone shifted in the sudden crack of discomfort.

Mather swirled the ale around his goblet. "Nothing," he confessed.

Kiefer held still. He hadn't expected that answer and, after a moment, dropped his gaze.

Feige leaped up in the silence that followed. She strode across the floorboards, the old wood not even moaning under her small frame, and stopped just beside Hollis.

"Go back to your stool," her brother snapped.

Feige ignored him, her eyes on Mather, calm certainty turning her youthful face into a dare. She was so small, yet Mather saw in her the ferocity that came when someone had seen years of bloodshed and battle. This girl couldn't have been more than thirteen or fourteen, but she was . . . weathered. That was the only word Mather could think of to describe her, but even that didn't entirely fit. Some awkward combination of worn and hard.

"Why?" Feige asked. "*I'm* not in denial." She glared at Phil and he instantly dipped away. When she was satisfied that he had surrendered, she turned to Mather. "What do you have to be in denial about, Once-King?"

Mather's grip tensed on the goblet. Hollis dropped back against his chair, his muscles coiled, bracing himself. All of them braced themselves, gulping ale and avoiding eye contact and holding their breath. For what? Feige?

Mather gave the only answer he could. "Failing you."

Feige laughed, her white hair bobbing in clumps that had likely never seen a brush. "At least you can admit it. No one else running this kingdom can."

"He isn't running this kingdom anymore," Kiefer mumbled to his lap. His eyes shot up, daring, challenging. "You may be a lord, but you're just one of us now. You're here instead of dancing the night away with the royals. They kick you out, Once-King?"

Mather dropped his eyes from Kiefer. No challenge here.

"But maybe that's why they don't let him do more than train the army now." Feige dug for something in her pocket, a wooden object she closed in her palm. "Because he's not the king, but the older ones know he can admit what happened."

Mather wanted to agree with Kiefer. He wanted to say he wasn't leading this kingdom, not anymore. But tonight should have been a chance at forgetting, so Mather stayed silent, his fingers tightening even more on the goblet.

After a long pause, Feige's amusement vanished. She tossed the object in her hand into the air, a chunk of wood that smacked onto the tabletop with a dull *thunk*. "I think you know we aren't really Winterians. We're different from them—we can't forget our pasts because it's all we've ever known. And I think the older ones realize you know that, and that's the reason they don't want you around. Because the people who are running this kingdom can't bear to have anyone around who might remind them of their great failure."

All the blood in Mather's body rushed downward, leaving him light-headed and gaping at this girl. This was why Phil had called her a ghost; it was too hard to believe she was real, this child throwing insults and truths with more accuracy than any adult.

Everyone at the table remained quiet, bodies slack. Mather tipped his goblet, the ale sliding down his throat in a bitter wave as Feige returned to her corner, curled on her stool like nothing had happened.

"Isn't enough ale in the world," Phil murmured. "Your sister will be our downfall, Hollis."

Mather reached for the carving in the middle of the table and cradled it in his palm. "No."

"My lord?" Hollis glanced up.

Phil rolled his eyes. "Suns, Hollis. He's one of us now."

The alcohol hit Mather's empty stomach and made him a little warmer, a little lighter, as if his body might float up out of the holes in the ceiling. Phil started drinking again, urging everyone else to start up before Mather could expand on his disagreement. Back to their evening, as if Feige's interlude had never happened. They could be just as good at pretending they didn't hurt as all the older Winterians.

Mather joined them. He wanted this, or thought he did, and forced himself to laugh at Phil's imitation of a Cordellan soldier. He wanted to focus on jokes and being around boys his age; the only person he had ever interacted with his age was . . . Meira.

She needed to know there were others who felt as she did, apart from Mather. That things were wrong, that they didn't fit here as perfectly as they should. He should storm back into the ballroom and swoop Meira into his arms and let everything tumble out.

Mather emptied another goblet.

Feige faded to nothing more than a shadow in the corner, whittling and rocking back and forth. Mather kept her carving in his lap, and though he toyed with the idea of pretending, he made sure he still had that small reminder that this wasn't real happiness.

Trace recounted Phil's failed attempt at sword fighting earlier today. Mather laughed and offered details, but kept his hand on the carving. No bigger than his palm, half a wildflower, half a snowflake, with four words etched on the back.

Child of the Thaw.

He wasn't sure why that mattered so much to him. But the more he drank, the more he could pretend Feige's words hadn't slammed into some hollow place inside him. The more he could pretend he didn't see how the boys gazed into the air when they thought no one watched, their eyes distant as if they saw the horrors of their pasts raging toward them.

The more he could pretend they weren't all Children of the Thaw.

Meira

I TRY TO stumble through the celebration, but Nessa
pleads with Sir to let me rest, and I can't even begin to say
how grateful I am for her insistence. She rushes to light
candles around my room, and Sir stays fixed in the doorway between Conall and Garrigan, who resume their posts
as if nothing's changed. As if I haven't had another panic
attack and basically doomed us to a Cordellan takeover.

Sir crosses his arms. "I'll go with you."

I drop onto my bed, one arm over my eyes as I listen to
the steady *flick-swish* of candles springing to life. "No. You
need to stay here, in case Cordell—" I stop.

Noam is staying to more firmly plant himself in Winter
in my absence.

I was such a fool.

"My queen, I implore you to—"

"You *implore* me?" I sit up. "But I guess that's proper, a

general imploring his queen. I'm too tired to argue this, Sir, so consider your imploring heard. But you're still staying here."

When I started speaking, Sir's demeanor had been hard, defensive, but now he slumps against the doorframe, his eyes glazed with an emotion I've never seen from him: pride.

He's proud of me.

The little girl inside me, the one always so desperate for Sir's approval, dissolves. But would he still be proud if he knew how hard I'm fighting to stay this calm? If he knew the raging battle in my mind, the fight between Meira the orphaned soldier and Queen Meira?

He's proud of someone who doesn't exist.

"All right," he says. "But Henn will go with you. And Conall and Garrigan, obviously."

"And me," Nessa adds, holding a lit candle. "And Dendera will want to go with Henn."

I nod. "Fine, but no more—I want people to stay in Winter in case Noam tries anything. I do plan on finding allies for us, regardless of the fact that he knows, but we need a firm presence here while I'm gone."

"We won't let my father get away with this."

The voice shoots into the room along with a sudden "Halt!" from Conall.

I fly to my feet as Theron darts in, his hair waving loose from its knot. Sir jerks up, as ready to yank him out of the room as Conall and Garrigan.

But I throw my hands out. "No, it's fine." I eye everyone else. "Can you excuse us?"

Sir pauses, his glare swinging from Theron to me. I prepare to argue with him, to plead my reasons, when he nods.

"Conall and Garrigan will be right outside," he says, more to Theron than me. "I should return to the celebration."

My shoulders cave forward. It still seems wrong when he doesn't fight me.

But he leaves, Nessa following him, and Conall shuts the door with one last cursory frown at Theron. When the door clicks, Theron relaxes, the strain in his shoulders giving way.

"I knew you were planning something," Theron starts. "But I never thought it'd be *that*."

All the hurt I've been keeping in check strains to flood the air between us, but I keep my face stoic. "How did you know?"

"Because when you stepped into the ballroom"—he smiles—"you had the same look on your face that you had right before you locked yourself in my father's study in Bithai."

I can't return his smile, though I feel how desperately he wants me to.

"I was wrong," I say. "I shouldn't have withheld what is owed to your kingdom. We *will* repay our debt to Cordell." *Eventually.*

Theron steps forward, close enough that I can feel the

heat off his body. "You don't have to talk to me like that. I'm on your side."

"No, you aren't," I snap, jaw tight. "You are Cordell, just as much as I am Winter. You'll always have to choose your kingdom over me."

"It won't come to that." The force of his words silences me. "I know you're angry with me for telling my father about the magic chasm, but I stand by what I did. Do you know why he let me stay here for this long? Because he expects me to report on your *progress* every time he returns, like you're property of his that I'm supposed to supervise. I will not continue living this way when an answer lies so close. We need that magic, Meira, and we need Cordell's support to search the world. Once we have the keys, *we* will be able to control opening that chasm. Not my father. We'll be able to give magic to everyone."

He's so determined, his confidence unwavering and blind. I trap a breath in my throat, biting my tongue as I war with telling him the truth. But if this is his goal . . . he needs to know what could happen.

"If everyone in the world has magic, they'll use it for negative things too," I start. "*That* fueled Angra—a Decay that was created by the negative use of magic. It'll return, and it'll darken the world. I can't let that happen."

"What?" Theron teeters. "How do you know that?"

How, indeed? *My dead mother told me through our connection to conduit magic because, by the way, Theron, I'm Winter's conduit. All of me.*

"While I was in Abril, I . . . he told me. Tried to break me. It worked."

Lies, lies, lies.

Theron squints. At first it seems like disbelief, but the longer the silence lasts, the more I realize he's analyzing me.

"Why don't you believe we're strong enough?" he asks. "Angra may have been fed by this negative use of magic— but what about the goodness in Primoria? Don't the good people deserve to be powerful?"

"It isn't about who deserves what—someone *will* use magic negatively. Surely you can't believe everyone in the world is trustworthy?"

"No—but I have to believe we're strong enough as a collective whole to withstand any evil that might arise. And if we're aware of what will happen and we all have magic to fight that evil, we can overcome anything."

The ferocity of his belief in the goodness of the world breaks my heart. Nessa has the same innocence, seeing only the good, ignoring the bad.

Recognizing that in him throws sand over the fire of my certainty. I want him to believe in the goodness of the world. I *need* him to believe in it, for the terrified boy who cowered in Angra's cell and represses such memories. Like my people's happiness, Theron's feels like a fistful of snow nestled in the cage of my hands. Only instead of being somewhere cold and wonderful where it can thrive, I'm somewhere hot and choking, heat licking my fingers and trying with all its might to melt the snow within.

I'll find a way to keep the world safe from negative magic use. I don't need Theron's help to do so—I need him to stay *him*.

"Goodness does need to be preserved," I say, an agreement that isn't exactly an agreement. "But I'm going to find allies to stand with me against your father, if the time comes. This could lead to war with Cordell, and I won't ask you to—"

One of Theron's hands cups my cheek, the other lands on my shoulder, catching me in a soft caress. But the distance created when he told his father about the chasm yawns between us, and I don't lean into him like I used to.

"You don't have to ask me to support you," he says. "I know the risks and they are, will always be, worth the repercussions. We'll set out to find the keys. We'll search each kingdom's monuments and archives and, golden leaves, even their vaults if we have to—but magic will heal only so much. This world has been divided for too long."

I frown. "What are you saying?"

Theron slides his hand behind my head, holding me here. "What if this trip wasn't merely a cover to introduce Winter to the world? What if it really is what you plan for it—a way to link allies, only *more*? We can go with an intention beyond finding the keys: to unite the kingdoms of Primoria in perpetual and lasting peace. If I draw up a treaty, we could present it to the kingdoms of the world.

For the first time in centuries, there is no war between any kingdoms in Primoria. We can seize this opportunity—and when the chasm is open, we'll bring magic into a world already well on its way to healing."

I've heard a speech like this before, only spoken from very different lips.

Mather dreamed of such things, when he was king and I was just a soldier. Only his wishes were for peace and equality to come through judging people based on their character instead of things like gender and bloodline. Back then, I was inexperienced enough to believe that we could achieve such balance—but I've seen too much now. Permanent peace and balance is an impossible goal. Far better would be to strive for a general state of equality, so that no matter what evils one kingdom might conjure, they would never be undefeatable.

And if magic is spread to everyone, evils like that will fill the world.

My body tenses in Theron's hands. "We've been without war for only *three months*, and already Winter borders on conflict with Cordell. Peace is . . . impractical."

Theron shakes his head. "Not if the world signs a treaty that binds them to one another. When issues arise, we intercede; when evils appear, we unite. And when we bring this to them, Rhythm and Season together, we will show them what that future can look like."

He curves his neck down and lays his lips across mine

in a hungry, powerful kiss, as if he's trying to impart his certainty into me. I can't process what's happening fast enough to decide whether or not I should pull away.

He wants to use this trip to search for a way to open the magic chasm under the guise-that-isn't-a-guise of uniting the world. Which sounds like a beautiful, admirable goal—if not for the sheer impossibility of it. I'm barely certain I'll find allies by bribing them, let alone getting Rhythms to agree to a state of peace and unification with *all* the Seasons.

A realization punches through me.

Theron found a legitimate reason to go to Summer, Yakim, and Ventralli. One that doesn't involve Winter—or at least, Noam would be able to argue that it doesn't.

Cordell doesn't need me on this trip. And we found the magic chasm—Cordell doesn't need Winter anymore either.

I pull back, pressing my forehead to Theron's. "Have you told your father about this?"

Theron closes his eyes, his arms dropping to encircle my waist. "No. It might be best to wait until after Yakim and Ventralli sign it. I can sign it for Cordell in his stead."

I exhale. Noam doesn't know.

Theron moves to kiss me again, and I find myself wobbling on a precipice I never imagined: if I disagree with Theron's plan for peace, will he run to his father for support like he did with the magic chasm, regardless of his own reasoning?

Theron's lips move to my jaw, creep down my neck in slow flutters. He moans, a soft sound that days ago would have melted every nerve in my body. But now I can't feel anything past the thoughts clogging my head.

This is politics. This is the life of a queen—hiding things, making sacrifices, keeping secrets, all for the betterment of my kingdom. It's what Dendera and Sir and everyone else seem to be shoving me into, at least—a life of pretending and hiding the truth.

Theron slides his hand up my spine, his lips hovering over my ear in a pause that beats awareness into me.

I launch away from him. "We should . . . we should get some sleep. It's been a long day."

Theron pauses. Realization dawns on his face and he shakes his head, his skin deepening to a heavy scarlet hue.

"Yes. We shouldn't . . ." He regains himself a little and puts an arm's length of space between us. "I won't push you to do anything you aren't ready to do."

My own blush heats every bare surface of skin. I haven't really thought about *that* at all. But as I look at Theron now, I realize I probably should have, if only to decide what I want our relationship to be.

"I know," I say. "I just . . . I don't want us to be together because we want comfort to chase away our nightmares or because I feel—" *Indebted to you.*

Theron saves me from having to explain by taking my hand. He's shaking, a tremor that catches in my own muscles and ricochets up through me.

"You don't have to explain," he whispers, his voice low and heady. "I know things have been chaotic, but I truly believe this trip will be the beginning of an end to that chaos. Soon all we'll have to think about is us."

Part of me wants to laugh at that, the idea of being so carefree that my only thought is of a boy. I can't foresee that ever happening.

Theron squeezes my hand and steps back, the moment gone. "We'll leave in a few days," he tells me. He bows at the waist, never taking his eyes off mine. "Lady Meira."

I dredge up a weak smile. "Prince Theron."

He offers one last grin and leaves.

This day has done its best to pick me apart, one emotional event after another. And as Theron shuts the door to my room behind him, the one leading to my balcony groans, and I'm hit with the numb thought that it isn't over.

A figure staggers in, swaying as if he's caught in a gale.

No, no, *no.*

Just one glance at Mather, and it's enough to undo the control I've built up this night. All I am now is the truth underneath: trembling and aching and frantically terrified. Was it only a few hours ago that I was glad for the way his presence unraveled me?

"What are you doing here?" I growl, but I frown when his bloodshot eyes have trouble locking on me. "Are you *drunk*?"

Mather pinches the skin above his nose and chuckles like he's shocked he made it. "Wait, wait—" He moves two fingers up to me. It takes me a moment to realize he's mimicking what he used to do when he snuck up on me as a child, two fingers on my neck in place of a weapon. "You're dead," he declares, sure enough. "And I'm allowed to drink."

I wipe away the nostalgia. "You climbed up my balcony while drunk?"

"I was perfectly steady," he slurs, and stumbles forward a step, bumping into the foot of my bed. The laughter on his face sloshes away as he remembers something serious, dark. "But why should you worry? I'm just one of your supplicants, humbly basking in your presence."

"Mather—stop it! Why are you here?" *How long have you been here? What did you see?*

A chill rushes through me, and my body feels light and heavy, tied down and floating.

He waves his arm out in a bow. "I'm sorry, my queen. My lady fair. My serene ruler. I'm sorry if I've caused you pain. It's nothing you haven't done to me, if it's any comfort."

"What are you talking about? I haven't—"

"Oh, you *haven't*?" Mather pitches toward me, a fierce anger dancing with his drunkenness to create this wounded, vicious animal before me. "Philip—Phil—and those Bikendi camp boys, they're all ignoring their pasts, and I don't want to do that anymore. I thought I wanted to just numb it all, but I don't want that, Meira—I want *you*. And I thought you did too—damn it all, today I thought we . . ." He stops, laughs brokenly. "Ice, I'm an idiot, because I come here, and even after what Theron did, you still want *him*."

I strangle the moan that eats at my throat, barely keeping myself together as splintering fragments dig deep. "I don't know what you saw with Theron, but that wasn't—"

"I messed up," Mather cuts me off, his face severe. "I know I messed up. I missed my chance, and damn it, Meira, I was fine to sulk off and lick my wounds and *forget* you. But Noam—the magic chasm—all these threats, they should be my problems. I hate that they're yours now, but I can't take it all back so you're safe. *I can't do anything*, Meira. There's a reason it's been three months since we've talked, and I need to force myself to see that reason. I'll still do what I can for Winter, but I can't live like this. I need you to know that I'm done. I'm not waiting for you to come back into my life."

All the pain and surprise of him being here explodes in me, sending shards darting out to every limb. But not shards of sorrow or grief—shards of anger.

He has *no idea* what is going on. And the worst part is—I might have told him, if he hadn't come here yelling at me, drunk, ripping holes in my already fragile shell of composure.

"I'm sorry you're miserable," I snap. "I'm sorry I hurt you. I thought I could talk to you because I *needed* to talk to you, and I didn't think about it more than that. But that's what got us into this mess, me not thinking things through, and I should have known better. So don't—"

His brow furrows. "What do you mean *you* got us into this mess?"

My head hums, body quivering in uncontrollable waves. "No, you don't get to sneak into *my bedroom* and yell at me and deserve any explanation at all."

I turn to the door, ready to shout for Garrigan and Conall to yank Mather out of my life. I shouldn't have talked to him earlier. Despite all he's undergone, all the things he's suffered, he's the only person I know who is still *himself*, who hasn't let our past change him. He's the Mather I grew up with, the Mather I fell in love with, and that makes me forget my own masks and want to stop trying so hard to contain myself.

The world blurs, warps, and I'm falling forward, bracing myself on the door.

I can't be around Mather. I can't afford to be around anyone who makes me feel like Meira the orphaned soldier-girl—which is why it's better for me to be around people like Theron and Sir. Who they are makes it easier for me to be queen.

Everything I'd been holding on to so tightly rushes free

and I turn back to Mather, searching for his eyes through my haze of tears. He hunches forward as if he expects an argument. Why wouldn't he? We're always wrong, him in one place and me in another and both of us screaming because we would only work if we went back to how things were.

Things didn't even work then, though, did they? He was the king and I was a peasant. Now I'm the queen and he's a lord, but he's still . . .

Completely, annoyingly, magnificently uncomplicated.

I pinch back a gasp. "I'd choose you if it wouldn't unravel who I need to be."

Mather's body loosens. All the fight drains out of him and he gawks at me, staring for a few beats of complete motionlessness before he jerks his head to the side, the muscles in his face tightening. The hole he's rending in me deepens as I notice he's holding back tears, that maybe the smallest part of him wanted me to fight for him and how it should have been. Meira and Mather, no titles or responsibilities.

His chest caves. "I think if we wanted to . . . I think we could have survived being unraveled."

I gasp, my own tears burning my cheeks.

His alcohol-reddened eyes meet mine long enough that I see the sorrow there, the reality dropping onto him.

"My queen," he says.

I fumble behind my back for the knob and open the door

to the confused faces of Conall and Garrigan, who only grow more confused when Mather walks past me, out into the hall.

He leaves. Just like that. No final good-bye, no last, lingering glance.

Like we never loved each other at all.

Meira

MUFFLED CRIES YANK me out of my sleep. Before I can do anything to help, the main door to my room opens, and in the hazy gray of night, I see Garrigan slip in. He eyes me but I wave him off.

"Nessa needs you more," I say, and he eases to the door that connects mine to the one Nessa claimed as her "proper maid's quarters." When he opens it just enough to enter, her desperate screams fly out to meet me.

"Shhh, Ness, shh," Garrigan's calming voice tries.

I roll onto my side, eyes shut, hands around my head. Over Nessa's continued weeping, Garrigan talks. But it isn't more reassurances—it's a song, one that pins me to the mattress.

"Lay your head upon the snow," he sings, uncertain at first, but with more confidence as he loses himself in the lyrics. *"Lay your sorrow in the ice. For all that once was calm, sweet child, will belong*

to you tonight. Lay your heart upon the snow. Lay your tears in the ice. For all that once was still, sweet child, will belong to you tonight."

I gasp when silence rushes in. Pure silence—not even a whimper from Nessa. After a few long moments of that delicate peace, the door opens again and I roll upright to face Garrigan.

He stops when he sees me, his body going stiff. "My queen?"

His concern catches me awkwardly before I feel warmth dripping down my cheeks. I'm crying.

"Where did you learn that?"

He steps forward, his shoulders slackening a bit. "Deborah found the sheet music in the rubble of the palace and played it one day, and—" He chuckles, a quiet, hushed sound so as not to wake Nessa again. "I remembered it. I think our mother used to sing it."

An image hits me. Something urged by the remnants of Garrigan's song on the air; something I see every time I look at him or Conall or Nessa, but can never admit.

Garrigan's life, how it should have been. Him singing that song to his child, raising a family alongside Conall's and Nessa's. And their parents, alive and happy.

"Do you . . ." My question wavers. "Do you regret who this war made you?"

Garrigan's face flashes with first wonder, then hurt. "No, my queen. Do you?"

"I . . . Never mind." I shake my head. "Good night."

Garrigan hesitates, but he doesn't press it. "Good night, my queen. If . . . Nessa has more nightmares, I'll be just outside."

I hear the words he doesn't say: *if you have nightmares, I'll protect you just the same.*

I smile, something true and simple, and he leaves with a bow. I'm left alone in perfect, unbroken stillness, even the magic in my chest blissfully quiet.

Garrigan doesn't regret who he is now. Sir doesn't; Dendera doesn't; Nessa, Conall, Alysson, Theron—they're all hurt by what happened to us, but none of them seem at all eager to do anything but move forward. Find the keys, open the chasm, create a new world.

I prod at the magic. It doesn't flare up at my gentle curiosity, maybe because I'm so exhausted.

Once, this would have been something I'd talk about to Hannah. She would have helped with this—or given me cryptic, maddening advice that I'd only figure out at the precipice of our destruction. But she was still someone I could lean on, someone resilient and strong.

Like Mather.

I ease back onto my bed, curling tight.

No. I'm strong enough on my own, I tell myself. *I'll find the Order and win allies for Winter—all as Queen Meira. This is me now. And if I keep trying, someday I won't have to fight so hard to be queen. It'll just be a part of me. It won't hurt.*

Someday.

Four days later, the palace is a flurry of departures.

The Autumnians prepare to return to their kingdom while Noam oversees the preparation of a caravan to take his son, me, and an amalgamation of Cordellan and Winterian escorts around the world. He already sent word to Summer, Yakim, and Ventralli to expect us, still holding strong our guise of meeting the world for Winter's benefit. He has made no mention of Theron's new plan, which eases only a small part of my anxiety as I descend the steps this bright morning, dressed in a starchy travel gown of wool and layered skirts. Dendera's idea.

People pack the area in front of the palace, a mix of workers rebuilding and the departing groups at the end of the yard. Winterians gather too, those who will be staying in my stead—Sir, Alysson, Deborah, Finn, and Greer. Horses and wagons stand before them on the dirt road, the snow cleared into piles as more flakes drop from the clouds. I quicken my steps down the narrow path.

Theron swings down off his horse when I approach. "I have—"

A cry of delight cracks the air. I glance over my shoulder in time to see a few Winterian workers grunt in shock as they fall out of the way of an unseen force carving a path from the back of the courtyard to us.

The source of the cry flops out from under one unlucky worker's legs, moments ahead of a rather flustered maid.

The whirlwind doesn't pause to see who she might be barreling into next. She leaps through the snow and launches herself at me, and once her short arms lock around both of my legs, she gapes up, all brown eyes and flopping green fabric and a large, gummy grin.

"MEE-WAH!" she squeals, and hugs me so enthusiastically it's a wonder my dress hasn't ripped off.

I widen my arms, unable to stop the smile that spreads over my face. "Hello, Shazi."

Theron grins as well. "I think you've made a friend."

"I'm not sure how good an impression I made when I dragged her and her parents on rather long tours of Jannuari, but she doesn't seem to hate me too much," I say, and Shazi squeals deep in her throat.

Her commotion draws the attention of the Autumnian courtiers, and one pulls away from the crowd. Nikoletta drops into a crouch and opens her arms, causing Shazi to release me and jump at her, sending them both toppling into the snow. But Nikoletta giggles just as much, if not more than her daughter.

Nikoletta sobers slightly and pulls to her feet while Shazi stomps on the snow, laughing at her own footprints. Theron beams down at his cousin, an adoration that mimics that of the Autumnian courtiers, still readying their horses. All these people's hopes heaped upon this one tiny head, with her infectious grin and the small sauce stain on her dress. Autumn hasn't had a female heir in two generations, and without a female-blooded conduit, they were almost as badly off as Winter. Shazi won't be able to use her conduit for at least another ten years, though—not until she's able to understand it and consciously push its power into her kingdom.

She feels me staring and clutches something at her neck. "Meewah," she declares, and waddles back over, trying to hand whatever is in her fist to me, but the chain holding it around her neck doesn't let it go far.

I drop to my knees and she plops a ring into my palm, a gold circle holding a pyramid of teardrop jewels and a small diamond. The cluster emits an auburn glow—Autumn's conduit.

A gasp sticks in my throat the moment it touches my skin. Images swarm at me, patchy things pouring from Shazi's memory into mine, exactly like what happens when Noam touches me.

Caspar chasing a giggling Shazi around a pale yellow tent. Awakening to the tearful face of Nikoletta as cannon explosions echo in the background, and people scream, urging them to hurry. Caspar kissing Shazi's head and pulling away with teary eyes, and some small jolt of terror slashing through her, knowing that if he leaves he might never come back.

I jerk to my feet, the conduit falling from my palm and dropping against Shazi. But she smiles and tightens her fist around the ring. "Stwong, Meewah!"

My eyes flick over Shazi's face. *Strong.* She wants her conduit to make me strong—she's probably been told since birth that it will make her strong someday.

I smile at her. "Thank you, Princess Shazi."

She grins again, satisfied with my response despite the lack of emotion that makes my words dry. Part of me feels like laughing—a toddler is trying to comfort me. Is my panic that obvious, or is Shazi already that observant?

"Thank you for coming," I tell Nikoletta, because I need to talk past the lump in my throat. "I'm sorry your visit couldn't be longer."

Her smile is worn, as if she understands. And since she grew up with Noam for an older brother, she just might.

"We hear that you are heading to Summer." Nikoletta eyes the crowd before stepping closer to me. "My nephew showed me a most intriguing treaty. It is an ambitious goal, but know that Autumn will help however we can."

My eyes widen and I snap my head to Theron as his hand drops to the small of my back.

"Autumn signed," he explains. "Shortly after I did. They are aware of its delicate nature."

I roll my eyes. I hate having to translate political-speak.

Caspar signed the treaty after Theron did—secretly, no less. Theron tried to show it to me yesterday, but I . . . well. Lying to Theron about what I think of his goals is hurting more and more, and I didn't want to have to fake added support of it.

But this is only the beginning.

"Yes," I manage, voice thin. I turn back to Nikoletta. "I . . . hope it will be fruitful."

Nikoletta nods, considering, before her demeanor softens. "I know how difficult it is to be a young ruler. It gets easier, I promise you that."

My chest cools a little. I wish I could tell her how grateful I am that she is nothing like her brother. "Thank you," I tell her again.

They leave shortly after, winding out of Jannuari and back to their kingdom, the first of many departures today. Their absence urges me into motion—I want to leave before I lose my nerve, and as I check the supplies on my horse, a task Dendera declares is "unbefitting of a queen," two sleighs roll forward.

I turn and fist a handful of my skirt when I catch Noam analyzing the sleighs, a grimace hardening his face. But he doesn't argue with their presence; he doesn't demand that the spoils within be moved to his coffer.

"I can't believe he's accepting of this now," I mutter.

Theron double-checks the straps on his own saddle and shoots me a sympathetic gaze. "He isn't—he's just taking advantage of the situation."

"How very Cordellan of him."

Theron winces, but he doesn't counter me, and I don't apologize.

Noam strides to us as if on cue, his arms tucked behind

his back. "One of my ships will be waiting on the Feni."

"So kind of you," I bite, teeth clenched.

Noam cocks his head. "Do not forget what we discussed, Lady Queen. The conditions of your return are nonnegotiable."

Bring me the keys or Cordell's charade of caring for Winter is over.

Fury burns from my stomach straight up my throat, but I say nothing. A queen wouldn't.

Noam pivots away, heading to his own caravan, one bound for Gaos so he can inspect the magic chasm entrance himself. I hope he tries to reach the door. At least once.

I heave myself onto my horse as Sir approaches me.

"Everything will be taken care of, and you'll be informed of any changes," he says.

I blink at him. Just orders now, orders and duty and *pride*, that's all Sir is.

The wind blows at me, swirling snowflakes through my loose white curls. I fight to keep the smile on my face, but the longer Sir stands there, spewing information about my absence, the less I can hold on to my resolve. One moment of truth, and I'll go back to being an obedient little queen. I'll be perfect and calm and emotionless—someone Sir will continue to be proud of.

"I understand why you did it," I whisper, cutting off his explanation of which new mines will be opened while I'm gone. "I understand why you hid everything from me and Mather and why it's all backward now. But what I don't understand is why you hated who I used to be so much. Why you knew how badly I needed you to love me, yet you refused to give me that. Did you blame me for everything?" I gasp, the air thin. "Maybe it was my fault. I caused a lot of our problems, I know I did, but I swear to you—I'll be a better queen."

Sir's frown slides off, his face blank, a stone statue come to life. "This is not your fault."

I wait for him to say more. To tell me he doesn't hate me, he never did.

"We will await your return most anxiously, my queen," he says with a bow.

I don't bother seeing whoever else wishes to bid me farewell. At a flick of my reins, the horse moves forward, winding toward the head of the caravan.

As I ride, someone pulls his horse alongside me. He leans across the space between us and puts his hand on mine, a small gesture that makes me glance at him, at his soft smile and the way his golden hair waves in the snowy air.

"It's going to be all right," Theron promises.

"Doubtful."

He shrugs. "We're the most capable people I know. We'll find the keys, and we'll win against my father, and the world will be at peace."

I throw him an exasperated stare. "Your optimism is annoying."

"That doesn't stop me from being right," he says, grinning.

I glance over my shoulder, eyes darting through the crowd, until I see the Winterians by the palace dispersing. Alysson heads toward the cottages, and Sir walks away . . . and Mather.

He stands with a group of boys, half listening to them and half watching me.

I spin away, eyes closed, and let Theron's grip lead our horses through the streets.

Mather

WILLIAM'S OFFICE WAS by far the dreariest room in the palace, just off an open-air walkway. Anyone moving past it would see what had once been a garden around the back of the palace, gray stone fountains coated in ice, dead plants frozen beneath layers of flakes, and the snow-covered buildings of the southern part of Jannuari. A nice view, all for a windowless, dark room lined with empty bookshelves and two sad sconces holding up jagged clumps of candle wax. A desk sat surrounded by three chairs, every free surface covered in papers and scrolls. It had been just as disheveled each time Mather had been there.

The other people in the room—Brennan Crewe and an old woman named Deborah who had been the city master of Jannuari before the takeover and had fallen back into her role without a blink from anyone—seemed willing to stay away from him, something for which Mather couldn't have been more grateful. Phil had gotten another few crates of ale from the Cordellans, letting all who had avoided the celebration a few nights ago relive that evening in the cottage every night since. Which was great fun during the drinking, but once morning came . . .

Mather pressed his fist against a throbbing vein that cut through the middle of his forehead. The ale left him feeling like he'd been dragged through a battle without armor, his eyes filled with bolts of pain, his body sagging from a raging headache. He leaned against one of the shelves, wincing to keep the bread he'd choked down for breakfast in his stomach. Thank the ice above that Meira's departure had delayed the Winterian army's usual training—Mather wasn't sure he could hide another morning of being hungover from William.

Alysson swept into the room, her pale hands cupped around a goblet. She walked up to Mather without any of the pleasantries he expected, and before he could clear away the fog of his hangover, she shoved the goblet to him.

"Drink this," she ordered.

Mather squinted at her, then at the goblet in his hands. "I . . . What?"

She placed her palm on his face, her skin cool against his clammy cheek. "Drink this," she said again, this time in the patient, careful tone Mather was used to from her. The woman who mended their injuries and nursed them back to health and sent them off on missions with this same tender cheek pat.

Hating William was easy. Hating Alysson took more effort than Mather had.

Mather raised the goblet to his lips and downed a swig before the horrid taste hit him. Like eggs left too long in the sun, like meat gone rancid. He hacked and doubled over, one wrong breath away from reliving everything he had consumed last night in reverse.

He gagged. "What is this?"

Alysson squeezed his shoulder. "A remedy for your ailment. It will take away your headache and nausea, but remember this delicious flavor should you insist on drinking so much again. Which won't be any time soon, will it?" Her tone pulled taut in a way that said she wouldn't accept anything but agreement. She patted his cheek once more as he stayed bent before her, arms around his middle, stomach churning like an angry sea. "Drink up, sweetheart. Every drop."

Mather collapsed onto the frayed carpet in a burst of dust. He looked up at her with hooded eyes as she scooted papers off a chair and sat next to Deborah, who shook her head at him disapprovingly. Brennan, on the other hand, leaned against the shelves and stifled a smile, no doubt enjoying Mather's torment.

When he met Alysson's eyes again, he knew this beverage

was meant to be more of a punishment than a cure. Honestly, he was surprised he'd gotten away with four nights of such behavior—though he had expected the punishment to come from William.

Luckily the study door opened again and William entered. All attention swung to him, everyone rising straighter, but Mather merely sank more heavily onto the floor and sipped at the repulsive concoction in his hand. His cheeks puffed in an uncontrollable gag. This stuff was awful even in small increments.

William walked behind his desk, pulled out the remaining chair, and stopped, like he couldn't decide whether to sit or run back out of the room. His forehead wrinkled, his pallor sullen, so like the William Mather used to know.

Mather set the goblet on the floor and stood, taking a single step forward in the silence. Before he could ask anything, William turned to them.

"Captain Crewe called this meeting," William began. "Though I am surprised King Noam did not delay his trip to join us."

Brennan shrugged. "As you might expect, my king is eager to secure the Tadil Mine and is already on his way to Gaos. He left me with explicit instructions to carry out regarding Winter's future in the face of this most joyous change."

Mather groaned. One thing he did not miss about being

king was useless political maneuvering. How everyone in this room knew exactly what the magic chasm's discovery meant—one more snare for Winter in Cordell's trap—but no one could counter Brennan without defying Noam.

Brennan pressed on. "My king has decided that it is not in Winter's best interest to train an army at this point in your rebirth. Cordell will continue defending Winter, and you will shift all focus to construction or mining, to benefit your economy and stability as a kingdom. You are to cease training, effective immediately."

William ground his fingers around the back of his chair, the only outward sign of his anger. "This is not a change we can agree to without our queen's approval."

Mather almost laughed. "This isn't a change we can agree to *at all!*"

Both Brennan and William shot him looks: Brennan, one of disdainful amusement; William, a narrow-eyed plea to be silent.

Mather frowned. Surely William would back him up in this. Surely he wouldn't let Noam stifle them even more.

Brennan wiped an invisible speck of dust from his sleeve. "Your queen's approval does not matter. On this issue my king is most adamant." He lifted his gaze to William. "And after the ceremony incident, it would truly be in Winter's best interest to comply. I must return to my men." Brennan made for the door. "Thank you for your time."

Silence coated the air after Brennan had left. Mather hesitated at the edge of the room, eyes fixed on William, waiting, hoping, *needing* for him to leap after Brennan and refute the orders.

But William only lowered himself into his chair, his body rigid.

Mather couldn't take it any longer. "You know this is Noam's way of keeping us weak."

William broke out of his stupor. "Of course I know," he barked. "Why do you think he waited until he and the queen had left to give the order? He didn't want to face any possibility of our conduit rejecting him."

Mather pulled back. "Our conduit? You mean *Meira*?"

William frowned at him. "That is how we must see her—as our connection to the locket. That is how the kingdoms of the world operate; their monarchs are links to magic, while a select few people truly run the government. We are a kingdom of the world now."

"When Meira finds out about Noam's order, she'll kill him," Mather countered. "She'll never allow this. We should keep training, Noam be damned."

William shook his head. "Acting against an explicit order will only hurt us after—" He paused, wincing at the memory of the ceremony four days ago. Mather had hated himself even more for leaving once he'd heard how Noam had reacted to Meira's change of payment—he should have stayed, gone to her, given her more support.

He wanted this, though. What he had told her in her room—he was done being in her life.

"We will obey this request until we can regroup in a way that does not outright defy Cordell," William continued. "Divvy up the trainees to aid with rebuilding or mining, but no Winterian is to lift a blade until I give the order."

Mather growled. "You mean until Noam gives the order?"

William's knuckles tightened on the arms of his chair. "You will not speak to me like that. I am the head of this kingdom in our queen's absence, and as such you will obey me."

Alysson and Deborah remained silent, and any rebuttal that Mather had was suffocated beneath his years of obeying William without thought. He wondered now if maybe he shouldn't have obeyed this man so blindly. If he should have been more like Meira.

"Is that why you let her leave?" Mather felt his insubordination like a fist to the skull. He realized in the looming silence how badly he *wanted* William to lash out at him, to be angry and put Mather in his place—to be himself again.

But William said nothing, and as Mather's eyes darted across his weathered skin, he felt everything Feige had said click in his mind. She was right, that demented girl. She was right about William carrying around his guilt so heavily that he refused to see anything that hurt. She was right about everyone around Mather being caught in a web of remorse.

That web would get them all killed.

"Of course not," William finally responded. "Our queen went because that is what she must do now—form alliances. You of all people should understand politics."

Mather grimaced. Yes, he should. But he only understood his own guilt at this moment, his own failings, his own pain, and how much he wanted to be rid of it all.

Every part of him trembled. "You're ashamed of failing Winter sixteen years ago, but you should be even more ashamed that you don't have the courage to face it. I won't ignore it. I will *not* end up like you."

He shoved past Deborah, who put her hands over her mouth, past Alysson, who watched him but said nothing. They let him leave, every one of them. Just like they had let Meira leave, because it hurt too much to focus on their problems.

The sounds of construction hummed outside, hammers and saws creating a steady tune. Mather hurried toward the training barn, darting past men carrying buckets of nails, women lugging wheelbarrows of scrap wood. For as tense as the air had been in William's office, it was far too light in the city. People chatted, moved about their day as if they had always been this normal. As Mather got to the door of the barn, he paused, a sad thought flashing through him.

Were most Winterians like William? Did everything they do just cover up their scars?

Meira shouldn't have left. If Mather had been more clearheaded, he wouldn't have walked out of her room four nights ago. He wouldn't have avoided her every day since, slumping back to join Phil and the boys each night. He would have sought her out, stayed with her as long as it took, demanding that she remain in Winter—for their kingdom. Not for him.

His mind flashed back to one of the last times Meira had left. He had watched in numbing horror as Angra's general had lifted her body, sneering down at her with an expression that said more than any threat ever could. And Mather had done nothing but scream for her while Cordellan soldiers hauled him back toward Bithai.

He would not fail her again.

Mather caught his thoughts and growled. *Winter.* He would not fail *Winter* again. Meira wasn't his to worry about anymore, beyond her status as queen.

Mather threw himself into the barn. Training should have started an hour ago; most of the men were pacing from having to wait so long. Except Phil, Hollis, Trace, Kiefer, and Eli—they looked perfectly happy with the extra moments of rest. Anger had forced Mather's hangover away—well, that, or possibly the forsaken drink Alysson had given him—but they still looked frazzled and exhausted.

Mather shoved his hands into his pockets. "Cordell has ordered that training cease immediately."

A murmur swept through the barn, a few grunts of displeasure. Mather opened his mouth to split the group into miners and construction, or even to explain why, to come up with a reason that made sense. But as he stared at the cracks in the worn wood floor, he couldn't think of anything, and the longer he stood in silence, the more the trainees glanced at one another, until a few started to leave in clouds of confused muttering.

"What caused that?" Phil asked when they were alone.

Mather tore his eyes from the floor. "Denial."

"Strange, isn't it?" Kiefer interjected, his attention on a passing group of Cordellans who peered into the barn and scoffed because they knew how weak Winter was. How broken.

Trace pressed his face into his knees where he sat on a barrel. "What's strange?"

Kiefer shrugged, shoulders moving against the wall of the barn. "We're home, but it doesn't feel much different from Bikendi. Scraping by, ruled by another kingdom."

Phil flinched, his head popping up from where it had been hanging lifelessly against his chest. "That isn't—" He choked, his mouth dangling open. "It's better here. We're free."

"Shouldn't have expected the queen to be any better than Angra. Just like royals, I guess," Kiefer continued. "Care more about their cushy lives than their lowly subjects."

"She's not like that." Mather regretted talking as soon

as the words left his lips, but Kiefer perked up—clearly he'd been waiting for Mather to respond. Even at night when the ale made most of them relaxed, Kiefer glowered whenever Mather looked at him.

Mather couldn't fault him for being angry. They all wanted someone to hate.

"Well, it seems she is," Kiefer snapped back. "Where is she now? Off to be pampered by the good-for-nothings of Primoria's other kingdoms while we're feasting our days away, right?" Kiefer swept into a bow. "Once-King Mather, please direct me to the feasting tables. I do so desire a plate of our queen's generosity."

Blood roared in Mather's head, the remnants of his anger with William adding fuel. "Stop it."

Kiefer laughed. "Tell me you at least got a little of *our queen's generosity* at some point."

Trace jerked his face out of his knees, Phil shoved up from his crouch on the floor, even Eli blinked at his brother in shock. Hollis's shoulders rose and one sweep of his body let Mather know he'd have support should he decide to tackle Kiefer.

Mather drew in deep breaths. It was just a weak outward sign of Kiefer's inner struggle. They were all tired, all in pain, and fighting him would do nothing.

But it would feel so, *so* good.

"Leave Meira alone," he tried. "You owe her your life."

"*Meira,*" Kiefer echoed. "Using her first name. She didn't

even know she was the ruler when you were with her, did she? She thought you were the king. Mighty King Mather. She probably did anything you asked of her."

"Quiet!"

"Admit it. It'd help knowing someone put her in her place while we were being put in ours."

Mather didn't remember consciously moving; all he knew was that he felt the smallest blip of relief that Kiefer had opened himself to this. Hacking at each other with practice swords worked out only so much frustration—real fighting, throwing true blows, released so much more, and as Mather's fist smacked into Kiefer's jaw, all his worries evaporated, if only for a moment.

Kiefer flew into the air, the force of Mather's punch bouncing him off the barn wall and onto his stomach. Mather let him have two seconds to right himself before jamming his knee into Kiefer's neck. Not hard enough to snap anything, and he dropped an elbow down on his spine. Kiefer flattened on a wheeze, the air knocked out of him, and Mather twisted so he had the boy's arms locked behind his back.

"Stop it!" Eli shouted. A few feeble punches danced across Mather's shoulders before another force swept Eli out of the way. The younger boy collapsed on the floor and stayed there, staring with terrified eyes at his brother and Mather and now Hollis.

"Stay back," Hollis snarled, and the younger boy cowered.

Hollis grabbed Kiefer's hair and yanked his head up, twisting it so forcefully that Kiefer cried out, the first sign of pain he had dared release. Mather admired him for being able to hold on so long, but then Hollis spoke, and anger flooded Mather's body.

"You saw those Suns attack your mother," Hollis growled, every word dark and horrible and so full of pain that Mather worried for Kiefer's life, even as he kept the boy's arms bent against his spine. "You saw them do that to more than just her, I know you did. How dare you wish that on the person who saved your pathetic life?"

Kiefer moaned, straining against the boys holding him, and when he did Hollis slammed Kiefer's head into the floor before standing. Mather jumped up, releasing Kiefer's arms and taking four steps back to put space between himself and the prostrate boy.

Eli scrambled toward his brother but snapped back when Kiefer snarled at him. Trace and Phil looked from Kiefer to Hollis to Mather, a gleam of pride in their eyes.

Mather ran a hand down his face. The rest of the former trainees might have eventually made good soldiers—but these boys would have definitely been successes. And now, who knew when Noam would lift the order? Or would he make sure Winter stayed crippled forever?

Mather's eyes narrowed as he took in each of the boys. There were only six of them, including himself. Already they had managed four nights of sneaking off early and showing up hungover each morning—they could easily go unmissed in the bigger rush and pull of construction and mining now that training had been canceled.

"New orders," he said, and the boys in front of him jerked to attention, drawn by the gravity in his voice or the brightness in his eyes or the way he smiled, *really* smiled. "We're not listening to the other orders. We're making our own."

Meira

FROM JANNUARI, IT'S two days of sailing down the Feni River to Juli, the capital of Summer.

The Feni stretches wide enough to provide an easy mode of transportation between the western Langstone River and the eastern Destas Sea. And Cordell, as the only Rhythm Kingdom bordering the Destas, has quite the navy—Noam travels to and from Winter on his own well-equipped frigate. But growing up on the run from Angra didn't provide many opportunities for me to experience sailing—the closest I've come to a boat was standing on a dock in Ventralli a few years back while Finn haggled over a barrel of salted fish.

The ship Noam arranged for us is a small schooner with only eight crew members, and adding our numbers makes the ship cramped. But the lack of space allows for an easier patrol of our crates of Klaryn stones, stores every Cordellan soldier eyes with amusement. They know exactly why the crates are here, that they're my feeble attempt at unseating Noam while we search for the keys, and every time I see the soldiers' snide expressions, my stomach knots.

Though that could also be due to the putrid stench of the river and the ebbing, rocking motion that makes Dendera vibrantly green. Every particle of air hangs heavy with the scent of fish and the moldier stench of stagnant water trapped at the river's edge. The palpitation of the wind filling the sails dances with the way the deep river licks the narrow boat in snapping waves, bobbing us back and forth, back and forth.

Just when my stomach—and Dendera's—can't take it any longer, the ship docks us on the northeastern tip of Summer, about half a day's ride from Juli, leaving us at the largest Summerian port on the Feni so we can buy supplies before trekking into the kingdom.

The abrupt shift from the bobbing schooner to the solid dock makes me falter. Theron grips me from behind, his fingers curving into my hips in a way that could be just to steady me, but could be something more.

I lurch forward, pulling out of his arms even as I see the small flash of hurt on his face. "I'm fine," I stammer, but he smiles knowingly.

"You'll be unsteady for a bit," he says. "Sailing can do strange things."

The ship's rhythm is only a small fraction of my problem,

though, and as I watch Nessa, Dendera, and the rest of the Winterians disembark, I see the same suffering descend over them.

I've never been to Summer, but the Rania Plains, where we spent so much of my childhood, were often sweltering and miserable, enough that I assumed I'd be able to deal with intense heat if I ever had to come to Summer.

I realize now how utterly wrong I was.

The heat ripples up from the earth itself. Sandy structures adorned with dried wood doors comprise the port city, but beyond it, the stark landscape stretches like the withered, cracked hands of a beggar, unfolding and reaching into the blue sky for even the smallest drop of water. When four of Theron's two dozen men return from the city with two enclosed carriages for the Klaryn goods and horses for us, I almost weep with relief. My Winterian blood couldn't handle walking through this kingdom—my body aches for cold as if each waft of heat drains the life out of me. Anything that lives here has to be just as harsh and determined as the sun, born of a fiery stubbornness that is either extremely brave or extremely stupid.

I only know a few things about Summer beyond its climate. Its male-blooded conduit is a turquoise stone set in a gold cuff, inherited by their current king, Simon Preben, after his father died four years ago. Biggest export: wine. Biggest import: people.

Their economy is all too similar to Angra's work camps,

only Summer uses some of its own citizens in addition to people from other kingdoms. I saw a few Summerian collectors on trips around Primoria, relentless human-hunters who scooped up living purchases. Only Yakim and Spring sell to Summer—the rest of Primoria's kingdoms find the practice of slavery repulsive.

Anxiety balls tight in my gut. Why did the magic chasm have to lead us here? I won't be able to see what Summer does to its people, to its *property*, without drowning in rage . . . and memories of my own slavery-filled past. Let alone the fact that Summer buying people from Spring indirectly supported Angra.

Maybe I'll find the key or the Order quickly, and not have to be here long. But what am I even looking for? The chasm's clue was only vines on fire. Am I looking for an actual vine on fire? That seems too literal. Then just a vine? Or just a flame?

This is something I'd normally talk to Theron about. Ask for his help regarding interpretation.

But I can't bring myself to trust him again just yet.

We lock our cargo inside the enclosed carriages and start south, making for Juli more slowly than I'd like. Each lurch of the horse leaves me shifting awkwardly, finding a new place where my pleated ivory dress clings to my skin. Thankfully Dendera let me change out of the starchy, high-collared monstrosity I wore for our departure from Winter—just the thought of being confined to wool and long sleeves in this heat makes black spots flutter before my eyes. But my bare arms are only a relief for the first few minutes before the unobstructed sun finds my fair skin, and I swear I can hear the rays chuckle with delight at such a tasty meal.

The heat would be bad enough, but after about an hour of riding, Theron's soldiers scramble in their saddles and start passing out thick cloaks. I sag when one falls into my lap.

"I'm not going to like what these are for, am I?" I ask Theron, who whips his cloak around his shoulders.

One soldier uncoils a length of rope and passes it back, connecting everyone in our caravan by looping it around the pommels of our saddles.

"No," Theron says, and his tone makes me tug my cloak into place.

Moments later, a gust of wind slams into us, giving a brief burst of relief against the heat before a greater threat swoops in—sand. Billowing, raging clouds of grit thrash and swirl around us, minuscule particles that turn into daggers and send me burrowing deeper into the cloak. The horses seem as accustomed to the sandstorm as any Summerian would be, trudging on with the help of the connected rope. I wrap the cloak across my nose, keep my eyes closed and my head bowed against the unrelenting storm that screams windy fury in my ears.

By the time it ebbs, I know what it would feel like for

a Summerian to experience a blizzard. The complete and horrible opposite of everything one's body is made for, and as I unfurl the cloak, sand cascading off the fabric in trickling rivers, I narrow my eyes at Theron.

Orange sand streaks across his face and he accepts my glare with a shrug. "I assumed you knew about Summer's sandstorms."

"I did—but I didn't think we would have to worry about one on our short trip. Some warning would have been nice."

He scrubs the sand off his cheek and shakes out his cloak as a soldier passes by, winding the rope back up. "No visit to Summer is complete without one, or so I'm told," Theron says, his grin fighting to cancel out my annoyance.

It works, and I roll my eyes in resignation. "As long as there are no more surprises—"

But I barely get the wish out before all my instincts scream.

The fading sandstorm reveals the measly shade of a forest around us. Scraggy, sharp trees cut into the sky like scars, tangled bushes reveal thorns as long as my finger— and raiders perch high in the trees, waiting for unsuspecting travelers to get disoriented by the storm.

Just as I shout alarm, the attackers lunge down like the sand particles, sporadic yet deliberate. Knives flash in the sun, throwing sharp beams onto the raiders' sand-colored clothes—orange scarves tied around their heads, dusty red shirts, billowing auburn pants that pouf around the raiders' knees but wrap tightly against their ankles. In a few seconds we're surrounded, our men holding weapons ready, the raiders staring up at them, knife to knife.

My fingers flex for a weapon, but I hold steady, keeping myself calm and rigid. A queen wouldn't fight—she'd face this threat logically, diplomatically.

"Hold!" one of the raiders shouts. From where I sit, high up on my horse, I can see over the shoulder-to-shoulder Cordellan men around me, all facing the raiders. The one who spoke stands near me, her voice cracking out in a sharp, biting command. Her brown eyes flick over us, the only part of her visible beneath her beige head scarf.

Her eyes stop on me and widen.

"Who . . ." Her surprise twists in the air, and as she lowers her weapon, all the raiders ease down theirs as well. "Winterians," she growls after a beat.

She glances down the road, her brow tightening.

A caravan rolls up behind us, turning from a road that runs south. Three wagons pulled by oxen, their lumbering bulks kicking up dust and mud into their long, hairy coats. The wagons are completely enclosed just like ours, boxes on wheels with two drivers each, surrounded by a dozen Summerian guards on horseback, clomping steadily down the road toward us.

The girl curses. By the time she pulls my attention back, her raiders have disappeared. I frown, but she doesn't react to their absence, just reaches up and tugs the scarf off her head, revealing tightly coiled red curls that spring around her face. Like Winterians, Summerian hair is vibrant, to say the least—it's as if they dipped each strand in the setting sun itself and came away with the most blinding scarlet I've ever seen.

Once her scarf is gone, the girl smiles up at me. Her demeanor completely shifts, any flicker of anger buried beneath that smooth smile. "Queen Meira, yes?"

"What's going on?" Henn snaps from his position next to me. "Who are you—"

"Forgive me," the girl interrupts. "Bandits run wild in these parts, and I've taken it as one of my duties to rid my kingdom of them. I am Ceridwen Preben, sister of Simon." She drops into a short bow, whipping back up so quickly that her curls dance around her head.

Her eyes flit to the caravan still approaching us, almost within earshot. Her face shows the briefest worry, but it disappears so swiftly I don't have time to wonder about it.

Theron turns in his saddle next to me. "I'm Prince Theron of Cordell. I come as an escort of Winter, who is most eager to make their kingdom known to the world. Your brother should already be aware of our visit."

I gape at him. *Do I sound that confident when I lie?*

Theron presses on. "I believe we've met before, in Ventralli? You were an ambassador there under King Jesse a few years back, weren't you?"

Now I *know* Ceridwen's face falls. She swivels away from

Theron just as the caravan reaches us, her lips breaking into a stiff smile.

"Ah, here we are," she says, swinging a hand to the nearest Summerian soldier. "Lieutenant, escort our guests to Juli."

The soldier blinks at her, clearly surprised at seeing her, or at her order, or at our presence in Summer at all. But he nods, surveying us with careful precision. He stops on me and his eyes flash wide, but not with confusion—with pleasure.

"Yes, Princess," he says, still watching me. "Our king will wish to speak with them."

Ceridwen waves her thanks and starts to disappear into the grove of spindly trees, but the lieutenant turns his too-pleased smile on her, and my skin itches.

"Princess," he calls, "your brother gave us orders that if we were to see you on our journey, you should accompany us to Juli. You can help us watch out for bandits, can't you?"

Ceridwen pauses before turning, and when she does her face is placid. "Of course, Lieutenant," she tells him, and strides forward. "I'll be needing your ride, though, I'm afraid."

The lieutenant's grin falls. But he relents, sliding off his horse seconds before she hops up onto it and pushes her new mount forward.

"Juli is a four-hour trip, but you'll have beds and food

when we arrive," she calls to us.

Our caravan moves again, with Ceridwen at the lead and the Summerian cluster at the rear. I cut my eyes to Theron.

"You know her?"

He makes a noncommittal grunt. "Not well. I went to Ventralli a few years ago to visit my cousin. She was there as an ambassador, and I remember being fascinated to see a Season accepted in a Rhythm court. I didn't get a chance to speak to her, though—I wish I had, at least to learn how she convinced Ventralli to host her."

"Maybe you'll be able to ask her now," I say. Sir never mentioned Summer sending ambassadors to other kingdoms. Rhythms sent ambassadors to other Rhythm Kingdoms on occasion, but war usually made it difficult for the Seasons to do such things. Yet somehow, Ceridwen of Summer convinced a Rhythm to host her as a political equal.

Ceridwen can't be much older than me—eighteen or nineteen at the most—yet she found a way to overcome the stereotypes and prejudices of her kingdom. She's even found a way to lead raiding parties against bandits despite being the king's sister. She's a Season and an ambassador, a princess and a soldier all at once.

I squint into the horizon, trying to make out which of the moving silhouettes is her.

Maybe Summer can help me more than I thought.

By the time night fully envelops the kingdom, we're passing through the tight clusters of outlying towns that surround Juli. Taverns buzz with music and laughter, but no one wanders among the buildings, everyone remaining shut within halos of light. At first it feels like they're simply tucked away for the night, but as Ceridwen gradually drifts back from her position at the lead, her dark eyes flicking periodically to the Summerian soldiers behind us, I wonder if it isn't the night that the Summerian citizens hide from.

Juli is drastically different from the smaller villages. No wall encircles the city, just a disorganized array of sandstone buildings leaning against one another on the bank of a tributary in the Preben River system, a collection of southeast-branching offshoots of the Feni, all of them too narrow to provide docking for the ship we rode in on. Fires burn in giant rooftop pits, and in roaring bonfires in squares, and even in the mouths of fire-dancers, keeping any rays of inky black night from encroaching on the never-ending party of Juli.

That's what this city is: a celebration. Each street we weave down is packed with people, their hair as red and wild as the fires they tend, their skin the same creamy tan as Ceridwen's. They stumble from building to building, giggling to friends, beseeching stall vendors for wine, the ruby liquid sloshing over the rims of goblets and staining the roads like puddles of blood. Women in corsets and lacy skirts lean against the doorways of buildings each in more disrepair than the last—glassless windows, gaping holes through sandy walls that show tables hosting card games and bowls for dice throwing. Like the party can't be stopped long enough to fix the city.

Conall and Garrigan, each holding a dagger, plaster their horses on either side of Nessa and me. Not that anyone tries to interrupt our travels—if anything, everyone seems to avoid us, not wanting to be involved in whatever has brought another Season and a Rhythm to their kingdom.

And what *has* brought us here makes me analyze the buildings we pass with more urgency. The key or a clue to the Order could be anywhere. What if one of the people we're riding past knows something? What if that dilapidated building has been around for centuries and holds a key in its depths?

Where do I even start?

Ceridwen remains stoic, guiding her horse through the ocean of people like she doesn't see them. She stays just ahead of the Summerian soldiers, which puts her close enough to me that I can see the way the skin around her eyes tightens with every cheer from the people around her, every distant, muffled laugh, every time one of the Summerian soldiers whistles at the women leaning in the doorways.

Summer's kings have been famous for using their conduit with little regard for the true welfare of their citizens. They don't control their people as completely as Angra did, forcing them to enjoy murdering and torturing enemies, but they do force a similarly damaging emotion: bliss, so much that their army is apparently a joke, their cities sit mostly in ruins, and their economy functions solely on the profits they gain from wine, gambling, and brothels.

When Sir taught us about Summer, my reaction was similar to Conall's and Garrigan's now as they growl at every passing Summerian. How dare they sit in this fog of happiness when so many in the world suffer?

If the city of Juli is a party, the palace is its hub. We pass through an open gate, the soldiers on duty throwing us uninterested glances from where they slump against the wall. A courtyard opens around us, a wide, dusty area with a stable on our right, a cluster of the same dilapidated, sandy buildings as the city, and before us, rising up in a mess of creeping green vines, stubborn spiny plants, and crumbling sand bricks, is the palace.

Ceridwen swings off her horse and passes it to a stable boy. "Welcome to Preben Palace," she tells us, waving her hand at the building. Her eyes linger on it, her face pulling with the same emotions I experienced when I first saw the Jannuari Palace. Worn down, dejected, and above all, tired. But she shrugs it off before it stays too long. "I will arrange rooms for you."

"King Simon will want to meet them as soon as possible," the lieutenant says.

Ceridwen's eyes flick over each of us in turn before she shoots a glare at the lieutenant. "I'd hate to interrupt my brother's revelry with political matters," she says before turning back to us. "No, introductions can wait until tomorrow. I'll be along around midday to collect you."

The lieutenant laughs again, an abrupt crack of noise alongside the continuing choruses of shouts and drumbeats. I groan at myself for having to hear the lieutenant laugh at the word *collect* to figure out what has been happening the whole trip.

These soldiers are Summerian collectors. And their wagons hold people.

Meira

THE INSIDE OF Preben Palace is no different from the outside—dusty, cracked, unkempt. The heat here is less intense, whether from the temperature decrease at night or the way the sandy stones are able to retain some coolness. Conall and Garrigan do a good enough job being annoyed about the similarities between the intentionally ruined Preben Palace and our war-ruined palace that I don't have to, holding my anger at bay so I can focus on meeting the king of Summer—and figuring out where to start looking for the Order and the keys.

Most rulers love showing off their kingdom's treasures, especially to visiting dignitaries as displays of power— Noam proved that with his absurd golden trees. Maybe Simon will be willing to give us tours of Summer's oldest, most treasured places, things that could have endured time and allowed a mysterious Order to have hidden clues or small relics in them.

But getting into such places will require being nice to the Summerian king, and I'm pretty sure I'm going to hate him as much as I hate Noam, if not more, based on what I've seen of his kingdom so far. Which doesn't make preparing to meet him any easier, and when morning comes, I have to consciously restrain myself from checking for my chakram. But taking a weapon to a political meeting . . .

Even I know that isn't a good idea.

My room is far nicer than the palace first appeared in the shadows of night. Flames crackle on a pile of logs in a pit in the corner, lit by servants despite the brightness of the morning, and bristly fire-red-and-orange blankets drape across a canopy bed. The tables and chairs spaced around the room are carved in dramatic swirls and sunbursts, curling in on themselves and shooting back out.

Dendera comes into my room shortly after I finish dressing. I expect her to be proud of how I chose a proper queenly outfit, but when she sees my pleated gown, she stops and sighs.

"Duchess?"

Her eyes flash. "Henn, Conall, and Garrigan will be with you, but—" She stops and turns to the trunk, the one she and Nessa packed full of my clothes. After a moment of shuffling through it, she pulls out a white shirt and coarse black pants, her face pinched as if she hates what she's about to say.

"Wear these. And take a knife, at least. Something small that you can hide."

I gape at her. "Is it my birthday?"

"What? No. I—" She groans and shoves the clothes at me. "I don't trust this kingdom."

"I'm sure I can find a chakram here somewhere." I grin.

"A *knife*," she corrects, waving her arms. "Fine. You don't listen to me, anyway. A chakram, a knife, a broadsword—snow above, why don't you just go in full body armor?"

I laugh and the softest smile rises to her lips. If it were at all possible to capture a moment, tuck it safely away in my empty locket, I know that the magic it would emit would be far, far stronger than anything from that chasm.

After helping me out of the gown, Dendera leaves me to dress myself. I change quickly, pausing with my hand over the knife she set out for me, something borrowed from Henn.

The queen of Winter, armed. But if Dendera, master of all things proper, thinks it's all right for me to take a weapon, just a small one, maybe . . .

I grab the dagger. It settles in my palm, a metallic weight that pulls up memories of an even deadlier weapon. As I slide it into my sleeve, I realize I missed an opening to ask Dendera where my chakram is. But if it's still back in Winter, it can't help me now.

Regardless, I have a weapon and I'm wearing my old clothes for the first time in months.

As I near the bedroom door, I can't help but breathe easier. Suddenly Summer seems a bit less suffocating.

Without much prodding, Dendera and Nessa agree to remain in their room. I would have been happy to have them with me, but Conall and Garrigan look stressed enough at the thought of having to guard me in this kingdom, let alone Nessa too—she'll be far safer in the room than parading around with us. So Dendera stays behind to keep watch over her while Henn, Conall, and Garrigan gather in the hall with me.

A few Cordellan soldiers stand at attention outside a room just down from ours, guarding the spoils of the Klaryns locked within. The door to the room next to it opens and Theron eases out, fingers digging small circles into his temples.

"Tell me you didn't try any of Summer's wine last night," I say, and he winces up at me but manages a weak grin.

"They didn't leave a bottle in your room too?" His grin broadens and he wipes a hand down his face. "I just didn't sleep well. Thinking too much, I suppose."

I almost ask him what he thought about, but I know. The treaty. Meeting Simon. Finding the keys. Everything that loops through my mind too.

Theron blinks through the strain as his eyes glide over my wardrobe. "Good," he exhales.

I snort. "Thanks. That's what every girl wants to hear."

He shakes his head, shrugging toward the rest of the palace and, somewhere in it, King Simon. The cacophony that greeted us last night has ebbed now, the halls empty of music or laughter or drumbeats. The quiet seems uncomfortable in this kingdom, more a pained, flinching silence than a relaxed, still silence.

"No," Theron amends. "I just meant that no event in this kingdom will be . . . normal. Gowns aren't the best idea."

Henn's pale eyes flash in the firelight from a basin not far away. "He means Summer has the same appreciation for personal boundaries that General Herod Montego did."

I lurch back, blinking at Henn as he leans casually on the wall like he said nothing of great importance. His focus flicks around, surveying everything, and I realize he *didn't* say anything of great importance—he's just giving me the facts of our situation, simple and straightforward. But the name of Angra's general leaves an itch on my skin.

Theron nods toward the room his men guard. "It's also probably best if we don't let word of our goods spread around the kingdom. Unless you feel Summer will make a worthy ally for Winter."

I bend closer. "And what of our other reason for being here?"

But Ceridwen appears at the end of the hall before he can respond, dressed so differently from the raider we met last night that I almost mistake her for as nothing more than one of Summer's court ladies. Orange fabric wraps around her legs, twisting up her torso to loop around her neck in two pleats. A leather corset hugs her stomach, matching the sandals that lace up to her knees.

She stops beside me, annoyance radiating off her before she even speaks. "My brother took his party outside the palace last night, and he has asked that you meet him in the city."

Theron straightens. "Of course. Thank you, Princess," he adds, stretching for formality through her apparent indifference. Well, not indifference, but . . . displeasure.

Ceridwen's scowl hardens. "Come on. Carriages are waiting."

Theron raises an eyebrow at Ceridwen's tone, but she strides away without waiting for us to respond. The rest of us—Conall, Garrigan, Henn, Theron, a handful of Cordellan guards, and I—hurry after her, having to keep a near-jogging pace to follow. She leads us down fire-lit halls, the orange glow making the sandy walls of the palace warm and closed in. We rush down two sets of stairs and take three lefts before Ceridwen comes to a halt.

Luscious pink hibiscus flowers sit in vases on tables along the walls, leading to a wide archway that reveals the courtyard outside. The light of day shows a few clusters of scraggly trees, stable hands running about, dust puffing up in clouds of orange. And beyond the wall, Juli rises, its buildings as sandy as the palace complex.

Ceridwen turns to us just inside the archway. "Prince Theron, if you will give me a moment with Queen Meira, I would like to congratulate her on reclaiming her kingdom. You will find the carriages awaiting you just beyond."

Theron's eyebrows pinch as he turns to me, putting his hand on my hip, but I squeeze his arm. I have reason to talk to Ceridwen too—and alone might be best. "I won't be long." I include Henn, Conall, and Garrigan. "I'll be all right for a few moments."

They seem unconvinced, but Henn's attention flickers from me to the otherwise empty hall. "We'll be just outside," he tells me. Conall and Garrigan follow him, and after a pause Theron trails them with his own guards.

Ceridwen turns to me once they leave, glaring with the same disapproving frown Sir always cast my way—brow tight, jaw crooked, eyes set to roll at the slightest threat.

"A Rhythm prince?" she hisses, so low that I barely catch the words.

My face falls. "What?"

She shakes it off, folding her arms. "Queen Meira," she

starts again, raising her voice like nothing happened. "Your conduit was difficult to come by."

I instinctively touch the locket. "Princess, what—"

"Your kingdom as well," she continues, keeping a fake smile on her face. "And your people. I should think a ruler such as yourself would be well aware of their value."

"Of course," I agree slowly, not sure what she's saying.

Ceridwen straightens, gazing at the hall around us like she can see through the walls, to the kingdom beyond. "Summer's rulers have never placed much value on their citizens or others. My kingdom has been branded by this shame, but where some see a brand as a scar, others see it as a fashion accessory."

I nod. "I am well aware of Summer's dealings."

"Are you?" Ceridwen steps closer to me. Gold paint rims her brown eyes, swirls along her temples in tight spirals that glitter as she moves. "That is why my brother has arranged to meet you where he is this morning, to show you how far Summer's *dealings* stretch. He will ask if you are willing to contribute to our"—she pauses, her lip coiling—"economy. Do you? Wish to contribute?"

It only takes a beat for me to understand the meaning of her words. I pull back, my mouth dropping open. "He— *what*? He wants me to sell some of my people to him?"

Ceridwen smiles. "I am glad to see where you stand, Queen Meira. The world is full of people who do not value the same things as you and I. And we do value the same things, don't we?"

"*Yes.*"

"My brother can be persuasive. I only hope your resolve holds."

"You have no idea how stubborn I can be."

"If stubbornness were all that was needed to be a good queen, I'd rule the world." She pivots toward the courtyard.

I stomp forward. "You were waiting to raid the caravan, weren't you? To free those people?"

She stops, the muscles in her bare shoulders bundling sharply. If she had intended to free those slaves, she'd want to keep her actions secret—but if she's someone who feels such repulsion for her brother's practices, maybe she's someone I can trust: someone who rises against opposition; someone who would sympathize with my plight and help me find the key—or the Order of the Lustrate itself—before Cordell does.

Before Theron does.

I flinch at the words I can barely stand to think.

Ceridwen twists back to face me, half of her face bathed in the archway's shadow, half in the courtyard's light. "She's smart too," she murmurs, and closes the space between us to jab something against my abdomen.

A dagger.

Where did she even hide a dagger in that outfit?

"Not everyone in the world has the power they deserve," she growls. "Do not misuse yours."

I clamp my hand over hers on the dagger, a slight pressure that grinds her fingers against the hilt. "I have no intention of misusing my power, Princess. I only wanted to offer my support. I know what it's like to fight for your kingdom's freedom."

She blinks at me, her face flashing with shock, then horror, then a cold, harsh smile that doesn't reach her eyes. She rips out of my grip and folds the dagger back into her palm. "We'll see, Queen Meira. As I said, enjoy Summer."

She's gone, dipping under the archway. The moment she slips through the door, Theron takes her place, flanked by my guards.

"What happened?" he asks.

I smile. "I think I just made a friend."

Wherever Simon wants to meet us isn't far. Two roads later, we stop in front of a four-story building that rivals the palace in terms of age. The sandstone exterior and brittle wood accents tell of years in Summer's harsh climate, but decorations drape from balconies, attempts to hide the dilapidation behind braids of crimson silk and bundles of vibrant orange and red flowers. It's these decorations that give the building more of a grand feel, an air of importance and stateliness, where the palace felt more forgotten.

The walls that looked run-down on the outside are perfectly kept inside, smooth panels of cream-colored stone with gold molding winking from every corner. A hall stretches down the center of the first floor, polished tiles glittering in a rainbow of colors on the floor and drooping plants keeping guard outside dozens of curtained alcoves.

I blink, certain I have to be seeing wrong. Every other part of Summer has been in a state of near collapse—but not this place? Why—and what is it?

An answer appears when one of the curtains to the alcoves shifts and a woman swaggers out, making her way to a staircase at the far end of the hall.

My eyes open so wide I feel them try to pop out of my skull.

She's completely naked.

Garrigan gags on his shock. Conall lurches toward me, realizes there is no immediate danger, and settles for tight-lipped glowering. Theron blushes so dark his skin turns a deep purple-red, such an odd expression for him that I almost laugh.

Ceridwen doesn't react at all, however. She marches down the center hall, throwing a nod at a man who rushes out to greet us. My contingent stumbles after her, silenced by our varying levels of shock and discomfort. The alcoves birth a few more people, curtains fluttering back to reveal the types of women we saw on our way into the city last night, the ones clad in very little, along with men dressed just as scantily. Most lounge on chaises, beds, their limbs strewn, hair askew, and outfits more so. And, usually, they aren't alone. The customers who populate their alcoves range from people in the tattered, dirty garb of peasants to the fine silk wraps of the upper class.

This place is a brothel. And apparently feeds Summer's economy regardless of class. How tolerant of them.

I suck in a breath and thank every piece of luck I've ever had that Nessa didn't come. I don't even want to imagine what Conall and Garrigan would have done, had their innocent, sheltered sister been thrust into a place like this.

Heat overwhelms me, makes sweat bead over my forehead and spread across my spine, waves of it dripping from the lack of ventilation and the way the noon sun heats the exterior of the building. This brothel feels more like an oven, and as we plunge farther down the hall, Theron next to me, Conall and Garrigan pressed against my back while Henn lingers behind, I half expect the sleeping men and women around us to start sizzling like they're being cooked.

Ceridwen leads us to an alcove in the back right corner. There, flimsy curtains part around silk-covered pillows that glisten as the people sprawled on them writhe in sleep.

She waves within. "Here you are," she snaps, and shoves back between us, leaving us standing there, blinking in shock between the alcove and her retreating form.

Theron's brows rise. "I'm getting the feeling we're not welcome here," he whispers.

I smile at him. "Maybe you, Rhythm prince."

He rolls his eyes and flickers a small grin at me before turning to the alcove. Five people sleep within, from what I can tell—they all overlap in a tangle of hair and limbs, shimmering satin and glinting gold jewelry.

"King Simon?" Theron tries.

No one moves.

Theron's jaw tightens. "King Simon Preben," he tries, louder.

Out of the hodgepodge of bodies, a head pops up. Even knotted in a web of pillows and other people's limbs, he's obviously young—not quite as young as Theron or me, but no older than his midtwenties. Scarlet hair cuts in a tangle across his eyes, one of which he cracks open with a rumbling groan before touching something at his wrist. After a moment, he sighs in relief and refocuses on us.

Did he just use his conduit to cure his hangover?

Simon surveys Theron, lifts a brow, and shifts his attention to me.

"Burn me to a crisp! Is it morning already?" His face lights up as he springs to his feet. The movement rocks consciousness into the people woven around him, eliciting moans of displeasure that he brushes off as he stumbles over the bodies to teeter before us.

At which point I make a noise halfway between a gag and a scream and duck my head to avoid seeing far more of the Summerian king than I ever wanted.

He's just as naked as the woman we saw moments ago.

Simon either misses my reaction or ignores it. "Queen Meira! I have been *most* looking forward to this—"

Theron clears his throat, not at all gracefully, and Simon barks laughter.

"Oh!" he says like he'd honestly forgotten. "Terribly sorry—one moment."

There's shuffling and a few more grunts from the still-sleeping courtiers in the alcove, and after a moment Theron nudges me, presumably because Simon has put away his . . . um . . .

The first time I ever see a man naked, and it's the tactless Summerian king. Lovely.

I risk a look up at him to see that he's draped a bundle of scarlet satin around his waist, and while he's still not exactly dressed, I'll take it.

"Queen Meira!" he tries again, and swipes a goblet from a table in the alcove. "It has been far too long since I've had the pleasure of a Winterian in my kingdom." He waves the goblet around, encompassing the brothel. "Which is why I thought it best to make introductions here. I don't imagine you've ever seen any of Summer's splendors. A true shame, but one we will quickly remedy. Today you will have the whole of Madame Tia's staff at your disposal—tonight, you will join me for a true Summerian celebration at the palace. We will have food, we will have drink—"

As my mind scrambles through his words to realize he intends to make us stay *here*, *all day*, Simon thrusts the goblet at me, wine sloshing over his hand. Some of the dark liquid coats a bracelet on his wrist, a thick gold cuff with a turquoise stone in the center, surrounded by a steady glow of scarlet light. Summer's conduit.

I want to tell him exactly what he can do with that goblet, but I manage some semblance of rationality through my fog of shock. He hasn't done anything threatening—and honestly, he's been hospitable. Just not the kind of hospitable I need.

Be nice, Meira.

A weak smile cracks my lips. "Thank you, but isn't it a bit early for all this?"

He downs the goblet's contents before chucking it into the mess of people and winking at me. "Not if you believe in yourself." His focus shifts over us, more analytical, and he visibly wilts. "Cerie didn't come with you? Flames on that girl. She used to be so fun. Did she even introduce herself? My sister, the most un-Summerian Summerian I've ever met, but when she *does* loosen up, guard the wine! Girl is a nasty drunk. In that regard, I suppose she's *very* Summerian."

"King Simon," Theron cuts in, angling between us. I bite back a sigh of relief. I don't even know Ceridwen that well, but I assume she doesn't take too fondly to her brother calling her a "nasty drunk." "We come with a proposition for you. May we plan somewhere to speak? Somewhere away from the bustle of the city?" He pauses, features angling. "I hear Summerian vineyards are most glorious to behold."

I frown. *A vineyard?*

Whatever link to the magic chasm or the Order of the Lustrate might be in this kingdom has to be somewhere that has survived the test of time—something important to Summer, or something at least as old as the door.

That's why Theron wants to go to their vineyards. Some of them have been around for centuries, and if any clues to the Order or the keys could have survived the trials of time—they could be at a vineyard. The carving of the vines on fire makes a little more sense.

My eyes lock on the tiles under our feet. The pride that wells on Simon's face.

"I don't imagine you've ever seen any of Summer's splendors."

Vineyards aren't the only thing Summer values enough to keep preserved for centuries, though. And maybe the carving wasn't supposed to be so literal.

My nose curls. Snow above, if I have to search Summer's *brothels* for the Order . . .

Simon stumbles out of the alcove and hooks his arm

around Theron's neck. "Quite glorious indeed! We'll make the trip tomorrow. Today, though—" His bloodshot eyes pin on me and he whistles, releasing a cloud of acidic breath. "I would very much like to get to know the new Winterian queen. Not that I'm not honored to host the heir of Cordell, but we Season monarchs have to stick together. Solidarity."

The scent of the wine on his breath makes me choke.

We're guests in his kingdom. We need to be here peacefully.

He hasn't done anything wrong. He hasn't done anything wrong.

But no matter how many reasons I stack like bricks in a wall, my impulses batter through.

We're guests in a kingdom built on slavery.

We need to be here peacefully—which is basically saying that we endorse his kingdom's treatment of people.

He hasn't done anything wrong—to me. But who else has he hurt? How many of the people here are slaves?

As if in response to my thoughts, one of the people in Simon's alcove sits up. She's dressed, thankfully, but her hair sticks out in the matted array of slumber, spiraling black locks that plaster to her tawny skin.

She isn't Summerian. She's Yakimian.

Heavy lines of gold paint around her eyes have bled down her cheeks and across her forehead. She pats her hair, and when she feels me watching her, she lifts hooded eyes.

I lock my jaw.

The smears of gold paint over her face almost make the small mark on her cheek unnoticeable. An *S* branded below her left eye, the skin singed but old, healed, something that she's lived with for a while. Maybe forever.

I flick my attention around the hall. Servants sweep up messes and straighten chairs; a few more of the scantily clad people in the alcoves are awakening. Most of them are Summerian, their hair spilling in tangled clumps of fire red around their tan skin, their liquid brown eyes; only a few people from other kingdoms move about. All are branded, their marks just as old as the girl's.

Summer brands its slaves. The servants who showed us to our rooms last night—were they branded? In the darkness, it was hard to see much of anything—and honestly, making sure the stones from the Klaryns got locked away distracted me. I focused on the things a queen would, not on the things a soldier would. The safety of our key to obtaining alliances, not the details of my whereabouts.

My body jolts with remorse. I should be glad that I acted like a queen—but all I can feel now is disgusted. How can I not remember whether or not the servants had brands? Or even if they were Summerian? But the Yakimian slaves here move around the brothel exactly the same as the Summerian slaves, with no inclination to fight back or strain against the life Simon chose for them. No matter how much he is able to make Summerians accept their lives, no amount of magic could enable him to affect someone he bought from another kingdom.

Have these Yakimians lived this life so long they don't know to fight back? Where are the people who don't accept this fate? Those have to be kept away from newcomers, so as not to spoil the illusion of pleasure. So anyone who visits sees the same fake perfection that made Spring keep its Winterian work camps inland, away from its interactions with the outside world.

That's it. That's all I can handle.

I whirl away from Simon, still wound around Theron's neck, and dive for the door, at the end of the long hall lined by the other alcoves. My guards follow, and I can't help but think they all sigh with relief to be leaving.

Ceridwen leans against the door, her arms folded and her eyes pinched. A Summerian slave appears beside her, whispers something in her ear. By the time I reach her, she shoves off the doorframe.

"Forgive her, brother," Ceridwen calls back down the hall. "She complained of the heat last night—our climate is a bit harsh for Winterians, you know."

I don't look back, and honestly, I'd run right out of the brothel if Ceridwen didn't catch my arm and hold me in place. From behind me, Simon chirps.

"Cerie!" Rustling, a solid bump as he slams into the wall beside his alcove at the end of the hall. "I thought you weren't yet back. You must come tonight as well! I miss you, sister."

The expression on Ceridwen's face makes it hard to tell whether or not he's sincere. She doesn't say a word, letting the silence stretch until Simon regains himself.

"But, yes, take a moment, Winter queen! Get some air."

A growl ruptures in my throat, and Ceridwen angles her head at me.

"Don't be stupid," she hisses.

I rip out of her hold. "You have no idea what—"

"I don't?" Her lips tighten and her voice dips lower than a whisper. "No, you're right. It's not like I've lived here for nineteen years. I have no idea what my kingdom is like. For instance, I have *no idea* that if you visibly act out against my brother, he'll retaliate. Unless you want him to start forcibly taking slaves from Winter, don't let him know you despise him."

"What?" All air drops out of my lungs. "He wouldn't dare."

Ceridwen snorts. "And what's to stop him? A few years back, King Caspar reacted to my brother as you did. Storming off, opposing him outright. Weeks later, I found a group of Autumnians secretly put in a slave house south of Juli. So, I reiterate, *don't be stupid.*"

I stagger, muscles coiling. "Did Caspar find out?"

This building feels too open yet too small all at once, and I have no idea if Simon can hear us. I glance back, briefly, to see him and Theron in conversation by the alcove. Theron dips his eyes to me once and offers a small smile.

He's distracting Simon.

My chest cools, gratitude nudging away some of the hurt I still feel toward Theron.

Ceridwen draws my attention back. "They were freed soon after," she says, neither confirming nor denying that she was the one to free them. "But those whom Summer brands don't have much of a life afterward. Don't risk your people. Tolerate my brother—put up with his antics."

I pause next to her, forcing my brain to process her words through this stupid heat, through my hatred of Simon, through my desire to tear out of this brothel and flee back to Winter.

She's right, though. I do need to put up with his antics—for now. Didn't I just wonder if this place holds any clue toward the Order or the key? I can't leave. Not yet, anyway.

My stomach roils with nausea and I keep my focus on the light gleaming through the front door as I raise my voice. "When I return, King Simon, I'd like a tour of this . . ." I can't say it. "Establishment."

So I can scour every surface for clues from the Order of the Lustrate and then run away.

Simon cheers behind me. "Excellent! Of course!"

Ceridwen smiles.

My face pinches and my voice drops again. "Why are you helping me?"

Her eyes flick to the slave who had spoken to her, hovering outside the brothel. He nods and ducks out of the courtyard, into the street.

"As my brother said, Queen Meira," she says, edging toward the door. "Solidarity."

Meira

THE TOUR OF the brothel takes three hours.

Three hours.

One wing of the building was built more than four hundred years ago. One caters entirely to people who like women; one, men; one, a mixture. The uppermost level holds private suites, one of which Simon reserved for us, but his offer was met with a firm, emotionless refusal. Theron figured out why I wanted a tour rather quickly, and spent the time analyzing details as much as I was. But not a damned alcove, plant, sculpture, or even tile seemed to contain anything related to the Order of the Lustrate—no symbols like in the chasm, at least.

So after far too many run-ins with nudity, I feigned exhaustion and Simon dismissed us to rest for the party that night.

If this is how our search is going to go in every kingdom, I don't think I'll survive the trip.

The celebration Simon promised—or threatened, more like—starts just after sunset. Again, Nessa and Dendera stay behind—this time, not for lack of trying on Nessa's part.

"Maybe if more of your court is with you, he won't be so . . ." But her words trail off as she wrings her hands. I didn't tell her everything that happened, just enough for her and Dendera to get the general idea of my stance on Summer.

I squeeze her arm. "No, stay here. I won't be gone long."

She holds my gaze. "You'll tell me about it, won't you? When you return?"

I bite the inside of my cheek. *If there's any part of it I can tell you.* "I'll be back soon."

Nessa's shoulders dip forward and she slides away, taking a seat next to Dendera in the corner of my room. She seems . . . defeated. Did she expect me to take her? Even if I wanted to, her brothers wouldn't allow it, and rightfully so.

But Nessa offers a smile as I leave. See? She's fine. It's just this heat—it's making all of us edgy.

Dendera let me stay in my very unworthy-of-a-celebration pants and shirt, modest and more suited to Summer than a gown. When I meet Theron and his men in the hall again, he wraps his arm around my waist and tucks his thumb into my belt loops as if it's his natural stance. I don't fight him, too preoccupied with trying to prepare myself for whatever lies ahead.

A servant leads us to a celebration hall, drums luring us in beats that vibrate through the sandy walls. Outside, faintly, more drumbeats can be heard, the start of parties reverberating through the city. Voices lift in laughter, and when we duck through an archway, a party unfolds around us.

Orange, scarlet, and gold fabric wraps around columns of the sandy bricks within a massive open-air room. Four stories of balconies lift up, ending in a swath of bluish-black sky in the process of sinking into night, encouraging fire pits that roar from every corner, torches that flicker along the walls, and fire dancers who spew strands of flames over the tightly packed crowd. Cheers and squeals of pleasure ricochet from every direction, peppered with the clinking of goblets.

If I thought it was hot in the brothel, it's absolutely searing here. The nearest fire is in the mouth of a dancer against the wall, but the heat I feel is strong and sure and close, pulsing over my skin with deliberate yet chaotic fingers. The heat comes from the Summerians, their bodies radiating waves of it just like the impenetrable cold that surrounds all Winterians. It swarms me, blistering, unrelenting. A heat that could drive people mad, warp images, and blur thoughts.

Theron leads me in. My eyes dart from person to person, noting every brand like a beacon. Just as many slaves populate this room as nonslaves, serving drink or food or dancing with courtiers. Even the ones serving refreshments seem to be enjoying themselves, swaying with trays over their heads.

Simon, dressed this time, sits in the center of a dais in the middle of the room. A grand orange tent caps the area, sunbeams sewn in gold thread glittering in the pulsing firelight. He reclines with the Yakimian girl who accompanied him earlier. She's the first to see us, whispering a quick word of warning to Simon, who snaps his attention to the foot of the dais and beams.

"Winter queen!" He leaps up, not even bothering to notice Theron this time. Why would a Season king so unashamedly disregard a Rhythm?

Cordell doesn't sell to Summer—which means they are of no use to Simon. And he obviously doesn't care about forging any connection, because when he saunters down the dais, he actually *shoves* Theron out of the way to put his arm around my shoulders.

"Meira! May I call you Meira?" Simon grabs a goblet from a passing tray and presses it to me. I take it only to avoid it spilling when he lets go. "Try this—you won't regret it. A ten-year-old red. Delicious."

He tugs me forward, trying to pull me beneath the

canopy over his dais, but I plant my feet on the floor, heat leaching steadiness from my body so I stumble.

Don't be stupid, Ceridwen's voice echoes from my memory.

"Thank you," I manage, and duck out from under his grip before he can touch me skin to skin. His is one mind I'd rather *not* see into. "But Prince Theron is more of a wine lover than I am."

Theron blinks surprise when I thrust the goblet at him, but he takes it, casting me a suspicious look. "Yes," he says, clears his throat, and turns to Simon. "Wine. I love it."

Simon smiles. "Really? Cordell does make a good ale, though." He turns back to me, eyes squished as he thinks. After a moment, he snaps his fingers in realization. "I know just what will entice you, Winter queen!"

I have to forcibly keep my nose from curling, but Simon spins me around and points to the far wall. "Food! Tables of Summerian delicacies. Don't even try to tell me that you don't like *food*."

His suggestion is so blissfully innocent that I actually smile, and he claps his hands, thoroughly enthralled with his ability to find something to "entice" me.

"Come, come!" Simon loops his arm through mine, hauling me into the fray without a backward glance. Theron falls in behind, along with our guards, and I can tell by the way he bites his lip that he's trying not to address the blatant Summerian brush-off.

The food table sits between two sandstone pillars wrapped in luminescent yellow fabric. Behind the table, nestled into the wall, a fireplace crackles, the flames licking far higher than necessary—meant to be more of a decoration than useful, I'd imagine. Slaves dart around the table, refilling platters and, in a few cases, providing entertainment. Off to the side, funnels of vibrant flames launch from the mouths of Summerian dancers while balls of fire gleam in cages at the ends of chains, flung in patterns as the slaves lunge and twirl and dip.

Simon beams at them. "Lovely, aren't they? Oh, try that—stew made of peanuts and sweet potatoes. Positively decadent!" He points to a bread bowl filled with lumpy golden mush and waves at one of the dancers. "Let's show our guests a true Summerian celebration, yes?"

The dancer nods, her smile unfurling even brighter, and motions to a cluster of musicians in the corner, the ones who have been pounding out steady, gyrating tunes. They see her cue and dive into an achingly fast song, drums thumping and tambourines shaking in a melody that throbs in me.

The performers dissolve into a choreographed dance, spitting fire on certain upbeats, swinging the lanterns in tandem. Flames and heat, feet stomping, hips spinning, a dizzying array of light and energy that mesmerizes everyone around. Simon, his courtiers, the Cordellan guards, even my own guards and Theron, who stare with something more like awe than like the passion of the Summerians. The dancers themselves, all Summerian, smile and laugh, engrossed in their own movements. The slaves not dancing watch with the same delirium, riveted with joy.

As I watch the dancers, their aura of happiness cracks here and there. One of the dancers steps wrong, landing on her ankle in an awkward twist, and a painful wince flickers over her face. But her smile returns, her body carrying on the dance like nothing happened. Another dancer fights cascades of sweat that roll down his face, his breath coming in gasps that shake his whole body, but he smiles through it, lips in a tight grin.

Enjoyment, enjoyment, everywhere—that is Summer's reputation, after all.

But so many of these smiles are forced by the man next to me, who grabs a platter of shredded pork and cheers with delight as he eats and watches his people dance through twisted ankles and exhaustion.

I grip my fingers into tight fists, every nerve taut.

A door covered by dangling beaded strands catches my eye—or more the person who materializes next to it, to the left of the performance.

Ceridwen.

Everyone else in this part of the room seems hypnotized by the dance. For a moment, no one is watching me. The awareness of this one chance at freedom sends a wave of tingling need through me, so strong and unexpected that I latch onto it before I can think of a more logical reaction. But all I see is a goal before me—saving Winter from a Cordellan takeover, finding the Order or its key before Theron. And Ceridwen is the first person I've met whom I might be able to trust.

Ceridwen turns to talk to a man behind her, the slave who was with her earlier. Together they duck through the door.

I cast a glance at the dancers, still hurling their bodies fast and strong with no hint that they might be slowing, and at the audience, still enthralled. Without another thought, I take a smooth step back, angle my shoulders, and fold into the crowd. No one notices me leaving, and I brim with a sensation I haven't felt in months—the thrill of sneaking, plotting, springing into a mission. Being *useful*.

I dive into the beaded doorway. The celebration dies behind me, this dark hall swallowing much of the noise. A few candles flicker on the tables, a few doors open into more rooms, but I'm focused on the end, where Ceridwen and her companion whisper as they hurry into the darkness.

I plunge forward, dodging out of the way of slaves who emerge from various rooms with trays of food and drink. Ceridwen and the man duck into a room on the right and I follow before I realize it isn't a room—it's outside.

The smell of straw, horse dung, and fire clogs the stable yard along with the occasional bout of cheering or complaining from a group of stable hands, bent over an intense dice game as they pass a few bottles of wine among them. Torches light the yard, revealing barns that wrap around the palace and out of sight. No Ceridwen, but I catch a glimpse of orange fabric and red hair on a barn's roof directly across from where I stand. It vanishes . . . over the wall? Where is she going? She's the princess—she should be able to leave through the front gate without question.

Meira the soldier wouldn't hesitate to follow her. But Queen Meira should return to the celebration and hope that no one noticed her departure so that she can bridge some sort of peace between Summer and Winter.

But the only Summerian ally I want is outside. If the muffled pounding of the same song is any indication, the dancing hasn't stopped—everyone is probably still entranced by it.

A stack of crates sits against one of the barn walls, providing an easy lift to the roof. I fling myself up, teetering on the old shingles, and step back to get a better view of the wall, hoping, maybe, that Ceridwen will pop back over. Faintness makes me sway and I wobble to the edge of the roof, heat draining me with each drop of sweat.

"Hey there, Winterian."

I whirl. On the ground below stand two men, red hair matted to their dirt-streaked faces.

One of them chuckles. "Your queen send you out to spy on us?"

The rest of the stable hands hover over the crate they used as a game table, sipping wine from glass bottles and watching us with cocked brows. I'm torn between worry that I didn't realize they snuck up on me and relief that they don't know who I am. Of course they don't—why would the queen of Winter be scaling barns, alone, at this time of night? She wouldn't. She *shouldn't*, for this very reason.

My dagger burns against my wrist, but I don't pull it out, don't want them to know I have a weapon yet. I swallow, hovering up on the roof high enough that they can't yank me down.

Unless they climb the crates and come after me.

The slightest tingle of fear starts at the back of my neck, but I shake it away. I've dealt with worse. I can handle this.

"How long till someone notices you missing, girly?" One man juts his chin toward me. "Long enough to have some fun?"

"I'm pretty sure we have drastically different ideas of what counts as *fun*," I manage, glancing at the door back into the palace. Empty and dark.

The men hoot laughter.

"She's got a tongue on her, this one!"

"What else can you do with that tongue of yours, eh?"

My legs shake and I step back, closer to the peak of the roof. The cold ball of conduit magic wiggles against my fear, clashing with their words and making me gag.

The empty stable yard waits, dark and ominous around me. Angra's face flashes through my mind as I realize how this area is so like Abril—vacant and eager. Horrible things don't happen in crowded places; they happen in the hollows of the world, where it's just a victim and an attacker and no one to hear any screams.

"Hang on there, sweetheart—we just want to talk! Come on down."

I rub my forehead, skin coated with grime, and draw in stifling mouthfuls of hot air. The sticky wetness of sweat on my hands grows thicker, a layer of moist heat that feels just like . . . blood. Blood like in Abril, when I killed Herod.

Herod looked at me like those men look at me.

The conduit magic flashes ice through me and I rub my hands furiously against my pants, wheezing on air that refuses to go into my lungs. What I wouldn't give for ice right now—

No, I'm fine—*I'm fine.*

A shadow moves on the other side of the barn's roof and I whirl, nearly losing my footing on the shingles as I rip the dagger out of my sleeve. Terror courses through me, lightning bolts of dread as the shadow moves forward. I lunge, but my vision blurs—the deep black sky, the distant flicker of a rooftop fire pit. My knees crack against the roof, the knife skittering down the incline, and the impact jolts a whimper from me along with—

Coldness.

Meira

BLISSFUL, WONDROUS COLD floods my veins, filling me from top to bottom. I cry out, so grateful for the sensation that for one frigid moment everything else disappears.

A face comes into my line of sight. It's not Angra, not Herod—Ceridwen.

She grabs my shoulders. "Meira," she calls to me, her voice distant. "Calm down!"

Blood roars in my ears, and my lungs squeeze like they're getting trampled beneath a herd of horses, deflating and barely refilling only to deflate again. The coldness retracts, my vision unable to process what I see. Ceridwen, yes, but also—snow?

Flakes of puffy white drift through the air between us.

We're in Summer—it shouldn't . . . it doesn't . . .

Ceridwen crouches, her face stricken. "What did you *do*?"

Her question comes jagged and harsh, and I just sit

there, my hands in the mushy snow that gathers on the roof, my body shuddering with coldness and horror.

Snow. In Juli.

I made it snow in *another kingdom*.

Conduit magic is linked to each land like it is to each ruler—it affects only its designated kingdom or people. I shouldn't have been able to call snow in Summer, but here I sit in piles of it, watching the flakes evaporate in the relentless heat.

"I—" I start, lifting a handful. "I don't—"

"My queen?"

I shove to my feet and fly up the incline of the roof. Garrigan lifts his hand to catch me if I fall, steady where he stands on the crates below. Sweat and dirt streak his face and he looks over his shoulder at the yard. The stable hands have left, nothing but their empty wine bottles remaining in the flickering torchlight.

"They're . . . gone," I pant. "They didn't see? Did you see—"

I motion to the snow, but it already looks like nothing more than a puddle on the roof.

Garrigan levels a masked look at me. "If they did see anything, I think they're drunk enough that it will be forgotten. But, my queen"—he pauses, exhales, and just when I think I might unravel if I have to explain it to him, he sighs—"are you all right?"

Thank you. "Yes," I say before I even know the answer. *Am I?*

I rub at my chest, prodding the magic gently. *No, I'm not all right.*

Ceridwen narrows her eyes at Garrigan before glancing back toward the palace. "I'm happy to see you didn't last long at my brother's party," she notes, and shifts to her feet, hands on her hips. "Though what, exactly, were you doing?"

Her eyes drop to the puddle at our feet, but she doesn't say anything more about it. Her silence feels like a challenge, daring me to bring it up, or maybe just logging the information for later use against me. Whatever her reason, I am in no mood.

I roll my shoulders back. "I was following you. You seem like the only sane person in this kingdom, and I wanted to find out if anyone in Summer is worthy of Winter's friendship."

Ask me about my magic. I dare you.

Ceridwen barks, her glare heavy. "And why would you pursue me instead of my brother? He is the ruler of this kingdom, the one with the power."

She spits the last word, still not addressing my magic, at least not outright. I recoil. I am so done with politics, with saying things without saying anything. I'm tired, and dried sweat makes my body stiff, and all I want is to run back to Winter and bury myself in a pile of snow.

But wishing for such things brought potentially disastrous results just moments ago, so I shove the wish away.

"I need help," I start, voice weak. "And not from your brother. Even though you're not the conduit-wielder, you still help your kingdom—"

I jerk to a halt.

She helps her people, though she isn't a conduit-wielder. She helps them without magic.

That's what I want, a wish I didn't even know I fostered—to rule Winter without needing magic at all. To be queen, to be *myself*, without having to depend on the unpredictable, frighteningly powerful magic that camps in my chest.

We spent so long fighting to get Winter's magic back that I never considered whether that would be best for our kingdom—but now that I have it, now that I've seen what it can do . . .

I'd rather we were enough as we are, just people, nothing more.

Ceridwen's eyes fall to the locket around my throat. When they leap back up to me, my body hardens, preparing for an attack.

"Even though I'm not a conduit-wielder?" she echoes, her attention falling to the street beyond the wall. Annoyed recognition flickers over her and I follow her gaze.

The slave Ceridwen left with darts out of the shadows of an alley. He nods once, holds up three fingers, and vanishes, all so fast that I would have missed it if Ceridwen's attention hadn't landed on him.

I turn back to her and squeak in surprise. She's close to me now, nose to nose, and glares with those endless brown eyes.

"Fine, Winter queen—you want to know what I do? That man is arranging to help a Yakimian family of three escape. But you've noticed the lovely souvenir Summer gives their property? The branded *S*? It means they can't return to their home—Yakim would send them right back here. The rest of their lives will be spent in a refugee camp away from civilization, and we can only help so many a month before Simon gets suspicious. Even then, he suspects me, but I have to keep helping *because* I'm not a conduit-wielder."

My pulse rises into my ears. "But would you use magic, if you could?"

Ceridwen squints at me and opens her mouth like she's certain of her response, but she pauses, jaw hard. "Why are you asking me this?"

I should've expected that. "I'm just trying to figure out where you stand, Princess. If you're someone . . ." *Who holds the same ideals as myself; who believes in the same freedoms; who would support my intention to keep the magic chasm closed.*

"If you're someone I can trust," I finish.

"How do I know you're someone *I* can trust?"

"Fair point." I cross my arms. "You don't."

Her wonder intensifies, but it's more curious, less affronted. She glances back at the now-empty street below. On a long, slow exhale, she rubs the skin between her eyes.

"My brother uses his conduit to make it sunny on cloudy days," she whispers.

I hold, letting her have the silence. She uses it to look at me, showing her true exhaustion in the way her shoulders dip forward.

"Which is . . . beautiful. I guess. But he also uses it to prevent any unwanted pregnancies in his brothels—unwanted by him, mind you, not necessarily unwanted by the slaves. He gets to pick and choose such things, and I used to think I'd kill for that kind of power. But . . . no." She shrugs, brow pinched. "I wouldn't change who I am. I'm trying so hard to clean up my brother's magic that I wouldn't want to be magic myself. Fighting fire with fire. Which, trust me, doesn't work."

Ceridwen blinks, breaking out of her admission with a swift lurch toward me. "And so help me, if any word of this gets to Simon—"

"No!" I cut in. "I won't. I . . ."

She doesn't want magic. Of course, she says that now, when she doesn't think such a thing would even be possible. But I need to trust her. I need help in this.

Noam's fear plays in my head. If someone familiar with the Order of the Lustrate hears us mention its name, it won't be difficult to piece together that we found the magic chasm. Not that I care about Noam's reason for keeping it hidden—I have my own reasons to want the rest of the world to stay ignorant.

My goal is more aligned with Noam's vision than Theron's. I've reached a whole new level of political revulsion.

"I'm searching for something," I start. "Something that could prevent . . ." *The end of the world.* ". . . Cordell from growing powerful beyond control. I think it may be here, in Summer."

"Summer has never had dealings with Cordell. Nothing of theirs would be here."

"No, not something belonging to them—something they're searching for too. It's imperative that I find it first."

The expression on Ceridwen's face is pure bewilderment. Eyes narrow, lips parted.

I groan and tap my fist against my forehead, eyes closed. "I don't even know what I'm searching for, honestly."

A key? The Order itself? Anything, really, but I have no idea where to start.

"That's the reason you came here?" Ceridwen guesses. "Not to ally with Summer."

I peer up at her. "I can't say the same for Cordell, but I'd rather stand naked in a sandstorm than ally with your brother."

She laughs. "I'd help you if I could, Winter queen." Her eyes shift to the puddles at our feet, but she stays quiet.

Yes, she's definitely holding my use of magic as something to keep me in check should I betray her. Neither of us is comfortable with the other yet—but this conversation is a start.

I'll take whatever I can get.

Garrigan brushes my elbow. "We should get inside, my queen."

That pulls my attention to how empty the yard is. Garrigan reads my questioning look.

"Henn stayed at the palace in case you returned. Conall went to search the east yard."

"You shouldn't have split up—" I start, but the reprimand flops lifeless at my feet. *I'm* the one who ran out on my own.

The look Garrigan gives me is cockeyed and exasperated.

"I know," I sigh. I move to the edge of the roof and drop to the crate beside him. We ease to the dusty ground, and the echoes of the distant parties give me enough of a break to relive the night in clarifying details.

I have no idea what effect my departure had on Simon. I could have been killed or worse if Ceridwen and Garrigan hadn't found me. And when I panicked and lost control of my magic, I'm lucky I only made it snow. But *how* did I do that? It's impossible—or should be. Each Royal Conduit can affect only its respective kingdom.

I need answers desperately. I need to find the Order of the Lustrate.

The guilt in my gut feels all too similar to the guilt that overtook me when I led Angra's men back to our camp in the Rania Plains. After Sir didn't want to send me on that mission, after I assured him and everyone that I could do it, I failed anyway, and we had to abandon our home yet again.

Someone could have been hurt by my recklessness tonight. That's what recklessness does—it hurts the people I care about.

I thought I'd learned that by now.

But as Ceridwen joins us on the ground, I alleviate my regret with the knowledge that I have aid, should I need it. Should I figure out what I'm even searching for.

I wipe away the sweat from my forehead and start across the yard, angling back toward the door. Something clinks against my boot, and when I glance down, one of the stable hands' empty wine bottles glistens in the nearby torchlight.

I frown and bend down to it. Finn had a few bottles of Summerian wine back when I was younger. I might have convinced Mather to help me steal one at some point. Tipsiness blurred most of the details after that, but I do remember the bottle: the glass a translucent maroon hue; the label peeling in tattered strips; grime caked so thick I had to scrub off a layer to get at the cork.

"They better enjoy that buzz," Finn had grunted at Sir once Mather and I were discovered, nearly comatose yet giggling uncontrollably. *"They just drank fifty years of aged Summerian tawny port."*

To be fair, we didn't drink *all* of it—we only managed a few sips before the taste became unbearable. And Sir had seemed more angered by the fact that Finn had the wine at all than by our drunkenness, as he proceeded to smash the bottle to bits and growl at Finn for buying goods from such a corrupt kingdom.

"They just drank fifty years . . ."

An idea surges to life in my head.

"How long do you age wine?" I ask Ceridwen.

She sees the bottle at my feet and dismisses it. I'd imagine thousands of them litter Summer. "Depends on the wine. Why?"

"What's the oldest bottle in Summer?"

"We have a few bottles and casks kept as tokens of the first batches. Centuries old, at least by now. I didn't take you for a wine enthusiast."

Centuries old. So . . . old enough to have existed when the Order hid the keys?

I stand, hands beating against my thighs. How much should I tell her? "I think . . . they could help me."

"I'd imagine so. Alcohol has been known to have its uses."

I laugh sardonically. "Not to drink. Where are they?"

Ceridwen relents, waving a hand dismissively. "Follow me."

I start after her but freeze. "Wait—they're here? Not at a vineyard?"

"Of course they're here." Ceridwen glances back. "The best wine in the kingdom has been kept in my family's private reserve for as long as Summer has been hot."

I hadn't expected it to be so simple, but Ceridwen starts walking again, and I follow dumbly.

She leads us back into the palace. We pause just long enough for Garrigan to run a message to Henn and Conall that I'm safe. Thankfully Ceridwen avoids the celebration, dipping us down a few dark halls and around the hubbub of the party to a stairwell that leads us deep beneath the palace. The air lifts degree by degree as we descend, each layer of coolness easing relief into my muscles. Maybe my Winterians and I can stay underground for the rest of our time in Summer—it'd certainly be far more enjoyable.

By the time the staircase deposits us into a wide space, my body buzzes with adrenaline, eyes snapping to every detail as if the Order of the Lustrate itself might be standing down here, waiting just for me. But darkness clings to the stones, so all I know is the reverberating echo of our footsteps hitting walls many paces off.

Ceridwen lifts a lantern and flicks it to life, the gold flames shooting light over a wine cellar.

Or a wine *warehouse* more like. Rows and rows of wooden shelves stretch in every direction, with more beyond the lantern's reach. Every shelf holds bottles swathed in dust or casks stacked in neat rows. The pungent tang of oak swirls around the musky stench of time, confirming that this place has withstood generations of turmoil and war, struggle and hardship. A place untouched for decades—or hopefully centuries.

"Welcome to the Preben reserve," Ceridwen says, her tone dry, and nods us on as she ducks down a row, her lantern's light swaying off the dust-covered bottles. Garrigan and I follow in silence, every step dredging up dust.

Left, left, right, left—Ceridwen makes so many turns I know I won't be able to find the way out on my own. This cellar has to stretch at least the whole width of the palace, if not more—maybe the whole area of the palace compound. The farther in we go, the thicker the layers of dust, the heavier the stench of age and mustiness on the air.

Finally Ceridwen stops and waves at a wooden rack that, to me, seems like every other wine-coated rack we've passed. The top few shelves hold bottles, neck out, while the bottom few hold small casks stored in horizontal rows.

"The oldest wine in existence," Ceridwen announces, clearly unimpressed with her own kingdom's possessions. "It's a point of pride for every king to leave them aging here."

I start to reach for one but stop, eyeing her over the flickering lantern light. For all my anticipation, I didn't process the fact that these are *important* to someone. Not things I can open and sift through. But do I even need to open them? Maybe the outsides will have a marking.

My hesitation makes Ceridwen's lip curl. She grabs a bottle and thrusts it into my hands, dust billowing off in a small cloud. "Do whatever you need with it. My brother has pride in a wine reserve, but caring for his people? I have just as much love for his priorities as he does for mine."

I snake my fingers around the neck. "He doesn't know where you stand?"

Ceridwen chuckles bitterly. "I'm pretty sure he knows, but he's never sober long enough to do more than idly wonder why I'm such a grouch. So what are you searching for, exactly?"

The question cuts hard into the air, weighted with the favors she's done for me.

I tip the bottle upside down, right side up, flipping and cleaning and searching every free space for . . . I don't even know what. The Order of the Lustrate seal, maybe.

"I'd rather you weren't involved in this until I have no other choice." My eyes shoot up. "You have plenty of problems of your own, it seems."

Ceridwen grunts in half-hearted acceptance.

I set down my bottle and pick another.

After twelve bottles, none of which give me more than a sneezing fit from the dust, I drop to my knees, facing the casks. Garrigan lingers behind me while Ceridwen gave up trying to help nine bottles ago and collapsed against the end of the wooden racks, head bowed against her chest, lantern resting on the floor beside her.

The first cask sloshes when I ease it out. There's nothing unusual on it, no Lustrate seal or keys stuck to the rim. The next one is the same.

And the next.

And the next.

I slide out another, brush my fingers over the exterior, analyze the wood. My certainty all but snuffs out as I ease it back in and reach for the next. Maybe I was wrong—there are only a few more casks. It could be—

But this one sticks when I tug on it, clinging tight to the shelf. I pull again, but it holds.

Ceridwen curves forward, drawn by the way the shelf shakes with every fruitless yank. "Need help?"

"I don't know," I admit, fingers flying over whatever parts of the cask I can reach. I brush the bottom, a smooth line of something like wax that bends along the curve of the cask.

My forehead pinches. Someone fixed this cask to the shelf? Why? Is it that special to Summer?

Or is it that special to someone else?

Every cask bears a cork in the flat side, facing out. I tap my knuckles on the cask, listening for a heavy thud to tell me wine sits inside. But the sound is . . . hollow?

Only one way to find out for sure.

I swivel onto my knees, bracing myself on the cold stone floor, and wrap my fingers around the cork. *Please, please, please . . .*

Ceridwen flies to her feet and squeaks in protest as I fling my whole body back, using every spare muscle to wrench out the cork. She freezes, hands splayed, expecting the worst—

But nothing comes. The cork sits in my palm, the opening in the cask wide and clear.

My lungs depress beneath the yelp of shock I release.

It's empty of wine. So what *is* inside it?

Ceridwen's arms flop to her hips, brows pinched, but she says nothing as I near the cask again. The edges of the flat side are expertly crafted, unable to be pried off, so I stand, turn, and kick through it with my heel.

The wood splinters with a silence-shattering explosion, cracking into a few frayed chunks. I whirl back around and haul them off completely, littering the floor with shards of wood. The lantern flickers from just beside Ceridwen's feet, casting light into the cask.

And deep inside, jutting up from the bottom, sits a lever.

Warning flares through me, biting sharply at the edges of my mind.

This is wrong, my instinct says. *This is dangerous. Don't pull it.* . . .

I inhale, wrap my fingers around the lever, and yank back as hard as I can.

The lever sticks for a moment but relents when I throw my body into it. The wood groans and slams toward me, moving only a hand's width, but enough that something deep beneath the stone floor grumbles and grates. Heat licks my boots, eats into my legs, crawling higher in a sudden eruption of warmth that makes my entire body throb with warning.

The floor cracks.

I whip to my right, where Ceridwen leans over me, confusion wrinkling her face.

"Move!" I cry as the grumbling in the floor and the waves of heat intensify, darting out to open in a chasm just beside me—right where Ceridwen is standing.

I fling myself at her, knocking her and the lantern back as the stone floor drops between the racks. A small opening, barely two arm lengths wide, but deep, and as Ceridwen trips onto the solid part of the floor, the lantern clanging along next to her, I plummet into the fall that would have swallowed her up.

"Meira!" she shouts as Garrigan bellows, "My queen!"

My fingers catch on the edge of the newly formed pit, taking all my weight as I slam to a halt against the side of the hole. Rock grates against my face, misshapen stones dig into my stomach, but otherwise, I'm unharmed. Shaken like a boulder down a landslide, but unharmed.

Ceridwen grabs my wrists. "Are you okay? Hang on—"

But I don't move into her assistance. This pit opened up when I pulled the lever, which means it's related to the key or the Order. Or it's just a mean Summerian trick hidden in a vat of their wine.

Nerves flaring, I cast a glance over my shoulder. Below me, about two heights down, light flickers up from the bottom of the pit in the form of a fire ring. *Did the lever activate this too? Why?*

The rest of the sides of the pit are rock, jagged and cut quickly, leaving large chunks poking out. Nothing else is unusual, no other flames or markings, and I drop my eyes back to the fire ring.

There, in the center of the flames, something glints in the light.

"Wait," I call up to Ceridwen and now Garrigan, who both have bent to their knees to help pull me out. They hold, and in their brief spurt of pausing, I release the rock wall. The unexpected tug of my weight makes them lose their grip on me and I drop, collapsing in a burst of grimy dust at the edge of the fire ring.

"My queen!" Garrigan's voice twists with panic and he shuffles toward Ceridwen. "Do you have a rope? A ladder? Something?"

Ceridwen grunts. "Sorry, Summer doesn't have a lot of climbing gear in our *wine cellar*."

"Then get some!"

"Calm down, Winterian, she's fine!" But Ceridwen's voice fades as she talks—she must be moving toward a storage area, or back up to get what Garrigan demands.

"Hold on, my queen," he calls down to me.

"I'm okay." I take a tentative step toward the middle of the fire ring. I didn't exactly expect the floor to drop out the first time, and I'm not about to be caught unaware again. But the jagged stone floor holds, the fire adding light and waves of heat that cause more sweat to bead down my face as I bend toward the object in the middle of the ring.

It's a key. Old and iron, as long as my hand, with lattice-work swirling at its top to encase a seal—a beam of light hitting a mountaintop. The Order's symbol.

I drop back, disbelief draining any emotions from my body.

I actually found it.

"Look out!" Ceridwen's voice precedes the smack of a rope on the stone floor just next to me.

A chain snakes out from the key's latticework. I grab the chain, shove the key into my pocket, and scramble for the rope, breath trapped against the possibility of any more surprises. But nothing happens again, like the key wanted me to take it, like the pit was waiting for someone to pull that lever and reveal all its secrets.

And maybe it was.

By the time I reach the cellar's floor, Garrigan is positively gray with worry. He takes my elbow and guides me to my feet, his mouth opening in another question of any injuries—

When a rumbling reverberates beneath our feet.

I spin. The pit is gone.

Ceridwen bites her lips together and pushes a muffled scream into them, pointing at the stones, then at me, then at the wine cask. "What—was—*that*?"

"I . . ." *Snow above, how am I going to explain this?* I fish the key out of my pocket and let it sway before me on the chain.

"I found what I needed. If that helps."

Ceridwen shakes her head and presses her fists to her temples. *"Which is?"*

"A key," I say, and she makes a *No, really?* grunt of obviousness. "A key to something . . . terrible. And old. And—" I stop, my fingers still clasped around the chain.

Hope sucks my breath away, a whirlwind that spirals through my lungs. I did it. I found the key—I found the clue the Order left for us.

I actually did it.

And this is proof, even more than the door, that the Order exists.

But . . .

Uncertainty gnaws at me, my ever-present worry growing in a new direction, and I look at the magically covered pit again. No heat anymore, like it never existed. Only the lever in the wine cask sits as a hint of the pit's existence.

Why was any of this in Summer at all? That still doesn't make sense, why the Order even put one of the keys in this kingdom. Why not Autumn or Winter or Spring? Why in Summer, in Juli, in the palace's wine cellar?

I look at the racks again. The age of this area, the dust on the bottles, the reverence Summerians—well, other than Ceridwen—apparently show to this wine, means it would have endured time. This has been one of the symbols of Summer for centuries—wine.

The Order put this key in a place significant to Summer

so it would be guaranteed to survive over the course of history. That at least explains part of the reason—why the cellar, not why *Summer*.

Will the other keys be in similar places?

"Meira," Ceridwen barks, and I jerk to her. Her shock is gone, covered by the same look she gave me when I made it snow moments ago. Logging my weaknesses for future use, analyzing me and trying to figure out a way to make this beneficial to Summer. It should feel like Noam's treatment of me, but she sighs, rubs her eyes, and shakes her head.

"You're involved with something dangerous, aren't you?" she asks.

I start to respond, but through the weighty silence of the cellar, a scream shoots out.

My head snaps toward it.

I know that voice.

"Theron."

Mather

"RELAX YOUR WRIST and exhale as you release." Mather positioned Hollis's arm, aligning the knife in his hand with the target at the back of the room. "Even though your hand does the throwing, your whole body should feel it. Your shoulders, your waist, your legs. Follow it through."

On an exhale Hollis let the blade fly, watched it spinning end over end through the air, until it struck the wall with a trembling *thwack*, five lines off from the center circle. Disappointment coated his features, but he didn't say anything, just marched down the line to yank the knife out of the wall.

"He's getting worse," Kiefer offered from his perch atop the table. It sat now against the front door of the abandoned cottage, opening the whole back half of the room while also barring anyone from bursting in unannounced.

"If you think you can do better," Mather said, and held out a knife to him, hilt first.

But Kiefer just shook his head and settled deeper against the wall, his legs spread out across the dents and stains of the tabletop. "You lot don't need my help getting yourselves killed. That Captain Brennan will find out about this, and I'm content to watch Once-King Mather discover what repercussions are for *real*, nonroyal folk."

Mather lowered the knife. "You're an ass, Kiefer."

"All my life," he responded, but even as he kept his eyes shut, Mather could see the twinge around the boy's lips. Flinches like that, knowing Kiefer was nothing but words and attitude, were all that stopped Mather from repeating their earlier fight in the training barn.

Mather surveyed the rest of the room. Hollis faced the target again, while a few paces to his left Trace and Phil sparred in the sad excuse for a sword ring. Nothing but a circle drawn on the floorboards in ash, the line blurred with every session as the boys slid over the boundary to avoid each other's practice blades, thin lengths of wood scavenged from the cottage's walls.

It had been four days since William had enforced Noam's order to cease training the Winterians—something Mather himself had suggested not long ago. But Mather had only meant it was pointless to train men who could barely hold down nutritious food, let alone hold a blade. The older ones, the fragile ones. He hadn't meant they should *all* stop—and honestly, most of what he had said since they had returned to Winter had been out of anger. Everything he had said to Alysson, to William—ice above, even to Meira.

But Mather had sixteen years of proof that even the smallest of groups could inflict damage. The six of them were better than nothing. Well, five, but Mather knew Kiefer would cave and start training eventually—already his brother, Eli, had given in, and sat against the wall next to Hollis, watching him work through each throw.

Thus far, it had been easy to evade William—so easy that Mather wondered why he hadn't tried to do it sooner. As long as he intermittently stopped by the cottage he shared with him and Alysson or was seen rebuilding the occasional structure, Mather was left alone.

Getting supplies was another issue, one he still worked on—the only usable weapons in Winter rested with the Cordellans, and he couldn't steal them without drawing attention, but he would figure out a way. He'd already managed to steal some knives at meals.

Trace swung his sword down onto Phil's. The force cracked Trace's blade in half, one piece staying in his hand, the other flipping up into the air. Mather cursed softly at losing another brittle sword when Trace's hand snatched the other piece of wood in flight.

Now equipped with two forearm-long pieces of wood, faux knives instead of mock swords, Trace's face lit up. He stabbed at Phil, who had barely managed to regain his balance and held his sword with wobbly arms. Trace slashed and lunged, a flurry of wood and limbs that made Phil stagger back.

Finally Phil collapsed, his sword skittering out of the circle as he threw his arms over his head. "I surrender!"

Trace pulled back, face streaked with sweat. His gaze flashed up to Mather and he grinned, panting. "Black suns, that felt good."

Mather beamed. "You should definitely fight with knives," he said, and nodded to Hollis, who watched with fascination. They had all shared that expression at least half a dozen times since Mather had started them on this insane venture—when someone blocked a blow, when someone hit a mark. More often they shared the flash of disappointment Hollis had shown when he'd missed the target. They needed to savor moments like these, when someone succeeded.

Trace marched out of the sword ring, still grinning as he joined Hollis.

Phil grimaced up at Mather. "Does this mean I have to spar with you again? I don't think my pride can handle so many losses in one day."

Mather laughed and walked forward when someone else beat him to the ring. Feige, who had been nothing more than a silent, observant shadow in the corner, smiled at Mather as she picked up Phil's discarded sword.

"I'll spar with our Once-King," she said.

Mather had made sure she knew she was welcome to train, but Hollis always made an excuse for her. Mather could never figure out why he didn't want her to fight, nor why Feige gave in to her brother when she had shown so much fire that first night. Since then, in fact, she had been nothing more than Phil's all-too-fitting nickname for her—a ghost lingering just beyond their interactions.

Hollis passed the throwing knife to Trace. "Feige, I don't think that's—"

"I didn't challenge you," she replied, voice cold. "I challenged the Once-King."

Mather felt Hollis's gaze on him, a weighty presence off to his right. His muscles twitched, and he already knew he would do this. The soldier in him needed to know what kind of a fighter she was, why Hollis kept her chained, if that flicker of eeriness in her eyes extended to more than wise words.

Without a word, Mather picked up a length of wood as Phil scrambled to get out of the way. Hollis hissed in protest, expecting Feige to obey him, expecting Mather to be smarter than this. Everyone else fell silent, and even Kiefer leaned forward with interest.

Feige entered the ring, appraising Mather. He took her in too, keeping his feet just outside the ash line. Her clothes hung loose around her skinny frame—the baggy fabric would be a hindrance to her, as would her loose hair. She either didn't realize these obstacles or didn't care.

A burst of coolness lit within Mather. Eagerness mixed with adrenaline, and he stepped into the ring.

Feige dove at him, her sword cutting through the air. Mather danced back, staying on the defense. She had grace, her movements fluid and methodical, like she had worked out every motion before she'd even stepped into the ring. Maybe these days of watching them train had let her develop her own series of attacks. Whatever the reason, she fought with a need that Mather had never seen before. Or—he had seen it, just never on someone other than an enemy soldier—bloodlust and desperation and hunger for a fight. Mather enjoyed the movements of fighting, using his muscles in a controlled, active way, but this girl enjoyed the *feel* of fighting, the threat of blood being spilled by her hand.

The realization sent the smallest jolt of fear through him, and he returned her blows. However eager she might be to fight, she was still no match for him, and he saw her realize that as he slowly beat her back.

The glee in her eyes dimmed to confusion, her smile vanishing in a scowl. Now she fought him with anger, which only led to accidents. He needed to end this before she hurt herself or one of the boys outside the ring, watching with wide eyes.

This was why Hollis hadn't wanted her to fight. The

others might have been broken and hurting, but none of them let that interfere with their training—if anything, their training seemed to help alleviate some of their strain. But Feige put every moment of her past into her fighting until Mather couldn't tell if she knew this wasn't real. Or if maybe she had set her sights on killing him just to see if taking this to its end would soothe her pain.

Mather swung the sword in what should have been a killing blow, the wood sailing through an opening and smacking against her exposed neck. But Feige didn't surrender, just batted his sword away and lunged. Mather blinked, surprised long enough for her to swipe at his legs. She sent one buckling under him and flung herself on his back. Her mock sword stung where she pressed it against his neck, jerking his head so he stared up at her on his knees.

Mather heaved her over his head, slammed her onto her back, and pinned her with one arm across her chest. He tugged her sword away and tossed his own, his jaw tight.

"You could be a good fighter," he snapped, "if you learn to control your anger."

As Feige glared up at him, Mather's instincts screamed. Once, as children, Meira had talked him into stealing a bottle of Finn's Summerian wine. When William found them, he had taken the half-full bottle and smashed it into the fire, and the wine had urged the flames from steady fingers of orange into a burst of roaring heat. Mather saw

229

that now in Feige—flames shooting higher, egged on by primal fear.

She snarled up at him. "Get off me."

Before Mather could react, Hollis flew forward and yanked him away. Mather stumbled to his feet as Feige shot up, her shoulders caved, her wild ivory hair reaching around her face.

Mather stepped forward but Hollis shot a hand out, his fingers digging into Mather's arm. "Feige, you're done," Hollis snapped.

"No." Mather felt everyone around him draw breaths in confusion. "We can't ignore things because we're afraid of them—your sister needs to learn to control her anger."

"I don't need to do anything," Feige growled. "I'm *fine*."

"You're not fine. None of us are. And until we admit that—"

He stopped and reached into his pocket, closing his hand around the carving he kept there. When he pulled it out, Feige stayed quiet, staring at her creation.

"Child of the Thaw," Mather whispered. He tightened his fingers around the snowflake-wildflower hybrid, tipping his head down to catch Feige's gaze. When she met his eyes this time, she seemed almost meek, and he couldn't believe one girl could show such a vast array of emotions in so short a time.

"You were right," he said. "None of us belong to Winter,

do we? Everyone else tries to cling to a Winter they once knew. But such things don't burden us—the Winter we know has always been one of our own creation, a kingdom we built on dreams. So you're right, Feige. We're all"—he paused, rotating the snowflake-wildflower carving to show the script on the back— "Children of the Thaw. Our own hybrid of the past and the future."

The smallest, most delicate smile fluttered across Feige's lips. It took Mather as much by surprise as her abrupt mood changes—the girl was a storm of emotion.

Just like the wild girl who had gotten him into all kinds of trouble as a child, a girl whose eyes flickered with the same desperate, blinding drive to succeed.

Someone who had only smiled at him like that once in the past three months—because he had chosen not to make her smile like that again.

He had slammed the door on Meira, locked the bolt tight. All that waited before him now were these people— maybe he could help them where he couldn't help Meira anymore.

Where he had never been able to help her.

"Children of the Thaw," Phil echoed, scratching his chin. "Like our own little group?"

Eli's eyes flashed with eagerness and he turned to Kiefer, still on the table at the edge of the room. Kiefer seemed to be rolling those words through his mind, testing their strength, mimicking the hesitation from the other boys. Like they needed to belong to something, but no one wanted to be the first to admit that need.

Finally Trace broke into a smile. "I like it."

Phil laughed and hooked his arm around Mather's neck. "The Children of the Thaw, led by the fierce Once-King of Winter! We'll strike fear into our enemies' hearts."

"And hope into the future," Mather added.

That sobered Phil, and he unwound his arm. "Aye, that we will."

The rest of the group seemed just as enthralled with the idea, smiling and tossing jokes about it as they went back to training. Even Kiefer moved warily closer to the throwing range and hovered beside his brother and Phil, all of them watching as Trace worked through throwing.

Feige returned to her seat in the corner, where she pulled out her whittling knife and hunched down again. When Mather turned away from her, Hollis waited next to him.

"You are our leader, my lord," Hollis whispered. "Do not abuse that power."

Mather swallowed. "I won't. We need this, Hollis. We need to face what we are." He motioned to Feige. "All of what we are, especially the parts that hurt."

Hollis stared at him, uncertainty framing his face. But he nodded and joined Feige in the corner. Somehow, that silence was more intimidating than if Hollis had threatened him. Feige might be a storm of emotion, but Hollis was the eye of that storm.

They would get through this, though. They had one another now.

Like their newly acquired name suggested, they would all thaw.

Meira

CERIDWEN LAUNCHES AHEAD, leading the way back through the rows of wine—and toward the scream. Thoughts leave me, giving way to instinct as I dash behind her.

Theron's shout fades in the ageless silence of the cellar. The last time I heard him yell like that, we were in the throne room of the Abril palace, Angra standing over him, snapping his ribs one by one with the Decay—

Maybe some spark of memory lingers from my panic attack. Maybe Theron screaming in the darkness of Juli is too close to Theron screaming in the darkness of Angra's palace. But as Ceridwen flies around a corner and slams to a halt, I spin past her, worry fading behind the focus that builds in my mind.

The stairwell opens two rows over, hazy light filtering

into the cellar. My eyes fix on a figure pressed against the left side of the wine racks before us. It takes only one beat of recognition for me to know it's him—the gold and green on his jacket—and I pin my body in front of Theron, instinct throbbing at how weaponless I am. Defenseless, again, forced to just watch as—

But there is no threat here.

I release my breath in short bursts, sweat pouring in freshly awoken rivers down my body with each passing second that I survey the shelves, the floor, even the ceiling.

Theron touches my shoulder and I immediately whirl.

Blood gleams on his hand like a beacon, glistening and fresh, sending a sharp spasm of concern through me.

He shakes his head. "No, it's not mine. When I realized you left, I came looking for you and . . ." His words scratch against a dry throat and he lifts his blood-covered hand to point at the mouth of this row, to a spot where neither Ceridwen's lantern nor the staircase's light reaches. "I tried to help him, but he was already dead."

I face the end of the row, heart rate slowing, limbs unwinding.

It all feels like it's happening at the edge of a dream— the Cordellan soldiers who rush down the staircase, holding lanterns that turn this dim cellar as bright as day, making every shadow slither away from the light. The relief that someone else heard Theron's scream; someone else could have helped him if I hadn't been here. Or if I had been, but failed, anyway.

All of it falls away when I drop to my knees next to the man. He isn't Summerian—the light from the Cordellan lanterns flickers on his face, revealing hair that hangs in matted black tendrils around olive skin, curling over a branded *S* on his left cheek. He looks with glassy hazel eyes at the rows of dusty wine bottles, unaware of the glistening blood wrapping around his throat in a gruesome collar. Heat wavers off his body, the warmth of fading life, and his blood hasn't yet dried, gleaming in a vibrant ruby hue.

He's only been dead for minutes.

I stand, hand to my mouth. He was murdered while we were down here. Anguish sticks to every muscle until my hand drops, useless. Where is he from? Autumn? No, his eyes are too light. Ventralli? Oh, please don't let him be Ventrallan—Theron is half Ventrallan, and I don't know what that would mean for him, seeing one of his mother's countrymen reduced to this.

"My queen?" Garrigan tugs at my arm, trying to ease me away from the body.

I push past him, one of my hands in a fist, the other bearing down so hard on the key's chain that the metal threatens to puncture my skin. Theron wipes the man's blood off his hand with a rag, his soldiers asking him the same kinds of questions Garrigan quietly whispers to me: "Are you all right? Are you sure?"

I can't bring myself to ask if the man is Ventrallan. If Theron hasn't realized that, I don't want to point it out. Maybe he didn't see the man's features in the dark. Maybe he won't look, and he can just assume the victim is Summerian.

Not that that makes the death any less jarring.

Ceridwen is the only one who doesn't seem to care about any of the living. She peeks around us, expression solemn with expected dread—until she sees the man's face.

She staggers back, dropping her lantern, the metal cage bouncing at her feet.

"Princess?" I start, but she spins away, fighting for composure at the edge of the torches' light. Does she know him? Or is she just upset by his death?

I look at him again. This isn't the slave who helped her, and I sigh relief. But still—who was he?

"Well, *this* certainly puts a damper on the party."

My shoulders tense and I glance back to see Simon at the end of this row, just beside the man's body. Half a dozen courtiers circle him, none of them guards, most clutching goblets of wine and watching us as if we're another act arranged for their entertainment.

Ceridwen stalks toward him, and I grab her arm before I can consider why. "You did this—" she snarls at her brother, but catches herself. Her gaze drops to my hand on her arm and she yanks away, toward the rows beyond.

Simon swaggers forward, his orange silk shirt catching

sheens of light, his conduit emitting a hazy scarlet glow as he swings his arm through the air in something like a dance. He stops just before me, eyes swimming in a sea of swollen veins and alcohol-induced redness.

"Winter queen," he starts, dipping forward. "Why did you come to Summer, if not to partake in all we have to offer? Surely not for—" His eyes shift to the body and his air of drunkenness unfolds to reveal someone observant, calculating. Deadly. *"This."*

It's an act. He may be drunk, but he's no less in control of his kingdom than Noam is of Cordell.

The realization sickens me even more. Because he'll remember I vanished from his celebration; he'll remember that Winter affronted Summer.

And he'll remember that he found me, down here, in his wine cellar, with a dead body.

"Of course not. We came down here"—I choke on the lie—"to see Summer's vast collection of wine."

Theron shifts and I look at him, still driven by my instinct to keep him safe.

Which is why I don't realize until now, too late, much too late, that he can see the key dangling from the chain in my hand.

Theron glances down, hardening when he sees it. He doesn't need to utter a word for me to understand everything he's feeling. It's written plainly on his face.

Eyes wide, lips leaping up in a half smile—surprised joy when I don't say anything to deter his assumptions.

Then, face relaxing, mouth parting in confused hurt that I went searching without him, that I'm doing nothing to confirm or deny the importance of what is in my hand.

Simon swaggers toward me. "I would have been happy to give you a tour!" His focus drops to my hand for a beat, though he clearly can't figure out why it holds Theron's attention. "Prince Theron and I were having the most interesting discussion before we realized you had left. Something about unifying the world? A lofty goal for a Season."

I squint at Theron. I thought he was waiting for the trip to Summer's vineyards to tell Simon about his treaty? Why did he tell him tonight?

Theron gives me no hint about why his plans might have changed—he just continues to stare at the key.

I arrange my fingers around the chain, the metal links digging into my palm as I try and fail to hide it now. "Someone should . . ." I motion to the body, not sure what I mean. Cover him? Take him to be prepared for burial or burning or whatever they do with bodies in Summer? Would they do that for him, though, if he's a slave? Acidic repulsion eats at me. I hate that I even have to wonder such things in this kingdom.

Simon's reaction emphasizes my worries. He flips his

hand as if the dead man is nothing more than a blotch of dust on the floor. "What were you saying, Prince Theron? There's a treaty to be signed?"

I glower at Simon as Theron blinks, nods, shaken out of his staring by the mention of the body and Simon's business talk so near a murder victim. "We . . ." He clears his throat. "We continue on to Yakim and Ventralli next. And eventually, Paisly and Spring. I have a—" His eyes dip to the body but instantly jerk back up and he angles himself so he can't see it. "I drafted a treaty, outlining the requirements of a united world. Support during times of strife; a council to be convened when war threatens—"

Simon applauds, cutting him off. He smiles, a giddy beam that catches like the spark of a flame, and soon all his courtiers are smiling too.

Do *none* of them care about the dead body?

Simon lifts his goblet in some sort of toast. His conduit emits hazy red light, dimmer than the vibrant violet of Noam's.

Anger flares anew. Simon is using his conduit to feed his courtiers' revelry. The only thing they feel, the only thing they will *ever* feel, even here, even with blood staining the floor.

"Such ambitions indeed," Simon chuckles. "I've never been one to turn down a Rhythm invitation. The parties, you see. And you'll be most interested in joining us, especially in Ventralli, won't you, sister?"

I flinch with panic. We weren't inviting him along—

But Theron doesn't correct him.

Ceridwen, still with her back to us, glares over her shoulder, her hard gaze biting into Simon. She ducks away, vanishing into the darkness of the cellar.

Simon grins again like her reaction was exactly what he wanted. "Excellent," he says, pulling up a conspiratorial smile. "You'll love Yakim, Queen Meira—they make the best whiskey! For now, though—there is wine to be drunk!" And with that, he saunters back into his group of courtiers, probably expecting us to follow him as he ascends the staircase.

The moment the Summerians leave the cellar, I turn to Theron's guards, the only others here I can give any sort of command to.

"Can you take care of him?" I ask, voice soft, eyes flashing once to the body.

The soldiers nod without scoffing or refusing the lowly Winter queen. At least they care. That compounds my hatred of this kingdom—Summer is making me like Cordell a little more in comparison.

While his men busy themselves with fetching someone to clean up the body, I pull Theron toward the stairwell, putting a row of shelves between the man and us.

"You're letting them come with us?" I ask, my voice tipping

low enough for only Theron to hear. "We don't need—"

He grabs my arm and lifts my hand. "Where did you get this?"

The key bounces against me, Theron's fingers tight around my wrist. The moment the key touches my skin, a scene flashes over my eyes.

I'm in the cell again. Angra crouches before Theron, his staff leaking black shadows that suffocate the room. Theron rocks forward, sucking in airy breaths and releasing ragged exhales. He blinks, disoriented, until his eyes lock on Angra, and the look on his face unravels me.

Not fear. Not resilience. Not even anger.

He's exhausted.

"He didn't . . . save her . . . ," Theron pants, sweat glistening down his neck. How long has Angra been torturing him?

And torturing him with what?

Angra reaches forward and cups Theron's cheek in his palm. I lurch back, shoulders smacking into the stone wall. Angra hesitated. *Before he touched Theron. The rarest beat of a pause, as if he was uncertain.*

Angra is—WAS—never uncertain or careful. About anything.

"What is this?" I shout, though neither Angra nor Theron pay me any heed.

"He could have saved her," Angra whispers, and his usual malice is gone. His voice sounds wrong without it, deflated, a flower without petals. "He had all the power. He could have sent her back to her kingdom—he could have helped her heal. But he didn't. And many like him exist in this world, many who don't deserve power." Angra leans closer. "Who

does deserve power, Prince Theron? Who?"

I stumble, slipping on the dusty stones of the cellar, just as disoriented as Theron was in the—vision? Memory? I don't know. I don't *want* to know—but I do.

This happened to him. These scenes are Theron's memories, however repressed or hidden by Angra's magic. The Order's key, the first of the three to open the door—it's a conduit? Or it has magic, at least, magic like the barrier.

Snow above. Theron took it. Sometime during my distracted state, he took the key from me.

I surge back to him, but he studies the key, rolling it between his fingers, unaware of my panic. He doesn't see anything when he touches it—he'd react in some way if he did.

In the darkness of the cellar, sweat glistening on his skin, he looks almost like the Theron in the vision. Broken, scared, *small.*

I can't find it in me to yank the key away from him— and I don't want to risk touching it and seeing more of the poison Angra pumped into him. Theron doesn't remember it; whatever his mind is doing to deal with what happened, he needs it. And right now, he needs this key, needs it in the way he grips it in his fist and sighs like some of the weight on his shoulders has slid right off.

"You found it," he says. "Where?"

My body goes numb, afraid to move, afraid anything

unexpected might shatter him. "In a wine cask."

A part of me doesn't want to lie to him, doesn't want to hide the truth.

But the other part of me, the logical queen part, jolts warning: *He'll know you went looking without him. You could have said you stumbled on it.*

Of course, that isn't unbelievable at all.

Arguing with myself. I shake my head, and Theron presses on, not dwelling on anything bad. As usual.

But as he starts talking, some of his men return with Summerian slaves who move to care for the dead man. Will they try to find out who killed him? This kingdom is dangerous. It could have been anyone, especially with the crowded party upstairs.

"I know you don't like Summer," Theron says. "But we'll need a unified front before—" He stops, tugs his voice to a breathy whisper. "Before the magic chasm is opened. My father won't willingly disperse magic equally—I *know* that. I know he'll fight. Which is why I'm doing this. We need a unified world to force him to submit."

I step back, eyes roaming over him. The set of his jaw, the sharp angle of his shoulders. Something in the most recent vision itches at the edge of my mind. Power—Angra kept saying that, over and over. *He had all the power.*

This is what Theron wants more than anything, isn't it? To not be powerless.

But while Theron's goal could be glorious, all I can see are the holes in it. The way magic will eventually be abused; the way we may strive for peace between every kingdom, but there will always remain differences that can't be glossed over with smooth words.

The goal I have is far different—magic used as infrequently as possible. No risk of the Decay being created; no fear of unstable leaders losing control of their magic and hurting innocent people; no fear of evil rulers enslaving entire kingdoms with inhuman power.

I can't bring myself to lie more. "Don't you find it odd that Simon agreed so easily?"

Theron shakes his head. "It's the Rhythms who will need convincing—the Seasons have always been desperate for peace. I never worried that we wouldn't be able to sway them."

That doesn't explain why Simon agreed so quickly—his kingdom, though Season, has always been on the edge of any conflicts, happily drunk at the outside of the war, only involved to make occasional purchases from Spring. They are also the only other Season to have a standing alliance with a Rhythm, however hidden or unofficial. So why would Summer even care about uniting everyone, when their place in the world is secure?

I press a hand to my forehead, questions adding wooziness on top of my ever-growing fatigue. Without another word, I head for the staircase. Should I go after Ceridwen? Finding her down here . . . I'd never be able to navigate it. She can, though. She'll be fine. I hope.

With Theron on one side and Garrigan on the other, I leave the cellar.

Meira

WE STAY IN Summer for a barely acceptable week. Emphasis on *barely*.

Every day is hot and slow, and every night is filled with the same parties. Theron still goes to Summer's vineyards, using the time to get Simon to sign his treaty. I opt not to join them, feigning heat sickness—well, not entirely feigning it, but still—and reveling in the time apart from both Theron and the boundary-less Summerian king, who assured me he assigned men to investigate the slave's death, but only after a flippant wave of his hand.

"Slaves often meet rough ends in Summer," he'd said as though he told me merely that Summer is hot, not that someone had *died* under his care.

If I had any power here, I'd do it myself—but already I stand on shaky ground with Simon. Especially since he knows that I asked him about the slave's death, and he told me he put men on it—if word gets back to him that I took it on myself, even after that . . .

I hate that I let that stop me. The old Meira would have simply dived into the investigation, sought out justice for the murdered man without a backward glance. But Queen Meira has to wonder—if Simon stole people from Autumn, would he do the same to Winter?

I'm not just *me* anymore. I'm a whole kingdom, and I can't make mistakes.

Summer's only redeemable trait is Ceridwen, whom I see even less than Theron and Simon, spotting her only once across the dining room during breakfast. Our allegiance isn't politically acceptable either, so I stop myself from calling out to her. My mind works in terms of politics so easily now. Hard-hearted politics that prevent me from talking to someone who could have been a good friend, from asking her if she knew the man who was murdered, all because Simon watches, wondering why I choose to speak to his sister instead of him.

Once we finally leave Summer, our caravan now containing two Seasons and a Rhythm, it takes six days of travel to reach Putnam, the capital of Yakim. The first few are spent under Summer's pounding heat, the oppressive air making the barren, parched world around us ripple. The next days, thankfully, lead us into the northeastern corner of the Southern Eldridge Forest, the wet, dense trees that cup Summer's left border all the way to the Klaryn Mountains.

The temperature difference is glorious. Though my Winterians exhale in the relief of being in a cooler climate, our Summerian companions twitch with a discomfort that will be long lasting—the Rhythms just entered their proper spring, which means there will be nothing but coolness for the rest of the trip. The thought alleviates a little of my stress, but where do I start in my search for the Order or the keys in Yakim?

The Summerian key was linked to their wine—what in Yakim might hold a key? Their lasting symbols of grandeur could be any of their hundreds of libraries, universities, or warehouses. Or what if it isn't in a historic place, like the key we found in Summer—what if it is somewhere completely different?

Three days out from Summer, we reach the tributary that shifts the Feni into the Langstone River. The Langstone runs along the eastern borders of both Yakim and Ventralli before it disappears into a lake near the northern Paisel Mountains, making it a popular guide by which to travel on the western bank. It's also wide enough, deep enough, and populated enough for trade ships and docks, and as our vast caravan of Cordellan, Summerian, and Winterian dignitaries crosses into Yakim along the congested main road that follows the Langstone, we get our first taste of the chaos of Rhythm industry.

People bustle around us, mostly workers milling from village to village on horse-drawn carts, their wagons loaded with straw or produce or tools. They gape as our caravan passes, staring with wonder at so many people from so many kingdoms.

"It's . . . a lot," Nessa pants, her wonder palpable as she leans forward in her saddle, her eyes so wide I worry she hasn't blinked since we entered Yakim.

The cool blue Langstone stretches so far off to our right that we can't see its other bank, a never-ending blanket of lapping water dotted by ships. That holds her attention—not the passing throng of people who stare with just as much amazement at her as she does at the ships. I see a few mouths form the word *Winterians*, see a few noses crinkle with disdain. Here the Rhythm-Season prejudice will not be skewed in our favor as it was in Summer.

I pick at a catch on my travel gown, the same one Dendera forced me to wear on our journey out of Winter. She let me wear my normal, comfortable clothes until today, when she cornered me and explained that, even though we're still a few days out from Putnam, it is imperative we make a good first impression. I agreed with every word she said.

No mistakes here. No risks.

"My queen!" Nessa points excitedly into the distance. "Is that a Cordellan ship?"

I nod, grateful for the distraction. One of the great wooden beasts bobbing in the river has a flag waving over its mast, the fabric flipping taut in the wind and revealing a lavender stalk with a golden maple leaf against a green background. "And that one is Ventrallan." I point to one just next to it, a rich violet flag bearing a silver crown. "And Yakimian," I say, motioning to a ship displaying a flag with a gold ax on a brown background.

The memories of my childhood lessons from Sir shoot a pang of nostalgia through me. It hasn't been more than a couple of weeks since I saw him, but my mind throbs with missing him, and I wonder if that pain has been here all along, and I just haven't noticed it.

He's probably busy overseeing Noam's control and training our Winterian army with Mather. The image of them crowded in a training yard, working through techniques and setting up sparring sessions, fills me with an all-too-familiar emotion—longing for Winter; longing for Sir and Mather and the lives they lead.

I shift up straighter, grinding my jaw. They aren't my family anymore—they're my general and my . . . whatever Mather wants to be. Something distant and formal and meaningless.

Nessa sighs, and I twist toward her. At least I still have her.

The wonder in her face shifts to a calm curiosity. "I want to see them all."

I smile. "You will, Lady Kentigern. You're a world traveler now."

Her body goes slack, but she just shrugs.

"If none of this had happened, I think I would've gone to one of Yakim's universities. I'd want to know as much as I could about the world."

"You could still go to one of their universities." I pause. Could she? I've heard of some Season citizens being allowed into Yakim's universities, but it isn't common. If she wants to go, I'll find some way to make it happen. "Nothing's stopping you from living anymore."

"I'm happy where I am. It makes me feel close to everything we lost." Her eyes wander to her brothers, next in line ahead of us, and I'm unable to tell whether they truly can't hear us or are just pretending they can't. "But if things were different . . . I don't know. I just like imagining the possibilities. That's part of freedom too—getting to dream, and knowing it could happen if I want it to."

How is she always so good at making me both sad and happy all at once? "This world traveling has made you quite astute."

Nessa giggles and I feel some of the distance between us lessen. For a moment we're as we used to be—just two sixteen-year-olds fighting to survive. When all this is over, I'll develop a university in Winter, or a library at the very least. A collection of history and science, words and books. A place where Nessa can be both who she is and who she could have been—one girl standing in a cavernous space, surrounded by swirling script and pieces of knowledge, staring up at each word with a strong, unwavering swell of hope.

Her smile eases, her hands tightening on her reins. She doesn't say anything else, simply holds my gaze and waits there, expectant.

But a horse pulls up on my other side, and I turn to Ceridwen, who stares straight ahead as if she isn't aware that she left the Summerian riders. Her posture is proper despite the way she grips a thick brown cloak around her shoulders, her white knuckles the only sign that she's as uncomfortable as the shivering, bundled-up Summerian soldiers behind her.

She doesn't say anything, and I cock a confused eyebrow at Nessa, who exhales, disappointed—had she wanted me to say something else? I start to ask, but she urges her horse ahead to ride next to Garrigan. Once she's gone, or as gone as someone can be in a constantly moving caravan, Ceridwen turns to me.

"I thought I should prepare you for Yakim, Queen Meira," she says, her face impassive. "I realize you have not had many dealings with other Rhythms, and this one is . . . unique. Queen Giselle is the product of a structured, logical society, and as such—"

"We're talking now?" I don't mean it as a rebuff and I catch myself, face falling. "Thank you for your concern, Princess, but I can handle a Rhythm on my own."

You don't have to help me. I won't drag you into my war.

My horse whinnies as I push it forward, but Ceridwen's hand snaps out and grabs my arm. She yanks it back as fast as it came and I loosen my horse's reins, keeping it even with hers.

The nearest Summerian is a few good paces back, out of earshot. I lean toward her nonetheless. "What's going on?"

Her eyes dart over mine, evaluating. "My brother already suspects me—and distrusts you. I can't fan the flame by being seen with you too often."

It's the same reason I gave myself for not approaching her. "I'm sorry."

She blinks at me, surprised. "For what?"

"You knew the man. The one we found in the wine cellar." I keep my spine tall, my expression not giving away to anyone who might be watching that I'm speaking of a murder. "I should have . . . I don't know. Helped you. I'm sorry I didn't."

"You shouldn't be the one apologizing." Ceridwen's face breaks, her expression unraveling. "He was under my brother's care—Simon is the one responsible. Just because someone has magic doesn't mean they're worthy of it."

She doesn't apologize or amend her statement to not include me in it, a monarch who has magic who might not be worthy of it, and somehow, that makes me respect her more. I need more people in my life who question me, who challenge me, who can admit I have faults.

"Did anyone find out who killed him?" I press, voice still soft.

She shakes her head. "Murders are not uncommon in

Juli." But her words hang in the air between us, and I know, were we alone, she'd expand on that statement.

Such talk is risky though, so I push for something light. "Tell me about Giselle?"

Ceridwen nods. "When you first met my brother, you noticed he tends to be . . . carefree?"

I glance at the Summerians behind us. Simon sits within a row of his soldiers, their leather breastplates accented with ruby-red cords. Behind him, tugged along by a pair of long-haired oxen, rolls an elaborate carriage of wine-dark wood painted with orange flames and golden sunbursts. Tassels hang at the edge of the slanted roof, and through those tassels a few faces peek. Isn't that Simon's personal carriage? Who are the people inside?

One of the faces turns toward me, and my jaw locks as my eyes catch on the brand on her left cheek. I swing to Ceridwen, who blinks in exhaustion.

"Yes, my brother brought a wagon of whores with him," she growls. "Yes, he does this whenever he travels. And yes, this makes me want to cut off his man-parts, but there's nothing I can do without defying him outright. But that wasn't what I asked."

I face forward, lips in a tight line. "The horrific heat of Summer distracted me quite a bit, but yes, I noticed that your brother was 'carefree.' Why does it matter?"

"Because Giselle is his exact opposite. There are benefits to being a kingdom focused on knowledge, but those benefits come at a price. The Yakimians who partake in their conduit's enhancement of understanding are the upper class or a handful of lower class who have proven themselves useful. That's the driving force in Yakim: use. Which makes them profitable and efficient as a whole, but when it comes to all the little pieces—" Ceridwen waves at the passing peasant folk, lugging their wagons or hauling along mules. "The way Giselle sees it, it is a wiser use of her resources to have a large population of poor who perform the bigger portion of menial labor jobs, and to have a smaller population of learned who perform the lesser array of specialized positions: physicians, professors, lawmakers . . ."

I squint. "So she lets most of her people live in poverty, though she has the knowledge and power to help them?" Ceridwen nods and I roll my eyes. "Why is it that of the handful of monarchs I've met, I've only liked one of them?"

She smiles. "Because it's impossible to hate a toddler."

I laugh, but my smile quickly fades. "But why?" I whisper. "Why isn't Autumn as corrupt?"

Ceridwen tips her head on a half shrug. "There are some good men out there," she says, her eyes fading to something beside my head, like she's watching a memory play out. "What's rare is to have a good, *strong* man, as opposed to a good, *weak* man. Those are the ones who ruin the world. Men who mean well, but buckle under others' opinions until their good intentions destroy an untold number of lives."

My hand goes slack on the reins. "You're not just talking about Autumn, are you?"

Ceridwen lifts an eyebrow. "I'll answer that question, Queen Meira, if you explain how you made it snow in Juli, and how you found a fire pit in my palace's wine cellar."

I tense. When I don't respond, she smiles dully.

"We all have things we need to hide," she says before she tugs her horse back to fall in with the Summerian party.

Meira

MY FOURTH-FLOOR ROOM in Langlais Castle over-looks most of Putnam, Yakim's capital. The other side of the castle stretches out over the Langstone River, allow-ing the churning water to spin great wheels that send power throughout the building. This water-fueled energy lets lights flare on with the twist of a knob, or hot water run from faucets without needing to heat it over a fire. One of the many things Ceridwen explained before we arrived, but having the explanation in my head doesn't make what's happening under my fingers any less bizarre.

Odd gadgets and décor fill the rest of the room—leather and polished oak make up the bed, a table, and chairs, along with accents of silver and copper buttons, knobs, and levers. But a device in the corner got me the most trapped—it's a replacement for a fireplace. A panel of knobs sits on one end while the other connects to the wall and the power source. The rest consists of snakelike coils of glass tubes that curl in two distinct sections. When one of the knobs is twisted, the right side of tubes flares hot; when another knob is twisted, the left side flares cold. When a combination of knobs is twisted, the temperature can be adjusted to whatever the resident of the room prefers.

When I got here it was set to heat to combat the chill of proper spring, and the amount of time I've spent twisting various knobs and oohing to myself about the instantaneous temperature change is not something I'm proud of. But giving in to the amazement of the gadgets proves to be a monotonous-enough activity that my mind clears, letting plans to search for the next key form over my building nerves at meeting the Yakimian queen.

I twist the knob to the right. Hot. To the left. Cold.

I've at least decided what type of building I want to search first. The clue that led Theron to guess Yakim in the magic chasm's entrance was a stack of books. There are dozens—maybe hundreds—of libraries throughout Yakim, but I can start with the oldest sections in Putnam's, searching for anything that seems unusual. But Theron will no doubt do the same. Should I try to work with him this time? But he still has the first key—if he gets the second one too . . .

I need leverage over Cordell. And I need to focus my search on the Order of the Lustrate and finding out more about magic.

This is what it comes down to. Choosing the well-being of my country over the well-being of my relationships.

The door to my room opens and I rise, grateful for the interruption.

Dendera leans in. "The rest have gathered not far from here. Come, I'll show you."

I lift the skirt of my pleated gown as Dendera whips back into the hall, flanked by Conall and Garrigan. She didn't offer to let me wear normal clothes again, but even I can tell that this place is far less physically threatening than Summer, and I can't rationalize bringing a weapon when so much relies on befriending Giselle. The only threats here are political or emotional: threats derived from prejudice and thinly veiled remarks. I hope.

The halls of Langlais Castle hold the same strange gadgets and furnishings as my room. The occasional panel of knobs sits in the stone walls, hazy yellow orbs emit steady light, a thick overlay of woven brown carpet covers the floor. Everything would be dreary and dim if not for the lights—their continual glow makes the hall feel bright and steady, as opposed to the usual flickering candles or fire pits I'm used to.

Dendera leads Conall, Garrigan, and me down two halls before stepping into a wide study. Leather chairs sit on a patterned auburn rug, the walls lined with shelves holding so many books that I'm reminded of Theron's room. These books feel different, though—where Theron's were cared for or laid out for doctoring, these are arranged deliberately, yes, but pages poke out of the tops, the bindings show thread and creases, and a few covers dangle off. I've never been particularly concerned with the things that Theron holds on to from his mother's Ventrallan side, but even I feel a hollow thud in the pit of my stomach when I see the state of these books.

Theron stands from one of the leather chairs and crosses the room to me when I enter. "One of the reasons Ventralli and Yakim have a rather strained relationship," he explains, his eyes sweeping over the shelves around us. He massages the back of his neck and winces like he's trying to fight an ache, whether from the state of the books or the growing stress of travel. "Difference of priorities—art versus information."

"I'll refuse to be fascinated by any of their other inventions," I promise, and he smiles.

"Been playing with the temperature gauge, have you?"

My cheeks warm. "Maybe."

He bobs his head in understanding. "The first time I visited Putnam, I missed a state dinner because I broke the temperature gauge and nearly burned my room down. Then I managed to trap myself in one of their"—he searches for the word—"lifts, I think they call them. Rooms that move up and down in lieu of stairs. This whole kingdom is one big trap."

I blink, incredulous. "Why haven't I seen these devices

before? I'd think Yakim in all their efficiency would sell these things to the world."

"They're willing to sell what they need to survive, but knowledge is power, and these things, however small, are their power."

"Probably for the best, anyway." I grin. Snow, it feels good—*normal*—smiling at him. "I'd hate to have any easily distracted princes injured by warm coils and rooms that move."

Theron lifts an eyebrow, but the pink tint to his cheeks tells me he's just as glad for this light banter. "And how long did you fiddle with the temperature gauge?"

"That's none of your concern."

"Thought so."

Dendera leaves to help Nessa unpack. Conall and Garrigan position themselves just inside the room, doing their best to blend into the background as Theron leads me to a thick sofa. Henn is absent this time, letting them have their first solo mission outside Winter, and I stifle a smile at the way Garrigan cannot keep his beam of pride from flickering across his face.

Simon and Ceridwen sit on the floor next to this room's temperature gauge, far less uncomfortable beneath the rays of heat wavering out of the coils. Everyone wears representations of their kingdom: Theron is dressed in Cordell's green-and-gold military uniform, I wear white and silver. But Ceridwen and Simon are the most dramatic.

Simon looks like he's purposefully adorned himself in every symbol of his kingdom. A square of scarlet fabric held in place by crisscrossing braids of red string forms a decorative breastplate that covers his otherwise bare torso. On the scarlet square an orange-and-red flame licks the fabric and Summer's conduit glows on his wrist. His eyes are lined with gold paint, his scarlet hair pulled into a high ponytail decorated with small sunbursts and clusters of rubies. He should seem regal in so much finery, but the way he leans against the wall, legs spread before him, head drooped, he looks like a little boy forced to dress up for a special occasion. I half expect him to break into a tantrum.

Ceridwen has changed from her layers of fur back into an array of straps and patches of fabric, with baggy pants around her thighs and sandals whose straps twist up her shins. Despite her simpler wardrobe, she looks far nobler than her brother—even with, or maybe because of, her only other adornment: a red flame painted beneath her left eye, in the place where all Summerian slaves are branded.

My eyebrows shoot up, and though I know she catches my surprise, she doesn't react, just turns back to the temperature gauge and holds her hands out to it. Is she usually so bold?

A throat clears, and I jump when I notice the only person in the room I don't know. A man towers inside the door, and from the startled expressions on the faces of my guards as well as Theron's and Simon's, no one else noticed him enter either. He trains fathomless black eyes on me, the wrinkles in his dark skin and the gray in the twisted coils of his dark hair putting him at around Sir's age. A thin scar runs from his temple down to his chin, cutting through his cheek in the smooth, pale tone of a long-healed injury.

He clasps his hands against his stomach. "Queen Giselle requests you join her in Putnam University's laboratory. Carriages await you," he says, eyes meeting mine. Though the connection lasts only a few seconds, I get the impression he's analyzing me.

We are in Yakim, though, which is known for study. And he's dressed as if he just came from a laboratory himself—a leather apron hangs over a white shirt rolled to the elbows and tight brown breeches. But now that I study him longer—don't most Yakimians have lighter tawny brown skin, not the dark shade this man bears? Maybe their skin tone varies and I just didn't pay attention during Sir's lessons on Yakim.

Before I can read more, the man sweeps out the door as noiselessly as he came.

We all rise to follow him and I turn to Theron. "The queen is at the university?"

He nods as if it's expected, one of his hands straying to brush over the breast pocket of his uniform. The action washes my responsibilities over me in a wave. The Summerian key. He'll want to go searching for the Yakimian one after we parade our lie-that-isn't-a-lie.

But for this kingdom, it won't be a lie on my part. I still want an ally to help me stand against Cordell—Ceridwen is helpful, but I need someone strong enough to offset Noam's hold. The goods from our mines are already locked up again, awaiting the time I can offer them to Giselle—without Simon present.

More delicate politics. More planning and scheming that make my head ache. But remembering that this meeting will be less fake for me than when we met Simon makes me stand a little straighter, build up more resolve.

"Giselle spends much of her time there," Theron explains. "She—"

"—wastes time inventing light switches when she could be curbing the poverty in her kingdom."

I cock a look at Ceridwen, who closes the back of our group behind Theron and me, her demeanor not hinting in the least that she just insulted the queen of Yakim.

Theron shrugs. "Some would say so," he offers, eyes flitting to the servant, still within earshot.

Ceridwen fans herself. "My, I forgot how thin the air gets when more than one Rhythm is in the same place."

Theron scoffs but throws a wink at Ceridwen. "Jealousy isn't a pretty color on you, Princess."

Ceridwen drops her gaze from him to me and back up again, her eyes rippling with true emotion. It's gone before I catch what it is, something that pulls at the mysteries she harbors.

"And a Season isn't a proper lover for you, Prince," she retorts.

All the air rushes out of my lungs. I'm still gaping as she leaves, pushing ahead of us to stand with her brother behind the servant. I can feel her words wiggle their way through the wall I've built around my feelings for Theron and point out how much distance remains between us, despite his lofty promises to bridge the gap between Rhythms and Seasons. Despite how I'm not sure I want him to.

Theron grabs my hand. "She doesn't matter."

I risk a glance at him, but he stares straight ahead, jaw set, eyes hard.

We wind through a few halls to descend into the castle's entryway, a short but wide room with two walkways on either side of an arched wooden bridge. Wheels spin in a bubbling stream that flows through the center of the room itself, a miniature version of the great, rolling ones that turn in the Langstone River. The water makes the room warm and moist, and as we cross the bridge and exit the castle, the air is only slightly cooler outside.

A yard stretches around us, green and buzzing with stable boys and Yakimian dignitaries, the gray stone of the complex wall rising at the edge of the grounds. Carriages await us at the bottom of the stairs, the servant already perching on the driver's bench of one. His eyes are on me before I notice him, and when I do, he levels that analytical gaze at me again.

I frown. Does he find me that fascinating? Actually, as I'm the recently resurfaced child-queen of the fallen Season, he probably does. That doesn't stop me from tightening my frown in an unspoken question.

His lips twitch in a smile that stretches through his scar and he faces the road ahead.

Within his carriage, Ceridwen waits, her chin propped in her hand. Another carriage holds a few Cordellan soldiers, while the last one is Simon's, the wine-dark wood connected to oxen. With a curl of my nose I climb in alongside Ceridwen, followed by Theron, Garrigan, and Conall. Once we're all accounted for, the carriages move out, dragged down the sweeping road that runs in front of Langlais Castle and out into the city.

Putnam is like every other Yakimian city I've seen. Thatched roofs, whitewashed walls, brown wood beams in Xs to support the structures and add some simple decoration. The buildings around the palace stand four and five stories in the air, tall things that reek of wealth, with giant clocks at the tops of towers and copper pipes coiling in intricate designs down the sides of buildings. The people who mill around these buildings are dressed as expensively as their homes, with tall brown hats, wide ivory skirts, pocket watches dangling from jackets, and canes tipped with gold. The fashion rivals Summer's leather straps and lack of clothing with its oddity, and I can't stop myself from staring as we roll past.

As we cross a bridge over a branch of the Langstone River, the buildings get a little drabber. Shorter, skinnier structures with cracked walls, tiles missing on roofs, dirt smudged on windows. The fashion remains much the same, only dingier as well, and more people work as opposed to stroll down the streets.

Across from me, Ceridwen leans her elbow on the window, our knees bumping with every jostling sway of the carriage. She surveys me as we ride, her eyes darting every so often to Theron, still holding my hand, but his attention is out the opposite window, his expression murderous.

We sit in heavy, choking silence, until at last Ceridwen heaves a long sigh.

"They built Putnam University away from the castle, in the center of the city," she starts, just to fill the air with words. We roll past a glass shop, a fire roaring behind a man who blows into a long metal tube. A bubble of translucent white forms before we're gone, rolling onto the next street. "Yakimians thought it better to divide their assets in case of war."

I shift and Theron's grip on my hand tightens, almost painful, refusing to let go of me. "Not so everyone in the city could have easy access to it?"

Theron glances at me, surprise cutting through his anger. Should I have stewed in silence? Besides, what she said in the hall of Langlais Castle wasn't wrong. Just blunt.

Ceridwen shakes her head. "Sadly, no. Only certain

Yakimians have access to the universities spread through-out the kingdom. The rest . . ."

She waves her hand out the window, at a group of children carrying wooden rods hung with dozens of heavy iron horseshoes. Their skinny legs barely seem strong enough to hold up their own bodies, let alone the weight of the iron, their faces smudged with soot, their clothes rumpled and stained.

My stomach tightens. "Giselle isn't trustworthy, is she?"

"She's similar to my father," Theron adds slowly. I squeeze his hand. "I often wonder why he agreed to marry a woman from Ventralli rather than Yakim. Yakim shares more of his beliefs—efficiency, structure, enterprise. But despite their commonalities, there is still one difference big enough to put off even my father."

"What is it?" I ask. But Ceridwen already points outside. I follow her finger to an alley back the way we came and the carriage rolling down it, deeper into the city. The wine-stained wood boasts the painted flame of Summer. It would seem Simon has opted not to meet Giselle.

I drag my eyes away from Simon's brothel carriage, unable to stop myself from guessing why it might be pulling away. Making money off its services? My stomach rolls over.

"For all my father's faults," Theron continues, his voice soft, "I can never say he isn't a good king. He views each and every Cordellan, no matter how small, as *his*, and turns green at the thought of selling anyone to Summer as Yakim does."

Ceridwen scoffs. "A Rhythm with a conscience. I wonder what other oddities will plague the world—maybe it'll snow in Summer."

Her statement at first sounds like just a declaration of absurdity, but when she meets my eyes for a beat, I feel the unaddressed issues she still has tucked in her mind. How I made it snow in Juli. How I uncovered a hidden pit in her wine cellar. I bite my teeth together, refusing to be ruffled by her.

Theron's face darkens. "Do not insult my kingdom when your own overflows with faults."

She gapes at him, startled, before she bares her teeth and crosses her arms defensively.

I lift both my eyebrows at Theron. "I thought your goal for this trip was unification. You know—breaking prejudices, being *nice*."

He blinks at me, the darkness in his face lifting on a shake of his head. His grip on my hand loosens and I wiggle free, stretching my fingers as he shifts forward.

"I'm sorry," he offers Ceridwen.

"I admire your father's stance, actually," she responds, her own version of an apology. She looks back out the window. "I wish more kingdoms appreciated their citizens that way."

Theron half smiles. "Maybe through this unification, they will."

I bite my lip, the images from the ride swirling in my mind. The fine upper-class citizens walking by their perfect homes; the children hefting horseshoes down the road. For the briefest moment, I'm sucked back to Abril and the sight of the children there. The only difference between them was their coloring. In a kingdom that claims to be so advanced, no one should bear any resemblance to someone from Angra's work camps. Not even peasants, not even the poor. There shouldn't even *be* a divide—there was no difference between Angra's other Winterian prisoners and me, and yet here I sit, riding in a fine carriage. What is the only difference? My conduit magic?

My eyes shift out the window again, to the sudden switch in scenery. No longer run-down buildings and child workers and poverty—now we're surrounded by high walls and fine brick buildings and more people in traditional Yakimian fashions—straight lines, brown fabrics, and copper accents. We must be at the university. That quick of a switch—no middle ground. Like the way most of Summer's people are forced into intoxication and the fog of happiness. Accept it or . . . suffer. Ceridwen is proof of that. This world is nothing but extremes.

There needs to be another option—something more than compliance or struggle. More than the abusive magic in existence today or the threat of everyone having magic. There needs to be a choice to just be *normal*.

Would people still divide themselves and hold prejudices

and foster hatred without magic? Of course they would. But if there were no magic, no Decay, nothing to make one person inhumanly different from another, things would at least be even. Just because it wouldn't cure everything doesn't mean it wouldn't make things better than they are.

I sit straighter in the carriage's seat. That's what I will ask the Order, if I ever find a clue that leads to them.

How to cleanse our world of magic.

Theron's hand envelops mine, jerking me out of my sudden epiphany. I jump, panic lancing through me before I can calm myself.

Just like that, just that easily, my magic gushes up through me, ice running in a jagged flow through my veins, crashing around my body in a frenzied assault of snow and chill. I rip free of Theron's touch, slamming back into the corner of the carriage, blind to anything but the unexpected influx of magic. I'm not threatened or scared or anxious—why is it reacting like this?

I gasp, unable to breathe past the knot of frost in my throat, and when I blink, I'm on the floor of the carriage in Garrigan's arms.

"My queen!" he says, and I don't know how long he's been calling to me.

The carriage door flies open. The servant teeters just outside, his dark eyes sweeping over me before he levels a gaze at me again—but instead of studious, it's sad. Sympathetic.

Poor, broken Winter queen, the look says.

No one counters him—if anything, Theron, Ceridwen, Conall, and Garrigan echo him.

Coldness roils in my chest and spreads down my hands, turning every muscle into crystalized ice. I shove out of Garrigan's arms, the magic thrumming and eager to rush out of me, to pour into him and Conall, to use them because that's all it does. Hurt and control and destroy, and I scramble back from them, pressing myself against the cushioned carriage seat.

"Go!" I shout. Maybe if they get far enough away, maybe if there aren't any Winterians close to me, the magic will just dissipate into nothing, and I won't hurt anyone. Or maybe I'll call down a blizzard in Yakim and it won't just be the Summerian princess who sees my magic's flaw—it will be a university full of Rhythm citizens.

My lungs burn but I hold my breath, refusing to give myself energy until I calm down. What would Hannah say if she were here? No, I don't want her here—*I don't want her.* She's part of the magic, and I am so tired of magic. I don't need her.

Calm down, calm, *please be calm*—

The icy chill rushes down my limbs and leaps from my fingers, barreling out of me before I can control it, before I can stop it. My ribs crack open, a bolt of lightning gouging through my flesh, incinerating my muscles, cutting my heart into two pieces as my eyes meet Garrigan's, Conall's.

But none of it compares to the sheer horror of watching what I do to them. Not just putting strength in them like I did with Sir—the command I screamed, *Go!*, reverberates through me. It gathers the magic and spews out of me on a surge of frost, ice crystals that slam into their bodies—

And fling them from the carriage.

Mather

THE CHILL WIND bit across Mather's face, fighting the sweat that beaded along his brow. He stood only one story in the air, but the wind snaked between the other half-repaired cottages, causing snowflakes to stick to his exposed chest, ice and cold melting into exertion and heat. The gust teetered him forward on the skeleton of this cottage's roof, and he used the movement to test the sturdiness of the boards he'd just finished nailing into place. They groaned but held.

"I'm not going to catch you." Phil slanted an amused eye up to him, his fingers fast at work salvaging old nails from rotted planks of wood on the cottage's floor.

"Your concern is moving, but I'm not going to fall," Mather panted. To prove his point, he stood straight up, balancing on the joist that made the base for the triangle frame.

Phil snorted. "Show-off."

Mather grinned, holding himself steady on the ridge board, the single long plank of wood that ran the full length of the roof, or what would eventually be the roof. From here, he could see the entirety of the square—a dozen other skeleton roofs and unfinished buildings crawling with Winterians performing the same tasks as he and Phil.

Mather's attention pivoted to the northeastern part of the city. The Thaw's cottage was still at least three sections away from being the focus of the repairs. They had another couple of months before they had to seriously consider moving elsewhere, or at the very least packing up their training gear until the builders passed them over.

They had been lucky so far. Lucky that few people went to the outskirts of Jannuari's inhabited section; lucky that as long as Mather and the rest of the Thaw occasionally helped with the repairs, no one noticed them missing on other days; lucky it had only been little more than a couple of weeks since they'd started their secret training so they hadn't yet needed real weapons beyond the few flimsy knives Mather had managed to steal.

A group of Cordellan soldiers circled the square, lapping the area as they had been doing all day. Mather glared at them, knowing his glare would go unnoticed but feeling better when he threw it. From the soldiers' hips hung one sword and two daggers each, perfectly sharpened weapons that dangled unused and taunting. Even the wooden swords the Winterian army had used before Noam's ban had been borrowed from Cordell. Would the Cordellans notice if a few of their swords went missing from their weapons tent? Probably.

Mather glowered as the soldiers marched toward this cottage, taking in the surrounding Winterians with a possessive air that felt like a dull blade running up Mather's spine.

Thwack.

Mather dropped his eyes to the cottage next door, the one Hollis, Trace, and Feige had been assigned to. Their roof was nothing but half a dozen joists running parallel to the floor, leaving the entirety of the one-story cottage open for Mather to gaze down into.

And when he did, alarm spiraled through him so strongly that he wobbled on the roof until his fingers caught the ridge board again.

"Still not catching you," Phil sang, analyzing a particularly stubborn nail.

But Mather ignored him. His eyes shot to the Cordellans, one building away.

Any sudden movement would only draw attention, which was the last thing they needed. Because Feige stood in a throwing stance, one arm wound back—and a knife in her hand. Another she had lodged into the wall on her last throw, the handle still vibrating from the force. Two of the pathetic blades Mather had stolen for their training, but *only* for their training in the Thaw's cottage, safely tucked away from Cordellan eyes.

Mather hissed at Trace and Hollis, who were out behind the cottage, one holding a beam steady while the other sawed through it. But with hammers pounding and saws grinding into wood, his signal got lost in the air, swirling away as uselessly as the flakes that danced all around.

"Well, what do we have here?" one of the soldiers ducked into the cottage just as Feige released her final dagger. It sailed through the air, knocked off course by her jolt of surprise, and clattered into the wall before dropping to the floor.

Feige dove for it, snatching it up and whirling with it held before her. The cottage wasn't more than ten paces from the front door, which the soldiers now blocked, to the back wall. Even Mather would have felt a spike of fear at that, but Feige's face was downright petrified. Her ivory skin grayed to a deathly hue, her eyes unblinking, her small body bent into a defensive hunch, both trying to protect herself and readying for an attack.

Mather moved the moment the first soldier stepped closer to her. He propelled himself off his roof and leaped into the air, clearing the space between the cottages.

"A weapon, eh?" the soldier asked, his boots gliding across the floor in daring increments. "What are you doing with this?"

Mather landed on the cottage's roof, momentum chasing him. He welcomed that momentum—because in the next second, Feige screamed.

This was the scream every Winterian wrestled into submission deep inside them, a scream that came from torture, from repeated and endless suffering. Mather felt it like a wolf's howl, the noise catching at his insides and igniting. It spoke to him in a way he hated and feared and cowered from, both because he understood such fear and because he knew the things Feige had endured had been far worse than anything he had experienced.

She lunged, screaming still, and sliced the dagger through the soldier's cheek. He howled, shock numbing him enough for Feige to swing again, the blade only battering against his sleeve this time. The soldier ducked Feige's next swing and angled his body to tackle her.

Mather gripped the nearest joist and swung into the cottage. The raw wood bit into his palms but he pushed on, locking his legs into a battering ram that he slammed into the second soldier. The man flew to the ground, the air knocked out of him enough that he rolled helplessly as Mather dropped and turned to the other soldier, who flew up from his intended tackle.

"What do you think you're doing?" the man bellowed, but Mather grabbed his collar and hurled him out onto the street just after Trace and Hollis darted inside.

Mather turned, skidding to a stop when he saw Feige curled into a ball in the corner, holding one of her daggers straight out. She still screamed that awful, sickening scream as though she had lost control of it. Maybe she had never had control of it to begin with.

When Hollis reached her, he knelt an arm's length from her and glanced back at Trace with the broken expression of a man who had expected a battle but gotten a war.

One soldier still rolled around on the floor in front of Mather, coughing to recover the breath he had lost. Mather grabbed his arm and dragged him out as the other soldier gained his footing in the yard, sword drawn, face livid.

"King Noam banned all weapons except those held by his army," the soldier barked.

Inside, Hollis's gentle murmurings were now interspersed with Feige's screams. Mather deposited the second soldier at the feet of the first and dug the heels of his boots into the snow in front of the cottage.

"She had a kitchen knife," he growled. "Nothing more."

They had drawn quite the crowd by now. All surrounding Winterians turned, pausing with nails in fists or hammers raised midswing.

"Besides," Mather continued, "if you touch her, I'll gut you."

"*We* will," Phil added, coming to stand beside him with Trace. Movement from just off to his right, and Kiefer and Eli ran forward as Feige's screams continued. They planted themselves alongside Mather, a single, united front.

"Mather!"

The pride swelling in Mather fogged his mind. His attention flicked to William, who shoved through the crowd alongside Greer. Alysson followed, pulling away from where she had been passing out water to the workers. All three stopped between him and the Cordellan soldiers.

"*Stop*," William hissed, and had they still been in their nomadic camp, the order would have worked.

But now, Mather staggered forward, all his anger and adrenaline fading to disbelief. "You're ordering me to stop? What about *them*?" He jabbed a finger at the Cordellans, who watched the dispute unfold with unadulterated rage.

"Don't make a scene," William growled, and swung to face the men. "I apologize for the misunderstanding. We will rectify the situation and comply with all of King Noam's orders."

The words made Mather snarl. "You can't be—"

But Greer stepped in as Mather launched forward. "Stand down," he snapped.

Mather tugged at Greer's grip. The old man held tight,

eyes set and dark. "Didn't you hear her screams? They did that to her!"

Feige had quieted by now, whether from Hollis's comforting or because the fear had snuffed itself out.

One of the soldiers seemed to come to the conclusion that winning this fight didn't deserve his energy, because he waved William off. "We won't be so kind next time, General."

William dropped his head in a bow. "Thank you."

The soldier clicked his lips in disgust before turning away, pushing into the crowd. His comrade followed, both of them throwing victorious sneers back at Mather. They had won something. A different battle, one that left Mather gaping as William turned to him.

Before he could get a word in, William heaved him out of Greer's grasp and bent his head to hiss in Mather's ear. "The Cordellans are our only allies until the queen gains others. If she can't, if Cordell is all we have, we cannot antagonize them."

"They would have hurt Feige," Mather spat back. "They would have—"

"You don't know that."

"I didn't want to find out! Would you have let them make her scream *more*?"

Behind William, the Winterians departed back to their tasks, chased off by orders from Greer. Only Alysson remained, her eyes flicking from them to the cottage where she smiled, the same comfort Mather had seen so often before. A smile that let him know he would be okay, because how could anyone look at him like that if his life was destined for misery?

Feige stood in front of the cottage now, her hands wringing against her stomach in quick, tight jabs. She didn't have her daggers anymore, and she stared at the snow packed along the road with eyes that weren't seeing. Mather took a step forward, but Hollis, hovering just behind her but not touching her, shook his head sharply.

"Feige?" Mather tried.

She flinched. Tears welled in her eyes.

"I didn't want to be defenseless again" was all she whispered.

Mather's heart cracked.

Hollis led Feige away. The rest of the Thaw lingered still, watching, hesitating, trying not to seem like they were still waiting for someone to break.

Mather had a sinking feeling he would be that someone.

"What if we never have other options?" Mather swung to William. "What if Meira comes back and our most powerful ally is still Cordell? What if Noam opens that damn magic chasm and becomes even more powerful? *What then?*"

William's jaw hardened. "We will not be in that position."

"We're already in that position! You did this to us once before, in Bithai. Angra had sent his army after us, and Noam had agreed to sell me, and you just stood there, because even though we had come so far, all you saw left to do was give up. We've come *so far*, so many times, but that seems to have only made you even more fearful. What are you afraid will happen? We've already lost everything, and we survived. We can survive without Cordell! We can fight them!"

"Just because we could fight Cordell doesn't mean we should. There are other options—paths that do not risk our people's lives." William shot forward, exhaustion vanishing in one last burst of certainty. "We did lose everything, and it took decades to get it back. We will not risk it again. We have it now; we will embrace it. Our kingdom, our lives, our families."

Mather's jaw dropped open. The way William said the word *families* like it was just another task, easily accomplished, made Mather look behind him, to Phil, Trace, Kiefer, and Eli. Ahead, William and Alysson waited. A definitive division.

"We were all each other had for sixteen years," Mather started, turning back to William. "All of us. Finn and Greer and Henn, Dendera, everyone who died too. And I never once felt like we wanted to be together. But we *didn't* want to be together—we didn't want to set up a permanent family somewhere else, because it might've made it impossible to get our real families back. But—we're supposed to be a family now? Just that easy?"

Alysson pushed closer. "Mather, we all loved one another—"

"I know we did," he cut her off, anger making his voice snap, and he wasn't sure he knew what he wanted out of this. No, he knew what he wanted, he could feel the question hovering on his lips, burning his mouth, filling him up, and bleeding him out all at once.

William just stared at him, didn't respond, didn't react, and Mather straightened, sucking in breaths and trying to calm his nerves. He couldn't though, couldn't stop what he had started, and the question burst out of him in a roar of need.

"Why do I feel more connected to six orphans than I ever have to my own parents?"

Alysson shook her head, not entirely understanding him, but hurting all the same. William just gaped, confusion making his muscles hard. Mather didn't want to hear their answers, didn't want to know, so he spun around, aiming to fling himself after Hollis and Feige.

William grabbed his arm. "Son, don't turn away from me—"

"I am not your son!" The words tore out of Mather so painfully that blood should have pooled in his mouth. "I want to be—you have no idea how much I want to be. But

I'm not, William, and I don't know why. Tell me why I never felt, *still* don't feel, like I'm anything more than a Winterian soldier to you."

William's jaw tightened, his eyes glazed. "You are a Winterian soldier," he muttered. His voice shook ever so slightly, like he couldn't hold it in, like maybe, just maybe, this broke him too. "We are all first and foremost Winterians. We need to accept our lives as they are *now*. You are our son. Winter needs Cordell. That's it."

Mather backed up, shaking his head, shaking it and shaking it because this was the split between him and William. This was the line, the mark, the place where their difference of opinion could rift a kingdom and get everyone killed.

"You're wrong," Mather said. "Our lives aren't that simple. We won our freedom, but we're still in danger, and nothing will ever be normal."

The rest of the Thaw closed in behind Mather as he stalked away.

That night, Phil beat him at sparring.

Mather wanted to pretend it wasn't because of the tension from earlier. But even Kiefer lacked his usual cynicism, and trained with a new sense of purpose.

So when Mather stepped left and Phil swerved right, Phil's mock sword sailing into Mather's chest, everyone in the cottage hurried over to smack excited hands on Phil's back. Everyone except Hollis and Feige, who stayed where they had been all evening—Feige on her stool, shards of wood flying around her like a blizzard, and Hollis on the floor next to her.

Mather took a step toward Feige. He didn't dare get closer—even a small movement in her direction made her wince, though her eyes remained fixed on her whittling.

"Feige," Mather tried. The boys behind him quieted and he held his hands out to her, a well of need springing in him. Need for Phil's victory to be felt by *all* of them. "Feige, don't be ashamed."

Hollis glowered up at him. "Haven't you done enough?" he growled so low that Mather almost didn't hear him. "She wouldn't have had the knife if not for all of this."

Mather dropped to his knees. "I know she wouldn't have had the knife if not for this, and she wouldn't have broken down today if not for what I've done to you. But she *would* have broken down eventually. Somewhere, somehow, something would have triggered her—just like something might eventually be too much for all of you. Horrible things have happened to us, are still happening to us, will happen every day for the rest of our lives, probably. What defines us is not our ability to never let them break us—what defines us is not letting them own us. We are the Thaw, and we will not be defeated by memories or evil men."

Feige's clear blue eyes lifted to his and she weighed his words one at a time. "We are the Thaw." She nodded decisively. "And we will *not* be defeated."

Beside her, Hollis exhaled, and when Mather looked at him, there was no blame on his face. Exhaustion, yes. But the start of what could be seen as . . . acceptance.

"We will not be defeated," Mather repeated, and he meant it.

Meira

CONALL AND GARRIGAN launch out the door, crashing into the servant, who topples to the ground as they continue through the air to collide with the brick wall of the nearest building.

Everything in me drains clean away.

I *threw* them.

Hands lift me, voices murmur, but my vision swirls, the magic aching in every nerve. I close my eyes, just for a moment.

But a voice I don't know bites a reprimand.

"Is she ill?"

It's a woman, her words high and feminine and close by. When I open my eyes, two people hover on either side of where I've been deposited on a chair in some grand room in one of Putnam University's buildings. I don't remember getting here, and disorientation makes me sway toward the woman who spoke.

She's in her thirties, her skin creased by wrinkles around her wide, watchful eyes. Thick, black curls tumble over her shoulders like perfectly arranged spirals of onyx, just barely brushing an ax on her back. Sharp and gleaming, two blades sweep out of a center of burnished wood. It emits the faintest gold glow, the same iridescent shimmer that comes from Noam's dagger in a violet cloud. Yakim's conduit.

So this woman is Queen Giselle.

My attention flicks to the other person—Theron. All I see on his face is concern, and it yanks me out of my bewilderment.

"Conall—Garrigan—" I mutter their names as my eyes dart around a room at least half the size of Jannuari's ballroom. The low ceiling, gray stone walls, and black floor accented by the other items throughout make this place eerie. Tables sit stacked high with glass tubes, and liquid bubbles in various bowls over open flames. Shelves and cupboards line the walls, stuffed with papers and books and jars, tools and goggles. No other Yakimians aside from Giselle are here, as if everyone got chased out to make way for me.

There are other non-Yakimians here, though, and my eyes sweep over them again. Ceridwen; the Cordellan guards; and—

I burst upright, stumbling enough that Theron leaps to his feet and grabs my elbow. Blood rushes to my head as

I force myself to look at Conall and Garrigan. They sway a little where they stand, Conall with his hand around his opposite arm, Garrigan with his fist to his forehead.

"What did I do?" I gasp, more breath than question.

Garrigan looks at me, starts to lift his lips in a smile meant to brush it off. But when he opens his mouth, nothing comes. What excuse would they even understand? I *threw them through the air.* I used my magic to launch them out of the carriage.

There is no reason for this.

The Cordellan guards see a reason, though. They shoot veiled eye rolls and quiet chuckles at one another, and I can practically hear the thoughts parading through their heads.

The weak child-queen can't even use her magic properly.

I dig my fingers into my stomach, eyes closing on an exhale.

No more. This is the last time I lose control.

No more.

As all this is happening, Giselle rises from her chair and turns her attention to a ledger on a nearby table, scribbling out notes as if foreign queens collapse in her university every day. Her outfit mirrors the décor of her kingdom— a tight-fitting brown coat stretches across her arms with gleaming brass buttons that reach all the way up the high collar to her chin. White linen explodes from under the coat in a thick skirt.

I don't bother caring about anything either. I barely have

the energy to stumble toward the door, and I'm halfway there when Theron grabs my arm.

"Meira—where are you going?"

To scour this kingdom until I find answers.

"Away," I snap at him. "Let me go."

He doesn't budge. "I know it's been an awful couple of months, but if you leave, we'll never know what we could have been capable of. Please—I'll escort you back to the palace myself after we've made introductions."

I'm so close to screaming at him, all the things I've already said that he didn't hear.

The goals you have will unleash the Decay over the world again.

Your father will never cede to you, no matter how much support you have.

You're wrong, Theron.

And I don't care anymore about protecting his innocence. I don't care about the way he shakes a little, so desperate to try, so desperate to hope.

All I care about is the way Conall and Garrigan shake too, because of *me*. Because of my magic.

I know my goal—keep my kingdom safe. And I will not be stopped.

"You're the only one who believes this venture is for peace," I growl. "Giselle won't care about some idealized scheme brought to her by a *child*. You realize that, don't you?"

Theron recoils but composes himself. "Sometimes one person is enough."

"I couldn't agree more, Prince Theron."

Ceridwen steps up next to me, her eyes trained on Giselle's back—Giselle, who seems to have forgotten we're in her kingdom at all.

I snap to Cerwiden. "I don't need your help. I need to *leave*. This meeting is pointless."

"Really?" She moves closer to me. "You need allies. Don't you?"

She looks briefly at Theron. More a gesture than a glance, and I wilt.

Cordell.

I still need allies. With armies.

How does Ceridwen already know how to threaten me? Because we have the same weakness?

But what will she get out of this?

"What do you want?" I yield, jaw tight.

"Who said I want anything?"

I roll my eyes and move to stand beside Theron, directly in front of her, not giving her the satisfaction of any more responses. Theron cocks a brow at me, his eyes sweeping over Ceridwen once, and I swear he mouths *thank you* to her.

"Good," he says to me.

No, it isn't good. I should be running out of here, tearing apart this kingdom for the key or the Order, and instead I—

Made the decision a queen would make. A careful decision, not a rash one.

So why doesn't my chest feel any less tight?

I dip my eyes to Conall and Garrigan, who move to stand behind me, trying for the normal stance they've taken so often. But when they think I'm not looking, they both tenderly prod at their ribs or the bruises on their cheeks.

Seeing them like this, damaged because of me yet still resolute beside me, provokes two different reactions in my body—gnawing remorse that I am so violently undeserving of them, and an even stronger rising cascade of fury.

I will be someone worthy of their loyalty. I will *make* myself worthy.

"Queen Giselle." Theron raises his voice and steps forward. "I—"

"This visit is quite unorthodox." Giselle doesn't break stride in whatever note she's writing. She probably heard everything we said, didn't she?

"Your Highness," Theron tries again, keeping his tone calm and even. "We come with the best of intentions—an opportunity for an alliance among all the kingdoms of Primoria."

And to distract you long enough to find a way to open the magic chasm without you knowing, I mentally add.

Giselle swings away from the notes, her eyes flicking between Ceridwen, Theron, and me. "Yakim has never been at war with any of you. Why should I care about something that does not involve my kingdom?"

Theron takes another cautious step toward her. "Because this isn't simply about peace; this is about equality. Doing away with old barriers and erecting a new standard among Primoria's eight kingdoms."

"Equality." Giselle clucks her tongue like the word tastes bad. "What would be the benefits of such an arrangement?"

I keep my eyes on her, though she doesn't seem concerned about anyone else in the room besides Cordell. The realization makes me bristle, and I remember what Ceridwen said about more than one Rhythm being together. Not only is it hard to breathe, it's hard not to feel like a child listening in on adults.

Theron draws a rolled-up parchment from his jacket and hands it to her. "A treaty, already signed by Summer, Autumn, and Cordell. The terms are quite simple, laying the groundwork for a world in which all eight kingdoms serve not only their citizens, but one another. In times of war, we gather in councils of peace; in times of trouble, we come to one another's aid. You'll wish to read it, I assume, so I don't ask that you sign it today."

Giselle takes the scroll from him, her eyes narrow in thought. This speech sounds grand, but I have to hold back my groan.

Will this change anything?

"Noam signed this?" Giselle asks, her tone sharp.

Theron doesn't flinch. "Cordell has signed it, yes."

Giselle sees the same hole in Theron's words that I do. She squints at him, silence looming, before she blows out an exhale.

"You look so like your father. Pity," she whispers, a brush of noise that might have been intentional, might have been accidental in its volume.

Theron frowns as I do. Was that a jab at Noam? From another Rhythm?

Before I can garner any hope that Yakim might be a better ally than previously thought, Giselle's eyes leave Theron to latch onto me. "Winter hasn't signed it?"

Damn it all.

She's right. I haven't signed that treaty.

Theron turns to me, smiling like he planned this.

"No," he says to Giselle. "But if this treaty is something Yakim agrees to, I had hoped to stage a joint signing ceremony between Yakim and Winter. A symbol to the world that Rhythm and Season both intend to make this work."

The curiosity on Giselle's face sharpens into analysis. "Why did Winter wait to sign with Yakim? I understand Cordell is involved with that Season."

Up until now, Giselle had seemed almost annoyed to have us here—but with that one question, her true feelings shine through.

She invited me to her kingdom via Finn and Greer's visit a few weeks ago—and I showed up, with Cordell, who proclaims unification of the world, declaring that they have a mighty vision for the future that would put everyone on equal footing. A counter to Yakim's attempts at unseating Cordell from Winter.

No matter how sincere Theron might be, no matter what Giselle meant by that odd statement about Theron resembling Noam, this visit is an insult to Yakim.

Regret overtakes my initial anger. I didn't think this through—

Theron smiles at her. "Winter waited because it brings a gift of its own to present to Yakim—a stake in the Klaryns."

Shock numbs me as Theron flings his arm toward the door, and Cordellan guards saunter in. One holds a crate—where was it? In their carriage?

He sets it at Giselle's feet.

"What once only Seasons owned is now Rhythm owned as well," Theron continues, ignoring my stunned glare.

He didn't tell me he would present Giselle with Winter's goods—*my* kingdom's goods.

He shouldn't have done this without telling me. I'd planned on giving away stakes in the Klaryns, yes—but I'd planned to do it *for Winter*, not for Theron's plan.

The Klaryns are not Cordell's to give.

Giselle eyes the crate, her flash of insult abating in what I assume is shock. Wide eyes, pursed lips, a slightly lifted brow. She looks up at Theron, her grip adjusting on the scroll. "Allow me time to consider your proposal" is all she says.

Theron smiles. "That's as much as I can ask of you."

But she's already turning back to her ledger. "Yes, it is."

Theron whirls to me, his smile blinding. "See? Not such a pointless meeting after all," he whispers.

The absence disbelief brought makes me empty and drained, and I can only gape at him and shake my head. "I need to go lie down," I say, and turn, skirt in my fists.

"Of course." Theron wraps his arm around my waist to support me, offering comfort and help so easily, so unabashedly.

It hurts worse that it doesn't occur to him that he did anything wrong. But why would it? I told him I'm on his side. I lied to him, and this is the product of my lie—he believes our goals are aligned. He believes that whatever needs to be done, I'll agree to.

But even if I were truly on his side, I wouldn't be okay with this. Because we *aren't* just two friends united in a goal of peace—we're a Season and a Rhythm, a queen and a prince. And Giselle just saw the Cordellan heir give away pieces of Winter.

Theron had no right to do this.

Resolve sweeps through my shock and hurt, hardening me as I stop inside the door, pivoting back and simultane-ously pulling out of Theron's arm. Conall and Garrigan stagger behind me, biting back their discomfort. And even farther behind them, Giselle stands with her back to us, the crate of Klaryn goods at her feet, Theron's treaty on her ledger stand.

Theron may have given away my one chance at gaining Yakim's favor, but I won't be that easily defeated. Theron said so himself—sometimes one person is enough.

I study Conall and Garrigan. They need rest—but they step back inside the room without a thought as to their own well-being.

Theron bends closer to me. "Are you all right?"

I don't look at him. "Leave one of the carriages for me."

He glances at Giselle, then at me. "You want to speak to her? I could—"

"No," I snap, hear my tone, and deflate a bit. "Thank you, but no," I try again, calmer. "Winter needs to build a relationship with them too, right? Let me do this. I just want to introduce my kingdom to her."

He still seems uncertain, but he nods. "All right."

If he adds anything else, I don't hear it, shoving past him and back inside. Ceridwen already left, presumably waiting in the carriage, so when Theron leaves, it's just Giselle, my guards, and me.

The door thunks behind me a moment later. Giselle stands by her ledger, pen scratching at the paper, presumably unaware of me when I stop on the other side of the crate, trying with every scrap of strength I have left not to look at it.

Silence creeps in, the bubbling of liquids in the glass

tubes gurgling loud and unhindered. I draw in a deep breath.

"Queen Giselle," I begin. Formal. Proper. A queen to a queen. "I wish to—"

"I know what you think of me, Winter queen," she cuts in, her voice emotionless and level. She lowers her pen to the ledger and pivots to me, eyes cocked in study.

I swallow. "Do you?"

"You disagree with the way I run my kingdom. You think I'm heartless."

She doesn't react at all, just that heavy gaze. Which makes it easier not to be shocked that she guessed how I feel, and I cross my arms, muscles hard.

"I'll admit, it is difficult for me to see kingdoms who treat their people in ways I would not treat mine, especially after I worked so hard to get mine back."

There, that was political and nice, wasn't it?

Giselle smiles. "You are very judgmental for someone so unfamiliar with the way the world works."

Now that wasn't political *or* nice.

"Excuse me?"

She bobs her head toward a door on the side of the room. "Come."

No explanation. She crosses the room and vanishes through the door, expecting me to follow like an obedient little Season royal.

I wave at Conall and Garrigan before they can even try

to move from where they both lean against a table. "Stay here."

Conall grunts. "My queen—"

"Stay. Here." I repeat, hating how strict I sound. Conall relents, sagging as I lift my skirt and march toward the door.

A hall cuts to the left, lit by a few more of those glowing orbs. Another door at the end stands open, casting a vibrant spill of white light into the dim brown interior. I push through it—and almost instantly wobble back.

The door opens onto a mezzanine that laps a room at least two stories deep, unfolding in rows of machinery, tables, and workers. Yakimians scurry about, cranking levers and prodding at the machines, every person moving in tandem.

Giselle knots her fingers into the iron latticework that guards the mezzanine. "One of Putnam University's test factories. My professors create designs for new devices, and they are crafted in prototype here." She glances back at me, one brow lifted. "Tell me, Winter queen. Do any of the people below us look despondent?"

I regain my composure and step toward the railing, eyes snapping over the room below. Giselle's tone grates at me, her air of superiority unavoidable—she expects to prove me wrong, to sway me to her side.

Whoever these workers are, they aren't the battered, dirty peasants I saw on the ride in. They're clean, neat, their white shirts crisp and their breeches well fitting. Only their leather aprons hang dirty, the byproduct of the thick black grease that coats some of these machines, the same sort of stuff we'd use to lubricate carriage wheels or riding equipment.

I look at Giselle. "Of course these people would be cared for—they're your upper class, aren't they? I'd be more willing to like you if *everyone* in your kingdom looked this way, but that hasn't been the case so far."

Realization throbs in me the moment I finish talking. Insulting the queen of Yakim is *not* the best way to make an alliance with her.

But Giselle laughs and her focus sweeps from my head to my toes. "You are quite young, aren't you? Yes, I agree that not everyone in my kingdom receives the same treatment—but these workers you see before you are not upper class. They are peasants who proved themselves useful—they are working through the ranks of society, and while it may look like they are menial laborers obeying the plans of a higher lord, they are free to work on their own projects in their spare time. They are *encouraged* to do such things. I do not devalue my citizens as you may think—I simply give value only when it has been earned."

I watch the workers, how they flurry around. None of them look anything but enthralled in their tasks. "Good for them. They've managed to work your system. Would this be a system they would choose, though, if you weren't forcing this need for knowledge into them?"

Giselle blinks, surprised for the first time. "My magic use is what you despise?" Her eyes narrow and, after a beat, she grunts like something occurred to her. "They all have this desire for knowledge in them. Everyone does—including you. I foster that desire. It is not like other kingdoms that force their people to bend to emotions or interests they might not otherwise harbor. Knowledge is a worldwide pursuit. Do not base your opinion of me on such unfounded hatred, Queen Meira."

"It's not unfounded—"

"But it is." She interrupts me with a wave of her hand. "Any of the peasants you have seen who live in undesirable situations can change their fate in an instant. If they prove they are of use to Yakim, they will be elevated to a befitting station. Use is not a right, Queen Meira—it is a privilege."

My mouth yanks open, ready to counter her accusations with my own arguments.

But I actually agree with some of what she said.

Not everyone is deserving of the same things. Not everyone is deserving of power—the whole reason I don't want the magic chasm opened. And if Yakimian society is truly based on people of any class earning their places, it might not be such a hateful kingdom after all.

"If you expect use to come from any of your people," I start, "why do you sell some of them to Summer?"

Giselle faces me completely, her lips lifting in a delicate, demeaning smile. "We all do things we ought not explain to outsiders for the safety of our kingdoms. If you dislike Cordell so much, why do you allow them reign over Winter?"

She has a reason for selling to Summer that affects the safety of her kingdom? What does she mean by that?

I bite down so hard on my cheek that pain lances across my face. "I do not allow Cordell anything. You seemed less than fond of Noam yourself." Here it is, an opening. "Which makes me wonder just how far that opinion stretches."

Her brow flickers in assessment. "If you seek to play on that opinion of mine, you will find little support here. I do not see the Seasons with the same disdain as my Rhythm fellows—the Seasons, like my people, have the possibility to prove their use to me. But what use does Winter serve me now? No, Queen Meira—your problems are your own. And know that as much as I value usefulness, I loathe interference, and I will do anything necessary to keep my kingdom functional. Do not try to bring your problems here."

I don't trust myself to talk again, so I stay silent. Her face remains blank and studious, as though she's simply reciting information, not threatening me.

"The Rhythms will destroy you, child, unless you stop them," she adds, not leaving herself out of the grouping. She turns and heads toward a staircase that will drop her into the factory. "You may go, Queen Meira. Tell Prince Theron I will consider his treaty."

I stay poised on the mezzanine, processing this interaction through a haze. Giselle's directness would be refreshing if it weren't for my instinctual hatred of her overall air of superiority. This whole thing was a test, wasn't it? She was searching for *usefulness* in me. In Winter.

And Theron presented her with the one thing that may have cemented such usefulness.

My anger at him bubbles up as Giselle reaches the factory floor. She walks the aisles, talking with workers, pausing to examine one particularly large machine, twice her height and bearing a number of long metal tubes sticking out in an even row. Each worker she encounters turns to her with apparent eagerness to show off their projects.

She does care for those who earn it. But it is an awful thing, basing worthiness on those who best fight for it. What about the children who are still too young to be of use and wallow in poverty? What about those who might not *want* to lead lives of knowledge, but who know that to succeed, they'll have to bow to Giselle's will? What about a weak, stupid Winter queen who didn't have the foresight to prevent this trip from falling apart before it began?

I rub my temples. My problems are minuscule compared to the others I listed. The perspective redirects some of my self-anger toward the tingling ball in my chest.

That's what makes me the most upset about the

world—how magic shoves people into lives they might not want. No one should have to beseech higher people for permission to be who they are, only to find their pleas ignored. No one should be forced to be something they aren't.

Meira

NESSA AND DENDERA help Conall and Garrigan into chairs as soon as we return to my room. Conall caves in on himself, holding as still as he can, his injured arm twisted against his stomach. Opposite him, Garrigan leans forward with his head in his hands, quiet, still.

My heart shrivels and I step closer to them before I flinch back, not trusting myself.

"How are you?" I manage.

Pain dances over Conall's features, but he smooths them out and nods at me. "We'll be fine, my queen."

Nessa puts her hands on his shoulders. "What happened?"

"I lost control. Again," I admit, my voice dry.

Dendera rushes to the attached bath chamber to fetch water for them.

It's Garrigan who squints at me, one hand in his hair.

"Does that happen a lot with conduit wielders?"

"I don't know," I say. "But I'll get it under control."

Dendera returns and dabs a wet cloth on Garrigan's forehead, wiping some of the sheen that has formed. She hands a cloth to Nessa, who does the same for Conall, and under their tender care, Conall and Garrigan seem to relax a little.

"You two, rest," I tell them, and turn for the door.

Dendera whips to me, her face instantly serious. "You aren't going out alone."

"Unless Henn is available."

"He's familiarizing himself with the grounds. He should be back in an hour."

"I don't have an hour." Theron could already be searching for the key. Finding the Order or the two remaining keys before him are my last hopes for helping Winter without Cordell's influence. Yakim is unresponsive. The possibility of forming an alliance with Ventralli still remains, and I'll try with everything I have left, but . . . Theron is half Ventrallan. Anything he says, they'll side with him.

I have to find the key or the Order. *Now.*

"I'll be fine—I promise. I was fine in Summer, and that kingdom was far more dangerous." Well, I was *barely* fine in Summer, but that won't help my argument.

My promises do nothing to ease Dendera's glare. "Take Nessa, at least."

And have her ask why I'm upset? Have her discover things

that might bring up her past?

"No." It snaps out of me, breaking the excitement off Nessa's face. Just when I thought I couldn't possibly hate myself more . . . "I mean—I need you to stay and take care of them."

Nessa slumps against Conall's chair, her hand on his forearm. She won't look at me, her lips set in a tight line. I hurt her.

What's left of my heart crumbles.

Dendera's lingering disapproval mars her words. "Tell me where you're going. The moment Henn gets back, I'll send him after you."

"Yakim's libraries. The ones in the palace, to start."

She nods, hearing my words for the harmless request they are, but Nessa frowns at me. They both know about the magic chasm, about the truth of our journey, to find a way to open it. They know that's what I'm doing—and doing it without Theron.

"I'll fetch someone to show you the way," Dendera says, and rises. "I won't let you go wandering aimlessly. And here." She tugs a small blade from Garrigan's sheath.

I lift a brow. For someone so adamantly against me using weapons, she's given me quite a few these past weeks.

"Hide it in your bodice," she tells me. Her eyes narrow and she adds, "Don't make me regret giving one to you again."

I take the blade. "I won't," I say with more sincerity than

she must have expected, because her tension evaporates into something like surprise.

She leaves and returns moments later with a servant who leads me into Langlais Castle.

"The libraries in the palace guard the oldest and most valuable books," the servant explains as we scurry down a staircase. "Putnam University houses the more functional tomes, meant for study and use. But for a Season's purposes, I do expect the books here will suit you."

A Season's purposes? All I told him was that I wanted to see Yakim's libraries. I frown at the back of his head, sorting through the meaning of his words, and roll my eyes when it hits me.

He doesn't think I'm interested in the books for *study and use*. Which I believe is a lofty Yakimian way of calling me stupid.

"Oh, quite," I return. "I just love looking at books. Sometimes I can even make out a word or two."

The servant cuts a quick glance back at me, his eyes sweeping across my overly serene stare. After a huff, he faces forward, and our journey through the palace falls silent.

Two halls later, we step into a behemoth of a room. Three stories high, with shelves of books that stretch in wrapping balconies, cloaking the bright, warm space in leather and parchment. No fireplaces or open flames of any kind sit in the room, the light coming from more of those unwavering orbs. Leather chairs cluster in rings on auburn rugs, in rows along balconies, like soldiers standing guard. And at the end of every shelf hangs a mounted oval of mirrored metal with numbers etched on it, identifying the books within.

The servant stops in the center of a ring of chairs and pivots to face me, hands behind his back. "This is the Library of Evangeline the Second, queen of Yakim six hundred thirty-two years ago."

Six hundred thirty-two years?

Adrenaline patters in me. Maybe these are the right libraries to start in after all.

Will Theron have figured this out as well?

The servant angles his eyes at me. He starts talking again, and I realize he meant for me to respond somehow—with proper oohing and ahhing, or some show of acknowledgment beyond absent, silent staring.

"Should you need assistance, the librarian in residence will be about," the servant says, his words slow, as though he's giving instructions to a child. "Do try to treat this space with the respect it deserves."

And he leaves, darting past me. Bluntness seems to be a Yakimian trait.

I start toward the first row of books and find I'm not the only patron here—but I am the only non-Yakimian. A few people glance at me as I pass, brief snatches that turn into shocked staring that unabashedly morphs into outright curiosity. Like I'm not a living person, but a statue, and they're trying to figure out how I was carved.

Four rows of maddeningly unhelpful numbers later, I stop. The rest of this row is empty of Yakimians for the moment, and I breathe in the solitude of not being looked at so curiously. To top it all off, I have no idea what I'm searching for. Again. These books all have titles like *Law and Justice* and *Civilities in Common Townships* and *Declarations from West of Ardith*. Nothing about magic, or even about the Klaryns.

I lean against a shelf, exhaustion muddling my thoughts. Maybe if I can convince Theron to let me see the key I found in Summer—maybe there's something I missed, a lead to the next one. But that would mean having to touch it again, and I don't want to risk seeing . . . memories.

"Find any more hidden pits?"

I jump, flailing off the bookshelf. Ceridwen crosses her arms at the entrance to this row, her lips lifted in a mischievous smile. Next to her, holding his body so he can see the rows behind us, stands the slave who followed her out of the party in Summer. He must be hers. Though I can't imagine she'd willingly keep slaves, not with her stance on Summer's practices. Maybe he's just her friend.

I tighten my jaw. If the man is her friend, he's probably trustworthy—but I keep my tone low all the same. "I told you. I don't want to involve you in this—you don't *need* to be involved in this. This isn't—"

"I just traveled here with you and Cordell," Ceridwen snaps. "I *am* involved in this. Or whatever your cover is, so I might as well be involved in the truth of it. And I helped last time, didn't I? Besides"—she smiles again—"I quite like you being in my debt."

I can't stop the way my mouth instantly turns down. But the spark in Ceridwen's eyes speaks more to camaraderie. I nod at her friend, who eyes me with cautious interest.

"I assume he's trustworthy?"

The man smiles, white teeth cutting brilliance through his tan skin, his *S* brand wrinkling under his eye. But Ceridwen gets to his introduction before he can.

"Lekan." She taps him in the chest. "He's been helping with raids longer than I have, plus his husband runs the camp where we send our freed slaves. He's trustworthy."

Lekan bows. "My princess trusts you, so I do as well."

One edge of my mouth starts to rise but cuts off when a realization flares through me. "You're Summerian, though," I state. "Aren't you affected by Simon's magic?"

I angle the question at Ceridwen too, because in all the chaos since I met her, I never thought to ask *how* she's able to think clearly when her brother pumps dazed joy into everyone else in their kingdom. My question makes Lekan's smile vanish, but Ceridwen laughs.

"Took you this long to ask me that?" She clucks her tongue. "You're not the brightest flame in the fire, are you?"

"Don't make me hit you in a library."

She laughs again. "Years of practice, learning how to distinguish our own feelings from magic-induced ones. It also helps that Summer's magic is, shall we say, *weak*, what with how much of it my ancestors have used on bliss. But most people are so accustomed to it that they don't need much help to remain happy anymore."

She says it all with no more pomp than if she had just told me it's hot in Summer. Lekan shuffles, slanting away from us, his reaction breaking Ceridwen's apparent lack of concern.

It's hard, what they do, resisting their king's magic. Harder than Ceridwen lets on.

Summer would certainly benefit from a lack of magic too, if their ruler was forced to govern simply by strength and will.

A throat clears behind me and I glance back, hand going to the dagger in my bodice.

The servant who led us to Giselle, who drove our carriage through Putnam. Those black eyes lock on me again, the studious way I'm more than a little sick of.

"May I help you find something, Your Highness?" he asks after a beat. He sweeps over Ceridwen and Lekan, decides they're not nearly as fascinating as I am, and focuses back on me.

I squint at him. "Who are you?"

The man folds into an elaborate bow. "Rares, the librarian in residence. You seem lost, dear heart—can I help?"

"*You're* the librarian in residence."

"Yes."

"And the carriage driver?"

Rares's smile doesn't even flicker. "I offered to accompany you to visit the queen—you're quite the specimen here in Putnam. A teenager who single-handedly freed her kingdom! I couldn't resist the opportunity to see you for myself."

"I'm glad I could provide some entertainment for you."

"And I can provide some assistance for *you*," Rares says. "What brings you to the great Library of Evangeline the Second?"

Ceridwen leans forward at that, just as eager to hear, while Lekan falls back to being uninterested, scoping the library like a guard.

I wanted help, didn't I? And now I have it from two sources. Neither of them could do any harm, unless I tell them straight out that the magic chasm entrance has been discovered—or they know about the Order of the Lustrate, which is a risk I'll have to take; neither of them will shatter at any information we find about Angra or the Decay.

What do I have left to lose?

I turn to Rares. "What information do you have on something called the Order of the Lustrate?"

Ceridwen frowns. "The what? Lustrate?"

"They're the ones I need help from. I just have no idea where to search for them." I pause, watching both her and Rares for any reaction. If either of them knows what the

Order is, they'll know now what I'm after.

Ceridwen's face doesn't change, her eyes drifting as she thinks. But Rares needs no time to absorb my question—his smile widens in delighted curiosity and he heads down the row, beckoning us to follow him. "Nothing in Evangeline the Second comes to mind, but this library is rather dull, and something like the 'Order of the Lustrate' sounds right mystical. The Library of Clarisse is just down from here, and that might be more suited to your research."

Neither of them knows what the Order is.

I hurry after Rares and tilt my head when he glances back at me. "What books are in this library?"

"Books of law and edict."

I roll my eyes. The servant took me to the *law* library? What about me says I want to spend time perusing books about rules?

Rares reads the annoyance on my face and laughs. "I do apologize, dear heart. Not what you were expecting?"

"No." I keep pace beside him as we duck down another row of books, angling toward the back wall. "You aren't what I was expecting either. Are you Yakimian?"

"No, dear heart. From outside Yakim, actually."

"Ventralli?" Ceridwen asks, her eyes analyzing his features. "You don't look Ventrallan."

He bobs his head in something like a nod. "You're familiar with Ventrallans, yes? It's odd that I'd be here, but *someone* should care for these books. Because, honestly, this is shameful. So I'm mending what I can, providing fodder for a kingdom that right *adores* studying unusual folks." He winks at me. "No manners, Yakimians. I'm afraid I've picked up a plethora of unseemly behaviors from them. Ah, here we are—the Library of Clarisse, home to books of history and records."

Rares pushes open a door at the back of the law library, revealing another room that stretches just as large beyond. An identical layout too, with balconies and chairs and orbs of light, the same mirrors marking each row with numbers. This library is far less crowded; the only other person here is a servant sweeping a carpet to our left.

Rares saunters in as if he knows exactly where he's going, stopping only to yank a book from a shelf and plop it into my arms. "A census record, but just for Yakim, and only through the last proper spring. The rest are in this row and around. They list people, businesses, even the occasional horse—if anything named the 'Order of the Lustrate' exists in Yakim, it'll pop up here." He turns to a row behind him. "And this row starts census records for Ventralli, that one for Cordell. They tried to do censuses in the Seasons, but you know how their relationship with you lot goes. Over here are a few for Paisly—old ones, and mostly inaccurate. Journey up there is a nightmare, I hear—even more imposing mountains than your Klaryns."

Rares whisks off to the next row, tugging me along. I throw a questioning look at Ceridwen, who stifles a laugh and shrugs as if to say, *You asked for it.*

"Now, this is good—Bisset's *Analysis of Secret Societies.*" Rares whips a book out of a shelf and stacks it in my arms. "It'll chill you to your veins! Though I'd imagine chilling isn't as uncomfortable for you as for the rest of us. Ah, now, this one should help—*A Study of the Unknown.* Oh, and you must have *Forgotten Worlds*—Richelieu clearly adored the sound of his pen scratching on parchment, but every few dozen pages he provides good information. Oh, and—"

By the time Rares is done, Ceridwen, Lekan, and I all have our arms stacked with books and more recommendations waiting on shelves. I gawk at Rares, my arms threatening to buckle. Though if I drop these books, I can spend time cleaning up the loose pages instead of reading all this.

Seeking information about the Order of the Lustrate might not have been one of my better ideas. How easily I forgot the misery of trying to read *Magic of Primoria*—but my brain remembers it well, already lurching with pain as I look down at the cover for *The Reign of Queen Eveline the First and Societal Cultures During Her Time.*

Merciful snow above.

Rares claps his hands. "When you're finished, dear heart, feel free to leave the books on the table, as disorganized as you possibly can." He motions to a table behind me, situated in a break in the rows of books. "The librarian in residence in charge of the Library of Clarisse is an offensively irritable man, and I would like nothing better than to make unnecessary work for him. Do let me know if any of these books help, or if you need more!"

"Wait." Ceridwen dumps her burdens on the table after Lekan and pauses, cheek caught between her teeth. "Lustrate," she says again, rolling the word around her tongue. "That sounds like a word Ventrallans would favor."

Rares's eternal smile cracks wider, like he can see what she's getting at, but I'm lost.

"Why?" I ask.

Ceridwen presses her hand just below her collarbone, eyes averted, and I can't help but think she's looking away more to avoid revealing something than to think. "Because of what it means—to purify by sacrifice. Ventrallan culture is full of words like that—luscious words for dark acts, dark words for luscious acts. Artistic, extravagant meanings." She turns to Rares. "Where are your books on Ventralli? And not censuses." Her nose curls and I smile. At least I'm not the only one who cringes at the thought of reading all this. If Theron were here, he'd dive in without hesitation.

My gut twists, but I brace myself against thoughts of him.

Books on Ventralli might be a good place to look, actually—the final clue in the chasm entrance was a mask, pointing to the Ventrallan culture of wearing elaborate ones. Maybe Ceridwen is on the right path.

Rares taps a finger to his lips. "Quite deductive of you, Princess. We'll make a Yakimian out of you yet."

Ceridwen's lips twitch in a snarl. "Don't insult me."

Lekan grunts and slaps her in the shoulder. Ceridwen glares at him, and he unabashedly returns her glare, an exchange that makes little sense to me. But after half a breath Ceridwen relents.

"Sorry," she mumbles, but while it would seem like the apology should be directed at Rares, Lekan is the one who nods and accepts it.

Rares overlooks this interaction and points to the back left corner of the library. "Last row, shelves labeled 273 through 492. You no doubt noticed the markers on the ends of the rows? Lovely, aren't they? Mighty helpful, you'll find. Anything else?"

"Not if life is at all kind," I groan, realize how ungrateful that sounded, and straighten. "I mean, thank you."

Rares winks at me. "Enjoy Yakim, Your Highness."

He leaves, angling back through the library in the opposite direction Ceridwen and Lekan head, toward the Ventrallan books. Since my only options are to stay and start sorting through Rares's choices or follow them, I unload the books from my arms and dart off into the rows without hesitation.

The orbs of light flash off the mirrored plates, the numbers dancing in the reflective surfaces until Ceridwen stops before a row labeled with an oval that proclaims "273–492."

"Order of the Lustrate, you said?" she asks as she starts surveying book spines.

"Yes—"

My attention sticks on the marker at the end of this row. Did it . . . change?

I step closer to it, head angling. The light from the nearest orb catches on it and—

I chirp surprise and hop up onto the chair that stands guard over this row, providing an easy lift to get close to the marker. Ceridwen turns to me while Lekan shrugs and goes back to watching the empty rows.

"What is it?" she asks, voice low in the stillness of the library.

I brace my hands on the bookshelf and tip my head to the side. Normal, just the oval with the numbers etched, nothing of importance. But as I ease to the other side, the light shifts, and a luminescent picture reveals itself. A beam of light hitting a mountain.

The Order of the Lustrate's seal, hidden in the reflective surface of the metal oval.

"It's here," I say, though I still don't know what *it* is. Something is here, though, in this shelf, or in a book on this shelf.

My pulse accelerates as I run my hand over the oval. My fingers glide down the edge and I spit unexpected laughter.

The oval *moved*.

I do it again, the mirrored plate spinning, crank by crank, under my fingers.

Ceridwen's attention returns to the shelf and she springs away in surprise. "Flame and heat! Keep doing that—there's a compartment opening behind one of these shelves."

I jerk to the side, eyes scanning the library's floor beside the shelf. "Watch out for—"

But Ceridwen is way ahead of me, testing the floor with her feet and holding on to the shelves should a surprise pit open up here too. She shoots a cocked eyebrow up at me. "Just keep cranking."

Books smack into the floor as she tears them off the shelf. I keep easing the oval, gear by gear, until it locks into place, the numbers upright again. Skirt flurrying around me, I leap off the chair and step into the row, careful to avoid the mess of books Ceridwen removed to make room.

The back of one of the shelves has swung out, revealing a hidden compartment.

Ceridwen, holding a cluster of books against her chest, turns to me. Her shock eases into smug amusement and she tips her head, curls bouncing.

"See?" she says, triumphant. "You do need me, Winter queen."

My surprise evaporates into the slightest tingle of unease as I wrap my fingers into the door and pry it the rest of the way open, the wood crying out with age and more than a few bursts of dust that spray into my face. I cough but open the door wider, allowing a nearby orb of light to shine into the narrow compartment. My fingers twitch to reach inside, but memories of my last encounter with the Lustrate's key make me hesitate. Is this one a conduit too?

In the back corner sits a smashed cloth. I ease my hand around it, waiting for the hard bite of metal to warn me of a key, but the thick weave of the cloth curves around something lumpy.

I pull it out and guide it open in my hands, my stomach knotted up with two different emotions. Hope that it will be the key—and dread that it will be the key.

The cloth unrolls and reveals a key within, identical to the one I found in Summer—iron, ancient, with the Lustrate's seal at its head.

So easy. *Again.*

Warning hums in my throat, the instinctual rearing of danger coming. But I should be relieved. I'm that much closer to finding the Order, or at the very least, having leverage over Noam. This is good. Not threatening—*good.* Maybe the Order wanted the keys to be found. Maybe they separated them only so they wouldn't be easily accessible.

But I only have two keys—no answers. No information about the Order itself, or anything that could help me with my magic. Yes, I'm a step closer to being able to keep the chasm closed, but I need more than that. And it's only luck that I found these two first—it could have been Theron with just as little effort. It makes no sense that the Order would bother to hide these keys with so little protection, unless they *wanted* them found. But why? And further—why

Yakim? Summer, Yakim, Ventralli . . . what do these three kingdoms have in common?

No—calm down, Meira. Right now, it's just two keys, nothing dangerous. I won't let myself worry until a viable threat materializes. I certainly have enough other things to worry about.

The cloth around this key shows a scene much like the tapestry the Ventrallan queen sent with Finn and Greer. Mountains circle a valley filled with beams of light and, in the center, a tight ball of even more brilliant light woven in yellow and white and blue threads, all of it swirling around.

Magic.

I exhale, hands shaking. The placement of the key in a tapestry depicting the Klaryns and magic, hidden in a row of books about Ventralli—it's purposeful. The final key is definitely there.

I look up at Ceridwen. "Now we—"

She winces before I even talk. I glance at Lekan, who eyes her with a lingering sympathy.

Ceridwen bobs her head. "Ventralli next. That was the plan, anyway."

"Yes," I say slowly. "But . . . you don't have to come with us."

Ceridwen sets the books in her arms on the floor. "Thanks, but I know someone in Ventralli who can help with that." She nods at the tapestry, her expression void of emotion. "It'll lead you to something, right? Admit it—you're helpless without me."

I start to smile, warring with pressing her discomfort regarding Ventralli. But I flinch when the stillness of the library shatters around the sudden chiming of music.

Meira

A PIANO DISTURBS the silence, the player unleashing the melody from close by, steady notes that tinkle like raindrops beating on a window.

I know who it is without needing to see him, some deep-seated link tugging even tighter. Just as the instinct hits me, I'm swarmed with familiarity—finding a key with Ceridwen, only to be distracted from the find by Theron.

In Summer, I brushed it off as a coincidence that Theron was in the cellar. He went looking for me—he probably asked a servant, who directed him there.

But for him to be here, again, just after we found the key . . . did he follow me? Why would he have followed me without revealing himself earlier, involving himself in the search?

My body quakes with another tremor of unease. No—I

won't distrust him that much. Theron is still my friend, he's still *him*, and he wouldn't do anything like that.

But he has already, my instincts whisper. *Twice, now—in Winter, when he told Noam about the chasm, and here, when he gave the goods from the Klaryn mines to Giselle.*

I curl my fingers around the tapestry. Is this key a conduit too? Probably—both my reaction to the barrier in the magic chasm and the first key hang all too memorably in my mind. But I only had visions when I touched the key *and* Theron—so if I don't touch the key, I should be safe.

I open one of the pockets on my dress and slide the key in via the tapestry. The iron thumps against my thigh, but the fabric of my gown keeps it from touching my skin.

"Guard this," I tell Ceridwen, and thrust the tapestry at her. "Please."

She hesitates, her eyes narrowing.

"Only if you explain what's going on. All of it," she demands.

I pause. She waits.

"I will," I relent, and even I don't know if I'm lying. "Soon. I promise."

Ceridwen considers, one beat, two. Finally she rolls her eyes, takes the tapestry, and closes the hidden compartment. "Fine. Deal with your Rhythm prince."

I start that she knows who the pianist is too, but she doesn't say anything more. Ceridwen leaves the books strewn about as she and Lekan duck out of the row, heading back for the main door.

Absently, I clutch the locket at my throat, the empty conduit giving me some sort of relief. Which is completely absurd—I'm stuffed with magic, and yet a small piece of useless metal comforts me?

I leave the row, letting the music pull me between the shelves. One last turn and a small opening reveals a few chairs with a piano against the wall. Theron leans over it, his fingers brushing the keys to make the music swell abruptly, cut off, and plunge down again. Each note . . . *aches*. Slow and palpitating, filling the empty air with melancholy, so even before he says anything, I feel broken.

He doesn't glance up as he plays, his head plunging side to side, lips tight in concentration. But I know he sees me enter the area—his shoulders jerk sharply, one note faltering under his fluttering hands.

He stops playing, the song ending on a crash of keys. "I went to your room to make sure you had returned all right, but Dendera said you left." He cuts his eyes to me, so fast I almost miss it. "You were gone. Again."

"I needed to be alone for a little while. I won't apologize for that," I say, and I only flinch a little at the hardness of my voice. "You're the one who should apologize to me. You had no right to give Giselle goods from the Klaryns."

"That was why we brought those goods." Theron pushes

off the bench. "We *had* to give her some of our mines— she's a Rhythm. She never would have—"

"Stop." My chest lurches with cold, and this time I welcome it, opening my body to the way every nerve fills with flakes of snow and shards of ice. I know my voice reflects the sensation. "They're Winter's mines. There is no *our*."

Theron lunges forward, cutting me off. Hands to my shoulders, yanking me to him; lips on mine, but not in a gentle, loving kiss—a hard, desperate kiss, his fingers stiff, his mouth unyielding, his body a formidable mountain with me trapped at the top, hopelessly lost in the clouds and wind and light.

"There is still an *us*," he tells me. "There will always be an us."

I heave back from him. "No," I state, voice hard. "There will always be a *separation*."

Theron's arms hang open in front of him, and he pants, yanking his hands up to rip through his hair.

"You need to stop doing this," he growls.

"Doing what?" Because I have no idea which part he's talking about. The lying? The choosing Winter over his own goals?

One of those I refuse to stop doing.

He groans to the ceiling. "Pushing me away. How do you expect—"

I throw my hand up. "Wait—you're upset because I won't open up to you?"

He nods, and fresh anger pools into the myriad of emotions in my stomach.

"I don't open up to you? I've *tried*, Theron. I told you how I feel about the magic chasm; I told you how I feel about your father. But you push away all the bad and ignore everything but your own hope. You do not get to be angry with me. I have to hold myself together because no one else is capable of handling the truth."

"You have to open up to someone," Theron continues. "I understand why you can't in front of your people, but you need *someone*. And I thought . . ." His words trail off as his tenseness eases, hesitates, waiting on the words that will follow. "I thought you would . . ."

Something changes in his eyes. Like an idea occurred to him, a shocking, ghastly idea that causes him to pitch up straight, snarling.

"Mather," he growls. "It's him, isn't it?"

"Mather?" I stagger, his name a gust of wind that lashes a chill across my body.

"All this time," Theron snarls, "I knew you loved him, but I thought you'd moved on—"

"I do love—I mean, I *did* love him once, but I—"

"—and I thought things would be better now. Everything is better now! We have the magic chasm and your kingdom is free and we can be *us*—"

"I can't do this anymore!"

I stop. Theron stops. We both gape at each other in the agonizing silence.

Theron exhales. "Do what anymore?" But he doesn't let me answer. "That's what I'm trying to tell you—you don't have to keep holding back. I'm here for you, and I—"

He talks so fast, and despite the comfort his words try to form, his shoulders droop and everything about his posture says he's talking merely to keep me from countering him.

"No, Theron," I whisper, and his jaw bobbles open, his words falling flat. "I can't . . . be with you. Not like this. I think I could, someday, if Noam requires our marriage; if it's in Winter's best interest. But I can't be with you *now*. Not when we're divided by so much." I dig the heels of my hands into my eyes as a warm wave of tears puddles against my lids. "I think I've known for a while, but you were hurting, and I couldn't add to that. I've caused you enough pain. But now I've only caused you more."

I lower my hands, sight blurred so I only see the hazy outline of a boy before me. "I don't know how to fix you. I don't even know how to fix *myself*. You may think everything's better, but it's not, Theron. I can't go along with what you want. I don't want the magic chasm opened—and I will do everything I can to keep it shut. We aren't united on this journey." My heart scratches at my throat, choking me, but not the ache of regret—the choking of words that needed to be said long ago. "I'm sorry. I shouldn't have lied to you, but I didn't want . . ."

I scrub my fingers over my eyes until he comes into focus, and when he does, a part of me shrinks. He watches me, his face hurt and distant and hard, and the combination drives nails into my gut.

"I didn't want to hurt you," I finish.

"That's the only reason you'd love me?" Theron spits. "If my father ordered you to?"

"*That's* all you took from what I said?" I wheeze, but as soon as I do, his face collapses. The wrong thing to say, and he angles forward, body coiled.

"I took that you were *using* me. I thought you of all people understood what it's like to be used so violently that you wonder if there are any pieces of you left. But you're just like my father." He gasps. "You're just like—"

"I am nothing like Noam," I snap. "Because I'm sorry, Theron. I'm sorry I lied to you. I'm sorry for everything, but I don't know *anything* anymore, and everything I do is my instinctual reaction to what I think will keep Winter safe. Has your father ever once apologized for the things he's done? No. So don't you dare compare me to him. I am *not* Noam."

Piece by piece, Theron's anger breaks, revealing the boy

beneath. The trembling shadows we all harbor within our all-too-fragile shells, terrified someone will one day see.

After another long second of neither of us knowing what to do or say that could make anything better, he slides back a step.

"The treaty," he whispers. "If Giselle agrees to sign it, will you? It *is* what's best for your kingdom."

"Yes," I say before he can go on. The treaty doesn't matter, honestly—if that will appease him, I'll sign it. But I hold, waiting for him to ask how I'll proceed on the next issue, the biggest one, the goal that makes him touch his pocket absently.

He still has the key I found in Summer. He doesn't know I found the one here yet.

I fight to keep from touching my own pocket, but I can feel the heavy weight of the key on my thigh. What will happen when he searches on his own and doesn't find it? Will we still press on for Ventralli?

"Can we at least agree to share what information we find?" Theron adds, his voice quiet.

"Information?"

He tips his head. "Information regarding the pursuits that might bring you to this library."

I swallow. He's never used that tone with me, an empty, formal timbre that plants clear expectations between two people—politics and propriety, nothing more.

My body hums with the magic still swirling through me. It isn't fed by anger now—it's fed by grief, bright and hot and expected, like now that I've outright admitted what Theron and I are, my body unwinds in resignation.

No more lying. He knows what I want with regard to the magic; I know what he wants.

So I don't tell him I have the key. At least, not directly.

"We should continue to Ventralli," I manage. "As soon as the treaty is signed."

Theron's brows launch skyward, understanding written in shocked lines over his face. When I don't elaborate, he snorts in incredulity and runs a hand through his hair, pausing with his eyes on the floor, his shoulders stiff.

"You'll see," he starts, "when the chasm is opened, that everything I've done has been to keep you safe."

I didn't think it possible to hurt more than I do, but an ache thuds in me, pounding where my heart should be.

"*I* don't need to be safe. I need *Winter* to be safe."

Theron drops his hand and looks at me. "You're more than that kingdom."

He's trying so hard to be sweet, to be the Theron I fell for in Bithai. But sweetness isn't all I want anymore. I want . . . Winter. I want someone who thinks of protecting Winter first and me second. Not the other way around.

"No," I say. "I'm really not."

Theron gapes at me, but snaps away his shock with a curt shake of his head.

He turns and marches toward the door without another word.

I watch him go, waiting for my grief to rear so high it paralyzes me, waiting to crack into pieces and fall apart. And at one point in my life, I think I would have. But knowing what he wants with the magic chasm, I feel more certain than I have in a long time.

There is very little that I would choose over keeping Winter safe.

And Theron isn't one of those things.

I reach into my pocket as the door shuts behind him. My fingers close around the key, a resolved, firm grip. I have one of the keys. I have a way to—

The old metal grinds against my skin, and I know as soon as I touch it that I was wrong. Whatever magic these keys possess—it isn't simple; I don't have it figured out.

Numbness launches up my arm, spreads across my chest, sends me toppling to the floor. I can't do more than reel as I tumble, too annoyed at myself for touching the key to be scared.

"My queen!" Henn's face darts into view. His lips move, saying something to me, but the magic is swift, a mad rush of sizzling nothingness that yanks a shadow over my eyes.

Meira

THE MAGIC COATS me in chill through a tangle of confusion that amplifies when a voice lights me up, a sun rising over night-drenched landscape.

"The magic must not be reached by someone of corrupt heart. No, their heart must be pure—no, good—no, no, none of those. The magic must be reached by someone of ready heart. They must be ready. And these tests—these tests will make them ready."

"What tests? Ready for what?" I ask. But who am I asking? No one is talking—no one but me is here. This is just in my head, knowledge coming in my own voice from—the key?

I think I'm holding the key. Asleep, somewhere, I'm holding it, and it's using my voice, droning on and on.

"And these tests—these tests will make them—"

The nothingness lifts, ripples away like curtains drawn back from a window until all around me is white: ivory-paneled walls trimmed in silver.

Winter. I'm in a study in the Jannuari Palace.

"I have to do this!"

Hannah stands in the center of the room, her body pivoted away from me as she talks at a man with his forehead pressed to the wall.

"You don't understand," she growls. "This is the only way to save them."

Seeing her now makes me realize how much I've missed her. She doesn't react to me, though—not when I say her name; not when I stand right in front of her, mouth agape.

"They need this, Duncan," she says, and her voice breaks on a sob.

I turn, but the man stays facing away from us, his long, white hair brushing across his back as he buries his face in his hands. Duncan. My father.

"I asked the magic," Hannah continues. "I begged it to tell me what to do. I don't want to just save them from Angra—I want to save them from all the dangers of the world." Her sobs abate, and she tugs her shoulders back, hardening. "I asked how to save Winter."

I know this already. The magic told her that when a conduit breaks in defense of a kingdom, the ruler becomes the host for the magic. They become their own conduit, a limitless supply of magic for their people. That was why she arranged for Angra to break her locket—she wanted to save our people from him.

"I have to let him kill us," she states, trying to convince herself as much as Duncan.

Kill us?

As I watch her, the rest of the story unfolds in my mind. One piece in particular jerks out in an uncomfortable lurch that rips the breath from my lungs.

How did I not see this before?

Hannah arranged for Angra to break her locket—but she also arranged for him to kill her. That was part of her deal with him—she promised him an end to the Dynam line, not knowing that she was pregnant, and that that meant killing her child too.

"When a conduit breaks in defense of a kingdom, the ruler of that kingdom becomes the conduit. And if the conduit were to break again—if that ruler were to die in defense of the kingdom as the last of that bloodline—the magic would seek out the next host linked to it—the citizens of its kingdom." She stops, winded. "They'll—you'll—never want for anything. I have to do this, Duncan. He has to kill us so Winter can be saved."

Us.

No—this is wrong. This is a trick—

"They must be ready. And these tests—these tests will make them ready."

My voice again, taunting me. I tangle my fingers in my hair, shaking my head to keep the information from sinking into my mind. But it does, and everything unravels.

If what Hannah said is true, if I hadn't been born—if Hannah had let Angra kill us both all those years ago—

Our ruined kingdom would be whole right now. Sir would have raised Mather as his son. Nessa and Garrigan and Conall would be filled with power, and Spring would have fallen, and the Decay would be a distant memory beneath all of Winter's conduit magic.

That's what the key wants me to see? How my very existence kept my people from safety?

"A ready heart," the magic says in my voice. "These tests will make you ready."

I bend forward and scream frustration, exhaustion, everything I have left. I don't even scream words, just noise, how tired I am of fighting a war when I can barely see one step ahead, how tired I am of being the only one who even sees the war, of being the only one who wants to live without magic.

And now—what? I should just let it all kill me so my people become their own conduits? This can't be it. This doesn't even have anything to do with the magic chasm—and these tests are supposed to help me reach the magic chasm, aren't they?

But the visions I saw when I touched Theron didn't have anything to do with the magic chasm either. He didn't see anything, though, and he touched the key—if he had seen something, I would've noticed him reacting. So why just me? Because of my own magic? Why would the Order have set up the keys to be conduits that only react with a conduit wielder? No one without magic can open the door? None of this makes sense.

"What is going on?" I shout. "Why do I need this? WHAT DO I DO?"

I'll never forget the first blizzard in Winter. Days after we returned, the weather kicked up as if celebrating our return. Snowflakes cut through the air, clouds darkened the sky, the temperature plummeted even more. Every Winterian in Jannuari ran outside to greet the gale, absorbing the chill with stunned ecstasy.

Standing in the courtyard of the palace, arms to the sky,

cold numbing all other senses and wind deadening all other noises, I closed my eyes. I had never, in all my life, felt so remarkably alone. But it was a perfect kind of alone, a delicate, dreamlike peace.

This feeling now, as I awaken, nearly drowning in my fear, blood roaring in my head—this is the exact opposite of that. Alone, but desolate and swirling deeper into oblivion.

I bolt upright, the canopy around my bed in the Yakimian palace jostling with the force.

"My queen?"

Nessa holds my hand in one of hers, the key lying on the quilt beside me, my fingers cramped from being pried open by her. I suck in air, lungs screaming like I held my breath for the entire dream. Or nightmare, more like, but I yank free of Nessa and scramble off the bed, eyes on the key, body shaking from head to toe.

"What happened—" I start to ask, but I know. I feel the knowledge all over, every muscle aching and drenched with it as I pace, my wrinkled gown swaying around my legs.

Nessa stands. "Henn said you collapsed in the library. Dendera fetched a doctor, but he couldn't find anything wrong with you. You were so still, though, and I couldn't believe it was nothing—nothing *natural*, anyway. So they all left, and I said I'd watch you, and I saw your fist all clenched up. It was that key—it did something to you. What is it? It has to do with the magic chasm—"

"Nessa," I stop her in a biting rush.

Hannah planned for us to die—but couldn't go through with it for me, for whatever reason.

I have no idea how to find the Order of the Lustrate. Not beyond these keys. There's something more to them, something I don't understand, and it terrifies me.

And if I tell Nessa any of this, it will give her even more fuel for nightmares. Theron already broke, and I can't handle her hurting more too—

"I can't tell you—"

"Why?" She ducks around the bed, closer to me, glaring, her cheeks red.

"Because this isn't your fight."

Her glare hardens. "Liar."

That makes me start. Nessa, my Nessa, is mad at me.

"I know you're hiding something," she continues. "I've known since we got back to Winter. Everyone else was happy and you were miserable—we won the war, yet you looked like you did in the camp, scared and waiting for something to break. It's the magic chasm, isn't it? Something about it has you worried. Noam? Angra? What is it?"

I shake my head, either in response or because I cannot, will not, admit this to her.

"Stop keeping it from me! I grew up in *misery*. I don't know why everyone thinks I'm so fragile. I can handle the truth!"

The door connecting my room to the one beside us

opens. Dendera, Henn, Conall, and Garrigan run in and freeze at the sight of Nessa shouting at me.

"You shouldn't have to," I tell her. "This shouldn't be your life. I'll make it better."

"That isn't your responsibility!"

"I'm the queen—of course it is!"

"No, *it isn't*." Nessa jabs a finger at me, every muscle in her face tight. "It's your job to make sure we have food and houses; it isn't your job to make every one of us happy. I deserve to know what's going on. You aren't the only one who loves Winter and wants to protect it."

"But I'm Winter's conduit, Nessa." My voice breaks. "I'm the only one who can—"

"Stop it!" Nessa waves her arm around the room at everyone gathered here. "You are not the *only* one. This is my kingdom just as much as it is yours. This is my war too!"

"This is my war too, Sir! You have to let me fight. I can help, I know I can!"

My own voice echoes back at me from Nessa, and I can't do more than blink at her. All the dozens of times I yelled at Sir, the exact same words.

I clap my hands over my mouth, shock freezing me in place. Dendera and Henn realize it at the same moment I do and their concern melts into the sad, hard set of truth.

I did to Nessa exactly what Sir did to me for years. What he did to everyone. He tried to single-handedly accomplish the most insane tasks—raids to get the locket half, scouting new camps, meeting with potential allies. He was always alone, stoic and hard and removed from our lives until he desperately, unavoidably needed us. He tried to keep the weight of our failures on his own shoulders so we wouldn't have to deal with the painful, wracking truth of what our lives were.

I hated him for it. We all did. I'd see Dendera exchange glances with Alysson or Finn snarl to Sir's retreating back, and I knew everyone felt, on some level, the same maddening urge to shake Sir into realizing that we *already* knew the dangers of our lives. If anything, his hesitancy to let us help dragged out the worst of it.

And I did the exact same thing. I tried to force a specific life on Nessa.

A guttural, scraping noise fills the bedroom, and Dendera's eyebrows rise at me. It's me—I'm laughing. I brace my hands over my mouth but I can't stop it, insane giggles bubbling up my throat and erupting into my palms until I'm doubled over, unable to breathe through the absurd twist that I've become Sir.

I collapse on the floor, my stomach cramping. Everyone in the room just stares, which only makes me laugh harder.

Nessa kneels beside me, her anger fading to a slight tint of red on her neck. "Meira?"

I lower my hands, laughter fading under the sudden trembling of my pulse. "You called me Meira."

She sighs, but her smile blinds me again, the kind that sends chill deep into my soul. "You've always been Meira," she says like it's the simplest thing in the world.

I shake my head as Dendera joins us, kneeling next to me on the floor.

"I tried not to be," I say, the words coming before I can consider a response.

Dendera takes my hand, her face blank, waiting. "Why?"

Her question, or maybe the dream, or maybe just months of being consumed with fear, breaks me, and it all pours out, every reason I cling so tightly to Queen Meira.

"When I got the locket half and led Angra's men straight to camp. When I fought marrying into Cordell even though it would've solved so much. When I barged into Noam's office and risked destroying our one alliance. Even in the Abril camp, when I brought down the ramps, I could've killed my own people. Everything I did, every selfish act, was impetuous and risky and I hurt *everyone*." Tears stream down my cheeks, hot, branding tears. "I was queen, all along, every moment of my life, and I could have helped everyone—but I didn't. I was so selfish. I could have done *more*, I could have—"

Saved everyone. I could have saved everyone in Winter, if Hannah had let Angra kill us both. But she didn't—she sent me away. She couldn't go through with it. She was weak, or maybe strong—I don't know what, but she didn't do it, and I'm just like her. I'm weak and scared and I try so hard, but it's never enough.

No part of who I am is enough, so I tried to be someone else.

Dendera silences me with a hand on my cheek. "You listen to me, Meira Dynam. Yes, you have made mistakes, but I have watched you succumb to this role over the past few months, and that, I believe, is the biggest mistake you have made. The biggest mistake we *all* made. We've all been afraid, and Meira, you look at me. *You saved us.* You, this beautiful, wild girl before me—*you* saved us. So be you again, and whoever that is will be exactly what we need."

You *saved us.*

Her words dangle before me, tempting, alluring. I haven't thought that . . . ever. I've never let myself bask in the good I did, only the good I *could have* done.

But . . . I saved us. *I* saved us.

I inhale, and this time, I feel it. This time, it rushes through me, life-giving and fresh and cool, filling me up with Dendera's and Nessa's certainty.

Dendera stands and moves to the trunk against the wall. Endless bolts of fabric sit within, some half-made articles of clothing, and she scrambles through it. When she pulls her hand out, the air I managed leaves my body in a gust that sends me scrambling to my feet.

My chakram in its holster, the great circular blade glinting sharp and polished, the handle worn smooth through the middle.

"My queen," Dendera says as she passes it to me, bowing over the weapon.

I ease my fingers around the chakram, my hand curving into place naturally, every muscle unwinding in a ripple of peace. I never should have been without it. This is me, whoever I am when I hold my chakram. Both the thoughtful, careful queen I've forced myself to be and the wild, passionate girl who pushed her kingdom to teeter on the edge of defeat—but also snatched it back from that edge.

A warrior queen.

I can be both. I *will* be both. I'm tired of fighting myself— I have far too many enemies, far too many obstacles, to spend so much energy wrestling myself into submission. I have far too few friends to alienate those closest to me. I need to start trusting them. And if they break . . .

We'll just have to pick up the pieces together.

I lower my chakram to my side and turn to Nessa. "All right, I'll explain everything. But first—" I exhale. "There's someone else who needs to hear the truth too."

Mather

CONFRONTING THE CORDELLAN soldiers must have been the final blow to William's resolve, because ever since, Mather had been swamped with tasks. Menial, mundane tasks, when during the weeks prior, he hadn't been missed. William gave him chores sent through other channels— Finn telling him that planks of wood needed sanding, Greer recruiting him to scrub dishes. Mather didn't see William at all, and in not seeing him, he grew more infuriated.

Mather deserved to have William shout at him for the defiant thing he had done—not that he regretted it, but had they been back at their nomadic camp and Mather had stood against him, William would have made him learn firsthand the meaning of the word *obedience*. That was how he punished them—well, mostly Meira, in all honesty: by making sure they learned how each soldier needed to be *perfect* for a mission to be a success.

But in this new life, William did not reprimand him. He didn't scold him or revisit what had happened—he just moved on from it, dismissing the event without a backward glance.

This was the final blow to Mather's resolve too. The final bit of proof that he was exactly where Winter needed him to be: building a defense. Because with leaders like William avoiding everything, it wouldn't take more than a handful of soldiers to tear down Winter.

And Winter already had far more than a handful of soldiers here.

Mather ducked down a narrow alley out of some lingering instinct to make his path scattered and chaotic so he couldn't be followed. Not that it would be difficult to figure out where he had been going every night after he finished his list of chores—there were only so many inhabited streets. But he still took his time until he popped out two buildings down from the Thaw's cottage and allowed himself a small sigh of relief.

His sigh bit off when he noted the figure slouched over the steps, shuffling around, metal clanking. A Cordellan soldier? Had someone finally found out about their secret trainings?

Readiness calmed Mather's nerves, the still of attack. He launched forward, grabbed the person's neck, and flung whoever it was out into the darkening street.

But he had felt long hair on the person's neck. And not

armor on the shoulders, but linen, and when the intruder hit the ground, there was a cry that sounded much too . . . feminine.

Though the sun had started to fall toward the horizon, enough light remained that when Mather's eyes locked on the intruder's face, he sprang forward and swooped her to her feet.

Snow, not a soldier at all—Alysson.

She blinked in a daze, her eyes catching his and crinkling in an unspoken question.

He grimaced. "I thought you—" he started, bit back the end of it. "I'm sorry."

Alysson put one hand on his shoulder like she wasn't steady until she touched him, made sure *he* was all right. "You thought I was a Cordellan?"

Mather frowned as the door to the cottage burst open. Phil stumbled out, everyone else behind him, but he didn't get far before his foot caught on a bundle leaning against the top step. The bundle Alysson had been crouched over.

Phil stopped, one of their practice swords clutched in his fist. They must've heard Alysson's cry of surprise during their self-led training, and as Mather looked up at them, all the blood in his body surged downward. Alysson was here, staring up at Phil and his wooden sword, and she would see just how much Mather had disobeyed William.

But Alysson didn't seem the least bit aghast. In fact, she seemed amazed.

Her hand went slack on Mather's shoulder. "You've gotten these results using *splinters*?"

Mather's jaw swung open, shut, open again. "What?"

"Hey!"

Rattling, the dull thump of iron. Phil bent on the top step, rustling through the bundle. A thick blanket fell away, revealing weapons. Swords, daggers, a bow, and a fistful of arrows.

Everyone gazed at the weapons spilling in a deadly waterfall down the stairs. Mather especially, his hungry eyes calculating how many swords, how many knives. Seven swords. Eight daggers—four sets.

He turned back to Alysson, who now had her arms crossed as she watched the Thaw pick their way down the steps, maneuvering around the weapons as though disturbing them at all would cause them to vanish.

"Where did you get these?" Mather asked, his hands shaking as if he already knew her answer, already felt the repercussions wafting through him. "How did you *know*?"

Alysson turned a soft smile to him and opened it in an almost mocking laugh. "I spent sixteen years in a camp surrounded by fighting. You think I can't recognize when a group of children, who should be just as scrawny as the rest of the malnourished Winterians, have the beginnings of muscle definition? When they should be unsteady and weak, but move down the street with, dare I say, *grace*?" She clucked her tongue. "I know I never picked up a sword myself, but that doesn't mean I didn't pay attention."

Mather choked. "You knew? You *know*? Who else—and where did you get—"

Ice above, just finish a sentence.

But try as he might, Mather couldn't get more than half-formed words to blubber out of his mouth. He knew the Thaw would eventually show physical signs of training, but he'd assumed everyone else would brush off the way his child warriors had begun to fill out their clothes more than they should as the effects of rebuilding cottages. But Alysson had noticed—Alysson, who had never done more than glance at a sword ring.

So who else knew?

She seemed to read the calculating horror on his face and put her hand on his cheek. "Of course William knows, but he's not seeing a lot of things lately that he should."

Mather shook his head, afraid he had misheard her. "You don't agree with him?"

But even as he asked that question, understanding burst through him.

"He doesn't know you brought these weapons." His mind rang with the softest vibration of regret, and he realized that he wanted William to know. He wanted William to address this, to see what he had done, for William's eyes to fill with the pride that Alysson's held.

That last bit made Mather gape. "But *why*?"

Alysson squeezed his shoulder. "You need them. And

you're my son, as much as you struggle to accept that. You have always been and will always be my son. That's how relationships work—when one person is blind, the other must see for them. When one person struggles, the other must remain strong."

Mather touched her wrist, amazement coursing through him.

Here Alysson stood, this woman he had always taken advantage of as someone who had helped the Winterian resistance in their camp, not the frontlines. Honestly he had never viewed her as a guiding source of strength. That had always fallen on William.

But Mather had been wrong.

About a lot of things.

"You shouldn't have to be the one to put us all back together," he whispered. The Thaw filled up the abandoned street in front of the cottage, testing weapons, laughing at how much heavier a sword was compared to their thin lengths of wood. He didn't want them to hear, didn't want to break this moment blossoming between him and his mother.

His mother. Frigid snow above, he'd almost thought it without balking that time.

Alysson's smile faded. "You need me more. William too. It's the nature of his position. I learned long ago that I have to be the one he leans on while Winter leans on him. And"—she hesitated, her brow rising conspiratorially—"if you want, someday I know you can do the same for Meira."

Mather reeled. Alysson knew about that area of his heart too. Had anything ever gotten past her?

She leaned closer to him. "You've fought for Winter so spectacularly. I am more proud than I have ever been to call you my son, and I will do all I can to help you as you help our kingdom. But don't forget to fight for yourself as well—there is no shame in that."

Mather closed his eyes, dropping his head in a bow—of surrender? Of agreement? Of gratitude? Everything. His body swam with remorse, but through that, he felt the tightest flash of joy—the Thaw had weapons now. Real weapons, and Alysson's support.

But he couldn't get the image of Meira out of his head, her face when he had left her bedroom the night of the ceremony. Her eyes wide and desperate, tears streaking in violent rivers down her cheeks. It had killed him to leave her—as it should have.

He never should have stepped out of that room. All the things he had wanted to do—run back to her, fight for her—were things he *should* have done.

He understood that now, understood through Alysson's silent strength.

Sweet snow, he had known Alysson his whole life, and never once had he seen her break. The most he could remember were a few stray tears flying down her cheeks when other members of their group died. But that was it, all the pain she ever showed, and Mather's other memories were of Alysson standing with her hand on William's shoulder, or a silent, firm nod before someone went off on a mission. Quiet and steady, and Mather had never noticed, not once.

He'd been blind for far too long.

So when Mather opened his eyes, he intended to tell her. He intended to fall to his knees and beg forgiveness for being such an ungrateful son.

But the peaceful tone of the otherwise empty street was gone, replaced with a sensation he knew all too well: alertness. The Thaw held their new weapons with purpose, their bodies forming a U-shape toward an attacker across the street from their cottage. Everything blurred as Mather whipped toward the enemy, already reaching for the dagger he always kept in his boot.

Alysson saw his movement. He knew she did by the way her eyes followed him as he spun, arms out, dagger ready.

But she didn't move, just wrinkled her brow, her mouth cracking open in a faint moan.

Mather couldn't identify her expression. No, he refused to, pushed it from his mind even as it slammed persistently into his skull. He'd seen that look before—he *knew* that look—

His eyes dropped to her chest, to the growing blotch of scarlet that stained her blue dress red. The tip of a sword gleamed against her body like a morbid bauble on a necklace.

The enemy hadn't been across the street. The enemy had crept up on them, close enough that Mather should have heard or seen or stopped them—

The blade ripped out through Alysson's back and she pitched toward him, her eyes vanishing into her skull as she collapsed in his arms. Mather's dagger tumbled from his hands, his heart surging numb shock through him as his fingers groped from Alysson's head to her shoulders, searching for a sign of life, a sign of explanation—but he knew. He'd known the moment he saw the weapons she'd brought, but he'd hoped she hadn't gone there, that she'd realized as he had what a suicidal thing it would be.

"She stole weapons," a Cordellan soldier confirmed from where he had stood behind Alysson. He was the same one who had threatened Feige days ago and his blade, heavy with maroon blood, glinted in the twilight. "And thieves will not be tolerated in a Cordellan colony."

A scream. A bright, piercing croak of noise, and Phil burst out of the ranks of the Thaw, sword blazing overhead. Mather shouted as the Cordellan soldier pivoted toward Phil, shouted because he couldn't fathom losing someone else, not now—

The soldier's blade swung up, the end poised at Phil's neck. Phil stopped a beat before he would've been pierced through, his chest rising in a desperate gulp of air.

Mather didn't have long to be grateful, though. The Cordellan sneered at him as shouts went up, as the clanking of armor ricocheted down the street and cries of victory echoed through the city. A horn blew, long and loud, a pulsing tear of noise that signaled—

. . . a Cordellan colony.

Noam. He'd officially taken Winter.

No, the only thing this horn would signal would be the end of Cordellan occupation in Winter. This ended now, *tonight*.

Arms tugged at Mather, voices shouted through his sudden, deadly fog.

"We have to run!"

"There are too many here—get up!"

Mather growled, pushing away whoever tried to grab him. Everyone was an enemy, everyone would die for this because Alysson's blood coated his hands and her body lay motionless where he arranged her on the ground. He scrambled to get his dagger again, his sight marred with murderous red as the Cordellan soldier ran away from him, the coward, to regroup with more soldiers who appeared at the far end of the street. Cowards, every Cordellan was a coward, and Mather would kill them all.

A face came into focus. "There are too many," Hollis pleaded. "You taught us that. You taught us to assess situations, to fall back if necessary. We have to run *now*."

Awareness sparked through him. At least a dozen Cordellans spanned the street to their north, blocking off any retreat into the abandoned parts of Jannuari. The soldiers marched in steady, taunting steps toward them—they were being corralled into the center of the city. From the shouts and cries of alarm ringing through the rest of Jannuari, Mather guessed the same thing now blocked every street out of the inhabited areas. An unbreakable circle of Cordellans finally preying on the Winterians.

Mather sheathed his dagger, swept his mother's body into his arms, and ran. The Thaw fell in behind him, all of them equipped with weapons they didn't entirely know how to use. But they gripped the swords with such lethal determination that Mather pitied any Cordellans who tried to stop them. But stop them from what? Where would they go?

The palace. William was there.

But Meira. Noam had irrevocably turned on Winter—had he opened the magic chasm? Had Meira failed him somehow? Was he here in Jannuari, or had he sought her out?

Was she still alive?

Mather bit back thoughts that threatened to cripple him under the body he carried. No, he couldn't think yet. Meira had to be alive.

And nothing in Primoria could protect Noam if she wasn't.

The palace's front steps flew under Mather's feet and he jammed his shoulder into the door, sending it banging into the wall. The lateness of the evening meant the main halls were empty, all workers returned to the cottages outside or to rooms deep in the palace. Seven pairs of feet thundered across the ballroom, up the marble staircase, down empty halls of ivory and silver that wrapped them in the encroaching shadows of night. The hazy grayness gave everything a dreamlike feel, encouraging the idea that this was wrong, *wrong*, and Mather could fix it. . . .

They sprinted down the long walk to William's office, the cold air of the balcony snapping around them. The door stood ajar and Mather stumbled to a halt paces from it, his arms cramping from how tightly he gripped his mother's body.

She's dead, William. Cordell killed her because you wouldn't listen to me, because you let them stay here, because I didn't try hard enough to protect Winter.

She's dead because we're both weak, William. Because I am your son in every way.

But none of those words came out as he walked into William's office, because William stood with his back to the door, facing Brennan, who held a sword pointed at him.

". . . for too long," Brennan was saying. "But my master no longer has need for this kingdom's freedom, and he has at last instructed me to take control of what rightfully belongs to Cordell. Congratulations—you are the first Season Kingdom to become a Cordellan colony, with Autumn soon to follow. I'm sure you'll see it as an honor."

A growl bubbled in William's throat. "I've heard men talk about their king as you do. '*My master.*' That is not Cordell. You don't serve Noam, do you?"

Brennan clucked his tongue. "Noam has his uses, but we all choose a rising sun over a setting one."

A rising sun? My master? Who did Brennan mean? The only men Mather had ever heard talk about their king like that were men who served Angra.

But Brennan had said, *What rightfully belongs to Cordell* . . .

It didn't matter—all that mattered was the weight in Mather's arms, the body still warm against his.

"William."

Mather's own voice shocked him by how worn it sounded. It scratched against his throat like dry air on a hot day, and when it did William looked over his shoulder, for a moment ignoring Brennan and his still-poised blade.

William's eyes barely glanced at Mather before they dipped to Alysson's body. Whatever emotion William had been feeling sank back into his face, the muscles relaxing, his brow drooping.

Mather had seen William react to death before, to their soldiers who stumbled into camp only to die hours later. He had been stoic in their passing, showing his pain through small gestures—putting a hand on their forehead, bowing over their corpse.

But this was how death truly felt, the way William gazed at Alysson's body as if he could force some of his own life into her through sheer need. Like he couldn't grasp the image of her, one of those fleeting blips of dreams before dawn. Like he had already planned her murderer's death, from the first blade drawn to the last moan from the soldier, a quiet, tortured plea.

Mather dropped to his knees, Alysson's body sliding out of his arms as William turned on Brennan. A knife appeared, the blade pressed between William's fingers. He ducked, grabbed Brennan's hand where he held the hilt of his sword, and twisted until Brennan screamed from the pain of his fingers dislocating. As Brennan moved to retaliate, as Mather felt the Thaw behind him draw a collective breath, William swiped his hand against Brennan's throat.

Brennan staggered back, slammed into the bookcase, his eyes fixed on the ceiling. He grabbed at the gash in his neck, and William watched him, standing over the Cordellan captain as the man slid to the floor, blood pulsing between Brennan's fingers on gagging spasms.

When he slumped against the wall, Mather shuddered with a single thought.

He died too quickly. He should have suffered—ice above, I wanted him to suffer.

William crouched over Alysson's body, Brennan's blood painting his hand red. Mather couldn't deduce anything from William's face—he'd see more staring at a wall. Meira had said that about Mather too, a few times. She'd thought it a conscious decision, but it wasn't, it was just *him* as much as it was William now, and Mather wanted to grab William's shoulders and shake him until real emotion tumbled out.

"You'll leave," William said. Mather blinked at him, the words not processing as William scooped Alysson's body into his arms and stood. "The queen will probably be in Ventralli by the time you reach it—head to the Feni River. You'll travel faster by ship—get aboard whatever you can. Do anything you have to, Mather. *Anything*."

Mather leaped up as William laid Alysson's body on his desk. Her head bobbled to the side, white hair cascading over her cheek, some of the strands clumped in tangles of blood and dirt. Her eyes sat open, staring unseeing at the study crowded with the Children of the Thaw.

How long ago had Mather stood in this same spot and called his mother a coward? She hadn't said a damn thing to stop him. Mather clenched his fists, trying frantically to remember everything she *had* said to him. He should've written it all down, should've branded it on his skin. Should've, should've, *should've*.

"I'm sorry," Mather moaned. That broke him. Not seeing his mother murdered, not the still-sounding horns of Cordell outside, signaling the ensuing takeover.

William spun away and grabbed Mather's arms, fingers digging like vises into his muscle. "You cannot afford to be weak. You will go to our queen and make sure she is safe." William shook him as Mather moaned, damn it, he was still so weak. "Do you understand me?"

Mather shoved out of William's hands. No, this man did not get to pretend he was the strong one. They both knew who was the strong one, and she was *dead*.

He wanted to say all that to William. Damn it, his mother had just died, and he wanted William to be a parent now, to pull him into his arms and assure him that they would get through this together.

But they wouldn't. This was who they were, had always been, and would continue to be.

So Mather turned his sobs into a snarl. "You aren't allowed to break either. If I sense weakness—" Could he do this? Could he threaten William? "I'll kill you. I swear, William—you already let this takeover happen. You don't get another chance. I won't let Winter fall again."

William turned away without a response, and Mather pushed out of the study. The twang of a blade being drawn filled the air behind him—William arming himself.

The Thaw followed Mather silently, and he exhaled thanks that they didn't try to talk to him. This horrified them too, he knew—their freedom had been so short-lived. But Mather pressed on, weaving into the dark streets, avoiding soldiers as chaos unfolded. Here Cordellans had to fight to subdue Winterians—there Winterians raised their hands in surrender. Here Cordellans barked threats—there Winterians fell to their knees and shouted compliance.

It made Mather sick, how many of them bowed without a fight. But he couldn't stop an entire army with only seven warriors. Their small number made sneaking out of Jannuari easier, but that was all they could do. They needed Meira.

He needed Meira.

"You've fought for Winter so spectacularly, and I am more proud than I have ever been to call you my son. But don't forget to fight for yourself as well—there is no shame in that."

Mather might not have remembered everything Alysson had said to him, but he remembered the last thing. He pulled those words like armor around him along with the promise he had made William—he would not let Winter fall again.

Meira

CERIDWEN CROSSES HER legs where she sits next to the coil of tubes in my room, the barest waves of heat licking off into her skin. Being in a room full of Winterians was "like being dunked into a bucket of ice water," she'd said, and after so long watching me pace back and forth and spewing nonsensical explanations, I figure she needs some comfort.

"So wait." She bobs her finger through the air as if pointing at all the information I laid bare. "When your mother's locket broke, you became the conduit. I understand that, I think. But these keys we've been finding are *also* conduits? And they're interfering with your magic somehow?"

"Not interfering." I lean against one of the posts that holds the canopy over my bed. "More like interacting. The Order made them as tests to help the finder with . . . something. My heart has to be ready, but I can't figure out what the things I saw are supposed to make me ready to do. Or what any of it has to do with the magic chasm."

"Are you sure the keys were made by the Order?" Conall asks, cradling the splint that cups his injured arm. "You said Angra might be Spring's conduit, as you are Winter's. What if all this is him? He was in the first visions you saw. This could be a trick."

"There's been no word of him anywhere, though," Henn counters.

Garrigan shrugs, his shoulders grinding against the chair he squeezed into alongside Nessa. "It *has* been more than three months since his fall. If he's alive, why wait so long? It doesn't make sense. It has to be the Order. Besides, the chasm entrance was hidden until a few weeks ago. How could Angra have set all this up without our knowledge?"

"He did have free access to your kingdom for sixteen years," Ceridwen says.

Dendera shakes her head. "He didn't touch the mines. When we reopened them, they had clearly been unused for more than a decade—filthy and dangerous and unstable. I don't think this is him."

I fiddle with my locket as they toss ideas back and forth. They've all handled this so much better than I could have hoped, taking in everything I know about Angra and magic and the chasm and Cordell with curious gazes and patient nods.

Well, almost everything.

I only told them I saw Hannah and Duncan in my last dream. I didn't tell them what Hannah said would happen if I die.

A shudder jerks my hand off my locket and I cross my arms to hide the tremor. I'll find another way to make my people strong. This world doesn't need an entire kingdom of conduit-people—keeping magic from becoming widespread is what I've been fighting for all along.

What Hannah said doesn't matter. I don't have to die for this. I *won't*.

Henn scratches his chin, pacing in front of where Dendera sits on a bench against the wall. "I agree. I think these keys are our best chance at getting any answers. Once we have the last key, we'll have more leverage over Cordell to keep the chasm shut."

"Will that be enough?" Conall leans forward, wincing as he puts pressure on his injured arm. "Noam could forcibly take the keys from us. How will Winter having the keys stop him?"

"We could get the first key from the prince," Garrigan offers. "Open the chasm. Retrieve enough magic to—"

"No," I say. "We'll continue to Ventralli, but we aren't opening that door. It isn't a risk we will take—there are other ways to unseat Noam. I can try to gain Giselle's support, or Ventralli."

My words seem weak now, and when Ceridwen shifts forward, I feel my fragile surety break even more.

"Hate to rain fire on your ice, but Yakim won't fight off another Rhythm for you. I've been begging Giselle for years to support Summer—to sell us food or supplies instead of people. She refuses."

"What if I prove useful to her? I'll give her whatever she wants. Snow, I'll give her as many mines as she demands."

"And what happens once she finds out that Cordell already has the magic chasm? She'll feel tricked, and you'll have two Rhythms mad at you."

I groan, pushing out my frustration. I hadn't had much hope for Yakim after my conversation with Giselle, anyway. "What about Ventralli?"

Ceridwen laughs. "You know who Noam's wife was, right? She may have died under Noam's care, but flame and heat, if the Ventrallans don't love Theron. Ventralli would no sooner go to war against Cordell than Simon would renounce wine."

"Both Yakim and Ventralli offered to host Winter, though." I squint even as I talk, recognition flaring back up through me. I realized the folly in our trip before, and now it makes every muscle in my body go slack so I drop onto the bed.

"I responded to their invitations." I rub my temples, eyes shut. "They invited me as a ploy to test Cordell's hold on Winter. Cordell responded with a treaty of unification, and I responded by *bringing Cordell with me*. Whatever door they might have opened . . . I not only slammed it shut, I built a damned Cordellan barrier over it. And now Winter's only ally is . . ." My eyes go to Ceridwen and she splays her hands.

"Hey, put me in a room with Noam and I'll end your problem real quick."

I snort. "Tempting. But that would cause even more problems."

Dendera stands. "What is our plan, then?"

I look at her, my mind swirling through everything.

No help from Yakim. No help from Ventralli. Paisly is too far removed to offer assistance. I have thin support in Summer, and an even shakier alliance with Autumn—but I don't think Nikoletta would rise against her brother, no matter how much of an ass he is. Unless he were to seize Autumn outright, but I can't believe he'd be that stupid.

Which leaves . . .

"The Order," I tell everyone. "They're our only chance at finding a way to seal the chasm door, or even get rid of magic altogether. Either one would halt the spread of Cordell's power and give us better leverage against them— or at the very least, give us a bargaining tool to negotiate Winter's freedom. We have to search for the final key and the Order, and if they say there is no way to seal the chasm permanently or stop Cordell without magic, I'll open the door myself. But let's not plan on that until we know for sure."

A slow smile creeps over Henn's face. "A thoughtful

decision, my queen. Where do you think the final key is? Ventralli, of course, but where?"

I bite my lip. "What stands as a symbol of Ventralli? Summer's was wine, Yakim's was books. The chasm clue that led to Ventralli is a mask. But the key we found in Yakim was wrapped in a tapestry, which is another symbol of Ventralli's affinity for the arts." I meet Henn's eyes. "Maybe . . . their museums? We'll start there. Their guilds might also be a good place to look, so we can move on to those next."

Dendera nods. "Good. We have a plan."

"Yes." Part of me itches to dive into a battle, to physically hack away at this threat with the chakram now strapped to my back. I've cast off all the shields I've built around myself—but I can keep some things, choose the beneficial parts and use them to strengthen who I am. I let Ceridwen, Conall, Garrigan, Nessa, Dendera, and Henn in, told them about the issues I'm facing; I will remain calm and careful, but let myself be reckless when I need to be. I will learn from my mistakes.

Unlike Hannah.

Unlike the way she lied to me and had everyone keep that lie for my entire life. Unlike the way she still kept things from me—for three months she could have told me the rest of her plan. Maybe if she had learned from *her* mistakes, we'd all be better off. Maybe, if she had never told any of those lies to begin with, we'd have been free years ago.

I straighten. *No.* I don't need to think about her—what she wanted doesn't matter. *What she wanted doesn't matter.*

"We should sleep," Garrigan says. "It's nearly morning."

"Wait." My eyes lock on Henn. "Will you return to Winter?"

He doesn't hesitate. "Of course. Why, my queen?"

I force the words out faster than my stomach can cramp with remorse. "Because Theron and I—things have changed. We're no longer as unified in our goals as we once were, and I don't know if . . . I mean, he wouldn't be that cruel, but he was our strongest Cordellan ally. Though that didn't do much for us. But now . . . just check on Winter, please?"

Henn grows solemn and bows his head in a slow nod. "Of course," he repeats.

Dendera rises to kiss him, quick and soft. He squeezes her shoulder and disappears into the adjoining room to pack for the trip, taking Garrigan and Conall to receive final departing orders.

Ceridwen stands and crosses the room to me. "I'm sorry."

I rise too, thumbs hooked in the straps of my chakram's holster. Snow, it feels good, having it back with me, so good that I can pretend I don't understand Ceridwen. "For what?"

She gives me a look half annoyed, half knowing. "Rhythm boys will break your heart," she says, but her face tightens with her own regret. "I stand by what I said, though. He wasn't a proper lover for you. You're too good for him."

Heat instantly surges up my neck and I throw a glance at Dendera and Nessa, the only other people still in the room, but they're both whispering quietly by the door.

"He wasn't my *lover*," I hiss. "Snow above, is that all you Summerians think about?"

"Trust me, when you find the right person, it *will* be all you think about." Ceridwen grins weakly.

I tip my head, voice low. "I've told you my secrets. Will you ever tell me yours?"

She blinks at me but recovers quickly. "That wasn't part of our deal, Winter queen."

And she leaves, brushing past Nessa and Dendera without another word. I stare after her, stunned, but shake it off when Nessa comes up to me.

She's been quiet through everything I said, like she's piecing it all together in her own way, and as I stand before her, I'm overcome by the prickling certainty that she will be the one to see what none of us have been able to.

Nessa wrings her hands together. "Are you still afraid of it?"

I touch the locket, the shell of what once was. Again my hesitation answers for me.

"I would be too," Nessa says. "Don't feel guilty for what you did; I don't think your magic is as bad as you think it is. After all, it's done a lot of good. It healed us, it helped save us, it fought off Angra in Abril. I know it doesn't make it any less frightening, but—" She pauses and shrugs. "It's a weapon we have, and we need all the weapons we can get."

I smile. "You really are too astute for your own good, Lady Kentigern."

Her cheeks flush and she backs away, skipping out the door, Dendera in tow. I'm left with the gears and knobs and twisting copper pipes of the Yakimian bedroom, the faint rays of the rising sun peeking through the curtains. I don't know how long we were up talking—hours, half the night, all night. I feel the exhaustion now, and my mind starts to sway and pull, the gentle fog between sleep and waking. The time when thoughts rush through my head, patching together meanings I missed.

Which is why Nessa's words resonate so strongly in me.

"It's a weapon we have, and we need all the weapons we can get."

I was right. Nessa did see the missing piece—the magic has done a lot of good. I've pushed it away for so long, feared it for so long, but . . . maybe it can help me, even in its unpredictable state. It's still magic; it's still power.

I have to at least try.

My gown pulls taut over my knees as I kneel on the bed. The Lustrate's key still sits on the quilt, silent and dark, and as I stare at it, everything I know about conduit magic rolls through my mind. How it came into me after Hannah died and Angra broke the locket. How it lay dormant inside me until I knew it was there, a passive magic founded in choice. And back before that, how Hannah grew so desperate that she surrendered herself to it so she could learn how to save Winter.

I frown.

She asked the magic how to save Winter. And this magic is about choice—she *chose* to ask about Winter.

A ready heart, the key-magic had said. Readiness is a type of choice, being prepared and accepting of things to come—is this what it wanted me to see?

Because . . . what if Hannah hadn't asked how to save Winter? What if she had chosen to ask how to stop Angra, or the war, or how to defeat the Decay? Would she have gotten a different response?

What do I need to be ready to ask?

I lean back into the pillows, my chakram pressing against my spine. The hazy vacancy of sleep ebbs over me, the events of the past few weeks unwinding in this one night of release. But I push past it, reaching out to the magic. A soft, careful touch, the beginnings of a bridge between it and me, and across that bridge I send a single thought.

What is the right question?

My chest grows cold, the magic responding with gentle fingers of ice that spread through my body like growing designs of frost on a window. When it speaks, it's not like Hannah, not clear words that ring in my head. It's like the key-magic, my own voice and emotions, waves of conviction that fill me with knowledge as if it had been there all along. I'm left with a heavy, persistent thought that rocks me into sleep.

When I'm ready to ask it, I'll know.

Henn leaves for Winter the next morning. And, much to my relief, I find I don't need to prepare to sign Theron's treaty—because Giselle refuses to sign it "until another Rhythm does." She says this without acknowledging that Cordell has signed and orchestrated it, and the blatant rift this puts between Yakim and Cordell makes our stay more than a little uncomfortable.

Without needing prodding from anyone, Theron agrees to head for Ventralli after only a few days in Putnam.

I know he hopes to get the Ventrallan king to sign the treaty and thereby sway Yakim—he still clings to his vision of peace. But as we leave Langlais Castle, our caravan banding together in another haphazard cluster of soldiers and people from three different kingdoms, I watch him from my group of Winterians. We haven't interacted with each other beyond the necessary planning for travel, and even now, we both stay firmly with our groups.

Theron feels my eyes on him and turns. Even from as far away as he is, the air still feels tight and uncomfortable between us, emotions knotted up, words left unsaid.

Dendera swings up onto her horse beside me. When she and Henn finally admitted to their feelings, it seemed like the easiest thing in the world. One minute they *weren't* and the next minute they *were*, and it was so right and so true that nobody batted an eye. Even now, it feels like I'm only seeing half of her, as her other part barrels fast for Winter.

It should be that easy. I want it to be that easy. I want to look at someone and know that every need and wish and desire I have matches his, not that my every need and wish and desire clashes with his. Unification *should* be the overall theme of a relationship.

So even though Theron watches me still, I turn to Nessa for something else to do, somewhere to look other than him.

After a few seconds, I feel him turn away.

Rintiero, Ventralli's capital, sits hardly more than half a day's journey north. Everything Sir taught me about Ventralli revolves around their love of art—color and life and beauty, art echoed through pain and imperfection. Their male-blooded conduit, a silver crown, belongs to their current king, Jesse Donati, a man in his early twenties. His wife, Raelyn, bore him three children—two girls and one boy, all under the age of three, which means they really wanted either children or a male heir as quickly as possible. Most likely the latter.

Ventralli's affinity for beauty is clear when we reach Rintiero at sunset. Whoever designed this city built it to complement the setting sun as perfectly as the stars complement the night. We crest a series of hills that make up the Yakim-Ventralli border and guide us down into the Rintiero Valley, giving an aerial view of a city that is more akin to a multifaceted jewel.

Rintiero curves in a crescent of spindly rocks and straight lines of docks that jut into the Langstone River, all of it capped with the deep, heavy blue of a sky about to sink into sleep. A chill blankets the air, the cold of a proper spring night. A soft, golden glow lights the streets—candles probably, but nothing like the violent flames of Summer's bonfires or the steady light of Yakim's lamps.

Four- and five-story buildings lean against one another or cling to cliff faces, all in the most vibrant colors I've ever seen. Teals stolen from the Langstone itself; the vibrant magenta of a court lady's blush powder; creamy peach tones that would make any orchard owner weep. Interspersed in among the buildings are Ventralli's guilds, at least a dozen domes made of glass, thick panes that reflect the unmatched beauty of the night sky.

The buildings flicker and pulse in the lights as if they're taking deep, calming breaths, and as we draw nearer to the city, I do the same. This kingdom instantly feels calmer than any of the others we've visited. The road isn't clogged with peasants on their way home from work, the small outlaying villages aren't dirty or rotten or poor. Everything is as it needs to be—whole, pretty, valued.

That must have been why Noam allied himself with Ventralli when he married Theron's mother. It would appear that Cordell and Yakim have more in common with their similar love for efficiency, but I've been in Ventralli for less than an hour and I can *feel* Cordell here.

We move through the winding streets of Rintiero and pass into a lush forest that wraps around the palace like a living wall. The complex itself is just as sleepy and calming as the city, and stable hands take our horses before servants lead us to rooms inside the palace. The rest of the crates from the Klaryns get locked away, a burden on our trip now that I know how useless they'll be, but everyone seems to have absorbed the relaxation of Rintiero. Without a second thought, we all crawl into our various beds and drift off under reflections of stars.

Meira

THE POWER OF Things Concealed.

The next morning, the bold, swirling inscription above the doors to the Donati Palace's throne room stares down at me. I lean against the wall directly opposite the two ornate white doors, their gleaming silver moldings and small sapphire accents adding beauty to confusion, and I touch the mask on my face.

"Are you sure this is necessary?" I ask.

"You don't like it?" Dendera touches her own, a half-face white mask with small crystal snowflakes clustered around her eyes.

Ventrallan servants provided an array of masks suited to every kingdom, stock they always have on hand for foreign guests. The servants seemed absolutely thrilled that someone would finally get to wear the Winterian masks—it had been decades, apparently, since they had been more than pretty shelf decorations. Conall and Garrigan didn't complain at all when they were forced to wear masks too, and they stand stoically beside me in simple white-silk half-face masks that blend into their ivory skin and hair.

"It's not that," I say. "I just don't see why it's necessary for us. We're not Ventrallan."

Dendera smiles but I can't see more than that in her expression. "It's respectful of their culture. Besides, if we don't partake in Ventralli's rituals, they would have the upper hand, wearing masks as they do."

I catch my reflection in one of the gilded mirrors that line this hall. The mask she chose for me is half a snowflake, the straight lines forming natural eyeholes before fanning around my face. She curled my long, white hair and left it down, and when one of the servants offered us a collection of dresses and shoes instead of my worn gowns or an unfinished dress of Dendera's, she teared up in the most perfect way.

Ventrallan fashion is unique, to say the least. Overlapping layers of pink and peach tulle make up this gown, with the topmost layer embellished by twisting strands of crystal beads. The sleeves are only one layer of the tulle, showing my pale arms through a haze of peach. I saw a few of the other dresses the servants gathered for us—slender, form-fitting things constructed entirely of jewels pressed side by side on flesh-colored fabric; skirts that dropped only to the wearer's knees; neck pieces that fanned around in giant cones of stiff fabric. Each gown had the same deliberate feel as the buildings in the city, like every piece of them was cared for.

At least this gown came with a pocket, and the key I found in Putnam sits within, wrapped in a square of cloth. I adjust the layers of tulle around my legs, feeling the weight of the key shift against my thigh. Yet another introduction awaits us, and the sooner we get it over with, the sooner I can start scouring Rintiero's museums for the final key.

Dendera straightens and turns, hearing footsteps as I do. Sure enough, the rest of our party starts toward us down the long, mirrored hall that stretches before the two ornate doors. Theron with his soldiers, all of them wearing their Cordellan uniforms, now accompanied by green-and-gold masks accented with golden maple leaves and lavender stalks. The mask makes it impossible for me to read Theron's face, but he meets my eyes as he approaches, his lips parting as if he wants to say something.

I pivot away from him, back rigid, and search for Ceridwen in the crowd. Simon and his guards have masks befitting their kingdom, snapping flames that weave around their faces, blending flawlessly into their scarlet hair. Simon wears the same outfit he wore in Putnam—but the gown Ceridwen chose perfectly combines Ventralli and Summer styles. Red tulle pours from a band of gold around her chest, wrapping around her body until it splits and falls in two sections over her left leg. When she walks, bloodred silk peeks under the split of fabric, showing an intricate fire design stitched all the way up to her hip. More gold straps crisscross her torso, a beautiful blend of gold and red and orange, flames and beauty and art.

Ceridwen doesn't look at me, staring at the doors as though they're an enemy, and I can't tell whether she's preparing to run or fight.

"Princess?" I start when they all stop before us. "Are you—"

"Isn't my little sister lovely?" Simon staggers to her and pats her cheek, resting the conduit on his wrist against her bare shoulder. "She's just nervous, that's all."

Ceridwen flinches. "I won't deal with you right now—"

The opening doors send a ripple of quiet over everyone, but for Ceridwen, the silence is harder, heavier, and she pulls into herself, head down, shoulders slumped.

"The king will see you now," a steward announces, his mask made of simple purple-and-silver silk. He spins on his heels and strides into the room, and we follow, a slow river of dignitaries clinging to uncomfortable silence like it's all that will save us from drowning.

I start forward when I notice Ceridwen lingering, her eyes stuck on the room ahead and slow, uneven breaths bursting out of her mouth. Everyone else passes us; even Dendera goes on ahead to give us space. Only Conall and Garrigan linger, and back by the wall, a man falls out of the Summerian group to hover behind Ceridwen. Lekan.

He meets my eyes, his own framed by a red silk mask. If he offers a warning in his gaze, I can't see it, and I turn to Ceridwen.

"You defy your brother on a near-daily basis, but it's Ventralli you fear?"

She shakes her head, coming out of her fog. When she looks at me, I recognize the same inescapable nothingness I'd feel whenever Sir refused to let me assist with anything. The dark, burning embers of not being enough.

"What's wrong?" I whisper.

She licks her lips, her hands wringing against her stomach. "The king of Ventralli gave me this dress," she says, almost as if she's not aware she's talking.

"It's beautiful."

"I shouldn't have worn it." She lifts the skirt and takes a few quick steps back down the hall, but she stops when Lekan and I start after her, and we all just stand there, me with one hand out, her with one hand in her skirt, Lekan coiled to spring to her.

"Ceridwen, tell me what's going on," I try again.

She glances back, her eyes bloodshot. Her gaze sweeps over me before she sniffs, straightens. "Nothing," she snaps. "Once this introduction ends, follow me. I'll take you to someone who can help with . . ." She touches her bodice, and I know she must have the tapestry tucked there.

I nod, still dumbstruck. "All right, but—"

She pushes past me, diving into the throne room before

I can finish. Lekan hurries after her, bowing his head to me as he passes, and I think I catch a mumbled apology.

My eyebrows raise so high I'm sure they're hovering over my mask. Conall and Garrigan seem just as confused, and Garrigan shrugs, offering me an encouraging smile. I take it and smile back at him, holding it on my face as I enter the throne room.

I grip my skirt in two tight fists, keeping alert in case whatever Ceridwen feared comes to pass. The throne room rolls out, a green-and-white marble floor swirling in a colorful dance beneath two rows of auburn columns. Sky-blue panels line the ceiling, broken only by a circle of gold in the center, bent to form a concave bowl that glitters in the light from the sconces around the room. Mosaics on the walls beyond the pillars create a kaleidoscope of green and brown that forms into shrubs, grass, maple and oak trees, and more. The gleaming golden dome above us shines down as a sun, casting us into an artist's version of a forest, perfect and untouched.

I stop next to Dendera, trying not to gape too obviously at the wonder around me. The more I look, the more details I see. Like the tiled deer hiding behind a tree in one of the mosaics, or the rotations of the sun carved into the dome above us, or the king and queen of Ventralli, sitting on thrones made of—mirrors? Palm-sized mirrors cover each of the two thrones, giving the illlusion that the thrones have been turned into diamonds. The dais beneath the thrones holds also an assortment of courtiers, a handful of men and women—but one stands closer to the king's throne than the rest. Her vibrant yellow mask does nothing to hide her obvious disdain, and she purses wrinkled lips at our arrival, bending low to whisper something in the king's ear. Sitting there with the courtier on one side and the queen in her throne on the other, the king looks . . . trapped.

My awe flies away and a pulse of anxiety moves me forward, my body humming with the need to talk to Jesse and Raelyn before anyone intercedes on Winter's behalf. Again. Dendera grabs my arm—the whole reason she came with me this time was to help me balance when to be impetuous and when to be calm. From the look she gives me, I can tell she wants to let the Ventrallan royals talk first.

As if sensing her cue, the queen rises. The older courtier woman pulls back from the king, eyeing the queen with some unspoken signal I can't read.

Raelyn Donati's gown swishes into place as if she controls every handful of fabric. A black bodice connects to cascades of black silk at her waist, the bundle falling down the back of her legs in an explosion of gleaming darkness. The front of her skirt is a riot of colors—layers of sunflower-yellow and blush-red tulle. Her mask combines her gown's colors and fabrics, fastened discreetly into her thick, dark curls. Sharp hazel eyes take each of us in as if she's sorting through different fabrics to pick the one she dislikes least.

She stops on Ceridwen. Even with her mask, Raelyn's entire demeanor changes, moving from slightly bored to annoyed with a few twitches of her lips. I risk a glance at Ceridwen, who keeps her eyes on the marble floor, her body so stiff she may as well be one of the pillars.

Raelyn takes a single step forward and turns to me, stopping at the edge of the short dais on which the thrones sit. "Queen Meira," she says, clasping her hands behind her back.

I brace myself. I expect Ventralli's displeasure now that I realize what bringing Cordell on this trip signifies, but I still don't know how they'll retaliate. Giselle only rebuffed us—what will Ventralli do? Throw their weight behind Cordell?

But, to my surprise, Raelyn's mouth opens in a sigh. "I am sorry to hear of your kingdom's suffering, but glad to know you have at last achieved a state of peace."

Her words are kind, but her tone is that of someone reciting the sentence at an execution. Dendera nudges me and I blink.

"Um, thank you." I clear my throat. "Thank you, Queen Raelyn. Winter appreciates your . . ." *Support? No. Empathy? Eh.* ". . . well-wishes."

She bobs her head in acceptance and turns to her husband. "My lord, our guests traveled all this way, and we haven't yet offered them a proper Ventrallan welcome." She puts her hand on Jesse's arm. "We have a celebration planned in their honor tonight, do we not?"

All attention is on Jesse now. But though we look at him, he only looks at Ceridwen, his eyes wide, his neck muscles tense, his jaw clenched. I feel as though we all stumbled in on these two, and we should duck out to allow them privacy for some affair.

Air lodges in my throat and I do everything I can to keep from coughing in the silence. That's exactly what I'm watching, what Simon implied, what Raelyn knows all too well, the way she touches Jesse and smirks at Ceridwen.

The Ventrallan king loves Ceridwen.

And from the way she glances up at him . . .

She loves him too.

That's her secret. That's why she seemed so disgusted by my relationship with Theron—we're the same. And her relationship is just as broken as mine.

The older woman leans forward to put her hand on Jesse's other arm, as if helping Raelyn hold him to the throne. Her touch shocks him and he launches to his feet, throwing off their hands in a way that makes both women blink in a sudden burst of surprise that no mask could hide.

Jesse looks down at the rest of us like he only just realized we were here. Like he couldn't see anything beyond the fire that is the princess of Summer.

"Of course, my lady." With his dark hair hanging loose around his shoulders and the simple red silk mask over his eyes, he complements his wife in every way. Every way except in how he keeps drifting back to look at Ceridwen, unaware of the fact that Raelyn moves to take his arm again, her slender fingers curving around him.

His hazel eyes flick over us once more and stop on Theron. "Prince Theron," he says. "Of course. We were . . . we expected you. Yes. A celebration, tonight."

Jesse turns to Raelyn, dipping his head in a bow again. "Yes. A celebration," he agrees before spinning around and diving between the mirrored thrones. The older courtier moves after him, hissing something inaudible, and all I catch in return from him is a brittle "Not now, Mother."

His mother?

A burst of silver reflects back—Ventralli's crown, hanging in a holster at his hip. Thin silver spires hold an array of jewels, from rubies to emeralds to diamonds, all of it emitting the faintest silver glow, the same hazy aura of magic that emanates from all object-conduits. How did I not notice it before? And why does it hang from his belt, not sit on his head?

Jesse throws himself at a door behind the dais, ducking out almost as if he's running from his mother, who follows in hot pursuit.

He doesn't behave like someone who has the power to change his country.

As soon as he's gone, Raelyn swings back to us. "We will see you tonight." She flips her hand in dismissal and moves between the mirrored thrones as well, catching the older courtier by the arm before they disappear beyond the door Jesse exited through.

I start forward when a hand grabs my arm. "I didn't get a chance to—"

But it isn't Dendera—it's Theron.

He hooks my arm around his as everyone else walks back down the throne room, pulling me along like we're doing what's expected of us, like we're normal again. Dendera talks with Conall and Garrigan, but she sees Theron holding me, and her brows rise, asking whether or not I want her to intercede.

I turn to Theron, making that my answer.

"We'll both get chances to speak with them," he says, his voice sinking on the way he divides us. "Give them time."

But as he talks, his focus wanders to the head of our group. Ceridwen lifts her gown and sprints down the room, followed closely by Lekan. She reaches the doors and bursts out, the clacking of her shoes echoing back, her brother and his men chuckling in her wake. My grip tightens on Theron's arm, an involuntary spasm as I fit together more missing pieces.

"You knew about them?" I whisper.

Theron looks down at me, his other hand rising to cup my fingers. No, I didn't mean to hold him like that, but he stares at me, and I can't read his expression behind these damn masks.

"The rumor is that it began after she became an ambassador in Ventralli," he says. "No one speaks of it. It's been the scandal of the Donati family for years, and Raelyn used to care—until little less than a year ago."

My jaw goes slack as I think back. "She gave birth to Jesse's son. She secured the Donati conduit line, and no one could threaten her station anymore." My lungs deflate, my eyes going to the door we're approaching. "And yet, Ceridwen still loves him."

I can feel Theron's eyes on me, anchors that used to ground me, that now feel more like restraints. "He still loves her too," he whispers. "No matter how many people tell him it's wrong. No matter how many courtiers despise him for it. He'll always love her."

It seems like a bold statement—how could he possibly know that? Then he runs his thumb up the back of my hand.

He isn't talking about Jesse anymore.

Thank everything cold, Nessa comes hurrying into the throne room, meeting us as we leave. "Meira," she says, taking my other arm. "I need to show you something."

She doesn't flinch or correct herself for using my name, and that alone makes me want to kiss her, but the exit she offers throws me willingly after her.

"I'll see you soon," I say to Theron, pulling myself away from him. Dendera, Conall, and Garrigan follow, and I let Nessa tug me out of the room, pretending the mask is enough to hide the pang that ricochets over Theron's face.

Maybe the masks aren't so bad, actually. They let us live in worlds as untouched as the forest throne room—controlled and glittering, unmarred and perfect. A world where I can focus on the things I need to focus on, not the fragile emotions of broken relationships.

"I have to go after Ceridwen," I tell Nessa, voice low, the moment we leave the ballroom. The hall is already empty save for the departing Summerian dignitaries, who turn left and head toward the front of the palace.

"I know, but this will help!" Her grip on my arm tightens and she hauls me to the left, dipping down a hall that branches off this main one. "I wasn't about to just unpack and wait for news—so I asked one of the servants what tapestries are in the palace."

She beams back at me, veering us left, then right again.

"Tapestries?" I ask.

"Like the one you found in Putnam. I thought maybe it would be a good place to start too! The servant said there's a whole guild dedicated to the art of tapestry making, but it's deep in the city. In the palace, though, they have hundreds, which wasn't a surprise. But he showed me the—"

"He?" Conall cuts in, angling forward as we all practically sprint down the hall.

Nessa blushes but tries to fight it with a roll of her eyes. "Yes, *he* was a cheery seventy-year-old butler. Really, you don't have to worry about me so much."

Conall pulls back, grumbling to himself.

Nessa continues. "Anyway, he showed me some of the ones they're most proud of and, well, look!"

She swings open a door to a gallery lined with tapestries: small ones depicting landscapes; large ones depicting battles; long tapestries depicting whole crowds. But none of them holds Nessa's attention, and she drags me across the otherwise empty room to the far wall, where eight tapestries hang, identical in size and shape.

The four on the right I understand instantly.

One shows scarlet-haired people adorned in orange and red, flames on their uniforms, the fabric of their clothes twisting and sparse beneath leather straps and sandals. The background shows a cracked desert, the blinding sun beating down in startling gold thread, vines wrapping in a frame around the whole scene.

The one beside that shows men in satin tunics of teal, burgundy, and brown, and women in wrapping bands of the same brilliant satin, their black hair and dark complexions making them blend into the background of shadowed red, yellow, and brown trees.

The next shows women in pleated ivory dresses, and men with bundled fabric wrapping in X's over their torsos. Snowfields cascade all around, the hazy, gray sky threatening more snow upon the scene.

And the last one—fields of flowers billow behind people

in airy dresses of subdued colors, rose and eggshell and lavender.

The Seasons. The parts of Spring I've seen have been shrouded in war and the Decay, but this tapestry shows what Spring should be. The aged quality to the threads, the worn texture at the edges, makes me think these tapestries must be centuries old.

My breath catches.

The four tapestries on my left show the remaining kingdoms. Cordell, with its green and gold and fields of lavender; Yakim, with its brown and brass and gears; Ventralli, with its eclectic styles and colorful buildings; and Paisly, with its . . .

Mountains.

Nessa skips down to the tapestry depicting Paisly and points up, bouncing. "You showed us the tapestry you found before we left for Ventralli. I know Ceridwen has it still, but I think I remember it enough. This is similar, isn't it?"

I stop before it, my mouth yanking open.

"Not just similar," I say. "Those are *the* mountains."

And they are. The exact same circle of mountains that I saw on the tapestry we found in Putnam gazes down at me—a ring of gray stones peaking sharply. But instead of a ball of magic stitched in the center, people stand within the ring, dressed in long, heavy robes of maroon and black with swirls of gold thread making intricate patterns up the bell sleeves. The high collars shoot around their ebony hair, the strands twisted into knots against their dark scalps.

"Paisly?" I ask. The tapestry showed the *Paisel* Mountains?

Or was it just a clue to lead us to the key?

I dive at the Paislian tapestry and run my hand over the thread. The dense fabric hangs from a clasp high up the wall, and most of the tapestry I can't reach. But I analyze the edges, searching where I can, lifting the bottom of the tapestry. Nothing sits in the wall behind it, no pockets dip from the material.

As far as I can tell, there is nothing specifically related to the Order in this tapestry.

"It can't be a coincidence." I turn to Nessa. "Can it?"

She shrugs, her face falling ever so slightly. "Maybe this was wrong? Maybe those aren't the mountains."

I back up, staring at the tapestry again. They *are* the same mountains, though.

"Are we supposed to go to Paisly?" I wonder aloud.

Dendera scoffs, "Snow, I hope not."

But that's all I can deduce from this. The Putnam tapestry led us here. Didn't it? Maybe we'll find something else if we search Ventralli's museums or guilds. Maybe this is just a weird coincidence.

My wondering stops dead as someone clears their throat at the door to the room. It's the steward from earlier, hands behind his back, chin lifted.

"The king requests your presence," he announces, and

swings back out the door, easing away at a fast clip so he's halfway down the hall before I even process what he said.

I snap my hands into fists and dive after him.

Dendera catches my arm. "Should we talk about this? We need to—"

"No," I tell her, tone even. "The key isn't here. I need time to figure out what to do next, and lingering around isn't going to help. Besides, I need to meet with Jesse too. He certainly can't make this any worse."

But I don't know what the Ventrallan king might want. Maybe he *will* find a way to make this worse.

We all follow the steward, leaving the Paislian tapestry behind.

Meira

JESSE WAITS FOR us in a study so cramped and chaotic that I can't help but feel even more curious about
this meeting. This isn't a room made for receiving foreign
dignitaries and impressing them with displays of power
and extravagance—this is his actual study, cluttered with
parchments and shelves crammed with well-used ledgers.

If there were any doubt over Jesse's relation to Theron,
this room would negate it. The mess peppered with bits of
art—a stack of masks in the corner, a tapestry rolled up on
the floor, a painting leaning against the wall—reminds me
so much of Theron's room in Bithai that I half expect him
to be here too. But only Jesse waits within, and it isn't until
the door closes behind us that he jumps and swings around.

"Queen Meira!" he chirps, and drops a ledger, sending it
crashing to the velvety green carpet. But it appears intentional, as he dives for a stack of papers on his desk without

bothering to note the book he dropped.

"I didn't expect the king of Ventralli to treat books with such disdain," I note, and Dendera snaps a quiet hiss at me.

But Jesse doesn't seem to hear me. "Oh, no, that's useless."

He drops the stack of papers in turn and moves for a scroll on his desk, mumbling unintelligibly.

"King Jesse?" I start.

He snaps up to me, blinking behind his red silk mask. His eyes cut to the door, closed after Dendera, Nessa, my guards, and me, and he surveys us in turn, his lips parting in tight, uneven breaths.

"Are they trustworthy?" Jesse asks, and thumps the scroll on his desk. "Of course they are; they're your people. You saved them."

"I don't understand—"

"Queen Meira, I need your help." Jesse moves out from behind his desk and crosses the room to me. He folds his arms behind his back to straighten into the most regal stance I've seen on him yet, the crown at his hip glinting silver. "I realize this is unorthodox, but I wish to form an alliance with you."

My eyes snap open so wide the snowflake mask shifts. "*You* want an alliance with *me*?"

Dendera sucks in a small gasp of surprised joy as Jesse nods.

"You freed yourself. Your people," he explains, shoulders

dipping slightly. "You overthrew a great evil. I need to do that. I need—help."

That quickly, my shock dissolves into wariness. "What exactly do you need?"

Jesse waves his amends, mistaking my concern. "No, no, I intend to reciprocate—whatever you need. Anything. I just—" His eyes drift to stare at a spot on the floor. "This has gone too far. My wife. She needs to be stopped."

I can't control my wheezing gasp. "You want help dethroning your wife?"

Jesse meets my eyes and nods.

My mind reels back to my brief time with Raelyn. She didn't seem particularly terrible, but we were only in the same room for a few minutes. If anything, she seemed . . . hard. Aloof. But this is Ventralli, after all—they built their culture on concealment.

"You're the king," I state, only because I need to remind myself that Jesse is, in fact, the most powerful man in this country. "Why would you beseech a *Season* for help with this? Can't you just order your own divorce?"

Jesse shakes his head in a tight, determined rebuttal. "You think I haven't tried ending things peacefully? She has support. Lots of support. Including my own mother, and that's what I was doing when you came in—trying to sort through all of my correspondences and figure out which allies I still have. But it's you I need. You overthrew Angra. You know of these things."

"I overthrew him in a bloody, costly war, not through politics. Why don't you go to Cordell?"

My gut twists. Here the king of a Rhythm is handing me an alliance on what may as well be bended knee, and I'm refusing him. But I don't have the extra resources to help—and anything he did take from Winter would come indirectly from Cordell, anyway.

"I did ask Cordell." Jesse pulls back and turns to his desk, shuffling aimlessly through the papers on it. His eyes lift to mine, softer now, some of his desperation receding. "But I fear my wife already has her influence in them as well. She does that—cuts off everything I have, infects potential supporters until I have no ally but her."

I step forward. "What do you mean she has her influence in Cordell?"

"That's why I needed to see you so suddenly." Jesse faces me again. "She's speaking to Theron at this moment. I needed to meet with you before—"

My brain lurches to a halt, though he keeps talking.

Raelyn . . . and Theron? She's who he went to in Ventralli, not his own cousin? But Finn and Greer did say that Raelyn was basically the kingdom's ruler.

But whom do I trust in this? I don't know enough about Raelyn or Jesse to choose between the two. Supporting the conduit wielder seems the natural course—his is the line that will always be in power.

Unless he dies, and the crown passes to their infant son.

Raelyn would no doubt act as regent until he came of age, and by then, she could be even more fiercely powerful.

Is she that kind of person? Jesse seems to think so.

I blink, surprised at myself. It seems I've gotten better at thinking through politics. I don't know if that's something I should be proud of.

Jesse hunches over papers on the floor, talking still. ". . . soldiers stationed just out west, who are loyal to me, I think."

All this swirls around me, the chaos of such heated politics rearing up out of what seemed a beautiful, picturesque kingdom. I turn to Dendera and to my surprise, she nods.

Accept him? I mouth.

She nods again.

But something about this still doesn't sit right. Unease seems to be my constant escort.

"Why now?" I swivel back to Jesse, who pauses in his sorting to look up at me. "Because I need allies too, King Jesse, and if I agree to this, I will need support quickly. Why is it so imperative you find allies to fight your wife now?"

His face drains of color. "Because she . . ." His voice fades, his jaw bobbing.

Every nerve in my body flares to readiness, a feeling that shocks me with memory.

I was four or five, young enough that my recollection consists of hazy flashes of images that may or may not be real. A canopy of heavy, wet leaves in the Eldridge Forest; Alysson's arms around me as we sat near a fire; and a sound, a violent, shattering noise—a branch snapping.

On its own it wasn't anything unusual; branches snapped all the time in the Eldridge. But something about it felt heavier, louder than any noise I had heard yet. Because just after it, Alysson shoved me off her lap and fell over the sprawled body of Sir, lying motionless in the undergrowth of the forest. He didn't move for so long, seconds that felt like days, until finally, *finally*, he turned over and murmured that his partner had been killed by Angra's men.

As I watched him, and his wife hovering over him and people running in a frenzy around me, all I could hear was that branch snapping over and over, the branch he'd stepped on as he collapsed by the fire. For years after, every time I'd hear a branch snap, my heart would drop and my eyes would tear and I'd expect death to come roaring at me.

Now, as I stand in the center of the Ventrallan king's study, I feel the noise before it happens. Not a branch snapping, but something just as commonplace—a noise forever associated with signaling that something's coming, something I can't control.

Two thumping knocks on the door.

I spin, the tulle of my gown whooshing against the force. Jesse leaps to his feet, his face sickly gray as he dives forward and yanks open the door.

Lekan stands there, fist up to knock again, sweat gleaming

on his bare face. He sees Jesse and jerks back—physically, violently *recoils*, lips curling, body hunching.

"I need the Winter queen," he snaps.

Jesse sags against the door. "Where is Ceridwen? Have you seen her? Can you—"

"I need the Winter queen," Lekan echoes his snarl, and shoves Jesse aside. *Shoves the Ventrallan king.*

I gape at Lekan. I know Jesse is Ceridwen's . . . whatever he is, and Lekan is her friend, but that was bold. And this coming from someone who once locked herself in the Cordellan king's office.

Lekan's glower softens when he faces me. "I need your help."

"I'm popular today," I say as Jesse leaps in with "Where is she?"

I squint at Jesse. The moment he saw Lekan, he asked where Ceridwen was. But, they are involved, aren't they? Wouldn't he know where she is? Or did something happen?

Is that why Jesse is so panicked to find allies?

"She does that at every turn—infects potential allies until I'm left with . . ."

Snow above. Did Raelyn do something to Ceridwen? She's left her alone for however many years, but maybe . . . maybe she finally acted against her husband's mistress.

I nod at Lekan. "Of course."

Jesse presses back a moan, torn between wanting me to help Ceridwen and wanting me to help *him*. But he relents, almost instantly, his eyes latching onto mine. "Please, Queen Meira," he gasps. "Consider my proposal. We can discuss this after we—"

Lekan turns on Jesse as the king reaches for a sword hanging on the wall. The pattern on the sheath and the jewels on the hilt scream "decoration only," and the lack of weapons on Jesse's person says he isn't a fighter.

"This doesn't concern you," Lekan growls. "Stay here. Do nothing. You're good at that."

Jesse's chest sags and he drops against the doorframe.

The old Meira appreciates Lekan's brazenness, but Queen Meira chokes. "He's the *king of Ventralli*," I half gag, half laugh.

But Lekan just grabs my arm. "He'll get over it."

And we're running, leaving Jesse with his hands over his face, his conduit dangling uselessly from his hip.

The halls of the Donati Palace are maddeningly long.

I'm already half out of my dress by the time I burst into my room. Conall and Garrigan close the door, and Dendera dives at the trunk in the corner, ripping out clothes more appropriate to search for someone. Nessa scoops it all out of Dendera's hands and shoves me behind a dressing screen.

"She loves him," Lekan starts. My heart fractures. "She has for four years. Well, more than that, actually—before he married Raelyn. But that's not important—she went to him just after you all met them in the throne room. She said she was done, that she wanted to end things. She's tried in the past, but something about this time felt different."

"What?" Dendera asks. "Why would this time be different?"

"Because Ventralli has started to sell people to her brother."

I bend forward, one hand bracing on the dressing screen.

The Ventrallan man who was murdered in the wine cellar.

Not only was his death upsetting for humane reasons, but it was also upsetting politically. His presence in Summer should have struck me oddly—I *knew* only Yakim and Spring sold to Summer, but I was too wrapped up in my own issues to see anything outside of myself.

Ceridwen should have told me how Summer's situation had evolved. What stopped her? Pride? My constant babbling about my own problems?

Dendera sighs. "He betrayed her."

Her words slant sharply, and I close my eyes as if that will stop them from hitting their mark. I don't need Dendera's observation to connect how similar Ceridwen and I are—both in our doomed relationships with Rhythm royals.

But Lekan grunts. "I don't think so. I think it was his wife. She's manipulative, to say the least, and she's always after ways to boost Ventralli's economy. And Jesse isn't heartless. He may be weak, but never heartless." He pauses, exhaling slowly. "But Ceridwen wouldn't listen to me. She went to talk to him, and that was the last I saw her. But the servants said that she hurried back soon after, and changed out of her gown and into . . . battle gear."

That was why Jesse was so riled. Ceridwen ended things with him, probably told him of his wife's arrangement to sell Ventrallans to Summer, and left.

Nessa folds my dress once it's off and I'm in my normal clothes, the black pants and white shirt I wore in Summer. The key, still wrapped in cloth, goes into my pocket while my chakram sits on my back, and as I step out from behind the dressing screen, I tighten the straps of the holster.

"I know where she went," I say.

Lekan flinches forward. "What? How?"

"Because I know where I'd go if my heart had broken," I tell him, "and I'm beginning to think Ceridwen and I are similar in more ways than one."

I know where I'd go if I had ended things with a man I loved, if my kingdom was constantly threatened by an evil far stronger than me. Weapon blazing, I'd march into war. It's what my body has screamed to do since I finally accepted all of who I am, a warrior and a queen. To face everything without hesitation, to seek out the fight instead of cowering from it.

I know we need to press on for the Order, for answers. But if I let someone I care about slip through the chaos, I've lost no matter what I do. I'd do the same for Nessa, or

Mather, or Sir—drop everything to race to their aid. The reckless part of me, the orphaned soldier-girl part—that's all she is. Someone who acts impetuously, but always with good intent.

I will be that girl and the queen, all the parts of me. I will help Ceridwen and my kingdom—I can save everyone.

I can save everyone.

That's it.

I blink up at Lekan, shock cooling me. I know what question to ask the conduit magic.

But it barely takes any effort to shove that to the back of my mind, the bulk of my focus going to Ceridwen.

"But where did she go?" Lekan asks.

My face tightens. "She's gone to stop her brother."

Conall and Garrigan protest when I order them to split up. Garrigan to stay here with Dendera and Nessa, should anything happen while I'm gone, and Conall to come with Lekan and me. Conall argues that Garrigan should accompany me, since Conall's arm, while not broken, is still sprained. That's the reason I want Garrigan to stay, though—he's more capable of protecting Dendera and Nessa.

Besides, I have my chakram now. That's all the support I need.

Nessa gives us a little wave as we slip out of my room, the soft, worn leather of my boots noiseless on the marble floor. Lekan knows where the Summerian caravan set up, so the moment we break free of the palace, he rushes in front of Conall and me and takes off down the twisting cobbled streets of Rintiero. He wears baggy orange pants and little else under his rough brown cloak, but he makes no move to grab different clothes or more weapons. I hope he's as prepared as he needs to be. Even Conall only needed to remove his mask before he was ready.

I follow Lekan as he ducks down an alley, scales a wall, drops down another street. Maybe we should have gotten more of Ceridwen's allies to help—didn't she have at least a dozen bandits when I first met her outside of Juli? Surely she brought more than just Lekan with her. But if she didn't plan on attacking her brother, maybe she doesn't have her whole retinue.

The odds of the four of us against one dozen, two dozen, an endless number of soldiers remind me of the other issue at hand: the question I want to ask the conduit magic.

As Lekan, Conall, and I hurry through Rintiero's medley of colored buildings and parks, as we pass Ventrallans wandering through markets or sweeping patios or drawing water from wells under the afternoon sun, the question surges through me, tight and relentless, until it's all I can think, and I can't believe I didn't ask it sooner.

Cautiously, desperately, I roll the words through my mind and push them one by one into the waiting ball of ice and magic and wonder.

How do I save everyone?

Because I want to save the world, not just Winter. I want everyone in Primoria to be free from Angra and magic and evil—to at least have a *chance* against such threats.

Maybe asking this question will give me a way to save Ceridwen from her brother's men. Maybe it will show me how to help Winter without needing to find the Order. Maybe it will fix everything, it *will* fix everything, because it is the right question. I know this through every part of me, even the parts that still quiver and quake in fear of the magic. This is right, just like what I'm doing now. This is how it was always meant to be.

The magic hears my question. I feel it react to me, to the way I relax in the wake of my words, a gentle surrender that shakes through me. The answer pushes into my head like I've known it all along, an instant recognition that consumes every other thought I've ever had.

I stop running, unable to move beneath the answer. The answer that will save everyone. The answer that I wanted . . .

No. No, I don't want it. I don't want it, and I fall to my knees, gripping my head as if I can dig into my mind and pull out the knowledge.

Hannah asked how to save her people, and the magic told her *how to save Winter.* She let Angra break the locket and kill her because she wanted to share the magic with everyone in our kingdom. She sacrificed herself without realizing there was another question to ask, a bigger sacrifice that could be made.

Sacrifice.

The word undoes me, and I think I feel Conall's hand on my arms, Lekan's voice telling me we're only a few streets away. My body moves while my mind whirls, and I'm running again, flying through Rintiero.

Magic is all about choice. Choosing to use it, choosing to surrender to it, choosing to take it from the chasm—choosing to let it break in defense of a kingdom. The most powerful magic of all is choice, and of that power, the strongest choice anyone can make is an act of sacrifice.

People took magic from the chasm. Just like it never occurred to anyone but Hannah to surrender to their conduit, it never occurred to anyone to put the magic back.

That is the most powerful choice anyone can make: relinquishing a conduit back to the chasm. Saying that I would rather be weak and human than stronger than others. I would rather the world be safe and magic free than deadly and powerful.

That ultimate of choices, an act of selfless sacrifice, returning a conduit to the magic chasm, will force the chasm to disintegrate and all magic with it. And since the Decay is magic, it will be destroyed too.

It should be easy, for a conduit wielder who wants to save the world. Just finding the chasm, tossing their conduit in, and walking out into a new existence.

But I am Winter's conduit.

And to destroy all magic I would have to willingly throw myself into the fathomless chasm of energy and power. The source of magic that, when people first made conduits, was found to *kill people* if they got too close.

I would have to die.

Lekan stops along a wall and I have no idea where we are. Somewhere deep in Rintiero, the sun pulsing above us, and I can't see anything but the blinding light of late afternoon casting golden rays. It's warmer now, not the sweltering heat of Summer, but enough that sweat breaks across my body—though I can't tell if it's from the sun or my own panic.

Lekan's eyes flick over my face. "Are you all right?"

I can't form a response. I can't feel anything around the knowledge in my head, how much I hate it, and how much I hate Hannah now too. I want to collapse on the road and wipe the word *die* from my memory, because that's all I can see now. Hannah intended for me to die to save Winter; the only way I can save everyone in Primoria is to die.

If Hannah had never asked her conduit the wrong question, if she had never let Angra break the locket and kill her and turn *me* into Winter's conduit, I could do it. I could save everyone and myself, and nothing would hurt as badly as my chest hurts now.

I fall against the wall next to me, the rough stone tugging at my sleeve as I cover my face with my hands. I want to live. I want to find a way to save everyone and LIVE. Is it so horrible that I want to save myself too? Is that such an awful request?

Lekan pulls my hands down. His eyes are soft, his brow drawn. "The caravan sits just around the corner. I realize this isn't your fight, Winter queen, but I need your help."

The caravan. Ceridwen. I'm supposed to help her. She has the tapestry—the Order is still out there. Maybe they have a way; maybe they know something that could help me.

Maybe, maybe, *maybe*. That's all I've been lately, one big swirl of possibilities, never anything definitive or sure. I won't waste time on maybes anymore. I'm done, I'm *done*.

The only definitive thing I know right now is that Ceridwen needs me, and that's all I can see. Not the new weight of the answer driving nails into my skull. Not the magic, trapped and confused and wanting to burst free now that I surrendered to it and asked a question and got my answer. But no, I am not surrendering to it anymore. I may have for a brief flash of a second, but I will not give in. I will not accept this.

Tears glaze my eyes. "All right," I tell Lekan.

Meira

LEKAN BOWS HIS head in thanks and starts to say something else when a flash of movement makes me spin. Conall whips a dagger into his good hand as Ceridwen comes racing up the street behind us, her face alive with toxic anger.

"What are you doing here?" she barks, though I can't help but feel that her anger isn't directed at us. It's just a part of her, hungry and wild.

Lekan steps forward. "We came to stop you from doing anything stupid."

I draw a shaky breath. *Focus, focus. Don't think about anything else. I am a soldier; Sir trained me to keep my emotions in check. I can do this.*

I don't want to die. . . .

"Lekan said you were missing," I start, my hands in fists that grow tighter to counter the tremble in my voice. "I figured you were off doing something reckless—like stopping your brother from collecting more slaves."

Ceridwen's lip twitches and she flicks her eyes from Lekan to me. "I'm not stopping *a* collection," she says. "I'm stopping *the* collections."

Lekan realizes what she means before I do. He glances toward the road beyond our alley and cuts a snarl to her when he sees the way still clear. "You can't take him, Cerie."

"I definitely couldn't take him in Summer, but he only has a fraction of his soldiers here. It's now, or I lose the opportunity. You know better than I do that this has to end."

Lekan runs a hand through his hair, the red strands bouncing wild around his fingers.

"How will this stop the collections?" But as soon as I ask it, I know the answer.

She's going to kill her brother.

"Ceridwen." I gasp her name like someone landed a blow to my gut.

She glares at me. "Don't. Don't you dare judge me. He's the last living male heir of Summer—if he dies, we'll be free of magic. Summer will get a chance to be more than fogged with bliss, and if someday I have a son, I'll make sure he's a far, far better king than my brother. You have no idea what it's been like, what he's doing now, and I can't—"

"Why now?" Lekan asks so I don't have to, his tone dark. "If this is about Jesse—"

"This has nothing to do with him!" Ceridwen's voice threatens a scream, but she catches herself, warping it into a sharp whisper. "Simon . . . he . . . you've seen it, Lekan." She squints at him. "Didn't you see it?"

Lekan shakes his head.

"With the non-Summerian slaves," she starts. "He can control them, like he controls his own subjects. I don't know how, but he cannot be allowed to continue this, especially if his influence is stretching into more kingdoms. It's too much."

"Wait—the others in Juli acted just like the Summerian slaves because *Simon* controlled them?" I clarify. She nods.

I thought the reason was more the slaves' own way of coping with their lives, but . . .

Simon *controls* non-Summerians.

Only one person has ever been able to influence people not of his own kingdom: Angra.

"No, Cerie. He just drugs them," Lekan says, uncertain. "Doesn't he?"

But Ceridwen dives between Lekan and me, sweeping out toward the road and, beyond it, the waiting caravan. Lekan grabs her arm and swings her to a stop, but she wrenches away, pointing a steady finger at him.

"I need you on the ground," she says, and pivots to me. "And you—you *owe* me, Winter queen. Your chakram would be better on a roof. Your guard, though, should be with me."

"I'm not here to fight for you," Conall states. "I'm here to protect my queen."

Ceridwen's lip twitches, her rage rekindled, but I grab Conall's good arm, my body moving independently of my spinning, chaotic mind.

"I'll take the roof," I tell him. "You can stay on the ground below me. Fight down here."

Angra. Simon controls people who are not his subjects? No, no, she has to be wrong. . . .

Conall doesn't seem at all appeased, but he hears the order in my voice and nods curtly.

Ceridwen grunts approval and takes another step backward.

Lekan moves after her. "Wait—"

The scowl she gives him could burn through a brick wall. "He's been hurting our kingdom for too long, and if he's using magic on non-Summerians . . ."

I want to scream at her, a wave of fear swelling in me. No, it can't be the Decay—it *can't be* magic. There's been no sign of Angra or his darkness for months.

But the Decay needs a host, like any magic. It has to be coming from someone. . . .

Lekan grinds his jaw, and the way he springs forward makes me think she pushed him too far. But he just hovers there, muscles hard, staring at her with eyes that say more than any words could. Finally he nods, one firm jerk of his head, and Ceridwen flashes a deadly smile before sprinting around the corner. Lekan moves after her, already holding a pair of knives drawn from somewhere within his cloak.

I watch until I can't see their shadows on the street anymore, the surrounding city quiet except for the distant murmurs of people moving about their day and, closer, the harsh voices of soldiers. I look at Conall, but he just waits. He didn't read the threat in Ceridwen's words. He didn't come to the same conclusion that drains me.

Angra's magic didn't dissipate.

He might be alive.

I force a nod at Conall and he moves to the corner of the building, blending into the shadows that put him between this street and the one just over, the one Ceridwen and Lekan ran for.

I don't give myself time to do anything else. No thinking, no chance to reflect on everything that threatens to destroy me from the inside out. For now, for this fleeting moment, I am just a girl helping to stop a terrible act. I am nothing more than the tightness in my arms as I pull myself up the side of a building, window to window, ledge to ledge. I am nothing more than the shiver that spreads across my arms as I stand on the roof in the unbroken wind.

Angra is alive.

He's alive.

He's——

Those words beat in my head alongside my pulse, and I take slow, careful steps up the inclined clay tiles of the roof, crouch down, and peer at the square, three stories below.

Just focus on this task. Help Ceridwen. Maybe I'll see something that will explain what Simon is doing—maybe it'll all make sense.

And that, honestly, terrifies me more than anything else.

Buildings form a cage around a small, open square of pale yellow cobblestones. Rintiero's vibrant colors gleam in the bright light of the day, the magenta and peach buildings providing a riotous backdrop for the people standing in the square.

Summer's stained wagon sits in the center of fifteen soldiers chatting merrily, only half aware of the fact that they're supposed to be on watch. A jug of wine passes between a few of them as laughter flies upward. More laughter radiates from the wagon along with other noises that make my stomach churn.

One of the wagon doors opens. Simon swaggers out a step, unmistakable in the soft scarlet glow that radiates from the conduit on his wrist. My eyes lock onto it, the disgust in my stomach flickering into dread. Maybe Ceridwen was wrong. Maybe he *did* drug the non-Summerians, like Lekan thought.

Or maybe Angra allied with Summer, has been allied with them, all along. Or maybe the Decay did kill Angra and sought out a new host, and I'm too late to stop any of it.

Simon snaps something to one of his guards before diving back into the wagon.

A gurgled moan emanates from across the square. My eyes snap up in time to see a Summerian soldier collapse, motionless, as a red blur sweeps out of the shadows. She doesn't hesitate before she moves in on the next one, and by now other soldiers have noticed her, shouting that they're under attack. No one sees Conall on the road below me, hidden in shadows, or me on the roof.

I shift onto my knees and yank the chakram out of its holster, no thoughts beyond calculating which soldier will make the best target, which man gives me the clearest shot. The chakram flies from my hand, an effortless and familiar burst of movement, and in that moment it doesn't feel like months since I threw it. It feels like I've done it every day of my life, and it licks across a Summerian soldier's leg before smacking back into my palm.

"Sister!" Simon's voice catches against the buildings around him, his cocky tone echoing. I pull down, eyes flicking over the scene as Simon steps out of his wagon, his men pulling back. They aren't attacking?

Ceridwen and Lekan realize the oddness too. They stand back to back just across from me, weapons glinting and bloodied, both of them panting yet ready for an attack. But Simon doesn't tell his men to charge again, doesn't let his soldiers attack the two intruders.

He steps toward Ceridwen, his voice carrying around the square with intention. "What brings you to the shadier parts of Rintiero? It can't be that you're the one behind all the attacks on my wagons. I know my sister would never turn on me in such a way."

Simon's words barely reach my ears when Ceridwen screams.

She crumples to her knees, weapons clanking on the stone as they tumble from her hands. Lekan surges toward her but soldiers pin him back and she screams again, writhing on the ground. No one is anywhere near her, touching her at all, not even . . .

It's Simon. He's using his conduit to hurt her.

And any magic used for the sake of harm feeds the Decay.

I lean backward until I spot Conall below me. He sees what's happening from his hidden view between the buildings, and when I move he jerks his eyes up to me.

I point at him, then back toward the palace.

Warn them, I plead. *Angra's dark magic.*

Were it any other threat, I wouldn't consider using my magic—but I can't be afraid of anything that might help me now.

Conall's face pales with shock when my order hits him, driving action into his body in the same way other conduit wielders use their magic to direct soldiers on a battlefield. He shakes his head sharply, but the resignation on his face cancels out his protest.

Go, I force into him.

Conall scowls and takes off, running into the streets, away from the Summerians.

Once he vanishes from sight, I pull myself back up the roof, fingers digging into the tiles. Ceridwen has stopped screaming, her eyes on Simon, who walks through his soldiers, taking slow, taunting steps toward her. He tips his head at her on the ground, pauses, and glances over his shoulder.

In that moment, I catch sight of the confusion on his face. He peers at his conduit, twisting the cuff on his wrist, and looks across from him, to my right.

My eyes snap to follow his and my heart sinks.

"Princess Ceridwen," Raelyn coos. Ventrallan soldiers swarm the square, filing around as she takes slow, controlled steps forward. "So glad you could join us."

Simon moves toward her. "This isn't the plan. She's my prisoner to deal with."

Raelyn's hair curls wildly around a silk mask that matches her gown, a swirling tempest of emerald and obsidian that ripples as she draws closer to Simon. Her soldiers take up positions around the square, barricading anyone from leaving. Even the people in the carriage, some Summerian, some Yakimian, all branded, are dragged out and corralled into a cowering group by the square's edge.

But Raelyn has eyes only for Ceridwen, joy mixed with fury mixed with satisfaction, and I don't realize why she's so enthralled until she tips her head and Ceridwen screams.

Simon isn't the only one using the Decay. Every time Raelyn twitches, Ceridwen screams, her body bending in unnatural angles. My hand tightens on the chakram, but I'm frozen on the roof.

A *non–conduit wielder* is using the Decay.

So is someone else the host for it? Based on the confusion on Simon's face, it isn't him.

When the Decay was first created, it fed on the fuel of the thousands of people who used their small conduits for evil. It made everyone's darkest, most sinister thoughts the *only* thing they thought—and those who had conduits were also given extra strength and power. It has always been able to affect people regardless of their bloodline—Theron and I saw that firsthand in Abril. Normal conduits cannot affect someone not of their kingdom; the Decay is the exception to that rule. It's the bridge between bloodlines, created during a time when everyone had conduits regardless of lineage or kingdom.

When Mather broke Angra's staff, maybe Angra became Spring's conduit, and the Decay became strong enough to infuse evil desires and magic into all people. The Decay, Angra, and Spring's conduit could be one now, a morphed, twisted entity of limitless evil that breaks through everything we used to know about magic.

Which forms the terrifying question . . .

If Angra is alive, where is he? Or after centuries of feeding off Angra, did the Decay just become strong enough to infect whomever it pleases?

A heavy weight settles in me. I can't save Ceridwen and

Lekan, not now, not here, because I can only use my magic to affect Winterians. So I just watch in helpless horror as Raelyn pauses over Ceridwen, her head tipping back and forth as she surveys the princess of Summer at her feet.

"This is better than promised," she says, raising her voice for all to hear. She enjoys the audience, the stunned Summerians, her leering Ventrallan soldiers.

Simon stomps forward, a few Summerian soldiers following with drawn weapons. "What are you doing? This isn't—"

Raelyn waves, beckoning some of her men to restrain the Summerian soldiers. When they're just as helpless as Lekan, she shoots a look at Simon.

He falls to his knees before her, gasping like an invisible hand slowly clamps around his throat. His face dims to a violent purple, and Raelyn pushes her long fingers through his riot of hair.

"Dear Summer king," she says. "I'm afraid nothing will happen according to your plan."

"Angra . . . promised me," Simon pants, his strain clear in his clenched arms, his face darkening more and more.

I crouch lower behind the roof, quivering so hard that the building must be shaking too. Simon's words echo relentlessly through my mind.

Angra promised me.

"To ally Summer with Spring." Raelyn reprimands him like he's nothing more than a misbehaving child. "Yes, I know. But you didn't honestly think someone so powerful would ally with *Summer*, did you? Angra only gave you true magic to keep you occupied while real rulers decided what would become of your land." She pauses, still stroking her fingers through his hair as he coughs and gags. "And we have decided Summer will best serve our new world without its conduit bloodline. So you see, Spring will not ally with you. We do not require you at all."

With Raelyn focused on Simon, Ceridwen's pain stops, her body relaxing. She eases onto her elbows, her fingers digging into the cobblestones as she looks at Raelyn as if the Ventrallan queen is more rabid beast than person.

"True magic?" Ceridwen dares.

"Spring." Raelyn turns to her, Simon gagging still. "They discovered the true source of power, and it is not useless baubles imbued with centuries-old magic. Spring holds a power stronger than any conduit."

Ceridwen shakes her head. "Angra's dark magic? After what he did to Winter, after the control he enacted over his own people? You're insane. This is just another form of slavery. Jesse will never let this happen!"

Ceridwen stops, her gaze frozen on Raelyn. That name echoes around them. *Jesse.*

"You're quite right," Raelyn snarls, and kicks her in the stomach. Lekan cries out, but no one pays him any attention, everyone enthralled by the building storm of the Ventrallan queen and the Summerian princess. "Jesse is too weak. He will fear this power, and he will doom this king-dom as he did when he bedded *you*. But we don't need him anymore—*I* don't need him anymore."

"No . . ." Ceridwen chokes, sucking air in uneven spurts.

Raelyn lifts her skirt and slams her foot against Cerid-wen's throat, pressing as she shouts words down on her. "I will kill him, sweet girl. I will kill him and those brats and every remnant of the Ventrallan conduit's bloodline, because I don't need them. The time of the Royal Conduits is over. The time of true power has come."

"Stop . . . Raelyn . . ." Simon spits out one gasping plea. "Leave her alone!"

In a swirl of green and black, Raelyn spins away from Ceridwen. As if she can sense what will happen, as if every moment had built up to this inevitable end, Ceridwen scrambles to get onto her hands and knees.

"No!"

Raelyn flicks her wrist, and Simon utters a single, trem-bling gulp before his neck breaks, the bone grating in the jarring snap of a quick and easy death.

Ceridwen's scream fades to silence and she hovers there, watching her brother's body fall lifeless to the stones. The other Summerian soldiers move to action, but the Ventral-lan soldiers are faster, and the square is soon coated in so much Summerian blood that it's hard to imagine the stones were ever anything but this gruesome red. The branded Summerian and Yakimian slaves drop to their knees, cowering, spared in their meek surrender—even Lekan is left alive, hanging limp from the Ventrallans who hold him, his eyes on Ceridwen in a look of pure sorrow.

Ceridwen doesn't react when Raelyn grabs her hair and jerks her head back to peer down into her eyes. "Isn't this why you came here? To kill your brother? I saved you the trouble of having to murder your own family. You should be grateful." Raelyn twists Ceridwen's neck back and she yelps in pain. "You will be grateful, Princess. You will beg me for death, and before I grant your wish, your last words to me will be *thank you*."

The chakram leaves my hand, my great, spinning blade swirling through the air, but I know as it leaves my palm that my aim is off, my horror sending shudders up my arm that make my chakram teeter and bend.

It licks off Raelyn's shoulder, a hand's width below my intended target. She screams in a deadly mix of pain and fury. All eyes in the square follow my chakram's path back to me, and as I leap to catch it, arrows fly.

I drop to my back, hidden by the point in the roof, the chakram to my stomach. Arrows pierce the roof behind me with sturdy *thwacks* and a few graze the point just over my head, sending sprays of tile raining down over me.

"Hold!" Raelyn cries, and the arrows cease.

I stay down, one foot lodged in a few clay tiles to keep me from sliding off the roof.

"Winter queen?" Raelyn calls, her voice taunting, and

I curse myself for letting my aim falter. "I won't kill you, Winter queen. That honor has been reserved for another Rhythm. I will, however, deliver you to him, so be a good child and surrender now. There is no escaping this revolution."

My lip curls and I pull whatever strength I can from revenge, for Raelyn's treatment of Ceridwen. From horror, for the murder of the Summerian king. From the hard, unavoidable realization that all of this, every moment of this trip, was a trap. A trap I not only fell into, but helped build. Who else has been swayed by Angra's power?

Raelyn said *Another Rhythm.*

Noam. Cordell.

I whirl to my feet and wind my chakram, knowing this time, I won't miss. Raelyn will die, her smug grin the last expression her face will form. But as I rise above the peak in the roof, my body lurches back, instinct realizing the threat before my mind has time to comprehend it.

Ventrallan soldiers. Five of them, climbing up the roof. Raelyn distracted me long enough for them to scale the building and gain on me.

I take off across the roof and slide my chakram into its holster. Arrows whizz past as I hurl myself onto the steep roof of the next building. My boots twist awkwardly and I slam onto my elbows, rolling down the incline. One arrow slices across my arm, a deep gouge that makes me wince, but I don't have time for it to hurt before I'm thrown off the roof, flailing through the air.

Another building, one story shorter, stops my fall, a few tiles crumbling when I crash onto it. But this one is infinitely flatter and I take off running again, ignoring the way my arm screams. A quick glance tells me the Ventrallan soldiers are just behind me, one roof away and getting closer. I leap into the air and grab the edge of the next building. Once I'm on it, I spot the palace to the northeast, its riot of colors standing out against the sweep of dense green park. I reel toward it and push myself into a sprint, aiming for the next building, a story taller than this one but easily reachable—

Until a Ventrallan soldier hops up in front of me, swinging to his feet and drawing a blade in one smooth movement. I rip my chakram out and let it sing through the air, but the soldier sees it coming, knows it's my weapon of choice now, and deflects it with his sword. The chakram drops with a *clunk* against the curved clay tiles, and the soldier kicks it behind him, sending it clattering to the street below.

I whirl to run back the other way but jolt to a stop. The other four Ventrallan soldiers stand at the edge of the roof, swords drawn. I'm surrounded, I'm weaponless, one of my allies is imprisoned—or worse—by the people closing in on me now. . . .

Which is why, when the soldiers in front of me start falling, one by one, I have trouble understanding what's happening.

Hands swing up from below the edge, grab the soldiers' ankles, and yank two of them down, while a knife whirls out of nowhere and lodges in one man's gut. Another soldier drops when a girl leaps on his back, slashes a blade across his throat, and spins her whole body around his, her legs whirling as she twists, shoves, and sends him flying over the edge.

I barely have time to register who these people are when the soldier behind me shouts. The roof trembles beneath his stomping feet, and I swing around into a crouch, arms up as if I'll be able to fight off his sword with my fists.

But he stops, body rigid, mouth lurching open with a gurgle. He grips a spot on his chest, a hole that slowly saturates his uniform with blood, before he collapses on the clay tiles, revealing a man behind him. A man holding a bloodied sword in one hand, my chakram in the other, his sapphire eyes pinned on me.

"Are you all right?" Mather asks.

Mather

ONE WORD FUELED Mather all the way from Winter to Ventralli.

When he and the Thaw reached the Feni, saw dozens of Cordellan ships freshly docked, soldiers disembarking to swarm Winter with reinforcements—*go*.

When they crept aboard the smallest ship, launched it out into the water in the dead of night and bobbed away from their newly enslaved kingdom—*go*.

When they sailed up the river, packed on that maddeningly small boat, nothing to do for days but pace the deck and stare at the passing scenery and plan, think, worry—*go*.

Go, move, fight—Mather's whole body was an arrow pulled more and more taut against a string, ready, so ready.

None of the Thaw tried to talk to him about what had happened. No one mentioned Alysson's death, or Cordell's takeover, or Meira's possible fate. They just patrolled the boat, quiet, obeying Mather's sailing orders—which were rudimentary at best as he'd only been on a boat a handful of times in his life.

When Mather had started learning how to fight as a child, it had seemed more like an elaborate game played with wooden weapons and clunky armor. It wasn't until his first kill, when he was eleven, that he realized the seriousness of it. He'd gone out on what should have been a simple reconnaissance mission with William and they'd run into a Spring patrol. Only three men, but while William dealt with the two who swarmed him, Mather drew his blade, instinct moving his muscles so that he didn't even feel like he was the one fighting. A detached, hazy interaction that had ended with blood on his hands and a body at his feet.

That shock of realizing that the things William had been teaching him weren't games, but tools to *kill people*, was one of the most jarring moments of his life. He'd always known what fighting would result in, of course—but he hadn't understood it, *felt* it, until that moment.

And Mather knew that was what had happened to his Thaw.

They had real weapons now; they had seen the reason for their training erupt before their eyes. This wasn't some game they were playing to pass the time. This was the difference between a free kingdom and slavery, happiness and misery, life and death.

This was the future of their kingdom. The seven of them, barely more than children, with only enough training to defeat soldiers if they had the benefit of surprise and numbers.

But Spring had been defeated by such a small number—though the refugees in Winter's nomadic camp had been populated with seasoned fighters, not teenagers.

There was no room for doubt. No room for worry.

Go.

They reached Rintiero a few hours before sunset, the seven of them flying off the boat in a swirl of white hair and desperation. The docks were mostly silent, boats bobbing lazily in the current, sailors tidying up their wares for the evening.

"Where do we go now?" Phil asked as the rest of the Thaw stretched and gawked at the city before them, their faces mixes of relief at being on solid ground and awe at being so far from home.

But Mather didn't have it in him to stop and let them wonder. He nodded at Phil's question and stomped down the dock, grabbing the first person he came across—a sailor winding rope up his arm.

"The Winter queen," Mather snapped. "Is she here? Has anything happened to her?"

The sailor yelped at Mather's fingers clenched around his forearm. "I . . . um . . . what? Who—"

Mather shook him. *"Is the Winter queen here?"*

"Y-yes!"

She's here. She's alive? Don't lose focus. GO.

Mather gripped the man tighter. "Is she at the palace? Where is it?"

The sailor nodded, trembling as his eyes shot over Mather's shoulder. The Thaw must be behind him, and Mather realized how odd this must look, a group of Winterians appearing on a dock and surrounding a poor Ventrallan sailor who probably was thinking of nothing but a mug of ale and a warm bed.

Mather released the man's arm, took a step back, hands lifting in surrender. It took all his strength to do so, his drive to *go, go, FIGHT* warring with his conviction not to unnecessarily terrify innocent people.

"I—I think so—" The sailor waved his hand toward the northwest. "The complex is that way—a forest, in the middle of the city—"

Mather clapped the man's shoulder in an act of goodwill, but the motion made the sailor chirp and cover his head with his arms.

"Sorry. Thank you." Mather took off at a sprint.

Everyone followed, Phil pushing forward to run alongside him. "He feared us."

Mather spared a glance at him, some of his tension easing as his muscles, cramped after so long on the boat, stretched in the run. "Yes."

Phil's chest puffed out. "Never thought someone would feel intimidated by *me*."

Mather cut down an alley, leading the Thaw northwest. "Could've been because we outnumbered him. Could've been because we surprised him. Or it could've been because he saw we were Winterians and expected retribution."

Phil squinted at him. "Retribution? For what?"

For something Mather couldn't bear to say out loud. *For allowing our queen's death on their soil.* "He could've been lying about Meira."

Phil swerved around a barrel in the middle of the cobblestone street as understanding washed over his pale skin. He didn't say anything more, just pressed faster, Mather matching him.

They stopped once more to ask exact directions to the palace, which took them to a lush thicket of decorative forest. A few smaller roads wound out of the greenery with one large, ornate passage open at the front, but Mather pulled the Thaw away from the main entrance, opting for some sense of stealth. Who knew what waited for them behind that forest?

A path to the left seemed the most promising—narrow, for walking only, most likely a servant entrance. But as Mather angled toward it, Hollis caught his arm.

"My lord," he whispered in a low growl, nodding to the right, where a slightly wider path darted out of the forest from farther behind the palace. Down that path moved a contingent of soldiers, dozens of them, all outfitted as if for war with weapons and armor and horses. Within the group rode a lone Ventrallan woman, her entire demeanor speaking of money and privilege.

The group rode out of the forest and into the city with the purposeful clip of a goal dangling just before their eyes.

Mather took a step forward, watching them vanish into the multicolored buildings.

"My lord?" Hollis questioned.

"What would a noblewoman need with a group of soldiers that large?" Mather wondered.

Trace grunted. "Nothing good."

"Exactly," Mather agreed, and pushed into the street, following the group. No one questioned why he chose to go after the soldiers rather than enter the palace, and honestly, the only excuse he could think of was that the knot in his gut compelled him on. So many men, led by a woman who, despite her Ventrallan mask, emanated an air of malice— nothing good could come from this at all.

And he knew Meira well enough to realize that she would most likely be wherever the bad things were happening.

They kept a few blocks between themselves and the soldiers as they moved deeper into Rintiero. Evening crept in, toying with their shadows to give them away. Mather pulled the Thaw back, dropping as far behind as he could without losing the contingent.

So when the confrontation finally happened, Mather

and the Thaw only reached the square as the Summer king's body fell, the conduit on his wrist proclaiming his station to all around.

"Damn it," Mather cursed, yanking Phil into the shadows of the alley that had almost dumped them into the fray. The rest of the Thaw crowded behind them in the darkness.

The noblewoman, whose threatening speech gave herself away as the Ventrallan queen, turned to a Summerian girl, immobile with shock, her eyes on the king's crooked neck. Mather didn't hear whatever the queen said to her, blood pounding in his ears as he gaped at the body on the cobblestones.

The Ventrallan queen had snapped the Summerian king's neck somehow. Without remorse, by the way she lorded it over the girl now.

Dread rushed up Mather's body and he turned to stone, one arm still pinning Phil to the wall beside him.

If the Ventrallan queen had killed the Summerian king . . .

What had she done to Meira?

Mather's eyes shot around the square, but no other bodies lay there. What about the palace? They needed to go back. Was this some kind of coup on the Ventrallan queen's part, or was the king also involved? Did he have Meira—was he tormenting her the same way this queen tormented the Summerian girl?

The dread in Mather's body caught fire, burned cold and hot all at once as he spun back up the alley. He couldn't see anything, couldn't hear anything, just the thumping of his heart pushing images into his mind of Meira's body lying in these too-pretty streets—

"Mather!" Phil grabbed his arm, but no, there was nothing else in this city, nothing else in this world, just him and Meira and he *would find her*—

"*Mather!*" Phil snapped. "Look!"

Phil whirled him around just as a projectile caught his eye, something flat and circular cutting a line from the Ventrallan queen to a roof across the square. The queen roared outrage and grabbed her shoulder, glaring at the object.

Mather lurched forward.

It was a *chakram*.

He noted the building it came from and every tightly wound muscle sprang into action.

"Follow me," he said, and shoved back into the alley, sprinting around buildings, cutting up side streets, making a haphazard path around the square toward the building from where the chakram had come. Adrenaline numbed everything but the barest, most instinctual thoughts—*Soldiers were climbing up the building, gaining on her, but only five, easily dispatched; were those swords clashing? The queen must have turned on the rest of the Summerians*—

A shadow flashed over him, drawing his attention to the

sky. A few more shadows followed, soldiers in pursuit, and Mather jerked to a stop.

"Trace, get to the next roof—you'll be our ranged fighter. Everyone else, go up the south side of the building—quiet, though. Surprise is all we have."

They dove into action, and just as Mather leapt for a window ledge on the building, something dropped off the roof and clattered to the road.

Meira's chakram.

He plopped back onto the cobblestones, swept it up, and scurried up the building with renewed force. She was up there—she was alive.

Frigid ice above, he hadn't realized how horrified he'd been until he felt the relief those words brought: like fresh air chasing away the rankness of a battlefield, like the cooling respite of herbs healing a wound.

Mather's grip on the chakram made his desperate climb awkward, but a beat after his Thaw made it to the roof, he swung up himself.

Their surprise had worked—the four soldiers at the opposite end of the roof went down without more than a few startled yelps. One man remained, bellowing fury with his back to Mather.

The soldier lifted a sword above his head and ran forward. Mather slid out his own blade and dove, impaling the man through the back and yanking his sword free. The soldier collapsed, rolling to the side, revealing—

Meira.

She crouched, her arms up defensively. Her eyes shot from the soldier's body to Mather, her brows furrowed, and he knew if he was having trouble catching up, she had to have been completely stunned.

Mather remembered their last interaction, the conversation that he regretted more than he could express. And while he had reconciled himself to loving her, she had told Mather she didn't want him and had spent the past weeks with Theron. Nothing had changed for her—so although every nerve in Mather's body ached to dive forward and scoop her into his arms, he stayed back, poised, ready, *hers*.

"Are you all right?" he asked, because he had to say something, had to break free of this moment before it consumed him whole.

She blinked, her confusion flowing off her face in a rush that left her gasping, trapped somewhere between screaming and crying. And before Mather could explain or ask anything more, she launched forward and knotted herself around his neck.

"You're here," she panted. "How are you here?"

The weapons clattered from his hands as he wrapped his arms around her, pressing her more firmly to his body. Ice above, he'd forgotten how she felt against him—she was so small yet so strong, all but choking him with her grip. He clung to her, drowning in the way *she* hugged *him*, how she buried her face in his shoulder, her lungs filling on raspy inhales.

Meira was alive. She was alive and safe, even if Alysson was not.

Mather leaned his forehead against Meira's temple, exhaling long, inhaling even longer.

"You're okay," he said, or asked, just needing to feel the words in the air between them.

Meira nodded, holding against him the same way he held his forehead to her. Breathing, resting, using each other like nourishment in a famine.

"Are you?" She pulled back but didn't unwind from him, so close to him, *so close to him.* "How did you—why are you *here*?"

The question sobered her and she spun out of his arms, gaping at the Thaw who had hung blissfully quiet behind them. Phil met Mather's eyes, a sly smile stretching his mouth. A waggled brow joined Phil's smirk when Meira took Mather's hand, held it absently like she needed some touch to keep her steady.

Mather didn't care to return Phil's teasing with anything but a smile of his own. He could breathe now, breathe where he hadn't in days, and the sensation made everything sharp and beautiful for a moment that he knew would be all too fleeting.

"Who are you?" Meira asked the Thaw, her voice awed and dazed.

Mather stepped forward, weaving his fingers more firmly with hers. She analyzed each of the Thaw with quick, studious sweeps, and as she did, her shock hardened into something like determination. The dangerous expression her face had taken so often growing up, but now, it held a resolved twist, like she had gone from simply being stubborn and wild to channeling that energy into a goal.

And as she looked at the people before her, Mather knew what that goal was.

Winter.

"These are the Children of the Thaw," he introduced. "And we have much to tell you, my queen."

Meira

WE SPRINT WITH all our might over Rintiero's houses and shops. The multistory buildings and mismatched structures make our path staggered, interrupted by bursts of scrambling up taller buildings or sliding down shorter ones. But we're moving, all of us, Mather and his Thaw behind me as I lead the way toward the palace, high above any possible blockades or soldiers in the streets.

Raelyn and her troop were gone by the time we returned to the square, nothing but bloodstains to show that the fight had occurred. She still has Ceridwen and Lekan—they have to be alive. They have to be, because I will not allow myself to believe that while I fled the soldiers, I let my friends get slaughtered.

Mather's tale plays through my head as I run. How Noam gave the order for the Winterians to stop training our army; how Mather trained this small group in secret, building a defense for our kingdom despite Noam's threat, despite my not even knowing my people needed it. My heart floods with a cool, violent emotion, one I could put a name to, but would undo me.

Mather watched over Winter. He saved them, like he always has—his own goal that has fueled him for as long as I've known him.

If we live through this, I'll have to find time to thoroughly think over how much of an idiot I was. For now, I hold the emotion from our embrace on the rooftop like a light at the end of a long and bloody mine shaft. Another goal to aim for.

Mather doesn't know what state Winter is in now, though. Whether or not Sir escaped; who even survived at all. My stomach cramps when I think of Henn, riding blind into a takeover—but he's just as capable as Sir. If anything, his presence there will help.

But the one detail that slammed through all others was the last. Mather's lips trembled but his face remained a stoic, impassive shield as he muttered, *Alysson's dead.*

The memory of his words makes me stumble now, but I kick myself faster. I should have known Noam would betray us. I should have known all this would happen—I *did* know all this would happen, felt it every moment of every day since Winter was freed, but I could never bear to face this. To tell my people what could come, what Angra could do to the world.

I underestimated them, I know that now. Some of them may have broken, but the ones behind me, as well as Garrigan, Conall, Nessa, Dendera—their lives have not beaten them down, but helped them grow into people who know how to survive.

Those people are the deadliest of all.

I stop on a rooftop a few streets from the palace to let the rest catch up. They may be fast and determined, but adrenaline courses through me in unstoppable waves, and I kneel on the roof, fingers prying at the curved clay tiles.

The king of Summer is dead. The Ventrallan queen is consumed by Angra's Decay and planning a coup. The Cordellan king betrayed and overtook Winter.

And somewhere, out in the world, Angra is alive.

Everything is falling apart. My attempts to find the keys and keep the chasm closed to prevent the spread of the Decay—it was all for nothing.

Maybe Angra did win.

I force myself to stand. Angra won't win until there is no one left to fight him, until *I* am dead.

I choke on the words.

No. I won't have to die. I am the queen of Winter; I am a conduit. And more than that, I am the girl who destroyed Angra's camps. I am the girl who, even when things seemed at their worst, managed to save everyone—including herself.

So when Mather and his Thaw catch up to me, when I'm surrounded by the start of what I know Winter can be—strong and brave and competent and deadly—I give them a firm, decisive nod.

I will stop this. No—*we* will stop this, because I'm not alone anymore.

I never was.

Carriages full of guests arriving for the celebration in our honor clog the courtyard of Donati Palace. Seeing the palace's walls glowing under the evening sun, guests in their extravagant, glittering Ventrallan outfits, footmen leading couples up the wide marble steps, I stifle a moan. The celebration. Everything going on as usual—proof that no one else knows what has transpired. Maybe Raelyn didn't come back—maybe she fled, ran off to regroup elsewhere. Maybe I'll have time to warn everyone.

But even as those words echo through my heart, I feel their weightlessness. Nothing is ever that easy.

I march up the courtyard, past the arriving guests, past the slack-jawed footmen who blink at my tattered pants and the arrow wound on my arm and my retinue of battered Winterians. A few servants rush toward me, try to stop me from bursting inside, and I silence them with a stern glare and a flash of my locket. They know what this is, and they know the only person who would ever wear it, even if that person has a chakram strapped to her back.

Once inside, I follow the flow of guests to the ballroom, meandering through tall, white halls with gilded mirrors. I catch glimpses of myself in those mirrors, forgotten flashes of a girl with a ragged braid of white hair, her hands in fists, her face set with a scowl. My body hums, the tense moments of peace before a wall of snow collapses in an avalanche, so I keep my mind on only the next step ahead, afraid if I think more than that, I'll dissolve.

Walk faster. Turn here. Chakram? No, no weapon yet. Slow down. Wait for Mather to catch up.

The ballroom appears on our right, a series of doors thrown open into the hall, letting airy string music drift out on waves of laughter and clinking glasses. I stop, staring into the teardrop-shaped room, my heartbeat an alive and determined creature trying to claw its way out of my throat. The ballroom's walls are pale peach, the floor a swirl of gold-and-white marble. Windows make up one of the swooping, concave walls of the ballroom, showing the fading light of evening and the glass garden beyond. Ceridwen told me about the garden on our way up from Yakim, how every plant is formed from glass—another example of the ways this kingdom tries to make things unnaturally perfect.

Thoughts of Ceridwen swarm me and I dig my fingers into my stomach. I'll find her after this. I'll save her like I should have the moment Raelyn marched into the square.

My eyes dart from the windows to the crowd. There are at least two dozen people here, mostly Ventrallans with their dark hair and hazel eyes, all wearing those maddening masks. They make scanning for a familiar face impossible, and I survey each person for a recognizable attribute—Cordellan blond hair, or the Ventrallan conduit hanging at a man's hip.

Arms clamp around my neck and fear flares through me before I recognize Nessa's voice.

"Where have you been?" she mutters. "Conall came back, and we thought—we thought something happened, and—"

I pull her off me as her brothers slip out of the crowd, their faces conflicting mixes of worry and anger. Dendera follows them, and she isn't at all conflicted about how she feels—she flies in front of me, her lips in a tight line, her fingers digging into my arm.

"Why in the name of all that is cold did you send Conall back without you?" She stops, her focus drifting to Mather and the other Winterians around me. When she looks at me, her eyes open wider, her worry giving way to concern.

"Raelyn killed Simon," I hear myself say. "And Noam—"

The music stops mid-song, the violins whining as their players jerk to an abrupt halt. The same deliberate type of noise as Lekan knocking on Jesse's study door, as the stick snapping under Sir's boot when he stumbled back to camp. It's the sound of things starting, and I rotate toward Raelyn on the musicians' stage in the corner, her hands clasped against her skirts, the green silk of her mask glinting in the light.

I gag on panic. How did she get back so quickly? We didn't make good time clamoring over Rintiero's rooftops—and she had horses, free rein of the city. Plus she's in control of this situation, probably planned every moment once she knew Ceridwen had gone to confront Simon.

Ceridwen. My panic twists, thrumming wild and chaotic. What did Raelyn do to her? Where is she?

"Raelyn!" Her name tears out of my throat and I surge forward, my eyes dropping to the barely perceptible bandage on her shoulder. Instinct courses down my fingers, filling my muscles with the need to pull out my chakram and slice through her neck, no missed marks this time. But there are too many people in the way now, and I'm appeased by the fact that she won't leave this room alive. I won't let her.

Raelyn cocks a smile as I carve a path through the crowd for my Winterians to follow. I feel them move behind me, the hush that falls over everyone when I reach the stage.

"Winter queen," Raelyn intones, tipping her head. "Are you not enjoying the celebration?"

The crowd murmurs confusion, ripples of discomfort at the unorthodox interlude. I don't bother to hide my snarl. I can no longer afford the luxury of propriety.

"You should've run, Raelyn." I motion to her arm. "I won't miss a second time."

The crowd shuffles next to me, and Jesse shoves through.

He's still wearing his clothes from earlier, not bothering to match his wife this time. His dark hair gleams in a tight ponytail, and he flicks his attention from me to Raelyn and back.

"What's going on?"

Raelyn sighs. "Oh, I suppose there's no harm in you knowing now, darling." Her words drip venom, poisonous spells that make Jesse take another step forward, and the crowd takes an equally large step back.

Raelyn faces the crowd, her smile just as deadly as her tone. "Thank you all for joining us. The Winterian queen, the Summerian royal family, and the Cordellan prince have gathered together in a tour of peace. Unification is indeed a feat to be celebrated."

She spots something at the rear of the room and grins. I flick my head over my shoulder.

Noam.

Mather catches me as I twitch forward, holding me back from starting a slaughter in the throne room. Noam sees my reaction, his eyes glittering behind his Cordellan mask, his lips twitching into the grin I've come to know too well. Condescending, controlling.

I'll cut that grin off his face.

"And today, we will rejoice in the knowledge that unification has been achieved." Raelyn's voice rings out. "King Noam, would you please join me on the stage?"

Noam, eyes still on me, jerks back. Confusion chases

away his grin, and that single shift of emotion stokes my instincts higher. Noam wasn't expecting Raelyn to call him forward. Why is he here?

Where is Theron?

Noam weaves through the crowd, flanked by two of his men. He reaches the stage, standing directly across from me over it. "What is this about?" he asks, eyes skimming around him. He can feel it now too. The wrongness.

"Raelyn," I snap, yanking her attention onto me. "Why don't you call the king of Summer to the stage too?"

The crowd, watchful, mumbles curiously. Raelyn tips her head, and the moment her eyes glitter with pleasure, horror plummets through my stomach.

She turns to an open door just off the stage, beckons to someone within its shadows. A soldier walks out, a brown canvas bag in one hand. He tips the bag onto the stage and with a heavy, wet *thunk*, Simon's head drops out, his lifeless brown eyes gaping up through tendrils of his flame-red hair.

The crowd breaks. Screams echo against the peach walls, glasses shatter in the fray, and everyone disintegrates into chaos as they tear their way to the doors. But we just stand there—my Winterians, Jesse, Noam, Raelyn, and their soldiers. Unable to move from the staring, empty eyes on the king of Summer's head.

Jesse wakes from his stupor first. He climbs the stage, and in the moments before he reaches his wife, every image

I have of the weak, desperate Ventrallan king splinters away. This man is muscle and power, his body tensing and winding, his eyes more flames than sight.

He grabs Raelyn's shoulders and lifts her off the ground. "What did you do to Ceridwen?" he growls, each word an arrow that should pierce his wife's heart.

But Raelyn merely laughs. The noise makes unease roll through me, another burst of instinct, and without knowing why, I spin to the door behind me.

"Theron," I say.

He enters the ballroom. He isn't wearing a mask, so there's nothing to keep me from seeing the worry that makes him gray, and when he reaches me, he doesn't seem to notice any of the other Winterians around me. As his mouth opens, Raelyn cuts in.

"Your whore is alive, for a little while longer, at least," she snaps at Jesse.

I exhale in relief, some of my worry ebbing at the knowledge that Raelyn hasn't fulfilled her threat yet. But just as my lungs deflate, Ventrallan soldiers march through the door the other soldier entered—the men who had accompanied Raelyn earlier.

Jesse blinks a few times before he realizes they're pulling him off her, that his own men are holding him on his knees. "Release me!" he commands to no avail, the glare he shoots at Raelyn filled with hatred. "What are you doing? Release me!"

"They don't obey you anymore." Raelyn straightens her gown, her voice twisted ever so slightly with annoyance. "Now, where was I—ah, yes. Unification. *Proper* unification. Weak leadership will no longer be tolerated, and the Seasons are no longer allowed to claim themselves as kingdoms—well, three of them, at least. Summer, Autumn, and—" She stops, glances at Noam. "Winter. May I tell them, or was that your secret to reveal?"

Noam seems just as shocked as I am. But when Raelyn addresses him, his eyes dart up to her, resuming a small flicker of his power. "Cordell is not part of any larger scheme. Winter is ours, and I came here to inform the queen of this development."

Theron steps in front of me as his father talks, his back to me, shoulders hunched so I can't see his face.

"The Seasons are, at long last, where they belong," Raelyn coos. "Isn't it wonderful? Winter and Autumn have been subdued by Cordell—"

Cordell overtook Autumn too?

"—Summer has been cleansed, and Spring—well, Spring is the only Season that has proven itself worthy of kingdom status. It will be the deliverer of a new world, and by its example, we will purify Primoria of insufficiency. We do not need the Royal Conduits anymore; we do not need the allegiances of weak bloodlines. We will form our own governments and kingdoms based on proper leadership."

Slowly Raelyn takes one step forward and bends down on the stage so she's level with Theron. "And Cordell *is* part of this bigger scheme. Isn't it?"

"Absolutely not!" Noam shouts.

Theron whips to him. "You know nothing of this!"

I can't tell whether Theron aims it as a question or a statement—it should be a question, him forcing his father to admit to not knowing about this. But the way it hangs before him . . .

No. It *has* to be a question.

Noam's control flickers, his jaw working. He turns to Raelyn. "Cordell has no need of the things you offer. We have true magic, not this infectious evil."

Theron coils his hands into fists. "It isn't just Cordell's magic. It belongs to the world—everyone deserves power. That's what I've been trying to accomplish on this trip—uniting everyone to show you how the world could truly be. I drew up a treaty, did you know that? A treaty linking the world together in *peace*."

Noam's shocked rage makes spittle fly from his mouth. "You naive, selfish boy! You go behind my back to make alliances for the world with that Winterian bitch whispering weak Season politics in your ear!"

Theron falters for one moment of brokenness before he lunges forward in a snarl. "Of course you refuse to share power. That's always been your problem. Cordell is important, but you cannot behave as though we are the only people worthy of life!"

Noam matches Theron's anger, his hands knotting into fists. "I always do what our kingdom needs. Do you know what happens when a ruler doesn't do what his kingdom needs? He ends up like that." With a disgusted wave, he motions to Simon's head, still silently watching the chaos unfold. "He ends up as a castoff other kingdoms take advantage of, and I will die before I see Cordell fall so low."

I keep myself from looking at Simon, my body slack under Noam's meaning. Summer is no better off than Autumn was for so long—helpless to use their conduit without the proper gender as heir. Assuming Raelyn doesn't just destroy Summer's conduit now, while no male exists who could provide a host for the magic, and kill Ceridwen to end Summer's lineage. The thought makes me sway.

Theron scoffs, the tight, pinched laugh of a man close to crying. "This is why my mother died—because you were too arrogant to admit that Cordell needed help in any way. She *wasn't* Cordellan, and no matter how hard you tried—"

"Stop!" Noam shouts. "I order you—"

"—you couldn't cure her. Cordell wasn't enough, but rather than admit that and let her go back to Ventralli to be healed by her bloodline's conduit, you let her—"

Noam's face turns a violent shade of red, spittle flying from his mouth as he shouts at Theron over the stage. "Silence!"

"You let her die!" Theron shouts. "And you destroyed our chance at peace, at ending this, because I just want us all to be safe."

I think Raelyn says something, or Jesse struggles to reach her—but all I see, hear, feel, is the look Theron gives me over his shoulder. His face twists with a sickened pallor— brows curved, lips twitching, teeth bared. And behind it all, rising up alongside his anger like light brought with the morning, comes every moment he stood against his father. Every second of being a pawn, of wanting one thing and watching his father do another, of being so tantalizingly close to changing the world, only to have it all snatched away by people with stronger agendas.

This is the boy I saw in my visions, crouched in Angra's prison, weeping over the power his father wielded. That was all Theron ever wanted—for everyone to be safe through unification.

Raelyn said that word specifically, as if she knew the weight of it.

"Today, we will rejoice in the knowledge that unification has been achieved."

Understanding rushes through me.

The key-magic said it was supposed to make whoever had the keys ready for something. So what if the scenes I saw were things that I, personally, needed to prepare me to open the magic chasm? Theron himself said before this began that if he had something this powerful locked away, he'd have made it so only the worthy could access it.

What if the keys are supposed to help whoever finds them become worthy of accessing the magic?

The keys showed me the vision of my mother so I would know there was more to magic than rulers transforming into their own conduits. So I would know to ask the bigger question and learn the way out that *I* needed.

Those keys held magic that bent specifically to me, because now I know that the only way to save everyone is to throw myself into the chasm—

And that Theron, *Theron*, all this time, has been a threat.

"I'm sorry, Meira," he groans. "I'm so sorry."

Panic slashes through me, bursting in the wake of all the emotion he shows me. I've only seen someone break once before. The exact, horrible moment back in Bithai when Mather decided he would rather sacrifice himself to Angra than let us continue to fight indefinitely. I stared into his eyes just as I stare into Theron's now, watching as he worked through the reality before him and arrived at the only possible solution.

"Theron—" I reach for him and he extends his arm, reaching for me too—no, not reaching for me.

He swings his hand over my shoulder to grab my chakram.

"No!" I shout.

But he shoves me back as I try to grab it from his hand, and in the beat between me stumbling backward and launching at him again, he aims the chakram at his father and lets it fly.

The blade spins through the air, twisting for so long I think maybe we'll all just stand here forever, poised between nothing and everything.

But it reaches Noam. It reaches him, and slides through his neck, a perfect blow.

Everyone moves. Mather scrambles for me but gets pinned back by Cordellan soldiers; Garrigan ducks around them, angling for me; Ventrallans shield Jesse and Raelyn, more Cordellans catch Noam as he falls, plummeting backward with unbelieving eyes. And I fly toward Theron still, my mind hooked around the need to stop him, but to stop him from *what*? He already threw it.

My fingers connect with Theron's arm and he whirls on me, rage tearing apart his features. He's never been this angry before, this inhumanly livid, and he grabs my arms, shoving me back until I slam into the wall, paneled molding biting bruises along my shoulders.

The shock of Theron treating me like this makes me numb when movement behind him grabs my focus. Garrigan makes it out of the soldiers, sliding into the place Theron occupied before he forced me away.

This has to be a dream. A nightmare. Because as I look at Garrigan, his clear blue eyes pinch with urgency . . .

And my chakram returns.

The entire world dissolves and rebuilds in the seconds

between Garrigan turning and noting the blade. He can't catch it, not that fast.

The chakram sinks into his body with a solid *thunk*.

His eyes slip down, dragged by the weight of the weapon sticking out of his chest. Even when Sir fell during the battle for Abril, his wounds weren't this certain.

Garrigan is dead before I can even think to use the magic to save him.

He drops to his knees, to his side, nothing but a body now.

The world speeds back up, a burst of noise and movement that jolts me into the present. Someone says words that don't make sense, babbling incoherently.

"He's dead. The king of Cordell is dead . . ."

I look at Theron, hands shaking, arms shaking, everything shaking in the earthquake of this moment.

Theron glares down at me, his eyes almost as lifeless as those of the people he killed.

Meira

RAELYN AND HER soldiers smile, the only people in the room not rocked by disbelief. They're *pleased* by this chaos.

My body stiffens with shock, that single emotion shoving the others away so that all I am, all I feel, is action. I rear my knee up and hit Theron in the gut, shoving him off me, and dive at Raelyn. Angra isn't here, and that lingering fact makes me dizzy, because if he's causing this much pain and he isn't even present, what's happening to the rest of the world? I may not be able to fight him now, but Raelyn—Raelyn will die. Someone will suffer for this—

I leap for her, but the ballroom shifts, retracts, and before my feet connect with the stage, a wicked force sweeps my legs out from under me. I crash onto my elbows, pain reverberating up my already bruised arms from my earlier chase across the rooftops of Rintiero.

Dazed, my mind swirls with the wrongness of soldiers

lowering Noam's body to the ground and taking Cordell's conduit out of his belt. The wrongness of Mather and his Thaw trying to get to me but struggling against soldiers, of Conall and Nessa kneeling over Garrigan, Nessa cradling his head in her lap and mumbling a lullaby through the turmoil.

"Lay your head upon the snow," she sobs, stumbling over the words, and the more she tries to force them out, the more my body wells with misery.

The force that yanked me to the ground pulls my attention, but I can't get it to make sense with everything else. I only see that word pulsing through me, *wrong, wrong, wrong,* and the numbing, empty blanket of shock that clings to me, becomes me.

Theron tips his head and surveys me like I'm an animal he brought down in the hunt, some prized trophy he's deciding how to skin. The expression itself isn't what makes me tremble—it's seeing that expression on Theron, who has never in all the time I've known him looked at me with such possession.

"My king!"

The voice precedes an object thrown into the air. Theron catches it, his eyes never leaving mine, his fingers tightening around the hilt of the dagger through the purple haze it emits. Cordell's conduit—*his* conduit.

He's the king of Cordell now.

That thought alone would be enough to cripple me,

but when another sight catches my eyes, I dissolve entirely. Every bit of fight, every last flicker of drive—it all evaporates as someone else emerges from the door beside the stage, stepping out of the shadows and into the light as if he'd been lingering there all along.

I could almost dismiss him as another vision or something in my own head, except for the way Raelyn looks at him too. And Jesse, and my Winterians, everyone staring with either joy or horror at the king of Spring.

"Convincing, King Theron," Angra purrs, meeting his eyes. "Convincing indeed."

I can't look back up at Theron. For once, I choose to focus on Angra, to keep gaping at him rather than face the horrifying reality that Theron is just as possessed by Angra's Decay as Raelyn. And now that Angra *is* his conduit too, the Decay is limitless.

Without thought, I reach for the magic within me and will it into the Winterians in the room, filling them up in a burst of icy chill. That was what stopped the Decay so long ago—the protection of pure conduit magic.

But Angra took Theron. Started working on him long ago, in Abril, when he used the Decay to worm into Theron's mind and pinpoint his weaknesses. Those weaknesses are all Theron is now, has been, for months. I should have seen the change in him . . . I should have pressed him more about why he was so hurt, should have *helped* him. . . .

But does he even know the Decay has him? Does he

realize that's what it is? He is the wielder of Cordell's Royal Conduit now, but if the Decay is already planted deep in his mind and he doesn't know to use the magic to block it or fight . . .

The magic is all about choice. It won't save him unless he wants it to.

I scream again and try to claw my way up the stage to Angra. There's nothing left inside of me but desperate, pure instinct, fingers curved in deadly hooks and teeth gnashing like a rabid wolf. I will stop this, I can still fix this, I can still—

Someone grabs me, fingers tight over the fabric of my shirt, and I wither, knowing whose hands they are, how very, abominably different this is to all the other times he held me. I catch a glimpse of Cordell's dagger tucked into his belt as Theron pulls me to my feet and Raelyn turns to Jesse, who watches all this happen with the empty eyes of a man in complete disbelief.

"Please stop this," Jesse murmurs, his voice sad and brittle.

"If you want your soldiers to obey you, *make* them." Raelyn's statement is a dare. "But you won't, because you are weak. And we will not stand for weak rulers anymore."

She signals one of her men to rip Ventralli's conduit off Jesse's belt. The soldier tosses the crown to Raelyn, who catches it. It's powerless in her hands, though—this object-conduit only reacts to Jesse. But she doesn't need object-conduits anymore. She has Angra's Decay.

"Such a pretty bauble," she coos, lacing her fingers through its spires. "And so fragile too."

I gape. She can't mean what I think she does—Angra wouldn't let her *break* it. Jesse would become like us, endlessly powerful.

Raelyn squares her shoulders. "Something awfully fantastic happens when a Royal Conduit is broken in defense of a kingdom, I've been told. But if it were to break by *accident* . . ."

Jesse dips forward, watching his wife in numb terror.

She turns to him and steps closer. Before anyone can intervene, she cuffs him over the jaw with the crown. Jesse rears back, blood exploding around his face as the ballroom resonates with the delicate sound of two of the crown's spires snapping off and hitting the floor.

It broke. His conduit broke.

The gray glow instantly snuffs out.

I stare at Jesse, waiting, hoping Raelyn was wrong. His conduit wasn't broken in defense of his kingdom, because he hangs there, not reacting at all, but maybe the magic still sought him out . . .

He looks from his conduit's broken spires up to Raelyn, blood dripping in ruby tendrils from his mouth. This is a man who wasn't defending anything, caring about anything, when his conduit broke. No emotion to spur the magic on.

What happens to magic when a conduit is broken

carelessly? When the conduit-wielder has no emotion in his eyes, no act of selflessness or sacrifice in the way he stares up at his wife, his eyes glazed with aching defeat?

The magic is all about choice. And if Jesse chose not to care, maybe the magic is just . . . gone.

My body sags in Theron's hands.

Angra's control is widening.

A crack slithers up my mind, letting a single question slip through.

Why?

Why now? If Angra has been planning this takeover since he fell in Abril, why wait so long to enact it? Why not just sweep through the world immediately?

Angra steps off the stage, smiling at me like a long-separated friend. "Why now, indeed, Highness?" he taunts, and I jerk with disbelief, slamming into Theron.

Angra heard me. He heard my thoughts. We possess— we *are*—the same type of magic now, though, so maybe we're connected? The thought is too disturbing to consider.

He leans closer to me. "You have such flimsy control of that magic, don't you? I expected more from you after the chaos you unleashed in Abril. But no matter."

"Meira!" Mather's pained shout comes from the ranks of the soldiers who have him and the rest of the Winterians. A clanking of armor follows as he thrashes to break free.

"You have a plan now, don't you, Winter queen?" Angra

purrs. He reaches up, running one finger down my cheek, and I brace for an onslaught of visions—

But nothing comes.

He grins. "Yes, such lofty plans."

Angra saw something, but I didn't?

He . . . blocked me.

I tremble, every muscle in my body an earthquake of horror.

He can control his magic more than I can.

This—the carnage of death at my feet, the victorious smirk of Angra before me—is everything I've feared my entire life.

And I can't move, can't fight him, every nerve limp with the knowledge that despite everything I've done, everything we've endured, we still failed.

I still failed Winter.

"I've always been more powerful than you," Angra spits. Theron adjusts his grip on my arms, fingers tight. "But you think you have a way to defeat me—by getting yourself killed, hmm? No, Highness. I'll make sure you stay alive for a long, long time, enough to watch me kill everyone else in your kingdom. Once everyone in Winter is dead, once I own every flake of snow in that miserable land—" He pauses, reaches into my pocket, and yanks out the key, wrapped in the square of cloth. He keeps his eyes on me as he reaches into Theron's coat pocket and takes out the one he had, holding them triumphantly before my face. "I will make you watch me destroy your mines once and for all. I will bring those mountains crumbling down."

My mouth pops open, a flicker of clarity pushing through my dismay. Our mines?

Angra's green eyes tighten on mine and all the questions break around the one answer I've been wanting for years.

When Spring overtook Winter, Angra never used our mines. He boarded them up and let them rot despite the riches they held.

Any time another kingdom tried to take the mines from Angra—whether by force, as Yakim and Ventralli attempted, or by treaty, as Noam did—he retaliated. Violent, destructive retaliation, slaughtering the armies that invaded or marching into the kingdom that dared negotiate with him.

Angra seized the one person in the world who wanted to give pure magic to everyone—Theron, who in turn killed the one other person who wanted to open the chasm—Noam.

The mines. The magic chasm.

That was the reason for the whole war. That was why Angra slaughtered Winter for centuries—because he knew one day we'd find it. Angra even let Theron continue on his quest for the keys, waiting to overtake the world so he'd be in thorough possession of the one way to open the chasm.

That's his weakness. That's what he fears.

Pure conduit magic as a counter to the Decay.

Angra catches my revelation—I see it in the way his face tenses with fury before smoothing into a forced grin. He flashes his eyes to Theron and leans in, hissing words just for me.

He doesn't want Theron to hear whatever he's going to say.

I beat down the thought, not wanting Angra to see any more revelations I might have.

"You will never defeat me," Angra whispers. "I will destroy everything long before you get that chance. You are nothing in this war, no matter how high you think yourself, but I will gladly let you be the one I blame for every moment I had to wait for this future. You are unable to stop this, Highness—you see that now. No matter what path you take, it will end the same for you—death and failure."

I yank against Theron's grip, unexpected strength leaching into my veins. Angra has a weakness, still. He fears something. "What you offer is evil. The world will know that—they won't fall to your control."

Angra's sickening grin returns. "King Theron," he announces, eyes still on mine. "Restrain our guests. They may need time to learn what you have."

"Theron." I writhe against him as he takes a step back, pulling me on. "Theron, *stop.* You've seen what Angra has done to the world! You can fight it—you have magic now!"

My voice crashes out over the ballroom, everyone holding

still as if they're just as desperate for Theron's response as I am.

He looks down at me, his expression flashing with a rapid array of emotions. Resolve, grief, hope.

"You'll see," he tells me. "This is the best way to unite the world. I've spent months going over it, Meira—I've spent months searching for other options. Angra is offering this power to *everyone*. No more conduits—no more limitations. You'll see. You *have* to understand."

I'd feel better if he sounded insane. If his words came angry and harsh, babbling of plans to make the world bow to him, like Angra. But Theron sounds like . . . himself.

Angra watches Theron as he tries to convince me, his smile softening. It catches me so off guard that I almost miss it. But no, Angra actually *smiled* at Theron.

Is there more happening here? Did I miss something in the visions of Theron's memory in Abril?

On the edge of my mind, I'm aware of Cordellan soldiers dragging Nessa and Conall away from Garrigan's body, Nessa's piercing scream when they kick his corpse in passing.

"You'll see," Theron says again, absently, and hauls me toward the door. The rest of the soldiers follow the unspoken command, the men holding Jesse taking him toward the other end of the ballroom, presumably to be dealt with by Raelyn later.

Theron drags me away, the rest of my party in the hands

of his soldiers. I can't even bring myself to offer some encouragement to them, my mind caught on how everything collapsed so quickly. Why didn't I see it happening? Why didn't I feel Angra's evil infiltrate one of my closest allies—one of my closest *friends*?

And now Angra has both keys. Theron had the key from Summer; Angra took the one from Yakim, and the one in Ventralli . . .

I jolt in Theron's hands.

Where is the third key?

Theron pulls me down the palace's gilded halls until we reach a door. Alongside every other beautiful thing in Ventralli, this one stands plain and blank, just a simple iron door with simple iron bolts, hovering in an alcove. The door to the palace's dungeon.

The colorful brilliance of the palace vanishes in favor of heavy gray stones that spasm in the dancing sconce light. A staircase shoots down, taking us deep beneath the palace, farther from any chance at escape. We reach a long, straight hall lined with doors, each one the same heavy iron as the one above. But these have windows, small, barred openings. Cells.

"Lock them up," Theron commands.

Nessa's screams die as a door slams on her, Conall, and Dendera. The Children of the Thaw are corralled into a cell beside them, Mather shoved in last. He fights the Cordellan soldiers, fights with every bit of strength I no longer have, kicking off the door and slamming the men holding him against the opposite wall. My body seizes in Theron's grip as a soldier lands a blow to Mather's cheek.

"Stop." Theron opens a cell and shoves me in. "Put him in here, then leave us."

I stumble forward, swinging around in time to catch Mather as the soldiers toss him in after me. He rights himself and spins in front of me, keeping one hand on my arm to hold me behind him as we both face the door. I cling to him, using him to ground me here, the way he crouches defensively, his cheek already red.

The Cordellan soldiers leave, as instructed, marching back up the long stairwell. Theron tips his head and the moment the door above slams shut, he enters the cell.

"Touch her and I'll kill you," Mather growls, taking a step back toward me.

But Theron walks past us, stopping at the wall on our right.

Leaving the path to the door open.

Mather notices it when I do, and every one of his muscles formerly poised to attack uncoils, dragging me to the door without hesitation. We get halfway there, so close to being out, to some advantage, when a noise makes me stop.

The heavy, solid click of a lock.

I yank free of Mather's grip. He whirls, panic tightening his features, but I turn to Theron, who faces the wall. Theron, whose hands hang by his sides, one wrist manacled to the chains that drape from the bricks.

He chained himself to the wall?

He slides onto his knees, face to the grimy stone floor. Tremors rock his body, make him sway forward and back.

"Theron?" I try, sure the desperation roiling through me makes my voice pinched.

His eyes pulse with the briefest, most fragile spark over his shoulder. "I can't hold on like this for long."

I fly forward as Mather launches at me. "Stop! What are you doing? We have to go!"

"No!" I shout, the word echoing off the empty walls. "I'm not leaving him here—"

"Yes, you are," Theron snarls, his fingers digging into the mortar between the stones. His knuckles turn white, sweat beading on his forehead. Light from the hall flickers off him, painting him in jagged streaks of light. "I shouldn't let you go. I should keep you here, but I—you need to go, *now*."

I recognize this for what it is. One last burst of clarity from the Decay. A final gasp for breath before it yanks him under.

I step toward him.

"No, you'll come with us." I step closer. "You have a Royal Conduit now—you can use its magic to get the Decay out of you. You just have to want it, Theron, you just have to—"

"I *don't* want it." He pulls the dagger out of his belt and tosses it away from him like it's a live flame and he a stack of dry wood. "I—I agree with him. I want his magic, not the conduits. *No more conduits.* I want the world to be free, *equal*—but I don't want . . . I won't hurt you. I *won't* hurt you." His strain releases in a sob that wracks his whole body. "I won't hurt you like I hurt my . . ."

He crouches over, hands in his hair, sobs mingling with jagged moans.

I open my mouth, but nothing comes. What can I say? What can I *do*?

I kneel before him, my hand on his where he cups his head.

He's a conduit-bearer now. And whenever I touch a conduit-bearer skin to skin, we're connected, the inexplicable magic linking us. Scenes fly into my mind, and I watch them, muscles frozen in anguish.

Theron in Winter before we left, giving the order to his men to take over Cordell in my absence. Whatever Noam did, or thought he did, he wasn't in control. It was Theron—and even Theron didn't know he was doing it. Entire moments and orders and wishes struck out and snuffed away, flames that lit, burned brightly, and extinguished.

Theron in Summer, talking to a man in the wine cellar. A Ventrallan slave with a snide, unnatural smile that spoke of a deeper possession.

"*You remember what happened, don't you?*" the man asks, easing out of the shadows. "*You remember what he showed you?*"

The wine cellar flashes away, a spurt of memory taking its place. "Father, stop!"

Angra, barely older than I am, screams at his father, a man who looks similar to how Angra himself does now, only taller and heavier. They stand in the entryway of the Abril Palace, shadows and flickering light making the scene hard to grab. An arm raises, falls, bone cracks on stone, Angra screams. His father storms away, stumbling across the darkness, leaving Angra crouched over a body on the floor.

Blond hair cascades down the woman's shoulders, one side of her head a mess of congealed blood. I recognize her from the paintings that hung in the Abril Palace, portraits of a little boy—Angra—and this woman.

She gazes up at Angra the same way Hannah gazed at me—this woman is his mother.

The scene fades and Theron teeters back, slamming into the shelves of the Summerian wine cellar, hands on his temples. "No . . ."

But his voice is uncertain, weak, like part of him does remember. Like part of him throbs with the memory, revels in it.

Angra's father killed his mother—and Angra used this similarity to break Theron.

"No!" Theron screams.

"You're the same," the slave encourages. "He's coming. He'll always come for you."

The flash of a blade. Theron stands over the man, the corpse, blood pulsing through a wound across the man's neck.

Theron didn't remember it any of it, the Decay tugging him this way and that as it tried to eat away at his mind.

Some of it he wanted—like a power strong enough to spread through the world. Some of it he didn't dare admit he wanted—like overtaking Winter, forcing my kingdom into a path he thought would make it safe. For me.

He remembers it all now, though. He sees it as I see it, my connection to the magic linked to his blood drawing out the memories as, moment by moment, heartbeat by heartbeat, the Decay crawled into his mind and settled inside of him like a dream he could feel but couldn't recall.

And now, after weeks of unconscious games, Theron can't fight anymore. He resisted—he fought it almost as much as he wanted the chasm opened. But one desire trumped all others, one Angra latched on to, wrestled into submission.

Theron's desire for a unified, equalized world.

He groans and I pull back from him, my throat raw.

"I need you here," he mumbles. "This is right. This *is* right, this will save everyone . . ."

"Theron?"

He turns to Mather, his voice deep and resonant. "Get her out of here!"

Mather obeys. He grabs me under the arms and lifts me, sweeping Cordell's dagger into his belt as he does. I kick against him, surrounded by the uncontainable certainty that I'll never see Theron again. Angra will consume him, the Decay will destroy anything good in him. Gone, like everything else Angra took, all the other parts of our lives that have been cleaved away.

Unless I save everyone.

I cannot live in a world where Theron is Angra's toy. And that's my only other option, isn't it? To not live in this world.

Mather shoves me out into the hall and slams the door on Theron, throwing the heavy bolt to lock him inside. As soon as it's in place, Theron's groans turn to shouts, the chain rattling in a cacophony of noise.

"Release me!" Theron screams. "Soldiers! The prisoners escaped—release me!"

I collapse against the door to his cell, listening to him shout, lost to the madness of Angra's Decay. Detachment consumes me, clouds every part of me, and all I can do is blankly gape at the hall.

Mather runs to the cells across from us. The soldiers didn't lock the doors with keys, merely shoved bolts that can't be opened from the inside. He tugs at those bolts now, and they groan but only budge a little as he snaps panicked words at me. "We don't have much time! We need—"

He stops.

A man stands at the bottom of the staircase. Thin black hair twists atop his head in loose coils, golden patterns swirl along the thick maroon fabric of his cloak, the collar rising high around his ears.

And a scar stretches from his temple down to his chin.

When the man steps forward, Mather flies toward him, raising the only weapon he has: Cordell's conduit. I fling my hand out to stop Mather before I even know why.

Rares. The librarian in residence from Yakim.

"You . . ." is all I can manage. His presence here makes no sense, clogging my mind with details that don't fit.

Like the way he watched me in Yakim, studious, amused. Like the outfit he wears now and how similar it is to something else, something that—

The tapestry in the Donati Palace's gallery. The heavy robes, the dark skin.

He isn't Yakimian.

Rares is *Paislian*.

He smiles, a quick flash of recognition. "The lie was necessary, dear heart. I didn't know you; you didn't know me. Of course, you still don't know me, but if you want my help, we must hurry." He swings toward the stairs, leaving me gawking after him, Mather staring with a wrinkled brow, and Theron shouting for freedom from his cell.

I leap forward. "Wait! What are you—"

Rares whirls back. "You wanted help," he states as if he's telling me winter is cold.

I shake my head. Mather's eyes flick to the staircase, waiting for the door to open, waiting for us to be caught and Theron's sacrifice will mean nothing.

"I—why *you*?" I gasp.

Rares reaches into his robes and pulls out a key. *The* key. The last one.

He was what the tapestry wanted us to find?

He steps forward and places a palm on my cheek.

Mather lurches and Rares would be dead if I had blinked instead of waving him off.

I can't breathe as I look into Rares's eyes, his skin warming my face. An image flies at me, a mountain, brilliantly gray and purple, bathed in a beam of yellow light.

The symbol of the Order of the Lustrate.

Rares pulls his hand back. "I had to make sure you could be trusted."

"How—" I croak through my shock.

He grins. "I'll explain all, dear heart, I promise. You will come with me now?"

My brows pinch as I feebly try to connect everything. This only happens with conduit-bearers, seeing images when I touch them skin to skin. No one else in Primoria has magic, and not even the Decay inhabiting someone could cause the same reaction, or I would have known something was wrong with Theron much sooner. But Rares has a key—so maybe the key's magic showed me an image again? But no, that only works when *I'm* touching the key.

Whoever this man is, he has magic. He's a member of the Order. And he's *Paislian*.

The Order is Paislian?

My mind flashes to that mysterious kingdom, the Paisel Mountains surrounding it.

Ventralli, Yakim, Summer.

Our Klaryn Mountains.

The kingdoms where the keys were hidden were the ones leading from Paisly to the Klaryns. The Order to the magic chasm. Was that why the keys were there? But why were they so easily found? So many whys—

But I know how to get answers.

And I know where the keys were leading me, all this time.

"Meira," Mather says, a warning.

My arms tremble. I've known all along the right things to do. If I had made better choices, if I had listened to my heart instead of my head and done what I *knew* my kingdom needed from the start, I could have stopped all of this.

So I nod to Rares. If he has magic, if he's part of the Order of the Lustrate, if there's even a *chance* that he knows things that can help me stop this horrible, deadly mess around me, I have to go with him. Whatever threat he might harbor, whatever danger the Order might possess—*I need answers.*

Staying would ensure the world's enslavement at Angra's hands. Leaving at least gives a possibility of hope.

Mather balks, Cordell's dagger going limp in his hand. "What?"

I spin to him. "You have to free them and get as far away from here as possible. And Ceridwen—the Summerian princess, you have to free her from Raelyn and—"

"Are you insane? I'm not letting—"

"I'm not asking you, Mather." I'm absolutely out of my mind to be doing this. "I'm *ordering* you. As your queen."

That undoes him. Whatever strength he'd been clinging to shatters, his eyes shaded with the glaze that broke me weeks ago when he stood in my room in the Jannuari Palace and cut the bonds that kept us together; when he left, shedding tears that hollowed every part of who I had once been.

But I'm the one leaving this time.

That difference doesn't make this any easier. I stumble forward, my arms going around his neck, a remnant of the hug when I first saw him on the rooftop. Touching him— it had been like coming home. Even now, holding him for this one short moment . . .

He'll keep my kingdom safe. He'll keep *our* kingdom safe, and knowing that, feeling that, makes me cling to him all the tighter.

He was a choice I should have made too.

Mather's fingers dig into my back, gripping me just as fervently, and for this one moment, we're us again. Meira and Mather, uncomplicated.

Determination chases away my sorrow, leaving nothing but pure, unmarred resolve. Rares rushes up the stairs without another word and I pull away as Mather works to open the cells again and Theron still screams for someone to free him. Chaos, just chaos, and I'm running away from it all.

No—I'm not running away. I'm running *toward* something, toward help.

I will fix this, I promise them. *Whatever it takes. Whoever I have to be.*

I will not let this world fall.

ACKNOWLEDGMENTS

SEQUELS ARE HARD. I swear they suffer from some bookish form of middle-child syndrome, which is why I owe this book's life to SO. MANY. PEOPLE.

Firstly, always firstly, to my agent, Mackenzie Brady, and all the people on the New Leaf team (especially Danielle, who gave me AWESOME notes). If every author could have an agent as awesome as Mackenzie, the world would implode with happiness.

To Kristin Rens, the lighthouse to my meandering, wordy cruise liner. This book HURT (again, sequels, blergh), but somehow, she got me past the pain and past the angst and helped nurse a coherent novel from my agony. She is eternally glorious.

To the fabulous Harper team—Erin Fitzsimmons (your designs are absurdly gorgeous); Caroline Sun (Publicist

Extraordinaire—thank you forever for wrangling all my scheduling craziness) and Joyce Stein (Publicist Extraordinaire the Second—your patience and persistence are invaluable); and the entire Epic Reads team for supporting my books with care, grace, and general badassery.

To Jeff Huang. Dude. This chakram. Your skills continue to leave me breathless.

To Kate Rudd, for not only giving voice to Meira but being so, so excited to do it.

To Kelson, the most supportive, patient, proud husband an author could ask for. I'm endlessly glad our romance turned out to be far less troublesome than Meira's.

And because I didn't get to include them in *Snow Like Ashes*'s acknowledgments: double thanks are owed to those who are now my in-laws. Annette, Dan, Trenton, and Caro—you guys make being married to Kelson so much fun. And to Mike, the non-in-law in-law—thank you times infinity for putting up with my crazy gaggle of author friends. Your house is lovely and so are you.

To my parents, again and always. Your continued excitement and support makes me think of twelve-year-old Sara, and how deliriously happy she'd be to know her weird little words morphed into a book. To Melinda, Sister of the Year—sorry your character wasn't in this book, but I promise, you'll be very important in Book 3.

To the rest of my family. Grandma and Grandpa, Debbie, Dan, Aunt Brenda, Lisa, Eddie, Mike, Grandma

Connie, Suzanne, Lillian, William, Brady, Hunter, Lauren, Luke, Delaney, Garrett, Krissy, Wyatt, Brandi, Mason, and Kayla the Librarian. Also, to Kelsey and Kayleigh—you girls made my signing day 100 percent more special.

To my writer-peeps (even though I abandoned most of them to move out east—I hope you still love me!): J. R. Johansson, Kasie West, Renee Collins, Natalie Whipple, Bree Despain, Michelle D. Argyle (your designs are beautiful), Candice Kennington, LT Elliot, Samantha Vérant, Kathryn Rose, Jillian Schmidt, and Cousin Nikki (and your kiddos, every single one of them).

To my new writer-peeps, in all of their varying forms. Claire Legrand (our books play so well together), Jodi Meadows (your calligraphy skills are EPIC), Morgan Rhodes (I still squeal over your blurb for *Snow Like Ashes*), Anne Blankman (neighbors! kind of), Lisa Maxwell (More! Coffee! Dates!), Martina Boone (always a YASI at heart), Joy Hensley and Kristen Lippert-Martin (fall debuts UNITE), Sabaa Tahir (ELIAS), Sarah J. Maas (East Coast FTW), and all of the YADCers (so, so, SO honored to be a part of you guys. And not just because of Pocket Jamie).

This may be the most important paragraph of the whole acknowledgments section: to my fans. You guys. YOU GUYS. I cannot properly express in coherent words how much I adore each and every one of you. The excitement and openness with which you've embraced Meira, Mather, Theron, and the whole *Snow Like Ashes* gang is mind-blowingly incredible. While I would love to put every person's name here, I know I'm going to forget someone and feel awful about it, but I'll try. THANK YOU THANK YOU to: the *Snow Like Ashes* Twitter fan accounts, Wesaun Palmer (your analysis of *Snow Like Ashes* will forever have a special place in my heart), Masha, junapudding, Ri, Iris, Celeste, Marguerite, Dessy, Stephanie, Katie, Eli, Crystal, Carol, Morgan & Fallon, Amanda, Kristy, Gaby, Jess, Julia Nollie, Sarah K, Jackie Larrauri—and I know I'm forgetting people, but I'm tearing up too much and YOU GUYS, I JUST LOVE ALL OF YOU.

And, of course, to the many, many bloggers who have made these books such a success (again, I know I'm going to forget someone—if I do, feel free to berate me harshly on Twitter): Lisa Parkin (Uppercase and HuffPo FTW!); Nikki Wang at Fiction Freak (always. ALWAYS); Rockstar Blog Tours; the Valentines; Jen at Hypable Books; Nova at Out of Time; Awkwordly Emma; Jenny at Supernatural Snark; Tween 2 Teen Books; Chyna; Ariana at the Bookmark; Karolina; and all the fabulous bloggers who have interviewed me, reviewed my books, and just generally made publishing a wonderful world to live in.

I told you, this book is owed to a LOT of people. But *Ice Like Fire* would still be nothing at all without YOU, dearest of all readers. You, forever and ever more, are stronger and better and far more glorious than any conduit. Thank you, thank you, a thousand times thank you for continuing to share Meira's story with me. I am thrilled to be here, with you, at the bittersweet place between the beginning and the end.

Let's finish this war together, shall we?

FROST LIKE NIGHT

Meira

THIS IS WRONG.

I'm still hidden in the doorway of the Donati Palace's dungeon and already I can feel the change in Ventralli, like the darkness of a storm moving in. But instead of staying to fight with my handful of Winterians, I left them to follow the man in front of me.

And I have no idea who he really is.

Any guards who might have been posted outside the dungeon are gone, drawn into the chaos of Raelyn's takeover of the kingdom. Rooms open to our right and left, far enough away that the people within don't notice us, close enough for me to catch glimpses inside. Soldiers corral courtiers into groups against the gilded walls, servants weep—but even more terrifying are the bystanders who do nothing at all. The ones who watch the soldiers swing threats like blades, declaring King Jesse deposed and his wife, Raelyn, the ruler of Ventralli because she has a stronger power now, one everyone can use—power given to her by King Angra of Spring.

"He's alive?"

"His magic is stronger than that of the Royal Conduits?"

"Is that how he survived?"

These questions rise above the soldiers' threats, mixing with the pounding of my heart in my ears.

"Angra helped the Ventrallan queen depose its king. He"—my breath hitches—"already has his influence in Cordell. He seized Autumn and Winter and had the Summer king *murdered*, and yet somehow, this makes people feel wonder, not fear."

The man I've been following—Rares, if that's even his name—looks at me.

"Angra has probably been planning this conquest for the three months he's been gone, so his retribution isn't as swift as it would seem," he says. "And you more than anyone know how easy it is for people to choose wonder over fear."

"I, more than anyone?" I choke. "How could you possibly know that?"

"Do you truly want to have this discussion now?" The scar that runs along the right side of Rares's face, from his temple to his chin, creases with his squint. "I'd planned on at least getting us past any immediate threat of death first. . . ."

Swords clash and a soldier shouts from up the hall. Rares dives around the corner without waiting for my response, leaving me to scramble after him.

I shouldn't be trailing some mysterious Paislian—I should be helping Mather release the Winterians in the dungeons. Or planning a way to free my kingdom from the Cordellan coup. Or saving Ceridwen from whatever fate Raelyn planned once she captured her after murdering the Summerian king. Or finding a way to extract Theron from the grip of Angra's Decay.

I falter, tripping over my many worries. While I always suspected Angra's death was a ruse, I never, not in any of my most delirious fears, thought he could be strong enough to give magic to non-conduit-wielders.

But his power is tainted by the Decay, which was created when there were no rules binding magic to bloodlines.

As Rares and I duck from hall to hall, I see the fruits of Angra's magic firsthand. The Ventralli of light and color that existed when we first arrived is gone, replaced by one that resembles the dark streets of Spring. Soldiers march with faces pinched tight by anger, their movements sharp. Courtiers huddle in trembling masses, fearful, with wide eyes and an eagerness to please their conquerors.

No one fights it. No one shouts retaliation or struggles against the soldiers.

This is Angra's doing. Though it looks as though he's only given his higher-ranking subordinates the ability to control magic, as Raelyn did when she killed the Summer king. The people who crowd the halls simply appear fogged, influenced by something beyond themselves, as if they all got drunk on the same bad wine.

This is what Angra is creating, a world of infinite power, where everyone is possessed by a magic that makes them pliable, overcome by their deepest, darkest emotions.

How do I stop him? How do I save—

It claws at me, the question I asked my conduit magic, and I'm sucked back to that moment, when I was running through the streets of Rintiero with Lekan and Conall. My biggest worries then were trying to keep Ceridwen from murdering her brother, and figuring out how to form an alliance with Ventralli, and finding the Order of the Lustrate and their keys in order to keep Cordell from accessing the magic chasm.

Then I asked that question—*how do I save everyone?*—and the answer blistered itself onto my soul.

By sacrificing a Royal Conduit and returning it to the source of the magic.

But I am Winter's conduit. All of me. Thanks to my mother.

Rares yanks me behind a potted plant moments before a contingent of men jogs out of a room just ahead.

"Not now," he whispers. He fishes for something in his shirt and withdraws a key on a chain, the one he showed me in the dungeon—the final key to the magic chasm in the

Tadil Mine. "You found me. You found the Order of the Lustrate—and *yes*, we will help you defeat Angra and stop all this. But first, let's just get out of here alive."

His words offer much-needed comfort, so needed, in fact, that it isn't until he darts back into the hall that I wonder—how did he know I was worrying?

It doesn't matter. I swallow, resolute. I will do this. I will learn what I can from the Order, and use that knowledge to either face Angra in battle and destroy him and his magic—or I will get the keys from him, enter the chasm in the Tadil, and destroy all magic in the only way I know how.

Either way, this is what I need to do. Angra is too strong—I need help, and the Order of the Lustrate is the only resource I know of that could help me grasp my magic in the same unstoppable way that Angra does.

Rares leads me inside an empty kitchen filled with thick wooden tables and roaring fireplaces and food abandoned by servants who are most likely hiding from the frenzy of the takeover. He pulls out a water sack and fills it at a pump in the corner.

"Who are you?" I finally manage to ask.

He points to a block of knives on a counter. "Arm yourself."

"With kitchen knives?"

He doesn't break stride. "A blade is a blade. Blood can be drawn all the same."

I frown but slide a few knives into my belt. My empty

holster still hangs against my spine—my chakram is back in the ballroom. Back in Garrigan's chest.

I grip the edge of the counter.

A hand cups my shoulder, and when I look up, Rares is watching me.

"My name is Rares. I didn't mislead you about that," he says. "Rares Albescu of Paisly, a leader in the Order of the Lustrate."

He glances over my shoulder, at the kitchen door that leads into the palace. Footsteps echo, growing louder, and I know we'll have to run before he can explain more.

"I will tell you everything," he promises. "But first we must reach safety—in Paisly. Angra won't dare follow us there."

"Why not?" I face Rares. "What are you planning—*why* is this—"

Rares cuts me off with a squeeze to my shoulder. "Please, Your Majesty. It's the safest place for all I must show you, and I promise, I will tell you everything as soon as I am able."

"Meira," I correct. If I'm going to risk my life for the foreseeable future, then I'm going to be addressed how *I* want to be addressed.

Rares smiles. "Meira."

We move to the other kitchen door, the one leading out to a garden. Rares starts to slip out when I'm caught by one last grip of remorse at all I'm leaving. By going with him, I *am* helping—the Order of the Lustrate is my best chance at stopping Angra—but it still feels like I'm running away.

Rares turns. "You can't save everyone by staying."

Other people have told me this before—*You can't save everyone; Winter is your priority.* Most loudly: Sir.

Grief stabs into me. Mather told me of Alysson's death, but what about Sir? Did he survive the Cordellan attack on Jannuari? What about the rest of Winter—what state is my kingdom in? I can't think about Sir being dead. He has to be alive, and if he is, he'll be doing everything he can to keep Winter together.

I hear what Rares said again, realizing now the exact meaning of his words, and I begin to see all the ways he differs from Sir. Rares's eyes are wider; his skin is darker; his hands are more scarred from years of fighting. And most of all, in Rares, I see something I never saw in Sir— something that made Rares add the two words that entirely changed the meaning of that sentence.

You can't save everyone by staying.

Not an end. A possibility.

"Who are you?" I breathe again.

Rares smiles. "Someone who has been waiting for you for a long time, dear heart."

Soon after we leave the palace complex, a horn wails through the hazy gray sky.

They've discovered I'm gone. Which means they found

Theron, chained to the dungeon wall, and Mather and the rest—

No. Mather wouldn't let anything happen to anyone in his care. Not because I ordered him to keep them safe, but because that's who he's always been—a man who, even after he lost his throne, still found a way to be a ruler. The way his Children of the Thaw look at him, with the unquestioned loyalty earned by someone born to lead . . .

He is the one person in my life fully capable of standing on his own.

What about Theron?

The question makes me stumble as Rares and I sprint out of the city, wiggling between two bright, lopsided buildings and into the lush forest that borders Rintiero to the north.

That question. It wasn't *me*. It sounded almost like—

I slam to a halt, Rares making it a few paces farther before he realizes I've stopped. But the voice in my head holds me captive, and I brace my hands over my temples.

A terrible fate, isn't it, being part of the same magic? If only you were stronger.

My vision blurs until all I see is Angra's face in my mind.

"No!" I scream, buckling, my knees slamming into the moist earth. Angra could hear my thoughts when we were both in the Donati ballroom, but he's nowhere near me now. How is he able to talk to me, *within* me? I should be able to stop him—

But you can't stop me, can you, Highness? My soldiers are coming for you. Winter is finished. Spring has come.

A single word ekes out in response. *Why?*

I've already asked that question, back in the ballroom of the Donati Palace, surrounded by the carnage—the Summerian king's head, Garrigan and Noam's bodies. But the only answer I got was the reason why Angra sought to destroy Winter's mines—he fears pure conduit magic countering his Decay, which is why he spent every moment he could working to undo that threat. That was why he attacked Winter for so long; that was why he turned on anyone who tried to open the chasm.

But what I ask now isn't even a conscious question—it's a whimper in the darkness as his face fills my mind.

Why is this happening . . . ?

I've seen my friends murdered for this war. I've watched my kingdom burn for this. I'm running for my life now for this, and after all these years, I still don't know *why*. What does he want?

Hands cover mine where I grip my head.

I open my eyes. Magic spreads down my limbs, cooling and deep and pure, turning my fear to shock.

Rares is pumping his magic into me.

His face tightens, beads of sweat breaking along his forehead. "Fight him!"

My heart knows I don't have to submit to Rares's magic, *shouldn't* submit to him, but everything else in me wants to, fear and panic coiling in a whip that tears apart my insides.

Fight! I will myself to stay open to whatever help Rares might offer.

A shock sends me flying backward. I slam against the ground, leaves sticking to my clothes, my head ringing as though someone struck a bell inside my skull.

I see Rares mouth my name.

"You . . . ," I think I say. "What did you . . ."

Pain flares behind my eyes and it's all I can do not to vomit on the soggy undergrowth. But Rares puts his hand over mine again, even when I glare at him through the agony that turns everything a vibrant scarlet.

Rest now, a voice says. It isn't Angra—it's Rares, in my head. *Rest, and trust me.*

Trust you? What did you do? You haven't told me anything!

But even as I try to fight it, unconsciousness comes, lulling me like the tempting aromas that waft from a feast. I'm half aware of Rares lifting me, of the jostling sway of being carried at a run through the forest.

You're more like Sir than I thought are my final words before everything goes dark.

Mather

SHE LEFT.

Channeling every bit of his panic into the task at hand, Mather threw his weight against the bolt. It released with a squeal and the cell door opened, freeing Phil, who barreled out, fists ready, a breath ahead of the rest of the Thaw. But Mather spared them no orders before he heaved open the bolt on the next door, releasing Dendera, Nessa, and Conall. Theron's shouts for help from inside his own cell would alert his soldiers at any minute—and Meira had left them.

"We need to get out of here," Mather said to no one in particular, but as he pivoted toward the staircase, he hesitated. Leaving that way would almost certainly land them right back in the dungeon if they encountered any soldiers. Was there another way out?

Phil stepped forward. "We can split up. Some of us go

up the stairs, the rest go deeper into the dungeon, see if there's a way—"

Another voice spoke. "Or you could follow me."

Mather was too numbed by the day's events to feel anything but readiness as he leaped toward the voice. He reached for a sword, but his weapons had been taken before the descent into the dungeon, and all he had now was Cordell's Royal Conduit. His fingers brushed the jewel on the hilt, his lip curling as he remembered how Theron had tossed it away so carelessly—a part of him would take such joy in tarnishing Cordell's pretty blade.

The person who had appeared in the middle of the hall folded her hands against the skirt of her gown, the silver looking almost like armor. A matching silver mask obscured her face, and when she spoke, she lifted her chin as authoritatively as a commander.

"If you wish to live, that is," she said.

"You're Ventrallan," Mather countered, stopping just shy of her. "Why would we trust you?"

The woman scoffed. "And you have so many options at the moment?"

Mather didn't get in another word before Dendera croaked, her eyes narrowing, "You. You're Duchess Brigitte, the mother of the king. I saw you with Raelyn!"

Brigitte rolled her eyes. "If I agreed with her coup, do you think I would bother to be in this filthy place"—she turned up her nose at the walls—"*alone*? I can either regale you with an explanation, or you can follow me. As I said, I personally do not care whether you live or die, but I think you can be useful to me, so make a decision quickly."

The door at the top of the dungeon's staircase rattled. Someone had finally heard Theron's shouts.

Mather lurched toward Brigitte. She took that as acceptance and spun on her heel, her silver gown flaring as she hurried down the hall. The rest of Mather's group followed without question—what other choice did they have? He had to get out of here to make sure Meira was all right, that whomever she'd left with wasn't part of a trap of Angra's. So many secrets had come to light—Cordell had turned on Winter, Theron had turned on Meira, and the Ventrallan queen had staged a coup. Could the man Meira left with be trusted? And beyond that, Winter was still under Cordellan control—how could they free it if they were Angra's prisoners?

Brigitte ducked into a cell on the right. Mather hesitated just long enough for his eyes to adjust to the dimness. If the old hag had led them into a trap—

But at the back of the room, a door cracked open, the stone on the outward side showing that, when closed, it would blend seamlessly into the wall.

"Shut the door behind you," Brigitte called before vanishing through the opening.

"Hollis," Mather hissed. "Take the rear. Stay alert."

Hollis positioned himself inside the room to let everyone

pass. Mather followed Brigitte, muscles humming with pent-up fight. The stone deadened most sound, leaving him with only the distant clicking of the duchess's shoes moving upward—stairs. He darted after her, hoping to put enough space between him and his group that if a trap did await them, he could give a warning with plenty of time for them to make it back down.

Alone in this narrow, dark space, a crack formed in his determination. It had all happened so abruptly—the man; Meira's unexpected trust; her desperate plea for Mather to free everyone. And he had agreed, only because he hadn't seen her look like that in months. Like the eye of a storm, terrifying and brilliant and severe.

The stairwell folded into a hall. One more hall led to another staircase, and at the top of that, Brigitte's footsteps stopped. Metal jingled, thin and light—keys. Mather waited a few steps back, bracing himself for soldiers, arrows . . . Angra.

He clenched and unclenched his hands, staring sightlessly down at them in the blackness. He had killed Angra himself. He had broken the deranged king's conduit on Abril's ground and seen his body vanish.

What had that truly done to him?

Brigitte opened a door. Mather forced his eyes to adjust, lingering long enough for the yellow light to reveal a little of the room beyond: a thick scarlet rug, a short mahogany table, blue walls. No soldiers that he could see.

Brigitte stepped inside and Mather followed, a beat behind.

"Grandmamma!" came a child's cry.

They were in a bedroom filled with mahogany furniture— a table and chairs, a wide bed, a few armoires positioned between floor-to-ceiling tapestries. This door stood behind one such tapestry while two more doors waited closed at other points in the room, unhidden.

Brigitte was the mother of Jesse Donati, the Ventrallan king. The king Mather had watched go from weak to infuriated and back to weak again while his wife seized control of his kingdom. The king who sat on a padded chair before Mather now, one child in his lap, another clinging to his arm as if it were a barrier she could hide behind.

A third child, the oldest but not by much, toddled forward. "Grandmamma," she said again, tears tumbling over her lace mask.

Brigitte stroked the girl's dark curls and looked over her shoulder at Mather. "I'll help you leave, but you'll take my son and grandchildren with you."

The Ventrallan king rose. The daughter who had been hiding behind him instantly latched onto his leg, and the boy in his arms, not more than a year old, stared with wide, calm eyes from behind a small green mask.

Phil moved beside Mather, and he felt the rest of the Thaw gather around. All the time they had spent in their clandestine trainings in Jannuari had let him learn each of them by heart, and he didn't need to look to know Trace's fingers twitched over his empty knife sheaths; Eli squared his jaw in a mimic of the glowers around him; Kiefer hesitated near the back, watching, cautiously ready to help; and Hollis and Feige hovered, quiet, on the edge of the group.

It was Dendera, Conall, and Nessa whom Mather had to check on. Dendera had her arms around Nessa, freeing Conall to stand alert, his face gray and hard. His brother had died as unexpectedly as Alysson.

Mather turned away from him. He wouldn't let his own grief rise any higher. Hopefully Conall could keep himself under control too.

"Mother," Jesse said, his surprise palpable even from behind his mask. "Who are—"

"Do we have a deal?" Brigitte asked Mather.

Mather narrowed his eyes. "You're saving us?" He had little to no experience with children, but even he could tell that getting them out of the palace would be nearly impossible.

Someone in his group stepped forward. Mather expected it to be Dendera—she, of all of them, was the most capable with children, but when Mather turned, he blinked in surprise.

Nessa faced Brigitte. "Of course we have a deal."

Mather had been on the verge of saying the same thing. Impossible or no, they wouldn't leave children here, defenseless. What surprised Mather was the ease with which Nessa moved forward and knelt in front of the oldest girl.

"Hi there," she said. "I'm Nessa. And that's my brother, Conall."

Conall gaped when his sister pointed up at him but managed a small bow at the princess.

"Melania," the girl told Nessa, rolling her *l* on an awkward tongue.

The smile Nessa gave her was impossibly soft for someone whose eyes still looked so haunted. "Well, Melania, how would you like to go on an adventure?"

Melania looked up at her grandmother. Brigitte's sternness melted as she smiled, and Melania placed her small fingers in Nessa's outstretched hand.

Things happened quickly after that. Brigitte pulled blankets and other meager supplies out of her armoires; Dendera and, more surprising still, Hollis eased forward to coax the other two children into coming on the same "adventure."

The room began to hum with movement, but the Ventrallan king stayed motionless before his chair. He didn't hold his son anymore—the boy now clung to Hollis—but instead stared at the floor with jaw-clenched ferocity.

"I have to go after her," the king said suddenly, echoing Mather's own looping thoughts.

Mather picked a dagger from the supplies, unsure of how to respond. No one else said a word. "Your wife sided with Angra," he tried. "Freeing her—"

"I don't give a damn about Raelyn," the king snapped, and something in his words made Brigitte, across the room, stop folding a blanket.

"No. I will not let you get yourself killed for—"

"For whom?" The king whirled on his mother. "You've called her many things over the years. Useless, harmful— a whore. But it would seem *Raelyn* is the one who most strongly embodies those attributes. So do not tell me not to go after Ceridwen."

By the time he finished, the room was silent. Mather felt that name dredge up memories of Meira's parting words. She had told him to save Ceridwen. Why would the Ventrallan king care about the Summerian princess too?

But the look on the king's face told Mather exactly why he cared.

Brigitte's lips puckered. She didn't utter another word before her son removed his dark green mask and pointed it at her.

"I'm not leaving until I break this mask and save Ceridwen."

Mather frowned. "Break your mask?"

The king didn't miss a beat, as though he had repeated this explanation to himself many times. "To break one's mask in the presence of someone you reject is an act of permanent separation. To say that you are finished with them in your life, so much so that you do not worry about them seeing your true face. You'll never see them again, so your secrets are nothing in their hands."

Mather nodded. It mattered little what the king wanted to do, honestly—if Jesse intended to confront his wife and save Ceridwen, Mather would follow, especially if it meant he could complete one of the tasks Meira had entrusted to him.

"Everyone else should escape while they can," Mather said, aiming the order at his group. "I'll accompany the king out of the palace. There's something I need to do as well."

"You're leaving us too?" Kiefer snapped.

But Phil stepped forward, his eyes on Mather's. "He's going after our queen."

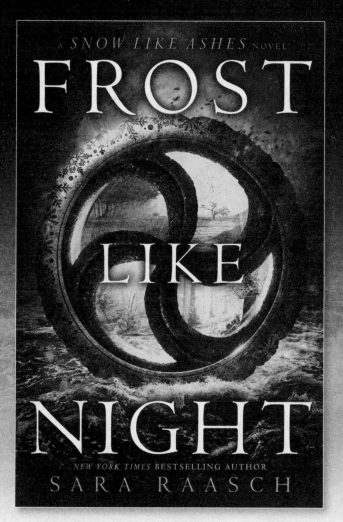